the best of friction

the best of

friction

the first five years

edited by jesse grant

alyson books
los angeles | new york

MANUFACTURED IN THE UNITED STATES OF AMERICA.

THIS TRADE PAPERBACK ORIGINAL IS PUBLISHED BY ALYSON PUBLICATIONS,
P.O. BOX 4371, LOS ANGELES, CALIFORNIA 90078-4371.
DISTRIBUTION IN THE UNITED KINGDOM BY
TURNAROUND PUBLISHER SERVICES LTD.,
UNIT 3, OLYMPIA TRADING ESTATE, COBURG ROAD, WOOD GREEN,
LONDON N22 6TZ ENGLAND.

FIRST EDITION: JULY 2002

02 03 04 05 06 a 10 9 8 7 6 5 4 3 2 1

ISBN 1-55583-761-1

COVER PHOTOGRAPHY BY STUDIO 1435.

Contents

Preface

I can hardly believe that the Friction: Best Gay Erotic Fiction series has been around five years. But I guess it has. So now we're doing a Best of the Best book, which is pretty exciting. In this volume I've collected what I believe are the most outstanding stories from the five books in the series, compiling what may be the most esteemed group of erotic authors ever found in one anthology.

That said, I need to add a disclaimer: These are *my* favorite stories. And although I think any sane and horny homo will agree that each and every tale selected is *h-o-t* hot, I also understand the maxim: "To each his own." Thus, if *you* were selecting for this book, you might have picked different stories. Which means that if you really want to experience the Best of the Best, you'll need to do exactly as I did— sit down and read all five of the previous volumes cover to cover. Helpful hint: Before undertaking this task, purchase an industrial-sized bottle of lube. (It's been over a month and I'm still chafed.)

Special thanks to Gerry Kroll, who created this series, to Terri Fabris for her administrative and editorial assistance, and to John Erich and Austin Foxxe, each of whom has been instrumental in the series' continuation.

Jesse Grant
Los Angeles
July 2001

Nasty
By Mel Smith

I looked up and he was staring at me from across the walkway. He was one of those smoldering straight boys whose blatant contempt for queers undoubtedly harbors a need to have his ass plowed until the cows come home.

His eyes never left me. The sneer never left his face. He wanted to hurt me.

Well, he was about to learn that this queer wouldn't sit and wait to be bashed. "What the fuck are you staring at?" I said.

"I'm staring at you." The voice matched the look.

As much as I hated to admit it, he was hot. Thick brown hair, a couple of days' worth of beard, black eyes that ripped through flesh, a body as sleek and powerful as a Harley Davidson, and a mouth that would look incredible with a cock crammed down it.

I hated him. I hated his repressed, hypocritical, breeding ass. I wanted to pound that ass with my cock, then pound his face with my fists. Or vice versa. Either way, the asshole needed to know that not all queers are easy targets.

I sat up straight on the bench. I knew my six feet two inches of iron-pumped muscle would be intimidating, even to a shithead like him. "You want a piece of me?"

He moved toward me, very slowly. He had no fear. This was going to be nasty.

I stood when he was about three feet away. I only topped him by about an inch. Up close, he was even hotter.

He put his face in mine. It dripped with loathing.

My hands balled into fists.

"Yeah, I want a piece of you." I could almost taste his hate. "My ass eats cock for breakfast and I'm wonderin' if you're man enough to feed it."

Okay. Now that is not what I expected him to say.

He caught me so off-guard I almost flinched, but I held it together and grabbed a handful of that thick, brown hair. I yanked his head back.

He snarled.

"I already stuffed five sluts like you this morning, and it ain't even 10:00 yet."

He licked his lips. I never saw anyone do it nastier.

I pulled his head back farther. "You want to do it here, pig, or does the little girl need some privacy?"

He dropped to his knees in the park in broad daylight and started chewing on my denim-covered cock. He sounded exactly like a fucking dog, panting and growling as he soaked my crotch with slobber. I pushed his head roughly against my straining rod. He chewed even harder.

I pulled him to his feet by his hair. I grabbed his crotch and squeezed.

He snarled again, his eyes shooting sparks at me.

His dick felt like a fucking bazooka. It took everything I had not to let him see me sweat. There was nothing I liked better than to tear up a big-dicked bottom. The bigger they are, the harder they cum.

"You're coming home with me, fuck boy, and when I'm done with your ass, it won't be able to eat for a week."

"You better hope that's true, because it gets awful ugly when it's hungry."

"Boy, you couldn't get much uglier."

The corner of his mouth curled up. He knew I was lying, but I couldn't let him get the upper hand.

I yanked his hair and squeezed his cock harder. He flinched and the sparks became rockets.

"I want to see what I'm getting before I waste my fucking time on a whore like you," I said.

Without a second's hesitation, he undid his fly and pulled down his pants. He wasn't wearing any underwear and nine inches of uncut meat sprang free, wedging itself between my legs.

I was going to fucking lose it before we even left the park.

I took hold of that meat and it throbbed in my hand like some living being. I lifted it and pushed it back against his stomach. I hefted his nuts with my other hand and tried not to let him see me giving thanks. They were huge and heavy, dangling like a bull's. I could see his loads of spunk hosing down my carpet as I fucked the shit out of him.

"I want to see the rest."

He turned away from me and bent over. I took the opportunity to catch my breath.

I lost it again as soon as I looked.

His ass was a fucking trampoline, tight and bouncy. If I slapped it with my cock, my cock would slap me right back. The cheeks were solid, meaty mounds that could be used like handles to steer while plowing.

I took a hold of those cheeks and dug my fingers into the flesh. My thumbs spread them wide and I said a silent prayer.

My prayer was answered.

A tasty, tight hole puckered and unpuckered at my thumb tips. It wasn't begging me to fuck it, it was daring me to.

I slapped his ass hard.

He yelped, then spit into the ground. Still bent over, he looked back and up at me. "Think you can fill it up?"

"Fill it? Asshole, I'm going to fucking burst it."

He stood and pulled up his pants. He left the top three buttons undone. A ripe mushroom poked straight up, peeking out of his foreskin.

This is the one, I thought to myself. I'd finally found a bottom nasty enough to survive my abusive monster. I was sure of it. This one wasn't going to be tamed.

Those eyes of his challenged me, while he slipped his finger and thumb inside his foreskin and teased the mushroom until honey oozed out of the slit.

My tongue almost came out, it looked so fucking tasty. But I stopped it just in time.

"I want to see what you got, too, before I waste the trip."

I put one hand around his throat and slapped his cock-teasing hand away with the other. I yanked his foreskin out as far as it would stretch. The mushroom bloomed inside.

"I don't fucking show you anything unless I want to. Is that understood?"

He smiled, but the cockiness had slipped a bit. A chink in the armor. I yanked harder on his skin. "Is that understood?"

"Yes, sir." It was still a snarl. Not even a hint of submissiveness.

God, he was perfect.

I took my key ring out of my pocket. It was big and loaded with keys. I pulled out his pants and slid the ring down onto his cock. I buttoned up his fly and could picture the keys digging into his balls. The tip of his mushroom was still visible over the waistband, dripping pre-cum like a leaky faucet.

I walked to my car and he followed. I got my extra car key out and I made him ride in the back seat. "You touch yourself and I'm booting your slutty little ass out of this car."

"Afraid you can't keep your hands off of me?"

He was pushing it. "When we get to my place, it will be more than my hands I'll have on you." I started the car. "Open your mouth again and I'm climbing back there and shutting it for you."

There was silence.

I looked in the rearview mirror. He was staring at me, the smuggest grin I'd ever seen plastered on his face.

He held my stare for a couple of beats more, then he slid down in his seat. His knees opened wide and his fingers spread across his thighs. His T-shirt was bunched up and I could see fluid from his cock filling up his bellybutton. The outline of my keys was visible through his jeans.

While he watched me watching him, he started pulling and arranging the seat belts. I thought, at first, that I had flustered him so much that he wasn't able to put his belt on correctly. Then I saw what he had managed to do.

His crotch was tied in a harness created by the seat belts. I could only imagine the kind of pressure it and my keys were placing on his stiff boner.

He licked his lips again, in that slow, tantalizing, shit-eating way he'd done before. Then he began to rock rhythmically, strangling his basket with every move forward. His head laid back and a low growl vibrated from his throat. The bastard was masturbating.

I had to give him credit. He wasn't touching himself.

I looked at the road and fought the need to squirm in my seat.

Could this be love?

We reached my house and he followed me in. When I turned around, he was on his knees, pulling at my fly.

I slapped his hands away. "I didn't give you permission to do that."

He looked up at me through long, dark lashes, his eyes still smoldering.

"Stand."

He stood.

"Take off everything except my key ring."

He did it slowly, his eyes rarely leaving mine. My keys jangled with his every move.

He was giving me time to look. He knew a man would have to be dead not to like what he was seeing. His skin glowed like highly polished wood. His nipples were exactly the way I liked them—familiar with abuse but still young and tender. They stood at attention, their shiny gold hoops twitching with every beat of his heart. His abs were carved into his flesh. I could've done my laundry on them. His thighs were powerful without bulging and his arms and legs were highlighted by the blackest hair I'd ever seen, giving his skin an even higher gloss.

I looked and I liked—God, did I like—but I wouldn't give him the satisfaction of showing it.

When he was done, he started to put his boots back on.

"I said, 'Just my key ring.'"

He stopped and looked at me, missing half a beat. Then he smiled, and rose to his full six feet plus.

I liked my bottoms completely bare. It made them look more vulnerable. But, as my eyes traveled over him one more time, I realized it only made this one look more incredible, like some natural beast, raw and wild.

I led him by my keys to a straight-backed chair sitting against the living room wall. A small table with a drawer stood a few feet away from it.

"Sit and put your hands behind you."

He obeyed.

"I don't want to see your hands in front. I don't want you to touch me. Is that understood?"

He gave me that look up through his lashes again. God, he was a tease. A nasty, slutty, fucking tease.

"Yes, sir."

I stood back, about a foot in front of him. I opened my fly and set the monster free. It thrust forward, like a lance, and hit him in the face.

His eyes grew huge and the smirk disappeared.

I thought, for a moment, that I'd lost him; that it was fear I saw in his eyes.

Then those smoldering eyes burst into flames and he whispered, "Chow time."

I watched my pre-cum inch down his cheek. "Does just your ass eat cock, or does your face get hungry, too?"

The smug smile was back. "It's just all one, long chute to me."

The image of my snake sliding down his throat and poking out his asshole made my legs shake. There was no way to hide it.

His smile grew bigger.

I was going to have to make him pay for that.

His hands were behind his back, gripping the rungs of the chair. I grabbed a handful of his hair with one hand and my cock with the other. His mouth opened wide and I shoved my way in with one long stroke.

He retched hard once and phlegm oozed out around my meat. His hands came forward, then stopped, and gripped the seat of his chair.

I felt the back of his throat convulsing against my cock. His knuckles were white and the fire in his eyes shimmered with moisture.

I was about to back off, when I felt his throat open up and my cock slide forward some more. His hands released the chair and returned to their place behind his back. The smirk was gone from his lips, of course, but now I saw it in his eyes. They twinkled at me.

I couldn't help but smile back.

As his lips disappeared into the hairy darkness of my crotch, I realized how right I had been. His mouth did look incredible with a cock crammed down it.

I held his hair and his ears and I fed him a feast. I fucked his face hard, slamming it with my body, over and over. The corners of his mouth started to tear and a trickle of blood came out of one of his nostrils. His hands, for the most part, stayed behind, occasionally getting knocked loose by my ramming.

I looked into his eyes, sweat blurring my vision, and I saw them glaze over. Then, unbelievably, he winked at me.

I almost lost it before reaching the main course.

I pulled out quickly and shoved his head in his lap. I closed my eyes and took some deep breaths, trying to keep it under control.

Still holding his head down, my legs started to quiver. His labored breathing and twitching hands, still valiantly held behind his back, were pushing me over the edge. I wasn't going to make it.

Then his body suddenly relaxed under my touch and I wondered—had he surrendered or had he gotten a second wind?

Not knowing gave me the strength that I needed and I knew I was going to be able to dole out the punishment he so dearly deserved.

I yanked him off of the chair and he landed, face first, on the carpet. My key ring went flying. He was on his knees, his ass sticking straight up in the air like the anxious little whore's hole it was. With effort, he tucked his arms under his head, covering his face.

Still I didn't know if he'd given in, or if he was just waiting for more.

I grabbed the chair and threw it across the room. I opened the drawer and took out a tube. I shoved the end in his ass and filled his hole with lube. The empty container followed the chair.

I rolled two condoms onto my cock; I'd had too many tear on me from the strain.

I looked down on his body, feeling pumped and voracious. Then everything came to a stop. His ass suddenly looked too vulnerable, too perfect. It was plump and full and pink with sweat. He couldn't control the tiny shivers that shook it.

No matter how much he asked for it, did anything so perfect really deserve such brutal treatment?

As if he could read my hesitation, his voice rose up to me.

"Don't worry. Guys with monster dicks like yours often suffer from performance anxiety."

That was all I needed.

I drove my jackhammer straight down into him. He howled like a dog and I pulled all the way out just so I could plunge it right back in again. My body slammed him into the floor with every ram of my cock.

He soon began making animal noises. All kinds of animal noises. Pig grunts, dog whimpers, rabbit screams. Did you ever hear a rabbit scream? It makes your skin crawl.

Still, I wouldn't let up. His hands were clawing at the carpet, but he couldn't get a grip. His knees gave out and he started to fall to the side, but I held him by the hips and kept him in place.

Every time I thought I would come, I'd picture that smug smirk or hear one of those cocky statements and I'd find the strength to hold on for a few more thrusts.

Suddenly, his body began to jerk and I heard those loads of spunk splattering onto my carpet. He let loose with several screaming sobs, his hands still searching for a hold. I pulled him up onto his knees as I dropped onto mine. I held him tight as I continued to pound his ass, watching in amazement as rope after rope of cum rocketed into the air.

Then I heard him gagging and I wondered if maybe he was right; that it was one long chute and my cock had reached up into his throat.

With that, my balls could take it no more. I pulled out and he fell forward. I ripped off the condoms and he rolled onto his back. I stood and held onto my hose, draining every ounce of fluid from my body onto his stomach, chest, and face.

I bucked with the power of an orgasm the likes of which I had never felt. I had devolved into something less than human, grunting and shouting and shaking as if possessed.

When I had squeezed the last remaining drop onto his twitching body, my brain started to function again.

The fog lifted and I looked down on him. He seemed barely conscious.

I knelt beside him and realized, with regret, that I had ruined another one. Like all the others, when he came round he would either run for the door, frightened and damaged, or he would become an obsessive puppy dog, shadowing me like I was his master.

Neither was the reaction I wanted.

His face had dried blood and rug burns on it, and it was sprayed with cum. Looking at him, almost comatose, he no longer looked hot and nasty. He only looked, quite simply, beautiful. I realized with a shock that beneath the sneer and the growth of beard, he couldn't have been much older than 20.

How could I ever have believed that he truly understood what he had been asking for?

I did my best to mask the concern in my voice. "Well, slut, did you get your fill?"

The eyes opened and embers flew out at me. His voice was weak but the sneer was still there. "I guess this can last me until dinner time."

I smiled. It was definitely love.

Damn, this was going to be nasty.

The Foreman and the Grunt
By Derek Adams

I zeroed in on the guy the minute he stepped onto the site. Here at Norris Construction we get assigned a crew of greenhorns every summer. Most of them are young, dumb, and full of come, and I generally steer clear of them. This particular guy probably wasn't much over the company's minimum hiring age of 18, and he was no doubt up to his eyebrows in jizz, but there was something about him that stuck in my mind like a burr, refusing to be shaken loose.

For one thing, he pretty much conformed to my idea of what a wet dream looked like. He was about a head shorter than me, built solid, with broad shoulders and narrow hips. His shirt sleeves were rolled up high enough to show the full curve of his biceps, and his lower body was giving a faded pair of Levi's a real workout. I mean to say, he was stretching those pants in all the right directions—side-to-side and front-to-back. His skin was burnished dark-brown by the sun, his eyes were blue as the summer sky, and his thick mane of hair was the color of wheat.

As luck would have it, the guy ended up working for me. My crew is responsible for getting supplies distributed to wherever they're needed on the site. The new guy was naturally gonna end up being the grunt—doing all the shit work that the rest of the crew foisted off on him. I sort of felt sorry for him, but he looked strong enough to handle it. Besides, the work wasn't gonna do him any harm.

"You're all done," old man Norris told the guy as he turned over the last of the employment forms he'd been filling out. "This here's Harry Andrews. He tells you to jump, you jump." Norris waved at me then walked off across the site.

"Morning, Mr. Andrews." The guy was a baritone but just getting used to the fact. He spoke softly, like he was afraid his voice might break if he shouted.

"Harry," I corrected him. "Just call me Harry. I'm the foreman, you're the grunt. The work ain't glamorous, but the pay's better than you'd get leaning on the counter in a convenience store. Basically, you do anything anyone on the crew asks you to do unless it's against the law or just plain stupid. You put in a good day's work, we'll get along just fine." I looked into his impossibly blue eyes and felt a tingling in my balls. I'd have to be careful around this one. "What's your name?" I barked gruffly.

"Sonny," he replied. "Sonny Regis."

"Come on, Sonny. I clapped my hand on his shoulder. Muscle jumped against my palm. "Let's get you a hard hat and some decent gloves."

I got him outfitted then sent him over to my crew. Every time I walked by to check on the guys, Sonny was in the thick of things, fetching and carrying. I knew my crew—they'd ride his butt hard, and he'd be sore as a boil for a few days, but they wouldn't let him get hurt. I went on about my business, checking inventory and ordering supplies.

At noon I stepped into the wire cage of the elevator and rode it up to the top. My boys liked to eat their lunch out in the sun, so they were always at the highest level that had been floored in. When the elevator shuddered to a stop, I opened the door and stepped out into the brilliant sunshine. Matt Preston, a practical joker from way back, turned around from where he was kneeling and motioned for me to be quiet. The boys were up to something—that much was clear from the wicked gleam in Matt's eye.

"We're doing us some initiating," he whispered, after he had crept silently over to my side. "The new guy is joining me and the boys in a little circle jerk."

"The hell you say," I muttered, shaking my head. It was such an old trick it had grandkids, but Sonny seemed to have fallen for it in a big way. I stepped over to where my guys were huddled in the center of the floored area, unable to resist the temptation to watch the proceedings.

Sonny was already blindfolded, a red bandanna bound tightly around his head. He'd taken his shirt off to soak up some rays, and I got a chance to study his body at close range. His pecs were squared; the small nipples capping them were burned just a shade darker than his skin. His belly was flat and hairless, ridged like a washboard. A few silvery hairs peeked out from under his arms, but for the rest, he was slick as a whistle. As I watched he slowly unbuttoned his fly, encouraged by the loud groans all around him.

When he pulled his whanger out of his pants, I damn near groaned out loud. It was nice and thick, the fat head covered with skin. A finger-thick vein ran up the middle of the shaft, pulsing slightly. His nuts were hanging low and loose in a bag that was damn near as hairless as his chest. Most of the hair on his body was concentrated in the dense curls that clustered around the base of his meat. They spilled out around the edges of his fly, gleaming like spun gold in the noonday sun.

After about five quick pulls Sonny's prick jutted out stiff as a poker. Nobody would ever tease him about the size of his business, that was for damned sure. It was a double handful, and Sonny's hands weren't small. He squeezed it, and a glistening drop of goo oozed out the slit in the tip. I licked my lips, knowing I'd be dreaming about this for days to come.

All the guys were groaning and moaning, pretending they were beating off, so Sonny got busy, determined to win the bet. You know how these things are supposed to work—first dude who comes up with a handful of scum wins. Thing is, there's usually only one dude doing the jacking, so the guy with the sticky palm is the goat. Anyhow, Sonny started off nice and slow, squeezing his piece from the base, right out to the hooded tip. By the third pull he was drooling juice. Once he had a skinful it oozed out, hung in the air, suspended by a glistening thread, then broke off and splashed onto the floor.

You could judge Sonny's progress by watching his body. His nipples were standing out on his squared pecs, delicate nubs of flesh that I longed to mash flat with my tongue. A couple of minutes into it, the veins on his biceps popped out like cords, slowly extending till they bulged from his shoulders to his wrists. A flush of red crept up from his belly and spread over his chest and neck. Within minutes his face glowed crimson and beads of sweat glistened on his forehead and upper lip.

"Shit, guys, here it comes," he gasped, his shoulders hunching as he raised up onto his knees and started fisting his prick so fast, it was a flesh-colored blur. "Oh, fuck, man, I'm coming. Better stand back!"

His hands dropped to his sides and his hips shot forward, his cock vibrating like a tuning fork. A big glob pushed out the come hole and started to drool down onto the floor. Then Sonny's muscles flexed, and he grunted.

I saw the sun glinting off the end of his knob, but I didn't see the arc of his first shot till it splattered against my forearm. The spicy, pungent smell of his juice damn near did me in. His second shot sailed past me and splattered on a girder. He pumped a couple onto the floor in the middle of the circle, then spit one onto the toe of my left boot.

"I win!" he shouted triumphantly, reaching up and taking off his blindfold. The expression on his face when he got a look at the other guys was priceless. "I'll be damned," he croaked as he took it all in. Then he started to laugh, his voice ringing out on the summer air. The other guys joined him, all of them cracking wise. Sonny had definitely passed the test and had been accepted as a regular part of the crew.

"Harry!" I turned and saw Sonny waving at me as I left the job site that evening. I waved back and he ran over to me.

"Survived your first day with flying colors," I remarked.

"Yeah." He blushed scarlet under his tan. "I'm really sorry about...about...well, you know."

"Don't worry about it, Sonny. It wiped right off." I chuckled and gave him a conspiratorial wink. "I don't even think it's gonna leave a scar. Hey, can I give you a ride someplace?" We had reached the parking lot, and Sonny was still following me. I liked having him walking along beside me, his shoulder occasionally brushing my arm. Every time I took a breath I could smell him, a heady mixture of sweat and pent-up spunk. My fingers ached to reach out and caress his skin, just to see if it felt as soft as it looked. Damn it, the guy was driving me right around the bend. "Where you headed?"

"Well, if you can give me a ride over to the bus terminal, that'll be OK."

"The bus terminal?" I stopped beside my old Chevy pickup and shot him a puzzled look. "You figuring on doing some traveling?"

"No, nothing like that. It's just that I'm sorta between places to live right now. The guy I was bunking with moved this weekend, and I couldn't afford the apartment by myself. I'll find something after I get my first paycheck. In the meantime, I've got my gear stashed at the bus depot. I was gonna wash up down there, then I figured I'd camp out in the park."

"That's pretty damned dangerous, Sonny."

"Hey, I can take care of myself." He squared his shoulders, and his handsome features settled into a scowl that wouldn't have scared an old lady.

"I don't doubt that you can take care of yourself," I assured him. "However, I don't figure a couple of weeks in a public park is going to do anything for your job performance. This is pretty hard work, just in case you haven't noticed. You'll be needing a good night's sleep."

"I'm sorry, Harry, but I don't have any options." He shrugged his broad shoulders and smiled a sad little smile.

"You can come and stay with me." When the words were out of my mouth I stood there, dumbfounded. With the brief exception of a disastrous marriage right out of high school, I hadn't lived with any-one for almost 18 years. I had a small one-bedroom apartment that was barely big enough for me. I don't know what the hell came over me, but I'd said it, and I'd stand by it. Besides, the grin that spread over Sonny's face would have melted a stone.

"That'd be great, Harry!" he enthused. "I'll be real quiet, and I'll pick up after myself. Hell, you won't even know I'm there."

Well, he was quiet and neat, but I sure as hell knew he was there. He sat beside me in the evening while we watched TV, he was across from me when we ate, and he was always slipping in and out of the bathroom while I was getting ready for work in the mornings. The worst thing was that he was always touching me. It was always real casual and natural, but it was driving me up the fucking wall. I saw him all day long, and after I went to bed he was etched on my eye-lids as I tried to get to sleep.

Today was Saturday, so I had to face the prospect of a whole day with him. I got up early, did a few stretches, then took off for a run, hoping that maybe a few miles would take the edge off the dull throbbing in my groin. I'd had a hard-on for days now. I beat off in the shower in the morning and after I went to bed at night, but I still popped a rod every time I thought about Sonny.

When I got back to the apartment, he was just getting up. He got up off the couch and gave me a sleepy grin. He was stark naked, his perfect prick hanging down between his perfect thighs. "Good morning," I said, fighting to keep my eyes off his butt. The cheeks of his ass were like two melons—firm, smooth and golden. They flexed with every step, a dimple in the left cheek winking at me teasingly. I stepped past him and headed for the bathroom, intent on a shower and maybe a quick hand job. Sonny followed along after me, obviously ready to talk.

"You've really got a great build, Harry," he said, leaning against the door frame, idly rubbing his belly. "Ever since I was a little kid, I always hoped I'd grow up to look like you."

"What?" I turned and looked at him curiously.

"Oh, you know, big and muscular with a hairy chest. Man, have you ever got great arms!" Suddenly he grabbed my arm, squeezing my biceps appraisingly. I flexed as his fingers dug into the muscle. He stood there, his hand on my arm, looking up at me with those big blue eyes. "Could I touch your chest, Harry?"

My throat muscles worked violently but no sound came out. I nodded my head slightly, too overcome by lust to remember any of my ironclad rules for living. His hand hovered over my left pec, brushing against the tangle of fur that grew there. He gradually pressed down till he made firm contact, his palm hot against my swollen nipple. Our eyes locked, recognition of our need sparking both ways. I put my hands around his narrow waist, my fingers burning as I finally touched him. He laid his head against my chest, and I was lost.

"Let's do it, Harry," he whispered. I picked him up and lifted him high in the air. He grabbed the shower curtain rod and threw his legs over my shoulders. I burrowed between his legs, snuffling hungrily at his prick and balls, taking in the heady mixture of sweat, jizz, and funk he exuded.

Sonny yelped when my tongue made contact with the tender rosebud of flesh tucked behind his big balls. I licked and teased, then thrust my middle finger deep, forcing my way past his tight ass ring and into the steamy heat of his fuck hole. Sonny squirmed and moaned, struggling to reach out and grab his meat so he could start jacking himself while I finger-fucked him. I refused to cooperate, purposely keeping him off-balance so he had to hang onto the bar with both hands.

"I wanna touch my prick, Harry. Come on, man, I really need to touch my prick!"

"Not a chance," I grunted. I drove my finger deeper up his hot hole, and his thighs tightened against the sides of my head. I licked his asshole and balls while I poked at his prostate. Sonny howled, and his asshole spasmed. With my free hand I reached into the medicine cabinet and grabbed a rubber. Opening it one-handed wasn't easy, but I managed. I plopped the lubed latex on the end of my meat and rolled it down the shaft.

After I'd licked and fingered him till his asshole gaped, I shrugged my shoulders roughly, dislodging him from his perch. The backs of his thighs slid down my sweaty chest, his asshole tugging at the hairs on my belly as it spasmed and throbbed. My aim was perfect—my swollen meat jammed right up Sonny's twitching hole as his butt slipped down to my crotch. There was a moment of resistance, then his eyes opened wide as I breached him and sheathed my fat piece in his hot, silky hole.

I dropped to my knees and fell forward onto him, pinning him to the floor, my dick buried deep. His smooth chest rubbed against my hairy one as he grabbed my arms and ground himself against me. His cock and balls mashed against my belly, the honey flowing out of him hot and thick. I'd only pumped him a few times when he closed his eyes and let fly with one of his high-powered loads. The first blast caught me under the chin, splattering on my throat and drizzling down over my pecs. I reared back and stirred my cock around in him slow and easy, watching him score his abs with creamy white streamers of jism.

After he was drained, I braced my hands on either side of his blond head and started fucking him, my prick sliding in and out of his un-resisting ass channel. He was hard again in seconds. I nibbled his succulent tits, and his asshole spasmed tight around my prick. Then I licked him, neck to navel, continuing down till I got the head of his piece in my mouth. I nipped the silky foreskin between my teeth and pulled it up tight over the fat knob. His balls rose up against the sides of the shaft, jiggling as I relentlessly pounded his ass.

"Fuck me," he squealed, grabbing his hard-on and jacking it furiously. I pummeled him, my balls slapping against his back. My orgasm began with a heat that permeated my skin and set all my nerve endings to throbbing. The sensation intensified as it swirled around my belly and coursed through my loins. I stopped humping when my groin muscles spasmed and my balls knotted tight between my legs. My cock flexed, and I began to shoot, flooding the rubber with my thick cream. Sonny's eyes rolled back in his head as he blasted my chest and belly with his second load.

I humped him till my balls were drained, then collapsed on top of him, my whole damn body tingling in the aftermath of the best screw I'd had in years. Sonny kissed me, his lips hot against my neck. When my dick slid out of him I rolled over on my side and looked down at him. "You just made me break every rule I ever managed to devise about keeping work and pleasure separate," I told him, tracing the curve of his chest with my fingertips.

"Hey, Harry, that's what rules are for, right?" He winked at me and sat up, stretching lazily. "Would the foreman like to shower with the grunt? Maybe we can come up with a whole new set of rules for you to live by."

"Yeah," I chuckled, getting to my feet. Sonny jumped up, slipped his arms around me, and began nuzzling my chest. "Maybe we could."

Joe Pornstar
By Alan Mills

A single white drop collects on the tip. I watch it, struggling to keep my eyelids from clamping shut. I concentrate, concentrate: Just hold back! And then, the sudden twitch of my pelvis, jizz rocketing upward in one long stream like Challenger '87, exploding mid-air, falling back to shower my stomach with seminal debris. I immediately think, this is exciting—me and this other guy, legs entwined, asses connected by a double-headed dildo, the sun on our naked skin, the two of us, on our backs, a couple of hot studs on a roof fourteen stories above Hollywood Boulevard.

I'd just delivered the come shot of my life. It was a perfect 10. I'd done everything right. Moved right. Tensed right. Groaned and moaned and swore right. Even my face gave a perfect expression at the moment of take off. I'm sure that I looked wracked and vulnerable, yet still totally a man, just like I'm supposed to. Now, it's up to the other guy. He strokes his cock quickly. It's smaller than mine. I lift my head and look at his face, saying with conviction, "Yeah, shoot that load, boy!"

"Oh yeah, oh yeah," he returns, his lashes shaking, his mouth gaping open. "Oh fuck, man, I'm gonna shoot my load, man." I know that rising in his pitch. "Oh fuck! Oh fuck!" It's happening. I grind my butt on the dildo, driving his end further up his ass.

"Yeah, shoot that load!"

He stops stroking, squeezes his cock with one hand, his nuts with the other. "Oh fuck!" He grunts, squeals, shakes all over, but nothing comes.

The shuddering stops, his body relaxes, and I just stare.

I stare, the cameras stare, the director can't take his next breath. I start to sit, eager to get the rubber out my ass. "Don't!" the director shouts. "Nobody moves until I get a come shot." He gestures to two cameramen. "Take a break, but be ready."

"Carl—" I start.

"Joe, don't move."

"Oh God!"

"Joe, you were great. Now, just stay right there. It won't take long." Carl turns. "David...sweety..."

David's still panting. "I...I'm..." He's a cute kid, but I could kill him right now.

"S-s-sh... Honey, I need you to come for me."

David strokes his softening dick and opens his eyes. "I think I did come."

"Not really you didn't." I hear bitterness.

"I did, but...just...nothing came out."

"I know you have more in you. Take your time. We'll wait."

And that's that. David goes back to stroking his little prick. The camera guys back off. Carl goes to get a donut. The various stage hands and hangers-on pace nervously somewhere behind the lights. And, after having already been through eight hours of this crap, I'm stuck, flat on my back, while cold come drips down my sides even as a thick piece of unforgiving rubber cruelly rests about six inches up my worn-out gut. As far as I'm concerned, this is a pretty fucked up way to spend a Saturday, or don't you agree?

My life isn't always exactly as easy as many people imagine. Really, I don't ride in limousines that often, and I've only been taken to Europe a few times since becoming a star. Sure, that stuff's glamorous, and whenever I show up at a party or a club, it's a major event, but most of the time, through most of my days, my life gets fairly boring and is often almost unbearable.

I don't think I've ever stopped to ask myself why so many hustlers and adult video actors die young of drugs or AIDS or suicide. Now I think it's because dying young becomes the only thing left to do. At least, that way, the party never ends.

Carl was a porn star, too. Now, like other survivors, he directs and does almost too much crystal. Not quite too much. Just enough to be a major mess while still making lots of money. Of course, that's because he's one of the smart ones. But, he's one of the dumb ones too. It'll catch up with him, but for now, he's doing great. He owns his own company, distributes all over the country, and works overtime to promote his product in a rather noble attempt to rob more major porn studios of their spotlight. I have to say I admire that. I'd like to think that I could do the exact same thing, but I don't. Thoughts about aging annoy me too much. It's futile, but I enjoy fighting back.

There's too much in my life to worry about right now. Even as I lie here with a burning pink dildo snaking closer and closer to my heart, I worry about what my roommate's doing. I imagine going home to an empty apartment. Aaron's definitely gone unstable. But then, none of us age gracefully. It's to be expected We're all just too gay—us porn stars that is—even the straight ones. We are the quintessence of gay. For decades, we've defined sexuality despite ourselves. And aging just isn't part of that picture.

I don't have much to worry about. I'm still 24. I've been in the business for three years, and that's been enough to make me famous. I look great. I feel great. I could go on being fabulous for another five years, but that's not usually how things go. Even I know that.

It's too bad being in porn is such a taboo. This industry works so hard to create its own little world, with parties, awards, a tight tribe that works extra hard to make us feel OK. I wish it was acceptable to enter into a brief, lascivious career after high school, before going on to bigger but maybe not better things. It could be like the army. We could give scholarships and student loans. How cool would it have been if my guidance counselor saw my potential way back when?

Thinking about it now, I'd leave, if there was someplace else to go.

"How you doing, Joe?"
"Just fine."
I feel like the whole building is sitting up my ass. Carl must know this. Some questions just shouldn't be asked. I lift my head and look at David. His eyes are closed and he's stroking his tiny, half-hard dick with two fingers and his thumb.

I had a David of my own once. Years ago. We were really only supposed to be fucking around, but for me, it was something more. It blossomed the normal way: a few six packs, a Saturday night, David asking, "I wonder what getting head is like."

I'm all, "I don't know."

He's like, "Seth gets it all the time."

And so, after the appropriate amount of silence, David says, "You know, it's not a big deal. It's like sticking someone's finger in your mouth."

I stare at him like a camera. He's a jock. I feel the most intense friendship. I think of him as a buddy and often wonder why other guys don't care as much about their friends.

"I'd do it to you," he says, "if you did it for me."

"OK, Carl," says David, "I think I'm getting there."

Carl violently gestures to his cameras. Cameras, lighting, grips move into position. I close my eyes, the first dick of my life passing my lips, spreading musk across my tongue, all the way back.

I feel the dildo going deeper. David's squirming, shifting side to side, fighting to exhume his load, driving my end deeper, harder against my prostate.

I feel David coming, the dildo like a jackhammer, his hips bucking wildly, David coming down my throat, the bitter salt, me exploding a second time, a second big time, my sphincter feeling like it'll never close.

I don't usually just come when I'm working on videos, but the situation seems to demand it. Most of the time it's like acting. I force it to be something unnatural and shocking. That's why I get paid. It is, after all, called a money shot. More shot, more money. At least that's my way of thinking.

This second time, however, is a bit different. I do it with my eyes closed. I do it thinking of the past, not keeping my mind on the moment, on the holding back, the tensing and releasing on cue.

Looking down at the mess, I know I did good, but still, I feel a need to go home, Ohio. Back to Kent State. Back to David, if he's still there, not with Nancy, not hitched to her. That's naive. It's not how the world works. Carl throws me a towel and says, "Hey Joe, get cleaned up and I'll take you to dinner."

I know what he's doing. This means he's paying the stupid kid more, the flavor of the month, hot little bottom, blond hair, fresh face. The cameras have yet to satisfy their need.

I quickly decide to take Carl up on his offer. He'll offer fast times, I'll order calamari and swordfish, drink as much as I can, but not really eat. I'll make him pay the difference.

Of course, he invites David, gives David a bag—I try not to feel hurt. It's all the kind of stuff you shouldn't take personally—drugs, sex, money. I set myself on "Don't care."

After a few drinks, I'm in the bathroom, filling a urinal with whiz. I'm fucked up in all sorts of ways, but not enough. I'm still connected to the world by a cord I want to cut, disgorging myself from the womb of reality, a crying fetus flinging myself into the great nothingness that has no sound.

See, better living through chemicals.

The door opens behind me, someone stepping into the small, brightly lit room. He moves next to me, about a foot back, to the toilet to my right. "Do you mind?" he asks softly.

"No," I say, "go ahead."

I hear the metal teeth gaping open, the metal clasp sliding down. I look over. He's a tall, broad, stud of a man. My chest tightens from the first sight of him, his fat, uncut cock still at the edge of my vision.

"Hey, you're—"

"Yeah," I say, zipping and walking to the door. I hear his piss fall, water collapsing into water, hormones rising inside hidden steam. I think of myself as a beast, sensing molecules in the breeze. I think of molecules moving, diffusing, forming compounds. It's indiscriminate, yet still makes sense.

I lock the door, a simple pushing of a tab. I move behind him, pressing close, taking his thick cock, his clean shaved sac cascading down my palm.

"You're fuckin' huge," I whisper as he continues to release.

"You too," he whispers back. "You're my favorite."

He's hard in my hand, so hard I just want to smack his cock against my face. "Don't mention it," I say, his piss trailing off. I squeeze the shaft, pump forward, shake, turn him around, his cock as the lead.

I descend to my knees, the smell of whiz still emanating from the bowl. I look right down his slit, piss still seeps from the end. I slap the meat against my cheek, rub it against my skin, feeling a light trickle drip down my neck.

I look up at him and lower his cock onto my tongue, the Eucharist. The bitter sting excites. I open my throat to it, submissive in the first moment, letting his cock enter me like the holy word. I suck on it, pull back until his foreskin is like gum between my teeth. I pump it in my fist, take one good look at its jaw-spreading size. I spit on it like it's life itself, spreading my spit across it with a fist. I spit again and notice, for the first time, a blazing tag along his fly reading Lucky You.

My mother still believes in signs. A tow truck or a bus. A street light flickering as she drives past. The stopping of a clock. I used to see them too, holding onto useless moments as if believing in preschool superstitions, the cracks in a sidewalk. But mother's signs were meaningless and inconsistent—omens undefined—and I tossed them all. But to this day, I think twice about a lot of things.

From my position on the tile floor, I look up at him. He grins. "I can't believe how hot this is," he says. "You look just like an angel."

I lower my mouth to his cock and cup my tongue under the head, lifting the weight with my chin. I lean forward, taking it all, the girth and length permeating my throat unnaturally. I feel plugged, shut up, picturing myself an angel, a cherub looking to Heaven, long lashes, pouty lips, cheeks overstuffed.

I lift myself up the expanse of his skin, letting my tongue enter the musky casing of his hard cock. I think I am a different kind of angel, a fallen angel at the feet of a fallen angel, a throne of corpses, me opening myself to tortures for sins for which I should permit forgiveness.

He grabs behind my neck and grips his nuts, his thumb hooked above his shaft. He fucks my face, not hard—steady—slow, deep. I moan around his flesh, spit dripping down my chin, drool rubbing all across my face.

"Oh God! Joe," he groans. "I always knew you'd be perfect."

And I think of him as alien, a divine figure who has watched me my whole life and is only now first meeting me. His love borders on obsession. I have always been his, but now, he has me.

Its pace increasing, his cock moves in time with hoarse breaths. I taste salt, like I'm swimming in the ocean. I think I'm a different kind of angel and I imagine myself painted by Caravaggio, light streaming down, the center of meaning not my serenity, but the lost passion on the forgiven man's face.

His cock escapes my throat. It is oblivion. I open to it, extending my tongue like in winter, catching snowflakes. Yes, it's all better living. His jizz strikes the roof of my mouth, behind my front teeth, falls on my taste buds, pours down my chin to the floor. My eyes closed, the vision taboo. All warmth. All chemicals. Jizz strikes my brow, slips through my lashes—I feel it clogging my nose.

I am without breath, without life, taken over by the seed of man's birth. I lower my head, clasp my hands, and wipe spunk off my face.

I stand. The emptied stud glances at my crotch. "Aren't you?"

"No," I say. "I've got a shoot tomorrow, and I've already come three times today."

"Oh," he says. "I understand."

"Thanks, um, Joe," he says, flushing the toilet. I look in the mirror, water running, my hands cupping it, bringing purity to form. I'm still so high, I want to suck off someone else. If my ass weren't so sore, I'd get fucked, and fuck too. I'd go to sex clubs and fuck everything, the men, the holes between stalls. "When you come out, I'll get you a drink, OK?" he asks, stepping into the hall.

"That would be nice," I say, rubbing his come from my eyes.

David steps in. "Are you still in here? I just ran into—"

He stares at me, silenced. I look at myself, used, the impurity of flesh, drunk and fucked up. I look at myself, crying a soft chuckle, breathing in, needing to blow spunk from my nose. I look at myself, this total slut, this pathetic porn star, this unbelievable creature stolen from myth.

Three-Penny Dare
By R.J. March

I gave Travis three pennies because he'd asked for them, and I watched him put them down his pants. "Davis said you'd get them for me if I asked nice enough. He said you'd blow me for 3 cents. That right, Kyle?"

"Fuck yourself," I said, feeling a flash of hate for him. I found it hard to believe that Davis would say anything about what he and I did, putting himself in any position so open to ridicule. But then Davis was kind of stupid too, and maybe he thought Travis would think it was funny, and maybe he didn't bother to mention how he'd lie back, letting me crawl between his legs to lick his crotch and jerk him off.

"They're in my underpants, Kyle. One's, like, in my pubes, and the other two are under my balls. I can feel them. Why don't you dig them out for me, Kyle?" We were in his basement. There was a game on television—Penn State was kicking the shit out of Michigan. It was such a slaughter, we lost interest, sprawled on old sofas, one for each of us, drinking beer because his parents were out of town.

I could have left, but we'd just smoked a bowl, and I didn't feel as though I could actually move myself. I looked up at the dumb little windows near the ceiling that were set in little wells outside; you couldn't see anything unless you stood just under them, and then all you saw was the overhang of grass from above. I was thinking it was just like being buried and having a window in your coffin, only your coffin was huge and had big old lumpy sofas in it and a TV and your ex-best friend trying to get you to feel him up.

"You are so stoned," he said.

"Quit fucking with me," I told him. What the fuck am I doing here? I wondered.

"I got a pudgy just thinking about it," he said.

"You're such an incredible asshole, Travis, you know that?"

"This game sucks." He switched it off.

"No shit now, Kyle," he said, sitting up, making his face look very serious. "He told me you'd blow me for a nickel. Is that true?"

I shook my head.

"It's not?" he said, sounding incredulous, and I wondered just how much that dumbfuck had told him.

He shut up then and didn't say another word about Davis or me or the three pennies in his undershorts. He got up awkwardly—to take a leak, he announced quietly—and walked funny to the bathroom back by the laundry room. I listened to him, liking the sound. In the middle of the room I saw the copper shine of a penny, and I scrambled for it and picked it up, sniffing it before putting it in my pocket. Truth was, I'd have blown him for nothing.

"You need to learn to keep your fucking mouth shut." I was up in his face, smelling the Italian sub he'd had for lunch, my finger tapping on the small patch of soft black hair that had grown on his sternum.

"What the fuck's wrong with you?" Davis said, backing up. He was my height and age, 19, but 20 pounds lighter—not that that gave me any advantage over him. He was unscrupulous and meaner than I could ever hope to be. "And my mom's in the kitchen, so watch it, asshole."

"We need to get out of here, then," I said carefully.

"Just settle down, Kyle," Davis said. He wiped his palms on his warm-up pants, looking around for something.

"Hurry the fuck up," I whispered hoarsely.

He gave me a cold look that made me bite the inside of my lip. "You better cool the fuck down, Kyle," he said, pointing his finger at me. He walked across the room and grabbed a gray sweatshirt off the back of a chair. "Come on," he said.

Outside, he walked to his car. "Mine," I said.

"Cool," he said. "I need gas anyway."

"And you're the one with the fucking secret," I said—whatever the hell that was supposed to mean. I'd taken us up to Bigger's Rock, a series of cliffs and clearings overlooking the Wallkill River. It was a party place for underage drinkers in the summer, but it was too cold to do anything now but look at the scenery. We called it Dyke's Peak because we saw Travis's sister kissing Amanda Betts there, slipping her hand up Amanda's Catholic-plaid skirt. I turned off the engine and sat looking out the window. I wasn't mad anymore, mostly because I'd noticed that Davis wasn't wearing socks. I took my hands off the steering wheel, turning toward him, and he got out of the car.

"I didn't say anything, Kyle, swear to God," he said over the roof of my Nova. "Why the fuck would I say anything? And to Travis, for chrissake? He's just dicking with you."

I'd already considered this—he really would have been cutting his own throat by saying anything to anyone. He stared at me, his hood up, eyes dark inside. He had thin lips that seemed always to be locked up in a smile, and his nose had a hard hook that kept him from being pretty but made him all the more beautiful. "Are we going up or what?" he asked.

"Maybe he wants some," Davis said. "He's just fishing. He's trying to get in your pants. You guys have been buds since, like, second grade or something, haven't you?"

I said, "Travis isn't like that."

Davis stopped on the trail, and I nearly ran into him. "I wasn't either—remember?"

I considered what he was trying to convince me of, but there was no way I was ever going to believe that Travis would do such a thing, not ever.

The sky was bright gray, and the hill across the river was dark. I was thinking that it would snow soon. Davis walked in front of me with his hands dug into the pouch of his sweatshirt, trying to stay out of the muddy ruts and keep his Pumas clean. I watched the way his butt flicked back and forth, how he walked on the balls of his feet, his hooded head bobbing.

There was a clean-edged cliff we liked. He was leading us there. "It's fucking cold," Davis said. The wind cut through my thin coat. He hopped around me, shouldering me, telling me how cold he was. "I'm cold too," I said.

"I wish we had a sleeping bag," he said. He pulled his hands out of his front pouch, and his sweatshirt lifted, showing the impress of his cock against the thin nylon of his warm-ups. He had a gigantic prick; I couldn't imagine doing much more with it than handling the thing, stroking it with both hands and kissing the fat bloom of its head, using the thick spit at the back of my throat for lube. He gave me a brown-eyed look, and I felt myself going all shy and buttery inside. He looked at me from the corners of his eyes, his head at a downward slant, his lips almost closed, breaths slipping out of him in small puffs. I glanced down and saw his hands fiddling inside his pants. I reached out, and he held open the waistband for me.

It was too late to do what I liked best, which was making him hard, feeling him go from a little spigot to a lead pipe. Now there was something I could do with my mouth, until he'd grow and grow and my lips would stretch and stretch. Not that I wouldn't have stayed on him and done my best, but he was always reluctant to have me stay on him like that—afraid, I guess, that he'd lose it and come in my mouth or something, like that was a bad thing. "Just jerk it," he would say, hands on his hips, bouncing on the balls of his feet, the muscles along his thighs going taut. Sometimes he talked to me while I pulled on him. "That Wallace kid on the team, remember him? Did you think he was good-looking? How about Secor—now that kid had a hot fucking body." He missed being in high school, missed soccer practice and the showers afterward—the wet, hairy huddle of guys who'd eye his plumbing furtively, enviously—the thickening rod, the great lathered balls. He'd linger as long as he could, until his dick threatened full erection. I wasn't the only one to notice but apparently the only one to let him know I'd noticed.

We stood face-to-face. I tucked his waistband underneath his balls and pulled on the hard shaft. It seeped and smeared my shirt cuff. I reached under his sweatshirt, where his skin was feverish. I found his nipple and toyed with it, rolling it between my fingers, something I think I liked more than he did. His nipples were pea-size and went hard quickly, and I loved getting one in my mouth to chew on gently. His stomach muscles fluttered under my fingertips, and I took his cock in both hands, a stranglehold that made the head bulge and go dark, and I bowed to put my mouth on it, wanting to lap up the big rolling drop of precome that had welled up in his deep piss slit. From there, I licked down his shaft to nuzzle his furry balls, the bag gone wrinkly from the cold. He liked the slide my fingers made over his dick head—I could tell by the way he leaked and from the roll of his hips. I looked up to find him watching me, his brown eyes tearing in the wind. He had something to say but wouldn't let it out. I covered his cock end with my mouth, tonguing into his hole, letting my lips go slack to slip down over his shaft.

"Stop," I heard him say, but I couldn't. I got as much of him into my mouth as I could, and he tried to break free from me, but I held him close and choked myself on him until I felt the hot blast of his come jettisoned down my throat. He pushed me off roughly then, shuddering. "Shit," he said. "Why the fuck did you do that?"

"Wanted to," I said, his residue dripping off my chin.

He wiped himself off on the inside of his sweatshirt, looking around us. I felt the cold, damp ground under me and the hot hardness I had in my jeans and wondered if he was ever going to take care of me.

"Get up," he said, his teeth coming together, the cold getting to him finally. "Let's go."

"I'm telling you, he wants it," Davis said. We were at the mall, standing in the store Travis worked in. We could see him standing by his register, picking at something on his knuckle, looking bored. "He wants you," Davis said as Travis looked across the store and spotted us. "Look at the way he smiles at you."

"Shut up," I said. He was walking over to us, swinging his arms wide.

"What's up, dudes?" he said, looking at Davis, then at me. To my amazement, there was nothing on his face, no trace of a smirk, not a reference to last week's three-penny dare. "I'm done at 5—what are you guys doing tonight?"

Davis looked at me, and I shrugged. "Why don't you come over to my place?" Travis pursued. "My dad went to Charlotte, and my mom's at my sister's."

"Sounds cool," Davis said.

"I just bought Redneck Ram-page—we can blow the fuck out of cows and shit," Travis said.

"Awesome," I said. Travis hitched up his shirtsleeve, baring his biceps. "Security just caught two guys in our shitter here fucking," he said, whispering.

"No way," Davis said.

"Absolutely going to town," Travis said, beaming. "They didn't even hear the guard, they were so into it."

"Fuck, man," Davis said, shaking his head.

"You got that right," Travis said, smirking.

In the car Davis said to me, "He's so fucking fixated, man, I'm telling you. He wants it, I know he does."

"Whatever," I said, putting the car in reverse.

I changed my mind like ten times about going with Davis to Travis's house. But there was something about the idea of the three of us getting together that was like an itch in my brain I couldn't get to. Waiting for 9 o'clock, I sat up in my room, listening to my mom and dad bitching at each other about where they were going for their vacation—Maine or Hilton Head. I sat on my bed, looking through a month-old Rolling Stone, wanting to call Davis up and tell him I wasn't going to go, and then I was looking at this Tommy Hilfiger ad—three guys playing at the shore in wet boxers—and I felt myself getting a little pudgy. I dug into my jeans and got a handful, loving the way the front of my briefs felt, all full and warm. I slid out of my jeans and went to the mirror on the back of my door. I ran my hand over the filled-up pouch, my cock hugging the curve of my balls, the whole neat and pretty package.

"No, wait," I heard. "Let's ask Kyle."

"Jesus," I said, yelling to my parents through the door. "Just leave me out of it!"

My father came walking down the hall. I made a lunge for my jeans on the bed and was trying to step into them when he opened the door.

"What do you think, son?" he asked.

"I think I'm going to Travis's," I said.

I walked over to Aeropagetica Road. Davis's car was parked out front, and the porch light was on. I let myself in.

I could hear the music from downstairs and Travis laughing. I walked through the living room and kitchen. "It hurts like that," I heard Davis say. I stopped still, standing at the door at the top of the stairs. My heart started beating hard in my chest, and I felt really, really stupid all of a sudden. "That's better," Davis said.

"I told you," Travis said.

I had to see them, to catch them in their naked embrace, because not only was I insanely jealous, but I was also poking out the front of my jeans again.

"Fuck, my head's gonna explode."

"Let me help."

I eased myself down the first step. Travis grunted. All I was thinking was, You couldn't fucking wait for me?

"Holy shit," Davis breathed.

I crouched down, trying to find them. The couches were empty. The guys were nowhere to be seen. I crept down two more treads and saw Travis's calves. He was clothed and standing, and Davis, I figured, was kneeling in front of him, which pissed me off even more, considering that he had never once made an offer to go down on me.

"I'm stuck," Davis said, and Travis moved, and I saw Davis hanging, his shirt covering his face, his torso bared, in some sort of hanging-boot contraption. "Get me the fuck down."

"They had one in *American Gigolo*," Travis said later. "Remember? Richard Gere?"

"You were, like, 1 year old when that came out," I said, holding the joint that Travis had handed me when I came in. "Who rolled this?" I tried to pass it to Davis, but he waved it on. I held it out for Travis, who said, "It's all yours, bud."

"I'm fucking zonked," Davis said, yawning.

"You want to try the boots?" Travis asked me.

I shook my head. "I'm afraid of heights," I said, cracking Davis up. He lay sprawled on the couch, and I leaned against it, sitting on the floor. Travis went over to the boots that were lying on the floor.

"They're fucking antiques, man," Davis said, his arm swinging off the couch and coming to rest on my shoulder.

I watched Travis put them on and reach for the bar overhead. His stomach was uncovered for a moment, and I saw the cuts of his abs. Where'd the baby fat go, I wondered, and how'd I miss it? He swung his legs up and got the boots hooked onto the bar. His shirt fell over his head, like Davis's had, and he tucked it into his shorts, but it kept pulling free so he took it off. And then he started doing crunches.

"Fuck," I whispered. I was awestruck and staring—I couldn't help it. His body was beautiful, and I'd never noticed.

Davis snored behind me, missing the show. I watched as Travis's stomach divided itself into neat, symmetrical sections, little rectangles of muscle. "Sweet," I said quietly.

And then he was done, getting himself out of the boots, asking me if I wanted to try. He had a mouthful of white teeth his lips struggled to cover. His hair, cut short, was the color of pennies. He twisted his shirt like a wet washrag, making the muscles in his chest jump.

"Your buddy's out, man," he said, looking at Davis's arm slung over my shoulder. Then his brows sort of came together, and one corner of his mouth went up. "He's like your best friend now, huh?"

I shrugged, feeling guilty. I couldn't pinpoint when it happened, when Travis stepped back and Davis stepped up. Maybe when Travis started dating Shawna Baylich and I realized we weren't going to be two boys together forever. Maybe when Davis started getting boners in the showers, looking at me from the corners of his eyes, maybe that's when I had to decide which was more important to me—dick or friendship? Isn't that what Travis had done?

"I'm hungry," he said.

"Me too," I said, not thinking.

We went upstairs, leaving Davis on the couch. Travis went to the refrigerator, and I hit the cupboards. "Dude," he said, all excited, and I turned and got a blast of whipped cream in the face.

"Fuck!" I shouted, and Travis laughed, pointed and laughed. He took a swipe at some off my chin and licked his finger, giggling convulsively. He came back for more, and I grabbed the can from him and squirted him from neck to navel. He stepped back and looked down at himself, and then he looked at me, cocking his head. "Oh, man," he said slowly. I put a dollop on each of his nipples.

"You really suck," he said, shaking his head.

"So you keep telling me," I said, impressing myself with the quick comeback.

"Can't blame me for trying, can you?"

The air went crackly—there was this static in my ears. I felt the whipped cream sliding down my cheek. He touched some again and licked his finger, and then he stepped close and put his face near mine, licking the line of my jaw.

I felt his tongue like a blow and stepped back, feeling pushed.

"I've been wanting to do that since, like seventh grade, I think," he said.

"Shut the fuck up," I said.

He hooked his finger into the waistband of my jeans and pulled me close. "Is this going to piss Davis off?" he asked.

I shook my head. "I'm in shock," I said.

"Do you need a blanket?"

"I'm having a heart attack, I think," I said, looking at his frothed tits.

"Have a taste," he said.

"Do I know you?" I asked him, looking into his eyes.

"Better than anyone," he said. "Least you used to."

I tongued away the whipped cream, feeling a little shameful, as if I were doing this to my brother. I licked his little brown nipple into hardness, and he held my head, telling me to bite a little. When I did, he moaned and pushed his hips forward, and I put my arm around him. He laughed, and I heard it in the cave of his chest. He pushed his shorts down, and his dick switchbladed up between us. I touched the cold, smooth skin of his ass. I licked down the whipped cream line to his belly button then nosed into his pubes, his dick pressing upward against my right cheek. I got the tip of it in my mouth. He had a nice pointed little dick head, shaped, I thought, like a Hershey's Kiss. It slipped easily into my mouth.

"Wait a minute," he said. "This is my fantasy."

He pushed me back against the kitchen table and started unbuttoning my jeans. He stripped me to my briefs, caressing the front as I had done earlier in the privacy of my room. He went to one knee, baring my prick. "You got bigger," he said.

"How would you know?"

"I was always watching, asshole," he said, putting his tongue on it.

I started thinking about the times we were naked together: the first time we got drunk, at Lisa Dinino's pool party, the two of us slipping off our shorts when everyone went in the house to watch Derek puke; at Disney World when our parents took a joint vacation and Travis and I had our own room; and now.

"Sit on the table," he said.

He spread my legs for me. My cock stood straight up, perpendicular to my body. He licked down the shaft, pushing his face into my bush, getting my balls in his mouth. He rolled them over his tongue, licking underneath them, his tongue long and serpentine and flicking at the hairs around my asshole. "Jeez," I said sharply.

His head bobbed up. "It hurts?" he asked, incredulous.

"No, it doesn't hurt," I said.

He pulled my shaft back, trying to get the head in his mouth.

"That hurts," I told him.

"Sorry," he said.

He stood, rubbing my thighs with backward hands knuckling against the pale skin. His cock poked up between us. He looked at me, my cock and stuff, and then he looked at my face. His face was almost sad.

"What is that supposed to mean?" he asked me.

I looked up at the ceiling.

"I mean," he said, lifting one hand to touch his hair, "I don't want to think too much about this, not right now anyway, but—"

"But what?" I said.

He made a smile out of his lips, glancing toward the basement, then he cocked his head in that direction. "Him," he said simply.

I closed my eyes, trying not to laugh. "Forget about it," I said, leaning forward. Our faces got close, and there wasn't anything else to do but kiss. At first it was tentative and foreign—I hadn't kissed another guy before, and I don't think Travis had either. We acclimated quickly, though, and soon our tongues were wrestling, and his hands went around my back and dropped to my butt.

"Come on, " he said. "Let's go to my room."

I hadn't been there in a long time, but it hadn't changed much. He still had his Flyers pennants up, and his poster of the Bay Twats, and a bunch of wall-mounted hubcaps we'd found together. The nostalgia I felt was spooky, like I was little again, or 15 at most. Travis pushed me onto his bed and lay on top of me. He said something that was muffled, his mouth against my throat. He pushed his hips against mine, and I got his shorts down to his thighs, and he was naked underneath.

"Can I?" he said, his mouth closer to my ear now.

"Can you what?"

"Can I fuck you?" he wanted to know.

I'd thought about it, of course, but I never imagined that it would really happen—not with Travis, anyway. I must have blinked up at him about 20 times before I actually answered.

"I guess" is all I said.

He pushed his cock against me, saying my name. I loved it. I closed my eyes, letting my head fall back against the pillow that smelled like him. His cock slid over my balls, and he pressed his belly hard against my dick. His hairs there were short and prickly, just trimmed, I figured. He licked my shoulder, across my clavicle, the other shoulder, biting me. His dick slipped under my balls, poking against my hole. I spread my legs for him, getting them around him, my calves on his cold ass, ankles hooking, drawing him closer.

"Does he ever do this?" he asked me, his face in my neck.

I said no.

"What does he do?" he wanted to know.

"He stands," I told him. "He stands and comes."

He leaned back as far as my legs allowed him, and he spat on the end of his dick.

"This is going to hurt, isn't it?" I asked.

"I don't know," he said. "It's different for everyone." He licked his forefinger and wormed it into my ass.

"Does that hurt?"

I shook my head.

He pulled it out and brought his hand to his mouth, sucking on his thumb, and then he put that in me. I moaned, and he looked at me. I got my hand around my cock. Every move of his thumb made me shudder, made me arch my back and want more of him inside me.

He reached into his nightstand and pulled out a rubber and a bottle of lubricant. I watched him roll the rubber onto his pecker. "You sure about this?" he asked me.

I shrugged.

"We don't have to," he said.

"I know."

He jacked himself with a little lube.

"You've done this before?"

He nodded.

"Who with?" I wanted to know.

"You don't know him," he answered.

He held himself, pushing against the spot he'd worked into softness. The slippery head eased in, but his thickening shaft made me gasp, and he stopped, touching my face gently. I turned away, not wanting any kindness that moment. I wanted to be fucked, and I told him so.

He pulled me to him, filling me with his cock, until he was in all the way and I was seeing stars. But there really were stars, these glow-in-the-dark stickers we'd put up on his ceiling years ago.

"Dude," he said. He put a thumb on my left nipple, rolling the little knob around. He shouldered my feet and managed to get more into me. I felt his balls bouncing against my tailbone, his pubes rasping my stretched-out ass lips, his breath blowing down on me, hot and sweet. He grabbed my cock and spat on it, drawing his palm up over the head. I touched his hand, shaking my head. "I'll blow," I said, and he smiled.

He fucked me slowly, bringing his cock head all the way out and pushing it back in. He leaned back to watch his own progress and the way my ass pulled when he tried to leave it. He gripped my ankles and lifted my bottom, slamming into me, making me grunt.

"Fucking beautiful," he said, turning us over on our sides, lying behind me. He held my hip and ground his dick up into me, rolling us over again so that I was on my stomach, my face in his pillow, and he was pounding me, licking my back, pounding and pounding my ass, his thighs between mine, spreading mine, coming up inside me.

"Oh, man," he said, pulling out, pulling off the rubber to show me. The end of it was filled.

He lay on his back and said, "Hop on." His cock was still hard, sticking straight up. He licked his palm and juiced up his stick for me, and I squatted on him, feeling a little self-conscious. He stabbed up into me, and I got my dick in my hand, jacking hard and fast and bobbing on his prong, keeping my eyes closed, not wanting to see him looking at me.

"Fuck," I said and started shooting. When I opened my eyes, his face was streaked, and he was laughing.

We took a shower together, washing each other's body. "I like this," he said.

Downstairs in the basement, we woke up Davis.

"We're hungry, are you?" I asked.

He nodded sleepily. "What time is it?" he asked.

Travis told him.

Davis sat up, rubbing his face, his cheek bearing the imprint of the Herculon weave of the sofa.

We walked out to the car. "I forgot my wallet," Travis said. Davis leaned over the backseat, his arm against my shoulder.

"I'm kind of horny," he said.

"You are?"

He nodded, grinning just a little. I reached over the seat and touched his crotch, finding him hard.

"Later," I said as Travis got into the car with us.

"Let's go, man, I'm fucking starved," I said, and we were off.

Fantasies
By Bob Vickery

The building's one of those converted Victorians, all the fancy woodwork stripped away, the facade covered with badly painted stucco. The steps are scattered with your standard-issue urban litter: fliers for pizza parlors and Chinese take-out joints, yellowing newspapers, that kind of thing. I take them two at a time, and when I get to the top, I pace up and down the stoop, breathing deeply. I'm getting an adrenaline rush like you wouldn't believe; my heart's pounding like a racing-car piston, and my brain's buzzing so much, I feel like I'm about to burst a blood vessel.

OK, focus, I tell myself. Channel the energy.

After I've calmed down a bit, I bend over and read the names on the strips of cardboard beneath each mailbox. Vinnie Castelloni is printed on the far right strip, vinnie written in bold strokes, castelloni all scrunched together. I push the doorbell and wait.

My hand begins to cramp, and I look down and see that I'm holding my Bible so tightly, my knuckles are white. I loosen my fingers.

Relax, I tell myself. Get into this.

I shut my eyes and take another deep breath. By the time the front door finally opens, I'm ready for bear.

The guy on the other side of the door eyes me suspiciously. He's in his mid to late 20s, too old for the street-punk attitude he's giving off. His black hair is greased back, there's two-day stubble on his face, and a cigarette dangles from his mouth. The tank top he wears hugs a well-muscled torso. There's a tear in it above his left pectoral, exposing a nipple the color and toughness of an old pencil eraser. His gaze flicks up and down my body and then settles on my face. He has the eyes of a fallen angel: dark and liquid but burning with a hard, cynical light. Mingled with the smell of old sweat is the unmistakable stench of a hell-bound sinner.

"Yeah?" he growls.

I clear my throat. I glance at the name card under the mailbox and then back at his face again. "Good morning, Vinnie," I say, making my voice as loud and hearty as I can. I raise my eyebrows and beam him my friendliest smile. "It is all right if I call you Vinnie, isn't it?"

Vinnie just glares at me with narrowed eyes, saying nothing.

"I'm here to share with you some wonderful news," I plunge on, "about how you can lay down the burden of life and let Jesus into your heart." I tug on the knot of my tie and inhale deeply. "I wonder if you'd be willing to give me a minute of your time?"

Vinnie just stands there in the doorway staring at me. He takes a deep drag from his cigarette and flicks the butt down the front steps. His full lips curl up into a nasty little smile. "Sure," he says, opening the door wider. "Come on in."

I push through before he has a chance to change his mind.

The apartment's small and dark: cheap thrift-store furniture, a threadbare rug, a beat-up old TV set. There are beer cans and newspapers scattered around the floor, and the kitchen sink is stacked with dirty dishes. A Hustler magazine lies open on the floor beside the couch, the centerfold model posed with her legs spread wide, showing pink (Just what was Vinnie doing when I rang the bell? I wonder).

I turn my head away and catch Vinnie watching me, smirking. He pulls a chair out from the table and straddles it, his forearms resting on its back. I sit down on the couch. I make a point of sliding my foot under the Hustler cover and flipping it shut.

"So what did you want to talk to me about?" he asks.

I run my tongue over my lips and put both hands on my knees. I'm feeling pumped. "Have you taken Jesus into your heart, Vinnie?" I ask.

Vinnie raises his arms above his head and stretches like some big jungle cat. The muscles of his torso ripple under his tight shirt. "No," he says calmly, "I can't say that I have."

I look directly into his beautiful dark eyes. "Did you ever stop to think that there may be a better way to live your life? Do you ever worry about your soul?" I raise my arm and shake my Bible at him. "The Bible says, 'Believe in the Lord, Jesus Christ, and thou shalt be saved.' " I realize I must look more like I'm trying to exorcise him than convert him, and I lower my arm.

Vinnie gives a little bark of laughter. He picks up a pack of cigarettes from the table next to him and shakes one loose. He looks at me over the flame of his match. "Do you really believe all that stuff?" he asks.

"Yes, I do. And it's worth your soul that you believe it too."

Vinnie looks amused. "What'll happen if I don't?"

I hold up my Bible. "It's all in here, Vinnie. If you don't believe, then you're just opening the door and letting Satan rule your life."

Vinnie seems to consider this. He takes a deep drag from his cigarette and exhales a stream of smoke. "Does Satan have a big dick?" he asks. "Do you ever wonder about things like that?"

"Well," I say, "if you're going to go on like that—"

"Does he?" Vinnie interrupts, his voice louder. He doesn't look amused now. His eyes drill into mine. "Is it thick and long? Do his balls hang low?" He stands up so abruptly, his chair topples back with a crash. He takes a step forward. "Do you ever wonder what it'd be like to suck it?"

I don't say anything for a while. "Is there a point you're trying to make?" I finally ask.

Vinnie's grin is boyish, but his eyes are two hard chips of stone. He walks over and stands before me, his crotch inches from my face. I can't help noticing the sizable bulge under the frayed denim of his jeans.

"Just answer the question," Vinnie says, his voice louder now. "Do you ever think about giving Satan head?"

There's nothing I can say to that. I close my eyes and start praying, the words spilling out in a steady stream.

"Do you wonder how Satan's cock would feel crammed down your throat?" Vinnie sneers. "Or shoved up your ass?" He's clenching and unclenching his fists now. "Is that what you want? To get fucked by Satan?"

"Sweet Jesus, but you've got a filthy mouth."

"I do, huh?" Vinnie growls. "Well, then, what about me? Maybe you'd like to chew on my dick for a while." With a quick movement he unzips his fly and yanks down his jeans. His hard dick springs out in front of him, inches from my face. "How about it?" he sneers. "How do I measure up?"

I stare at the thick shaft before me. "I've seen bigger," I lie.

"Bullshit!" Vinnie snarls. He grabs my shoulders and pins me down on the couch. I struggle, but I don't have enough purchase room to break free. Vinnie straddles my torso, his meaty red cock looming above my face. He grabs it by the base and slaps it against my left cheek. "Aren't you supposed to turn the other cheek now?" he jeers.

"Why are you doing this to me?" I cry out. "I only came here to help you!"

"Shut up!" Vinnie snaps. He glares down at me. "You Jesus boys make me want to puke! Damned hypocrites!"

He stands up and kicks off his sneakers and jeans. He pulls his tank top off last; I watch as it slides up over his body, revealing a hairless torso packed with muscles. I stare at his naked body: the sharp cut of the muscles; the smooth, chiseled abs; the dark, meaty cock jutting straight out before him.

"Now, I want you to get on your knees before me like you're going to pray," he says, "and lick my balls. Lick them for Jesus."

I don't move. I can't take my eyes off his body. With a snarl Vinnie pulls me off the couch and onto the floor. He yanks back my hair, and when I open my mouth to protest, he drops his balls in. The fleshy scrotum fills my mouth, and, as if it had a mind of its own, my tongue starts bathing it, rolling it around, savoring the taste and heft of his ball meat.

"Yeah," Vinnie growls. "Give those balls a good washing."

I burrow my nose into his crotch and inhale deeply, breathing in the ripe scent. The smell travels down into my lungs, intoxicating me. It has the stench of Satan: raw, animal, musky. I can't get enough of it!

I wrap my hand around his dick and begin stroking it, feeling the living tube of flesh throb in my palm. I look at it hungrily, tracing the veins up the shaft, noticing how the head flares out, red and angry. This is what Satan's dick would look like, I think. Just as meaty. Just as dark and threatening.

I slide my tongue up the fleshy shaft and swirl it around the engorged head. Vinnie grunts his approval. I squeeze his dick, and a clear drop of precome oozes out. I lap it up and then swoop down, taking Vinnie's dick deep in my throat. Vinnie gasps, and I feel a twinge of smugness that I've knocked him down a peg. I begin bobbing my head up and down, sliding my lips along the thick shaft.

Vinnie seizes my head with both hands and pumps his hips savagely. His cock rams against the back of my throat, slamming down it. I grab his ass cheeks with both hands and give them a good squeeze, feeling their hard muscularity. I tug down my zipper and pull out my own stiff dick. I start beating off furiously, timing my strokes to Vinnie's thrusting hips.

We quickly settle into a fast-paced rhythm of cock sucking and pud pounding. It's been too long since I've had a dick in my mouth, and the old hunger sweeps over me again.

Vinnie is relentless; he plows my face like there's hell to pay, but as brutal as he tries to be, I take it all eagerly. Old skills that I haven't used for some time come back now, and I give Vinnie what I'm willing to bet is a truly righteous blow job. Vinnie's breath comes in ragged grunts, then low whimpers.

I look up and see the sweat dripping down his face, his eyes glazed, his mouth open. My lips slide down his shaft, and I bury my nose in his pubes, keeping his dick deep inside my throat, working it with my tongue. I cup his fleshy balls in my hand and squeeze them. Vinnie groans, and his legs begin to tremble.

I take his dick out of my mouth and stroke it quickly. Vinnie's groans rise in volume; then he throws back his head and bellows as his jizz shoots out, splattering against my face, coating my cheeks, my mouth, my neck, my chest. His body shudders a few more times and then grows still.

A few quick strokes with my hand is all I need before I feel my own load pulsing out, oozing between my closed fingers. I groan loudly. Vinnie bends down and kisses me, pushing his tongue deep inside my mouth. He wraps his arms around me, holding me until the last of the spasms pass.

We lie like that for a few moments, Vinnie propped up against the couch, me cradled in his arms. I can feel his chest rise and fall as he breathes. He looks down, and our eyes meet. There's a moment of silence, and then we both laugh.

Vinnie runs his finger along my cheek, scooping up a dollop of his come. "Jeez, what a mess!" he grins.

I laugh again.

Vinnie disentangles himself and leaves the room. He comes back with a hand towel and tosses it to me. I wipe his load from my face.

"Well, did you enjoy yourself?" he asks.

"You have to ask?" I say, grinning. I toss him back the towel. "I think that was our best fantasy yet. Better than the TV repairman. Even better than the census taker."

Vinnie laughs again but says nothing. He picks up the fallen chair and puts it back by the table. I just lean back against the couch, watching his naked body. Even after just squirting a load, I feel myself getting turned on again, he's so handsome.

"You're a natural at this," I say, "playing out these little fantasies I set up. You should go into acting."

Vinnie shakes his head. "No, thanks. The escort business pays better."

Vinnie lets me use his shower. When I'm cleaned and dressed, I hand him the $100 I owe him.

"I'll give you a call in a couple of weeks," I say, "after I work out another fantasy. Maybe something involving a cop next time."

Vinnie shrugs. "Whatever you want, Gary." Now that he's out of character, he's amiable and relaxed. He's actually a sweet guy when he's not acting out some role.

He walks me to his door. Next to it stands a table cluttered with envelopes, notepads, an appointment calendar. There's also a framed photograph I hadn't noticed before. I look at it briefly. Vinnie and another man are standing on the deck of a cabin cruiser, the sea and a sunny sky behind them. Both men are laughing and have their arms around each other. Vinnie's friend has those all-American good looks found in milk commercials: wavy red hair; boyish face; compact, muscular body. The two of them make a very handsome couple, and I feel a pang of envy at how happy they look. I know nothing about Vinnie's personal life and have no idea what romances he's involved in when he isn't working.

I pick up the picture for a closer look. "Your friend's good-looking." I glance toward Vinnie. "Where was this taken?"

Vinnie gives me a polite smile, but there's a tightness to it that wasn't there before. "Cancún," he says. He takes the picture from me and puts it back on the table. "Well, good night."

I can take a hint. We shake hands, and I leave.

About a week later I run into Vinnie on Castro Street. Well, run into isn't exactly right. I see him on the other side of the street waiting in line in front of a theater. It's a little after 9 on a Saturday night, and the neighborhood is just beginning to come alive. The restaurants are full, and the music from the bars spills out onto the sidewalks. It's a warm evening, unusual for San Francisco, and the uniform of the night seems to be tank tops and shorts. Vinnie's no exception, and the gym shorts and T-shirt he's wearing show off his body to good effect. Vinnie's with someone; in fact, he has his arm draped around the guy's shoulder. The gesture is too casual to be erotic, but it's that very casualness that makes it look so intimate.

I'm in no rush, and because I'm a nosy little fucker, I stop and watch them from the doorway of a doughnut shop. There's something familiar about the guy with Vinnie, but I can't quite place him. I look at him closely and suddenly make the connection: He's the man I saw in the picture with Vinnie. Only I can see now that the photo was incredibly flattering; in real life he isn't nearly as good-looking. In fact, he's actually kind of scrawny and worn around the edges. This surprises me. A guy with Vinnie's looks could easily do better. Hell, he could get anybody he wanted.

Vinnie's friend says something to Vinnie, and Vinnie grins. Once again I'm struck by how fuckin' beautiful Vinnie is; it breaks my heart just to look at him. After a while I move on.

Later, in a bar, as I'm talking with friends, that scene with Vinnie and his friend flashes through my mind. What does Vinnie see in that scrawny little fucker? I think. But someone says something to me, and I let the thought drop.

The phone rings and rings, and I start to wonder if Vinnie's out. It's been more than two months since we acted out our little Jehovah's Witness fantasy, and my dick is hard and juicing with the thought of him naked in bed with me. I'm a regular client, and I usually don't let so much time go by between sessions, but with business trips and a two-week vacation to Hawaii, things just got in the way.

But now I'm ready to make up for lost time. No fantasies, no role-playing, just down-home sweaty gruntin' sex.

Someone finally picks up the phone. "Hello?"

"Yo, Vinnie," I say. "It's Gary."

"Hi." Vinnie's voice sounds oddly flat.

"How have you been?" I ask.

"OK."

There's a long silence. I begin to wonder if Vinnie's put off with me for some reason. Last time, I told him that I'd call in a couple of weeks; is he pissed because I've taken so long?

"Is everything OK?" I ask. "You sound kind of funny."

"I'm fine." Another pause. "So what's up?"

I clear my throat. "I was wondering if we could get together tonight. Nothing fancy, no fantasies this time, just a regular roll in the hay."

There's a long silence on the other end of the line. For a moment I wonder if we've been disconnected. "All right," Vinnie says after another long pause. "What time?"

His tone is really putting me off. He sounds so remote. "Around 10 o'clock?" I say. I hear my own voice taking on a certain coolness, matching his.

"Yeah, that'll be fine," he says. He hangs up without saying goodbye.

I sit there with the phone still in my hand. That was weird, I think as I return it to its cradle. Vinnie's usually a friendly guy. I don't know what the hell is going on with him.

I go through the evening thinking about that conversation and getting more and more annoyed. A large part of Vinnie's charm as an escort comes from his being a down-to-earth guy, a rare trait for someone in his line, especially if they're as hot as he is. If he's going to suddenly start copping an attitude with me, that'll kill the mood for sure. I begin thinking about the possibility of canceling with Vinnie and finding someone else. God knows, the city's full of handsome guys willing to turn a trick if the price is right.

The latest issue of the local gay rag is on my coffee table. I pick it up and start flipping through the pages toward the back section where the escorts advertise. I find myself in the obituaries, and I'm about to turn the page again when one of the notices catches my eye.

I recognize the picture immediately: It's Vinnie's red-haired friend. In fact, it looks like the photo's been cropped from the framed photo I saw on Vinnie's table. I sit down and read the obituary all the way to the end. The man's name was Steve Benson, and he was 26 when he died, the cause of death "complications due to AIDS." The obituary ends by saying that Steve is survived by his mother, his father, a sister, and his loving partner, Vincent. I see that the funeral was today.

I look at the picture of the laughing man for a few seconds more and then close the paper.

Oh, shit! I think. Poor Vinnie.

Vinnie answers the door in his bathrobe. He smiles apologetically. "Hi, Gary," he says. "I'm running a little late. I just got out of the shower."

He stands aside and motions for me to enter. I walk in and sit on the couch.

"Do you want a beer or something?" he asks.

I shake my head, watching Vinnie closely. He seems pretty normal, maybe a little subdued. As always, I'm awed by his good looks. I think of the muscular body under that terry cloth robe and feel my dick begin to stiffen.

"It's been a while," I say.

Vinnie smiles. Some of his old charm returns. "Yeah, I've been wondering what happened to you. Everything OK?"

I nod. "Sure. Things are all right." I let a few seconds go by. "How about you?"

Vinnie shrugs. "Yeah, things are fine."

Both of us are silent for a few moments. Vinnie finally walks over to the couch and slips off his robe. It falls to the floor around his feet.

I sit back and look at him: the beautifully sculpted body, the thick dick hanging down between his thighs. "God, you're handsome," I say.

Vinnie gives a small smile. "Let's go back to the bedroom."

I undress by the night-light next to Vinnie's bed. Vinnie is already lying on top of his bedspread, legs splayed, hands behind his head.

Once I'm naked I slip in beside him, kissing him lightly on the lips. My mouth travels south, down his neck, stopping for a moment at each nipple, then down across the hard, rippled expanse of his belly. Vinnie lies motionless. I rest his dick in my hand and kiss it too; even soft it has an impressive thickness. I put it in my mouth and start sucking, twisting my head from side to side for maximum effect. Vinnie's dick stays limp. After a couple of minutes I give it up. I look up at Vinnie's face.

Vinnie's staring somewhere over my shoulder, his expression unreadable.

"Vinnie," I say softly.

He turns toward me. His eyes have the stunned, baffled look of a plane-crash victim's. Beneath the shock all I see is despair.

"Oh, Vinnie" is all I can say. I reach up and stroke his cheek. After a few seconds I add, "I saw his obituary."

Vinnie stares at me for a long time without saying anything. Suddenly his eyes brim with tears. He reaches down and pulls me up against him.

We lie in bed, our naked bodies pressed together, my face against Vinnie's neck. My hands stroke his back up and down, kneading the skin. There's nothing erotic in my intent; it's the only way I know to comfort him. I feel his hands rub against my back as well. We lie together like that for a long time, his heart beating against my chest.

I'm not quite sure exactly when it happens, but there's a subtle change now in the way Vinnie's holding me. He slowly lowers his head and kisses me, pressing his lips gently against mine. He does it again, more passionately, this time slipping his tongue inside my mouth. His pelvis starts grinding against mine, and I can feel his dick thickening, getting harder. He starts dry-humping my belly, pushing his now-erect cock against my body. My own dick is stiff and ready for action.

He breaks away and opens the drawer of the nightstand, pulling out a condom package. I take it from him, tear it open with my teeth, and roll it down his dick. Vinnie pulls a tube of lube out of the drawer and squirts a dollop onto his palm. He reaches down and massages my ass, probing into my crack, pushing a finger up my hole. I groan. When I'm nicely lubed, he wraps me in his arms again, rubbing his body against mine. He works his thick, hard dick between my legs, and I take over from there, holding it with my hand, guiding it in. I breathe deeply, letting myself relax, welcoming the sensations of Vinnie's dick pushing its way up inside me.

Vinnie wraps his arms around me again and begins to pump his hips. His hands travel over my torso, kneading my warming flesh. With his eyes closed he kisses my face, his lips gently pressing against my mouth, my eyes, my hair. He has never been this tender before.

His thrusts pick up speed, and I move my body in time to them. Vinnie sighs his gratitude. I squeeze my ass muscles hard around Vinnie's thick root, and he kisses me again, shoving his tongue once more down my throat. I push my tongue against his, holding his face between my hands. Vinnie's eyes are still closed, and it doesn't take a rocket scientist to figure out who he's pretending I am.

With a quick movement Vinnie flips me on my back and lies on top of me. His muscular torso, slippery with sweat, squirms against mine. He plows my ass with deep, quick thrusts now, his dick pulling almost completely out and then plunging all the way in. Vinnie grinds his hips against mine, his balls pressed against my ass, his thrusts pushing me hard against the headboard.

And yet, even with the increased tempo, the tenderness remains. His hand is wrapped around my dick, and he beats me off with long, slow strokes. I reach down and cup his balls in my hand. They're pulled up tight against his body, and I know it won't be long before he blows.

He pulls out again and then skewers me deeply, his hips churning. I feel his body shudder, and I pull his face down to mine, kissing him hard, biting his lips. Vinnie cries out as the first wave of jizz slams into the condom up my ass. His torso heaves and bucks against mine with each succeeding spasm. Vinnie's strokes take me closer and closer to climax, and then I'm shooting too, squirting my load into his hand, my groans muffled by Vinnie's mouth over mine. Our bodies strain and push against each other and then fall apart.

I glance over at Vinnie. He's lying on his back, staring up at the ceiling. I get up and pull my clothes on. Vinnie doesn't say a word. For a moment I think he's fallen asleep, but when I look at him, his eyes are still open.

When I've finished dressing, I pull my wallet out of my back pocket and fish out a wad of $20 bills. I sit on the edge of the bed and shake Vinnie's shoulder. He turns his head and looks at me, saying nothing. The misery in his eyes hasn't changed.

I never know what to say at moments like this. "Here's the money I owe you," I say, feeling very awkward.

Vinnie pushes my hand away. "Forget it." He manages a small laugh. "Tonight it's on the house."

I squeeze his arm, but I can't think of anything to say.

"Good night, Gary," Vinnie finally says.

I stand up. "Good night, Vinnie."

I walk out the bedroom door. When I'm in the living room, I glance at the picture of Vinnie and Steve laughing on the cabin cruiser. I slide the money under it and leave the apartment.

Outside I see that the fog has rolled in and the night has turned chilly. So much for our Indian summer. I zip up my coat and jam my hands in my pockets. It's late, and nobody else is out on the streets.

The last time I was with Vinnie, I think, I was a Jehovah's Witness. Tonight I was his lover.

I decide that I just might take a break from fantasies for a while. I climb into my car and drive down the deserted streets toward home.

For the Asking
By David Wayne

People are always asking me how I met Travis, and I always tell them that we met here at The Pub, which is true enough. If they want more details...well, I generally make them up fresh every time. That's why there are so many conflicting stories about Travis and me. I always loved a mystery. I've discovered that I love being a mystery even more.

But you say that Jamie told you to ask me. Well, that's something else entirely. That means I'm going to tell you the true story of Travis and me and the night we might, and I swear, Scout's Honor, that it's the real true story.

And maybe, by the time I'm done, you'll understand why I'm telling it to you.

I first met Travis right here, on the very spot you and I are standing now. It was a Thursday night—The Pub is always cruisiest on Thursdays for God-knows-what reason. The place was packed from bar to back room with men, but Travis caught my attention the instant he pushed through the door. He just didn't fit in. Hell, he didn't even make the effort to fit in. If anything, Travis's appearance was a concerted effort to hide just how handsome he was. In a room full of stretch Lycra, he was dressed in a pair of work-stained Levi's and a worn leather jacket. Beneath the stubble on his face, though, his jaw was hard and square; his T-shirt, time-worn and damp with sweat, clung to a torso that was finely muscled. I remember all of these details in retrospect, but at the time, they were eclipsed by one thing: his eyes. Piercing, playful and squinted just slightly, Travis's eyes surveyed the room; I was acutely embarrassed when his gaze locked onto mine as if he had sensed my stare. I became even more embarrassed when he began to wade toward me. He walked through the crowd like he was haunting the place. People shivered and stepped away as he passed, but no one turned to see what had disturbed them.

At last he reached me. His eyes scanned me up and down, then he turned and pressed his firm belly against the bar railing.

Jamie was the bartender that night, like he is every Thursday night. I knew Jamie in the usual ways that gay guys get to know each other. He was the ex- of an ex- for one thing. Furthermore, I'd sucked him off once in the sauna of one of the local bathhouses. I was pretty sure, though, that Jamie didn't remember that little incident. The point is that the bar was a din of chattering voices and drum beats, and Jamie was having trouble keeping up with the orders. He appraised Travis's threadbare appearance and filed him in the "light tipper" category before turning his attention to the other clamoring customers.

I found myself shouting, "Jamie, two beers."

Jamie looked at me, looked at Travis, then raised a disapproving eyebrow; but he dropped a pair of wet, brown bottles in front of us and scooped up the bills I'd laid out.

"One of these for me?" Travis gave me a half smile.

"If you want," I answered.

Travis stared at me for an uncomfortably long time.

"Yeah, I want." He took a swig from the beer I'd bought. I watched his Adam's apple bob as he swallowed, and I felt something kindle in my groin. Those flames were fanned when Travis shrugged out of his jacket, revealing a broad chest and beautifully muscled arms.

"My name's Jack," I said, sticking out a hand in greeting.

Travis took it, his hand warm and firm in my grasp.

"I'm Travis. It's a pleasure." He released my hand, letting his fingertips graze my palm. He looked me in the eye as he did this, his eyes kindling with thinly veiled amusement.

I was at a loss. I hate that awkward moment when you meet someone in a bar and it's not clear whether or not you're going to fuck, so you have to find something to talk about.

"So, what do you do?" I hazarded lamely.

"What do you mean?"

"You know, your job."

He snorted into his beer. "Am I going to have to fill out a credit report too?"

His lips curled in amusement, signaling that he was enjoying my disorientation.

"Just curious I guess," I finally managed.

He was silent for a moment as he stared out into the crowd. "I hate pissing contests. No offense, but you don't care about my work. Fact is..." He turned to look at my face. "Fact is, I'd be disappointed if that was all you wanted."

His left hand slid down his side, his thumb catching in the belt-loop, leaving his fingers curled next to the none-to-subtle bulge in his jeans. He watched me staring at his crotch, and then I felt his eyes slide down my body, giving me a similar appraisal. He gave a friendly laugh.

"Look," he said. "I know what you want; you know what you want. Why don't you just ask?"

His face was blank, his expression very matter-of-fact. I felt my stomach churn. I felt something twitch a bit further south, too. He stretched casually, his T-shirt slithering up his torso to reveal his abdomen and the recess of his navel.

Maybe you'll find it difficult to believe how hard it was to say what I wanted. In my mind, I could see him naked. I could hear the rumble of his throat as passion lowered his voice to a growl. I could smell the musk of him. I could taste the sweat of him. The desire burgeoned within me, but the words couldn't get past the watchdog of my tongue.

He downed the last swallow of his beer and waggled the empty bottle. "Thanks for the beer."

He started to slip on his jacket, and I knew with absolute certainty that he would leave—and that he wasn't going to make this any easier.

"Last chance," he said. "Just ask. What do you really want to do?"

"I...I want to sleep with you."

He smiled, a look of victory in his eyes.

"Well, I'm hoping that 'sleep' is a euphemism...but close enough. Come on." He took my hand and guided me through the dancing throng. As we passed through the door, his hand slipped from my grip and moved to the small of my back, shepherding me through the densely packed vehicles—a Gordian knot of steel and fiberglass that wouldn't be untangled until closing time.

"There's no way you're going to get your car out of here," I said uselessly.

He gave me a wolfish grin. "Who says I have a car?"

And with that, he pulled me into the darkness of the alley behind the club. Moonlight spilled into the narrow space between the buildings like a waterfall into a grotto. The light glinted off the cases of empty bottles, and I could smell the stink of stale beer. As we slipped into the shadows, my hands trailed along the wall, and it pulsed beneath my fingers to the occult rhythm of the drum and bass seeping through the mortar.

The alley dead-ended, and we found ourselves in the darkened alcove of a disused back door. Travis leaned his back against the wall and pulled me into his grip. In the darkness, our lips met. Travis's arms encircled me, and I succumbed to his embrace as our tongues danced. The kiss seemed eternal, but eventually, painfully, it came to an end. I opened my eyes to meet Travis's stare.

"There's one condition," he said.

"A condition for what?"

"Sleeping with me."

I was no longer thinking about sleep, but I played along.

"What's the condition?"

"You can sleep with me tonight, but first you have to fuck me as hard as you can."

"What, right here?" I said incredulously.

"Why wait?"

His hands were already pulling at my belt. It cinched tighter about my waist, then went loose. As his hands unfastened the top button of my jeans, he leaned into me, pushing me against the wall. One hand crept into my jeans and tugged playfully at the hair growing from my groin.

"No underwear?" he teased. "Naughty, naughty boy."

I heard my zipper descend as his hand slipped deeper into my pants. Like a curious dog, my cock rose up to sniff the stranger's hand. He grasped it firmly, noting its heft, then pulled it out through the open 'V' of my fly. He squeezed and I swelled in his palm. With my stiffening cock as a leash, he pulled me toward him. Our lips met and his free hand grasped the back of my head, pulling our faces tighter. Our kiss was frenzied, and all the while he jerked roughly at my exposed prick until it stood out from my body like an embedded knife. I clutched his hips and thrust my groin against his, feeling something stiffen in reply within the denim enclosure of his jeans. I sucked his tongue into my mouth, chewing on it and bathing it with my own saliva. Without breaking the coupling of our lips, my hands slid around his waist to rest at the top button of his jeans. He wasn't wearing a belt, and his fly seemed to burst open of its own accord. I pushed his jeans down his flanks, and was amused to hear the clatter of change as his pants pooled around his ankles. My fingers traced across his abdomen, dipping downward to find the root of his cock. I pushed at the base and found it as stiff and firm as my own. Our fingers brushed as we brought our cocks together within the confines of our two palms.

I broke our kiss, moving along his jaw line to the tender flesh beneath and behind his ears. I bit gently and he moaned, crushing against me. He spread his legs, and I nudged my cock between his thighs. I drove forward, my prick forging through the coarse hair that forested behind his balls. The sensation of his rough hair against my cock's tender head was excruciating and exhilarating. The fingers of both my hands worked their way into his crack, and my right index finger found what I was searching for. His hole gaped open, and with just the sweat of our bodies, the tip of my finger slipped inside him. He gasped, and I pushed deeper in reply. I strained forward with my hips, hoping to let my cock join my fingertip in the warmth of his asshole, but my dick's reach stopped agonizingly short. Travis's knees buckled slightly, but even that wasn't enough. There was a whisper in my ear, and it took a moment's concentration to recognize it as Travis's guttural chant of "fuck me fuck me fuck me..."

I pushed him away with my free hand, keeping my finger tucked into the opening of his chute. Wordlessly, I pushed on his shoulder, signaling him to turn around. He pivoted on his heel, but the tangle of his pants snared him. He tripped forward, catching himself with his hands on the wall opposite me, and let out a started yelp. I drove my finger deeper inside him, and he yelped again, his muscles tightening. I pulled back slightly and he relaxed, then eased himself down onto my finger. I hunched my hips forward, and let my cock burrow between his cheeks to crowd my busy fingers. He sensed the pressure and pushed backwards against me. I thrust my hips, nosing my dick in deeper and deeper into his crack. I was leaking lube, and with a few strokes he was wet.

He turned his face, and, in the moonlight, he was unmasked. The guarded irony had slipped away, and all that remained was desire. I didn't have to ask if he was ready. Pulling my finger out, I positioned the head of my prick at his opening. I thrust forward, and his knees buckled as I stabbed into him. There was a moment of eerie calm, as we adjusted to each other's bodies. We were frozen at the brink of ecstasy. And then, clutching one another, we fell into it.

I won't say that that first time with Travis was indescribable—just that description doesn't do it justice. I'm sure you know what it's like to fuck a man, and I'm sure you know that even though the mechanics are roughly the same every time, every time it's different.

God was this different.

I didn't fuck Travis so much as ride him. He moved as if electrified. I grasped his writhing hips and plunged into him again and again, battering against him as if he stood between me and ecstasy; my cock was a battering ram and his body the unyielding door. The alcove was cramped and the sounds we made were echoed and amplified. My ears were filled with the moist slapping of our bodies and the guttural sounds that had supplanted language. I felt something exploding behind my balls, and I pressed my face into his back, wishing that I'd gotten his jacket and shirt off so that I could taste his flesh. All sensation was eclipsed as I felt myself ejaculating inside him. I accented each spurt with a savage twist of my hips, and found that I was still thrusting long after I was spent, as if I'd forgotten how to do anything but fuck. At last my body stilled, and I slipped out of him, my cock deliciously raw. As I took in gulps of air, my spent passion turned to tenderness. My hands circled his waist and I kissed his neck.

"I kept my end of the deal," I whispered.

"Mm-hmm..." was his only reply.

I backed away, breathless, and leaned against the opposite wall of the doorway. Travis was still spread-eagle against the wall, his back heaving. In the monochrome moonlight, posed against the decaying brickwork he looked, for all the world, like a Bill Costa photograph.

As I reached to pull up my trousers, he turned toward me. The first thing that caught the moonlight was the rigid shaft of his cock, so engorged it actually jerked with each beat of his heart. The second thing that caught the light was his face...and that wicked, wicked smile.

Travis is fast, everybody knows that. You can tell by his feline, feral bearing. But unless you've actually seen him move, you just can't appreciate it.

He was on me before I could let out even a squeak of surprise, and we fell in a tumble into the open air of the alley. I tried to say something—anything, but his lips silenced mine. His body was heavy on top of me, and I could feel the heat and insistent pressure of his cock between our bodies. At first all I could think was, This jacket is calfskin, and then I just didn't care anymore.

My eyes closed, and I just let go.

Just as suddenly as he had leaped on me, he was gone. I opened my eyes in bewilderment, lifting myself onto my elbows. Something yanked my pants down around my ankles, then pushed my knees up to my chest. Instantly Travis was on top of me again, back-lit by the moonlight, which was dim compared to the demonic light flashing in his eyes. I kicked feebly, my legs trapped by both his weight and the tangle of my pants. Something poked at the opening to my ass. I thought it was a finger until the sheer girth of it became apparent. I panicked, tightening against it. Travis's face dropped down to mine, and something in his kiss told me "trust me."

Again, I let go.

Travis's hands were braced on my shoulders as his cock slowly worked its way into me. I was hungry to have him inside me. I writhed to accommodate him, but pinned as I was there was nothing I could do to speed the process. His cock crept into me with the stealth of an assassin and I was powerless beneath its advance. At last I gave up movement and laid still. It seemed like an eternity, but at last I felt the solid brace of his pelvis against my backside and knew that he had reached his limit. I felt his cock flex inside me, and I reveled in the fullness of it.

Just as slowly as it had entered, Travis's cock began to retreat, leaving a void as it withdrew. I would have begged him to fill me, but I'd forgotten language as such. I simply moaned in distress. When he actually popped out of me, I gave out a cry. Travis laughed low in his throat, then kissed me. His tongue drove itself into my mouth, and just as suddenly, his cock drove itself back into my body. Soon he had worked out a rhythm, his tongue and cock collaborating to fuck me at both ends. I felt an uncomfortable pinch in my groin and realized that my stiffening prick was trapped pointing downward. I reached between our bodies and pulled it free. Still wet with semen, it slipped easily between our bodies. I managed to get in a few strokes, before Travis pinned my arms over my head.

I think Travis could have continued until dawn at that excruciating pace, but as if cued from some external source, he began to increase the tempo of his thrusts. Unable to move my limbs, I focused my movements on my tongue and lips. I was intoxicated by the slide of his tongue as it mirrored the slide of his cock through my ass. With each thrust, the rough texture of his belly sent a thrill through my cock. Travis broke the kiss, gasping for breath, but the intensity of his thrusting into my body didn't abate. My mouth uncovered, I began to cry, to howl. Travis was silent, but I could feel the barely audible rumble of a growl in his chest.

I looked up, and the stars were eyes, looking down on us, and I knew that Travis and I, at that moment, were the center of the universe—that everything was watching us. The epiphany pushed me over the edge, and the orgasm hit me like a tidal wave. Travis cried out, and he thrust deeper than he'd been before. I felt my bowels fill with the warmth and wetness of him. He hovered above me, trembling, and didn't move or speak until his softening cock was expelled from my body.

I opened my eyes to look at him, and found myself frozen in fear instead. Above us, there were no stars—only eyes and leering faces. Five, ten, fifteen men encircled us. Travis sensed my tension and looked around us. He said nothing, simply extracted himself from my embrace and stood up. He offered me his hand, still keeping a wary eye on the onlookers. I accepted his help, and pulled myself to my feet, feeling foolish with my pants around my ankles, and thinking that I didn't want to die like this.

One of the faces stepped forward, and there was a familiarity to him that I didn't immediately recognize. He looked different in the night air, away from the strobe lights and smoke machines. It wasn't until he spoke that I recognized him.

"Um..." he said. "Can I be next?"

My God, I thought. It's Jamie.

So that's how I met Travis, and that's how me and Travis's little organization got started. Weekly meetings are held every Thursday behind the pub. No trouble with the cops because we've got two cops in the club. No trouble with the bar because...well, because we've got Jamie.

Jamie liked you enough to tell you to talk to me. I can see Jamie made a good choice, and I can see by the look in your eye what your answer is going to be, but I have to ask you the question anyway, because it's club rules. Yeah, I can tell by looking at you just what you want, but it doesn't mean anything if you don't say it yourself.

So here's your chance. Just ask. What do you really want to do?

Constantine's Cats
By Dominic Santi

I didn't lose my wallet to the pickpockets at Termini station, but I was still marked as a tourist the minute I caught my backpack in the door of the Rome Metro. Even a whistle shrieking as the door opened and closed again didn't cover the snickers in the packed-to-the-gills coach. I was used to disdainful sniffs at Americans. I flushed to the roots of my hair, though, when I realized the slender young Roman god standing next to me—I mean, the most gorgeous hunk of man I'd ever seen in my entire fucking life—was laughing so hard, his eyes were watering.

"New backpack," I muttered, reaching up to grab the overhead railing next to the godling's hand. I wasn't fast enough. The train lurched forward, and I tipped nose first into the armpit of hunk boy's leather jacket. As I groped his waist, trying to find my balance, my nostrils filled with the heavenly scent of warm, healthy male sweat, my hands gripped washboard abs that made my dick twitch, and I figured my short life in macho het-boy Rome was over. I was stunned when a surprisingly strong arm reached down and pulled me to my feet.

"Hold the pole, like this."

My Roman wet dream's voice was buttery smooth. So were his deep-brown and, fortunately, still smiling eyes. I felt myself falling into them as he firmly lifted my arm up beside his on the railing. I grabbed hold automatically, bracing myself next to him as I mumbled my thanks.

Even when he looked away my greedy photographer's eye soaked in his aristocratic features—the warm Mediterranean gold of his Italian skin and the thick brown hair that fell to his shoulders. My eyes kept traveling all the way down to the firm, perfectly rounded ass that showed how God had meant a man to wear jeans.

Dreamboat's face now held the same emotionless mask of his fellow travelers, but his eyes twinkled as they swept over my crotch, obviously aware of what I'd been doing.

"American?" he asked.

"Yeah," I coughed, trying to regain my composure. "Photographer."

He nodded, and the hand on the railing pressed gently against mine.

"You like Italy?"

"Very much," I smiled, letting my quick glance downward show what I liked best.

This time a smile cracked the edges of his lips. While I basked in the glow, the train jolted and I bumped against him again as we slid into Cavour station. This time he didn't move away. Instead, he pressed against me as the door opened and the additional incoming passengers crowded us closer together. When we jerked forward I felt a hard dick press against my leg. I decided that if my Roman idol was a pickpocket, he was welcome to whatever he found, so long as he took his time searching.

"What do you photograph?" His conversation was light, but the bulge brushing my thigh had my shaft bending uncomfortably against my buttons.

"Cats."

He stared at me blankly.

"Il gatos." I knew I was mangling the plural, but my Italian sucked. I'd been taking advantage of the fact that most of the locals in the tourist areas spoke at least a smattering of English. "I'm on assignment for International Feline. I'm going to take pictures of the cats by Constantine's arch."

He quietly pressed against me. "I did not think such was your interest."

I turned and resituated slightly. This time it was my hard dick pressing against the side of that firm, shapely ass. I locked my eyes on his. "Lots of people like pussies." I was still looking at him as the train again ground to a stop and the doors opened. I jumped when he pushed me toward the door.

"Colosseo—this is your exit."

"Thanks!" Without thinking I pushed my way into the crowd streaming through the door. When the whistle blew I turned to catch a final glimpse of my Roman wet dream—and someone plowed into the back of me.

"Excuse me," I started, then I saw who it was and laughed. "I didn't know you were there." His grin lit his face all the way to his warm, sexy, velvety brown eyes, and my dick throbbed so badly it hurt. As the throng pushed forward around me, he grabbed my shoulder and pulled me toward the exit.

"Come on, American. I will show you the cats."

"I'm Steve," I said, smiling back at him.

"Tonio," he laughed. "Now walk and pay attention."

We stepped out of the station, and I almost stopped breathing. The Colosseum rose above me to the left, the afternoon light casting eerie shadows in the archways of the age-darkened stone. A full third of the building was swathed in scaffolding, but the view was still breathtaking. I drank in the site of the ancient ruins, sharply contrasted against the bright-green grass and the darkly wet streets slick from a passing spring rain. I didn't even notice when the sidewalk ended. A firm hand yanked me back as a bus zoomed by my nose.

"Are Americans blind?" Tonio's gorgeous locks swirled in the sunlight as he shook his head. "Come. It is late. The Colosseum is dangerous after dark, and you do not pay attention so well."

"Sorry," I blushed. "I was just admiring the scenery." I again looked pointedly down his body. "Hope you don't mind."

He grinned lecherously at me. "I like your artist's eye." He nodded toward the huge arch next to the Colosseum. "This way." Constantine's arch was directly in front of us, the lower half of one of the stone legs also covered with scaffolding. I followed the sexy sway of Tonio's ass up the short stone walkway, past the few tourists the rain hadn't chased away. I didn't know what kind of shots I'd get in this light, but my job was rapidly taking a backseat to my cock as we reached the excavations at the base of the monument.

"Gladiator quarters." Tonio pointed down into the maze of ruins, toward the newly uncovered walls, shoulder-high amid the steel supports and plastic sheeting.

I forced myself not to think about naked men living and training in those trenches. Fat pigeons and fatter-still cats strolled the paths and lounged in the damp grass at the edge of the dig. I pulled out my camera and started shooting—orange tigers, golden-yellow tabbies, panther-black tomcats. They were everywhere, stretching and preening, obviously wild, but with no fear of the human intruders.

I shot three rolls, including several pictures of Tonio pointing out particularly photogenic specimens. I focused on his ass, especially on the profile of his succulent round globes against the Colosseum. His grin told me he knew exactly what I was doing. Tonio had been right, though. We didn't have much time. The light faded, it started to rain again, and suddenly it was dark.

"We could go in there," I said, nodding toward the Colosseum as I shoved my camera back in its case. Tonio shook his head.

"Too many guards and drug dealers." He grabbed my arm as I slipped on the slick stone path. "Come." With a quick tug he jumped down into the excavations and dragged me under a low sheet of corrugated plastic. As we knelt on the wooden work plank, he wrapped his arms around me and his hot tongue swept into my mouth. I kissed him back hard, sliding my hands under his jacket and holding him close in the darkness. Surrounded by the sound of the rain, I cupped his ass in my hands and pulled his cheeks as far apart as those skintight jeans would allow. "I want to fuck you."

Tonio wiggled against me, still kissing me, his dick hard against my crotch. His mouth was hot and wet and sweet. I wanted to tongue his lips, wanted to tongue his ass lips as well.

"All Italian men are tops." Tonio's breath was warm against my face as he wiggled his ass back into my hands.

"I won't tell," I growled. I reached down and yanked the front of his jeans open. His gasp caressed my ear as I skinned his long, beautiful cock and leaned over to take the salty, slippery head between my lips.

"Mmm. You taste good."

It was hard to see in the shadows. I closed my eyes and ground my nose into his pubes, inhaling the clean, heavy man scent emanating up from his balls. My dick was so hard I couldn't stand it anymore. I tore my jeans open and pulled out my throbbing, leaking cock.

"Bello," Tonio gasped, thrusting up into my throat. "So good." He put his hands on my head and started pumping. I felt his dick getting stiffer, and I didn't want what we were doing to end too soon. I pulled off, saliva dripping from my tongue, and sat back, yanking

Tonio's jeans down to his knees.

"Turn around and bend over."

He didn't argue. I lifted his jacket and shirt, licking up his warm, smooth butt as I worked my own pants down over my hips. Then I grabbed Tonio's firm mounds, pulled them apart, and buried my face in his crack. He squirmed right away, moaning softly, his talented ass lips kissing me back as I feasted on his "virgin" hole.

"I like rimming Italian pussy," I growled, sucking softly on his loose, receptive pucker as he arched his ass at me. "You sure all Italians are tops?" I poked in hard and tongued him ferociously, pulling his ass cheeks even wider as I dug in deep.

"Fuck me," he gasped. "Now!"

I indulged in one final taste, then leaned back and dug a rubber out of my jacket. As soon as I was sheathed, I grabbed his hips and shoved in, hard. Tonio's ass lips slid down my dick like they were swallowing a sword. My groans were as loud as his as I sank in all the way to the hilt.

"Nice ass," I gasped, pumping into him, my hands gripping his hips. Tonio's shoulder moved as he took his weight on one arm and started stroking himself. I reached down and pulled him upright, gasping as loudly as he did when my dick slid over his joy spot. Tonio shook in my arms. I sank my teeth into the back of his neck and slammed my shaft up into him. "Come for me, pussy boy. Take me deep and make your dick spurt." It was a quick, hot fuck—too hot to last. Tonio's body tensed around me, and I thrust my hungry dick into him hard and fast.

"Americano!" he cried out softly as his body tensed and his asshole clenched hard around me. His hot Italian pussy spasmed over my shaft. I buried my cock up his ass, grinding against him as his asshole sucked me deep and my guts clenched. The smell of his jism filled my nostrils, and I was gone. I shook as I emptied my balls up Tonio's quivering ass.

We didn't stay around to see if any of the local guards had noticed us. I tossed the rubber in a trash box, and we yanked up our pants and scrambled back onto the walkway. Nobody was there but a fat tabby strolling nonchalantly by with a few loose feathers in its mouth. Tonio and I innocently made our way back to the well-lit

Metro station and the last of the tourists and commuters heading home.

When we reached the entrance Tonio stopped and smiled at me. "Are you hungry, American? There is a good pizzeria a short bus ride from here." He paused, looking at me deliberately as I once more melted into his soft-brown eyes. "By my apartment."

I licked my lips before I realized what I was doing, then all I could do was laugh. We were still laughing as I followed him onto the bus and the shadows of the Colosseum disappeared into the distance.

Getting Even
By Simon Sheppard

"Greetings! You have mail!" NstyLthrMan dragged his mouse and clicked. E-mail from one of his editors: that damn anthology was delayed yet again. He'd have to wait a month or two longer to see his story in print. And even longer than that to get his check.

He grimaced, found the "dirty gifs" folder on his desktop, and opened DutchguyWS's picture. The monitor screen glowed with the image of a perfect dick, long foreskin, a bright stream of piss. Seeing DutchguyWS always made him horny. He reached inside his boxers and tugged at his swelling dick.

Obviously, it was time to hit the chat rooms. He dragged the uncut dick to one side of the screen and brought up the list of online chat rooms. M4M Dungeon. Full. M4M Unusual. Full. Even M4M Feet was full. Daddies and Boys. Full. Hmm. Daddies and Boys. He pushed the Who's Here button. The list of screen names came up. Oldrtopman. CuteLngIslndStd. Long Island? Across the continent. Ah, NaughtyboySF. He clicked Find Info and brought up the boy's profile: 34; 6 feet; 170; bl/bl; muscular, gym 3-4 times a week; kinky; submissive; looking for Daddy. He opened the InstaMail window, addressed it to NaughtyboySF, typed in "Hey, boy. What's up?" and clicked on Send.

NstyLthrMan waited, stroking his hard dick. The boy might be involved in three or four other chats. In any case, NaughtyboySF would want to read his profile before responding. He spit in his hand and stroked his dick head, pressing into the swollen tip. He moaned with pleasure; he sure knew how to drive himself crazy.

With a little chime, a response appeared in the InstaMail window. "Hi, Gramps. What're u doing?" Gramps? Gramps?

"What a cheeky boy!" he typed back. "I'm more than man enough for you." Send. Second thoughts: it sounded too much like a challenge. Maybe NaughtyboySF didn't mean anything nasty by

"Gramps." He typed in an additional line. "Just cruising around. You?" Send.

A second or two went by. Chime. "Cruise elsewhere."

How fucking rude. He took his hand from his dick. "Sorry to have disturbed your immaculate self." Send.

Chime. "Fuck you. It's trolls like you that made me stop going to gay gyms."

And, he thought, it's attitude queens like you that keep ME away from gay gyms. "First," he furiously typed back, "I am not a troll. Second, my regular boy is a lot younger than you. And nicer. Someday you'll get to be my age, if you're lucky, and then I sure hope someone treats you the way you're treating me." Send.

Chime. "Troll. Go pick on somebody your own age."

"You really are an asshole. What are you doing in the Daddies and Boys room, anyway?" Send.

A warning beep, and a window appeared. "NaughtyboySF is no longer online."

NstyLthrMan gritted his teeth in frustration. The rude little asshole had the last word and there was nothing he could do about it. He logged off and reached down for his now-limp dick. Fuck it! He was too upset to even jack off.

"Greetings! You have mail!"

NaughtyboySF clicked open his mailbox. Spam. A new fat-burning pill. An opportunity to make thousands of dollars while sitting at home. A web site featuring all-nude girls. That was misaddressed. Delete. Delete. Delete.

Chime. An InstaMail window opened unexpectedly. A message from someone he'd never heard of. Gr8hardbod. "Hey, buddy. Liked your profile..." He pulled down the Members menu and clicked on "Open Member's Profile."

"Gr8hardbod: 25; 5'10"; 175; San Francisco; handsome, masculine, ripped; looking for kewl guys into good, dirty fun. Sounded good. Sounded great.

"Hey Hardbod," he typed back, "got a gif to swap?" Send.

Chime. "Sorry, no. So if you don't want to send yours, I'll· understand."

NaughtyboySF felt disappointed; there'd be no exchange of pictures.

Another chime. "But I'm fucking horny and I'd like you to suck my hard-on. Wanna make a date? :-)"

NaughtyboySF felt his dick starting to stir. But he felt wary, too. There were a lot of liars and losers online. Men who'd send someone else's gif or promise to come over and never show. Predatory old guys and worthless trolls, guys like that grandpa who'd InstaMailed him the other day, a pathetic leather daddy he'd had to beat away with a stick.

Chime. "You still there?"

He decided to take a chance. After all, there wasn't much else to do on a slow Sunday afternoon. He started to unbutton his fly, thought better of it, and started tapping on the keyboard. "Sure am, stud. What're you into?" He clicked on Send. And reached for his fly again.

It was a second-floor apartment in a nondescript building. Gr8hardbod rang the bell, announced himself through the tinny speaker, and was buzzed in. The hallway smelled of frying hamburgers.

Apartment 207. Gr8hardbod knocked, and the door opened immediately.

OK, so NaughtyboySF wasn't a perfect match for his online self-description. Of course not. Still, he wasn't bad. 34? Yeah, probably. Six feet? Well, maybe a short six feet. 170 pounds? Kinda skinny for 170. Bl/bl? If his hair had been blond, it had grown out. Muscular? Trim was more like it. And looking more like an aging MTV boy than a hunky gym bunny. Short brownish hair, skinny sideburns. Cutish, but a little shifty-eyed. And, surprisingly, a piercing through his lower lip, one of those...it begins with an "L." Kinky? Submissive? That remained to be seen.

NaughtyboySF, on the other hand, was clearly impressed. His ad might have said "looking for Daddy," but he smiled broadly when he saw the breathtakingly handsome, well-built young redhead at his door. Gr8hardbod wasn't being immodest; when he glanced at himself in the mirror behind NaughtyboySF, that's what he saw—a breathtakingly handsome redheaded guy.

"Mmm, I love redheads. C'mon in." NaughtyboySF's tenor voice was just the faintest bit femmy. Gr8hardbod stepped inside and closed the door behind himself. In a split second, NaughtyboySF was all over him, grabbing at his butt, rubbing his hard crotch up against his leg. They kissed like a car crash. Gr8hardbod could feel the little silver piercing-ball pressing into his chin. He wondered where else the guy was pierced. He knew he'd soon find out.

"Want something to drink?"

"No, I'm fine, thanks."

"Come on with me, then."

NaughtyboySF waltzed him through the tasteful, slightly barren apartment, and into the bedroom with its huge bed, its big-screen TV, and little else. Now NaughtyboySF was tugging at him, pulling him down to the bed while trying to unbutton his shirt.

"Wait, let me get my backpack off."

"Oh, yeah, your...toy bag."

Gr8hardbod put the pack down on the floor beside the bed. And immediately NaughtyboySF was all over him again, undressing him, shoving his tongue down his throat. "I'm glad you're into older guys," NaughtyboySF whispered.

"Nine years isn't that much older. And anyway, age is no big deal."

But NaughtyboySF had already moved on to another topic, muttering about how pretty his nipples were. It was time to take control.

"All right, take your clothes off and get on your knees."

Yes, SIR!" said NaughtyboySF. He peeled off his tee-shirt and jeans. There was already a wet spot on the front of his Calvins. "Underwear, too?"

"Underwear, too."

"Yes, SIR!" He smiled, and the ball stapled to his lower lip winked with light.

"What're you grinning at, fuck boy?"

"Nothing, Sir!" He was pulling down his briefs. His hard dick bobbled as he pulled his underwear over his ankles. A hard, short, chubby dick, nowhere near the seven-and-a-half inches he'd promised, but fat enough, with a Prince Albert shining from his piss-slit.

"Now get on your fucking knees." Gr8hardbod kept his tone calm and level, knowing that a true Master didn't have to raise his voice.

"Yes, Sir." The guy dropped to the floor with a thud and knelt with his hands clasped behind his back, a purposefully blank expression on his face. His fat little hard-on jutted from his well-trimmed pubic hair.

Gr8hardbod spat in his face.

"Thank you, Sir!" NaughtyboySF said, spit rolling down one cheek.

This is going to be easy, Gr8hardbod thought. The guy didn't even notice I left his door unlocked.

Spit rolling down his cheek, NaughtyboySF looked up at the redhead's face. He couldn't believe his luck. He hadn't found it easy to hook up with younger guys who'd want to top him. Certainly not such a handsome, hunky, nasty guy. And a redhead to boot! God bless the Computer Age.

"You want to taste your Master's dick, fuck boy?"

"Oh yes, Sir!" said NaughtyboySF. And he meant it.

"Just a taste, then. If you want any more, you'll have to earn it."

NaughtyboySF stared straight ahead as his new Master unbuttoned his jeans and pulled down his jockstrap. A great dick, a beautiful dick, with a big mushroom head. And a bright red thatch of pubic hair. To stop himself from grinning, NaughtyboySF opened his mouth. Wide.

The redhead teased him with his dick, bringing it right up to his lips, then pulling it away. NaughtyboySF stuck his tongue all the way out and waggled it in a way he hoped looked seductive, not ridiculous. The big head slipped into his mouth. He nursed at it, swirling his tongue around the dick flesh. Gr8hardbod grabbed the back of his head and slid his shaft all the way in, filling his mouth and throat.

"Mmm," NaughtyboySF groaned.

He felt something around his throat. A collar, a leather collar. His Master was collaring him, claiming him. His chubby dick leapt. He'd do anything for this young man. Anything. Within reason.

With a tug at his collar, his new Master pulled out of his mouth.

"That's enough for now, fuck boy." Gr8hardbod's voice was soft and serious. "Now lie down on your bed. Spread-eagle on your back."

He did as his Master said, stretching his limbs wide, his throbbing dick pounding against his belly. He turned his head to watch Gr8hardbod, who bent down, reached into his backpack, and stood over him again. His hands were full of leather and rope. "Keep your head still and your eyes straight ahead," he commanded.

NaughtyboySF felt rather than saw the leather restraints being tightened down around his ankles and wrists, the ropes being fed through the restraints' metal D-rings.

"It's sure as hell time to tie you down, fuck boy," his Master said, looping the ropes around the legs of the bed, drawing them taut and knotting them till NaughtyboySF was stretched out, tied-down, and vulnerable. Vulnerable to this handsome young man he wanted so much to surrender to. He could feel more rope now, winding around his torso, then his legs, binding him down more securely. And he could feel the long cord being drawn through the ring of his Prince Albert, the ends being tied to the wrist restraints, his hard, sensitive dick being stretched out. The first slap on his dick made him jump.

"Stay fucking still." The same deadly calm tone.

"Yes, sir."

Another slap. He tried not to move at all, to conquer his reactions, to give his captor whatever he wanted.

And another slap.

"Maybe it would be easier if I blindfolded you."

Without waiting for assent, Gr8hardbod reached into his toy bag again. NaughtyboySF looked up into the redhead's face, into something dangerous gleaming in his eyes. The blindfold appeared between them, and then the familiar contours of his bedroom vanished into the dark.

NstyLthrMan and his two friends had waited long enough. He opened the door of Apartment 207 and the three of them walked inside, locking the door with a little click. It wasn't hard to figure out where the bedroom was. NstyLthrMan smiled with satisfaction. A naked young man was tied spread-eagle to the bed, a web of ropes around his body. Lean. Big nipples. A line of dark hair leading down to his pierced dick. Blindfold. Ball-gag. Ear plugs.

Gr8hardbod looked up and smiled.

NstyLthrMan smiled back. His boy had done his job well.

NaughtyboySF felt the ropes being unwound from his torso. Unable to see or hear, he had no idea of what was happening. Was the scene over? His hands and feet were being untied from the corners of the bed. And someone—a second someone!—was pressing leather-gloved hands against his chest. Then he realized with a shock that there were more than two of them there, that a third person had entered the scene. He started to panic, jerked his body upward, only to be firmly held down. By more than one pair of strong hands! How many of them were there? He tried to yell, but the gag muffled the sound. He squirmed against the powerful grip. He yelled again. A hand came down hard on his cheek. He tried to arch his body upward, his still-hard dick throbbing against his belly. Struggling was useless. He was no longer spread-eagle, but his wrist restraints had been clipped together, pinned down above his head. His ankle restraints were clipped together, too. Ropes were being wound around his legs. How many of them were there?

His hands were forced down to his crotch and the wrist restraints were tied to the cord running through his Prince Albert. Struggling too hard could rip the steel ring through the flesh of his swollen dick. What the fuck was happening? What had he let himself in for? Reflexively, his hands closed around his dick, a feeble attempt at self-protection, but soon he was stroking his cock's veiny meat. He was sweating, rivulets running down from his pits. What had he let himself in for?

He felt strong hands lifting him off his bed, the air hitting cold against his sweaty back. Levitation. It was like flying, flying blind. There were at least three of them—no, four. His body was no longer his own. Whatever was happening, he had no say in it. He was powerless, along for the ride. He was being lowered down now, being stuffed into a box, a trunk, something. He was being manhandled, stuffed into a fetal position, his hand still firmly on his dick. And with a ka-chunk, the lid came down.

From the motion of the trunk, he could figure out that he was being carried, being hauled down the stairs, out to where? The street? A waiting car? It felt like the trunk was being slid across a surface. Then the clunk of a closing door. An engine revving. A van, then, he was being taken somewhere in a van. How did I get myself into this?

the trussed-up boy wondered, on the thin edge of panic. His naked body was slick with nervous sweat. How the fuck did I get myself into this?

His weight shifted as they took the curves.

"He's a heavy fucker."

"Nah, it's the trunk that's heavy," said NstyLthrMan. "He's a real lightweight." He grinned. Everything was going as planned. Though, thinking of what his captive must be going through, he felt a little guilty. Oh well, if you didn't feel a little guilty, you weren't really having fun.

The four men wrestled the trunk into the abandoned warehouse. One of them shut the thick metal door behind them. And shot the bolt.

The lid of the trunk is flung back. They grab him, pull him out of the trunk. Take his blindfold off. There are four of them, the redhead and three others, leathermen who look as though they've stepped out of a Falcon video. Incredibly buff, handsome, masculine. They undo his restraints, his blindfold, take the gag out of his mouth. Fling him onto a table, get him on all fours. The redhead whips out his dick, that big, pink mushroom head again. He opens his mouth for it, sticks his tongue out expectantly. The redhead's meat plugs his throat. He feels hands spreading his cheeks apart, lubing up his hole. Fingers going up inside him, opening him out. The redhead pulls his dick out, leaving him hungry. The four strong guys are lifting him up, throwing him onto his back. "Who fucks him first?" a voice asks. "I do," says the redhead. Two of the leathermen grab his ankles. Lift his butt in the air. Spread his legs wide. The fourth man straddles his head. Pulls out an enormous dick. Shoves it into his mouth. He feels the redhead's big dick head slide inside his ass with a pop. The two men let go of his ankles, move to either side of him. He reaches for their big, hard dicks, starts jerking them off. He has cock in each hand, cock in each end. "Who wants sloppy seconds?" the redhead asks. The guy in his mouth pulls out, goes around to his butt. The two guys he's been jacking off move up to his head. They both fuck his face, taking turns while the redhead's dick is replaced by an even bigger one. The redhead laughs and starts slapping his ass. No, he doesn't laugh, he...

"...You'd like that, wouldn't you?"

NaughtyboySF snapped out of his gangbang fantasy. It was almost as if whoever had spoken had been reading his mind. He'd been pulled from the trunk and was now standing up, naked, hands suspended above his head, cold concrete beneath his feet. The earplugs had been taken out. The gag and blindfold were still in place. But nobody had fucked him. Nobody had slapped him. They'd hardly even touched him. Not yet, anyway.

"Do you have any idea who I am, boy?" A firm, angry voice coming out of the darkness.

Who he is? Who he is? I have no fucking idea...

"I'm Gramps. The troll. Remember now?"

Oh God, which one? When?

"Remember?"

And then he did remember, more or less. And began to get deeply, truly scared.

"Remember, you little fuck?"

The blindfold came off. Before him were standing three men. Three men dressed in leather, their faces half-hidden by leather masks. Two white men, one black.

The first white guy had a neatly trimmed salt-and-pepper beard, a hairy beer gut peeking out from his leather vest. The second white guy was tall, lanky, sinewy, a leather harness over his smooth torso. And the black guy, wearing just boots, chaps, and a studded codpiece, was built like a brick shithouse, incredible shoulders and pecs. Nipple rings gleamed against his dark chest.

"That's my Daddy. My Daddy and his friends. Like them?" The redhead spoke softly, tauntingly, in his ear.

Which one was he, which of the three? He didn't remember any of the details of whatever-his-screen-name-was's profile.

"So you'd better watch who you insult online, asshole," the redhead continued. "'Cause you never know who you're talking to. Hell, it could even've been me, using my Daddy's account."

The redhead stood before him. The three older men moved closer.

"And now I bet you think you're in for a gangbang, huh? No such luck, asshole." The redhead smiled. "See, my Daddy wants me to do this...." And he held up a gleaming hunting knife. A long, long knife with a sharp, sharp blade.

NaughtyboySF felt a shiver of fear jolt through his body. He tried to kick the redhead, but his ankles had been shackled to the floor. Gr8hardbod slowly lowered the knife. Watching the descent of the blade, NaughtyboySF began to tremble.

"Hold still or things'll get really messy."

Don't hurt me!, NaughtyboySF wanted to shout, but the gag made it into a muffled "Mmph." Tears were in his eyes.

The knife was against his thigh. The brutally sharp edge rested on his flesh. Slowly, slowly the blade ascended, up toward his balls, his dick, tracing a thin line in its wake. The knife was just an inch from his balls. The redhead smiled. The knife edge pressed into his soft ball sac. NaughtyboySF couldn't help himself; he lost control of his bursting-full bladder. He let loose a stream of hot piss.

"Some naughty boy!" The redhead's voice oozed contempt. "Pussyboy is more like it, a pussyboy who wets his fucking bed."

Laughter. Derisive laughter. The leathermen all were laughing. Laughing at him. His face burned hot with mortification.

Then the redhead spat in his face, which didn't cool it down at all. One by one, the three older men came up to him, very close, and spat at him, too, big gobs which mixed with the tears running down his cheeks. This was very different from the games he'd played back in his apartment. This was, he feared, for real.

"You look like shit," said the redhead. "And your dick's nothing special when it's soft."

Flash. One of the leathermen had a camera in his hands. A second flash. And the redhead stepped up close to him again, brought the knife back down to his crotch. He could feel its cold, sharp pressure against his cock flesh. The pressure increased. Oh my God, he thought. Oh my God. He closed his eyes and shivered, waiting. Waiting for a pain that never came.

"You learned your lesson, asshole? You had enough?" Gr8hardbod sneered. "My Daddy wanted to really work you over, but his friends talked him out of it. They figured you just weren't worth the fucking trouble. And they were right." The blade retreated from his cock. "So we're just going to get rid of you. No, not kill you, shithead. Too much of a hassle. We figure you won't make any trouble for us if we let you go. You won't, will you, pussyboy? Because it'll just be your word against mine, and I've saved our online flirtation on my hard disk. And then there's the pictures we just took. I don't think you'd like them to be posted all over the Internet. So you'd better behave. No more rudeness to your elders and betters. Got that?"

He slapped the boy's face.

"I said, 'Got that?' "

NaughtyboySF nodded, new tears burning his cheeks. He meekly allowed himself to be blindfolded again, to be bundled back into the trunk. The lid clunked shut.

Back in the van, NstyLthrMan looked at his friends, at his boy at the wheel. They were all laughing and joking. So why was he feeling so ambivalent? The boy in the trunk had been asking for it, needed to be taught a lesson. But had he let NaughtyboySF's insults get to him? Had he been ruled by his anger? Had he compromised his dignity? Maybe gone too far? Oh well, if you didn't feel a little guilty, you weren't really having fun.

The van drove on through the night. A light rain had begun to fall.

NaughtyboySF felt the van screech to a stop. The trunk was being lifted out, carried somewhere, then lowered with a thump. When the lid was opened he felt the chill of the night against his nakedness, the cold dampness of a light rain. He was lifted out, laid on cold, wet ground. The unseen men tied his wrists and ankles together. And then, minute after cold, wet minute, nothing. Nothing at all. At last, he tried the knots around his wrists. They came undone easily. He untied his ankles. rose unsteadily to his feet. Pulled out the gag, the earplugs. Took the blindfold off. He was standing, stark naked and all alone, in the middle of his own backyard.

NstyLthrMan sat staring at his computer. The gif on the screen showed a man in his 30s, his face contorted in fear, though it was hard to see that he'd actually been crying. His naked body was suspended by its wrists, and if you looked closely you could see a pool of piss darkening the concrete at his feet. There was a sign above his head, like the "King of the Jews" sign at the Crucifixion. It read "I am a rude, silly queen and a pushy bottom. NaughtyboySF."

In the few days that had passed since the scene, NstyLthrMan had gotten over his guilt. Now the humiliated boy in the trunk was mostly just a pleasant memory, a memory he'd even jacked off to once or twice.

And now the time had come to send the gif to NaughtyboySF. It was time to go online.

Suddenly, he felt particularly old.

"Greetings! You have mail!"

It was from NstyLthrMan, and it had a file attached. As he downloaded it, an image took form on his screen. An image of him, naked, kidnapped, tortured, humiliated. A taunt. A warning. A softly glowing souvenir of the worst, most unforgettable night of his life.

He felt his dick getting hard.

His left hand stroked the shaft while his right hand dragged the mouse.

There it was, the "Daddies and Boys" chat room. And there was room for one more. He entered the chat room, scrolled down the list of who was there. He found a likely screen name, checked out the profile, opened the InstaMail window. And he began to type:

"Hi there, Gramps. What's up?"

Thug Life, Thug Fiction
By Lance Rush

It was the era of Prohibition and bathtub gin. The worse of times for many, and the best of times for some. Men of power wielded big dicks and bigger guns. In this Jazz Age, the decadent rich and piss-poor alike sported hats and dressed to suit their aspirations. One such powerful, sharply dressed man (carrying a big rod) was steppin' lively in his black fedora down a dark street. A happy sack, he'd just had his big, thick, impatient dick blown to completion, and this cuckoo world had begun to make sense. Yep. The big galoot was starting to believe in love. Soul-deep, butt-fucking, nut-busting, Love—before it all went horribly wrong.

A blazing riff of Satchmo's horn wailed like an omen. A rage swept through Harlem that hot August night in 1931 as the wheels of a late model Packard cried, turning the comer of West 129th Street. Something big was going to happen. Inside those late night surroundings, Depression crippled dandies, cats, chicks and spines all scattered. Residents dropped to the concrete, taking cover as the .45s and tommy guns commenced their willy-nilly blasting. It was an awful noise. The frantic shots riddled the windows of Juicy's Juke Joint. A fedora flew like a frightened bird from an important man's skull as a violent hail of bullets ripped at his proud chest. The car sped away in a cloud of smoke, leaving bits of shattered glass and carnage in its wake. The head waiter at Juicy's stumbled out the door, bleeding from a nick to his neck and cursing at the dust, "Juicy's gonna get you motherfuckers!" Maybe. Or just maybe not.

When he looked down, he saw their target sprawled below him. As he bent down, he recognized the face. It was a famous kisser. A notorious mug. A face that made him shiver in his size 13s. But behind that puss was a human being, and the waiter listened intently to what seemed to be a dying man's last words. "Die men. D-i-i-ie. Men. Diamond..." he said, before his eyes closed as slowly as two falling stars on a dark and wounded night.

Was it about jewels? Was he shot down over a few lousy rocks? Or was Diamond a person? If Diamond was a person, then there was only one: Roundtree. Earl Diamond Roundtree. Most everyone in Harlem's cafe society knew that cat. But Diamond was a mean piano man, not a murderer! Or was he? If this man on the ground meant Diamond Roundtree, then that pretty-boy Negro had better grab his hat, take a quick A-train, and ride it the fuck out of town!

A couple of months earlier, Earl Diamond Roundtree was ticking the ivories in the main room of Lucky's Lounge. The atmosphere, as always, was one of austere sophistication. In sartorial splendor, Lex "The Checker" Martin emerged from his chauffeured Bentley, accompanied by his driver, friend, and head henchman, Fats Brown. Once inside Lucky's gold-painted doors, they were treated like kings. A girl took their cashmere overcoats and lit their fat stogies, while another seated them at a table in front. Fats perused the dive, but Lex stared straight ahead, transfixed. Earl Diamond Roundtree sang and played the piano. Lex sat, hypnotized. He felt a heat all through his chest, and it wasn't from that hot sauce on his spicy meal. Nope. Diamond Roundtree was taking his breath away. Stop the night! Lex Martin wanted to get off!

"Damn! Who's the face?" he wondered. "Lucky's usually features Colored entertainment. This here singer ain't Colored. Or is he? Well, damn! Shit! Motherfuck! Maybe he is Colored."

Lex usually liked his men darker than blue. Earl Roundtree was light, bright, damn old fey! Still, the boy was fine as amber-colored moonshine, and at right that fuckin' minute, he was giving "The Checker" a high, hard one. Lex's big ole uncircumcised, country-bred peter started to drip down the leg of his elegant custom-made vines.

When the show was over, Lex quickly scribbled a note and told Fats to deliver it backstage. Lex had a whole other kind of act in mind—a performance of the hem-blowing kind, and Earl Diamond Roundtree was being summoned.

15 impatient minutes later, Fats returned. "Here he is boss. Checker Martin meet Earl Roundtree. Folks call him Diamond."

Lex was duly impressed. Tall. Immaculate posture. In snow-white tie and tails, Diamond was one natty Negro. A lean, polished dude, his manly elegance matched Lex's own.

Up close, his face struck Lex like a bolt of lightning. His eyes were a sexy pale-green, and his skin was a light, dusted gold—amazingly smooth but for the thin pencil mustache above his moist, full upper lip. His pomaded hair was a Harlem night-black arrangement of polished waves. This here was one of the most handsome men Lex had ever seen. Earl. Even the name suited him.

Diamond waited for Lex's big mitt before giving up the skin. Lex grabbed it, firmly, willing Earl to look him dead in the eye. Earl took him in; dark copper tones and sable eyes flashed back, defying a careful smile. A mop of manicured black curls framed his exquisitely manly mug. A slight crook in his nose made him look nearly Egyptian. The romantic in Diamond wanted to believe that, in another life, Lex "The Checker" Martin might've been a Pharaoh.

Hmm, Diamond thought, not to shabby for a low-class kingpin who's probably never read a book in his fuckin' life. He's fine, though. Nice threads. Is that a real sapphire and diamond cross? Nice chest, though. But look at all those tacky gems fighting for attention on his fingers! And, what the hell is that thing? Is the thug packin' a .45 or is he just thrilled to meet me?

It was both. Despite the things he found to pick apart, Diamond was strangely attracted to this pin-striped gangster. "The Checker" in the flesh. You couldn't pick up a paper or turn on the radio without hearing of his exploits. The tax evasion charges. That nasty turf feud with Juicy Carlito. Hints, whispers of racketeering, number running, money laundering, extortion. And when the smoke lifted over all those mysterious shoot-outs up in Harlem, a whiff of the Martin name wafted above the scene like a bad smell, but the G-men and copper's couldn't take him down.

"Ya sing good. Let's blow this joint and crack open a bottle of hooch. Grab your coat!" Lex ordered brashly.

Who the fuck did he think he was? Diamond had a problem with orders. Didn't like 'em. If they were to keep time together, Lex would need to learn that little fact. Still, Earl grabbed his coat, and they set out in the Bentley. Fats watched them with a jaundiced eye. Something was going on between them. Fats could see this. And whatever that something was, it worried him.

The whole queer night was a slow, seductive dance of desire. Later on, Brown chauffeured the hot twosome to the Dorchester Hotel. Lex was putting on the Ritz, big time. He had a suite there. Diamond was impressed as hell, but didn't show it. Lex cranked up the Victrola, and Miss Bessie Smith began to wail the "St. Louis Blues." They sat on a velvet divan, sipping a bottle of Chateau Rothchild, listening to the Empress belt out those sad and bawdy Blues. Lex stared at Diamond, his rod dancing like some big, thick, horny baton. Diamond couldn't help noticing.

"So. What did ya think I asked ya back here for?" Lex asked.

"Don't know. A personal concert, maybe. Where's your Steinway?"

"I think you're smarter than that. Got a dame on the side, or what?"

"Don't date dames," Diamond stated plainly, looking Lex dead in his eyes.

Then Lex, a little woozy, a little bolder, stood and slowly unbuckled his trousers. The sound of the metal fastener opening excited Diamond. Suspenders fell like dangling vices to the floor. Off came Lex's satin shirt. The hard mold of his muscled torso was covered in a field of wiry black tufts. His aroused nipples poked through that plush pelt like two fine-chocolate candies. Lex turned slowly, revealing his sweet gem of an ass. The impeccably rounded spheres undulated hotly before Diamond's eyes. Diamond stared intently at that taut, slow-moving ass. Yep, it was as a gangster's rump ought to be. Hard, supple, full of meat. The perfect receptacle for a long dick, except for one dark, raised scar, a souvenir. But if Lex's ass could take one of Juicy Carlito's bullets, it certainly could handle the sting of the hard projectile about to pierce it.

"Ya like, huh? Like this ass?" Lex asked, his voice never losing it's tough guy tone."

"It's copacetic," Diamond replied, cool as cucumber kept too long in an icebox.

Lex stood right in front of him and kicked off his pants. His purple-headed club shot out, quivered and banged against Diamond's cheek, leaving a slimy trace of dick-juice behind.

It was a real big one. Big, with a hot, butt-ugly appeal. A vein-stitched, 11 inch bruiser, extra long on skin. "C'mon! Ya know ya want it. C'mon baby. C'mon and suck this big black dick!" Lex hissed.

Lex Martin was used to getting his way. So, when Diamond Roundtree didn't jump to it, Lex pried those tightened lips open and thrust his wide, salty cock inside, sending that choke-thick shaft ramming past Diamond's tongue. He held Diamond's trembling chin and forced that big thuggish prick down his throat. Roundtree gulped. He needed air. It was too much dick at once. Shit! That hard, heavy mocha python was close to a foot long!

Diamond couldn't have designed a better cock for a Colored gangster. Hard and resilient. Crooked, veiny, thick of skin. Huge, potent balls. Roundtree went down on it again, licking, lapping, lacquering the shaft with a violent swirl, jacking it with a vengeance. Lex groaned and shivered, bucking his hips, sending his cock deeper down Roundtree's clutching gullet.

Diamond quickly whipped his dick free. The long, hardening lance lunged forth and vibrated. Aroused by the sight of it, Lex pulled his prick from Diamond's wet lips, turned and shimmied his ass onto Roundtree's waiting erection. Its head felt slick to Lex's cheeks as Diamond beat his long hard cock to that taut, gyrating drum. Diamond got off on the contrast of his beige meat and those warm copper cheeks. His precome left a long sticky smear there, like a brand. Lex's ass was his and his only, for that night, at least.

When Lex faced him, the heads of their cocks met in a come-dripping kiss. They embraced tightly and ground their dicks together. The cock on cock friction became intense and put an unbearable heat on their skin. Before the two lugs spontaneously combusted, Lex fell before the long, hot, twitching bone punching obscenely out of Diamond's silk boxers. Hot to suck that long motherfucker, Lex poured champagne along the rigid dong, soaking its shaft in amber suds.

Diamond shook savagely as Lex slowly glided around the crown and sucked it with a mad slurp. Lex gripped the base and licked the jutting column up and down, slapping his face with it. Like a thug in love with a brand new rod, he lost himself to the smooth, pulsing feel of it.

"Oh yeah. Suck it! Go all the way down. Yes! Swallow all that long, hard meat!"

Earl held tight to Lex's head and pushed. Lex gulped hard, savoring the long ride down. He grabbed the bucking spheres, adoring the feel and the fierce mold of Diamond's ass. Its hairless seam was perfect, deep—the firm mounds so buttery smooth. Lex intended to fuck it thoroughly before the night was through.

The men fell to the divan. Earl took hold of Lex's throbbing prick. Pulling the long flap into a pinched nipple, he flicked his tongue inside. Lex groaned. A former horn player, Roundtree took a deep breath, flexed his jaw muscles, and engulfed the entire rod. The big cock head, thick blood engorged shaft, and corded veins pounded hard on Diamond's tongue.

They were passionate dick slurpers, bobbing and sucking with a ferocious rhythm. Even an explosion from a felon's gun couldn't keep them off each other. Lex jabbed two blunt fingers deep up Earl's steaming cleft. He and his big, fat, anxious rod anticipated a plunge into paradise. What he got instead was Roundtree's Rule on The Subject of Fucking: "Hey! Don't do that, baby. I don't get fucked."

"What? Bullshit! I'm getting some of this ass, tonight, baby!" Lex insisted.

"Sorry, Lex, but you won't be fuckin' any of this here ass tonight!" Diamond panted.

"But you gotta give me some. Hell! I earned it. I sucked your cock! Checker Martin sucked your fuckin' dick, man! I don't do that shit for just anybody!"

"Well, holy smokes and gee-whiz, thanks, but I don't get fucked. I do the fuckin'!"

"Fuckin' sissy! You suck dick better then a professional, and you don't get fucked? Ain't ya man enough to take it up the ass?"

"Look, I take it in the face and like it, and I'll fuck you till you sing the low down dirty Blues. If that ain't man enough for you, you can catch a hat! Scram! I ain't stoppin' you!"

Well didn't this beat the mood all to shit! Both their dicks were harder than 1929, and Diamond didn't get fucked! Lex's horny mind worked overtime, the thug in him thinking: I could just take it, by force if necessary. He'd whine and yelp, but eventually, he'll grow to love this big mother-fuckin' asshole-splitter. Most men did.

But, instead of force-fucking, instead of words, Lex took Diamond's hand and led him to a king-sized bed. Lex sprawled upon red satin sheets, his glorious colored ass rising and falling; its pink pucker calling Diamond forth. Diamond mounted him, running his hands along firm, hair sprinkled globes. Slowly, he pulled the dusky cheeks apart. He held his dick, tapping it right on Lex's butt crack. Then he eased it in, the head of his cock piercing that anal knot. Lex unleashed a wild yow! Pushing past tightness, Earl's tubular flesh disappeared inside a lush tunnel. As Earl wiggled his pole inside, Lex banged the mattress. He pulled back and let his prick deliver a slow, stabbing punch to that fuck hole.

He jammed it in, squirmed it out, slowly, rhythmically. Lex started gyrating, grabbing the back of Diamond's sweating neck. He held on tight and swerved his hips to meet each kinetic thrust. Raw anguish mixed with ass-deep pleasure. Diamond thought Lex would protest, howl out loud as men did when he fucked them, but Lex never feared pain.

Diamond's fuck speed increased. His long, hard dick continued banging, the rigid shaft jabbing, jabbing forth in deep and stabbing thrusts, again and again. Lex writhed against it. Diamond reached around and clutched Lex's rigid rod. Earl fisted it swiftly as Lex held on for dear life. His fingers slipped from Diamond's wet neck and he crashed face-first to the sheets.

"Let me see you," Earl grunted. Lex turned onto his back, eyes all shiny with lust. Man! He never looked tougher than when Diamond's dick reentered him. Pulling Lex's legs apart, he went in for the burn, his balls and thighs slapping Lex's cheeks. Lex pounded his rod to the vision of Earl, tightening his legs around his man's wide, glistening back, drawing him in.

Diamond lost himself in the wild field of Lex Martin's bushy chest as steam rose off their heated bodies. They were shooting silent messages through their eyes—ga-ga love notes each had forbade the other to read out loud. These two lust-sick stumblebums fucked intensely, vigorously, wantonly, fucking for more than an hour—an hour charged by "Oohs, ahhs, and aw shits!", an hour filled with the sounds of "Yes! Yes! Fuck yes!"

Diamond's dick rammed deeper, harder. Lex could feel every inch of it, moist droplets of precome oiling his overheated asshole. The friction was too good, and Lex fired recklessly upward. Gooey spunk ropes splashed Diamond's bucking torso, the force of his load surprising them both.

Roundtree followed, shooting a deluge, his hips writhing, his come-slit creaming, chucking forth a bountiful gush of hot ivory lava. Lex wondered if the oozing would ever stop. They stared in silence at each other, panting like two hot animals, trying to decide if they'd be lovers or lethal enemies. Savage beats thumped inside their chests. In a desperate rush, they each hurled fiery tongues toward the dark of the other's mouth. Yep. Fats Brown was right. Something had indeed happened between them. The turbulent times, the violent world outside disappeared as they lay against satin sheets.

Some would say they were crazy—and maybe they were. But what they did was behind closed doors, and it had to stay that way. What they felt in that moment was crazy, cuckoo, dangerous. Yet, they lay grinding, kissing and clutching at the unlikely possibility of a small time thug and a saloon singer being happy together.

Fate, however, had other plans.

Roundtree stared at the sleeping man beside him. As shafts of light poured onto the planes and valleys of Lex's face, Diamond studied his lover's parts and wondered, Why had Lex chosen this life? But what choices were left to Negro men with ambition, smarts and style? Maybe this seamy life was chosen for him? In that light, Lex looked tender, masculine, glowed with almost angelic ethnicity. If times were different, Lex Martin could've been a fucking movie star. He could've owned a rib joint, a car dealership, a fancy night spot. Something! He could've done a thousand other things, safer things. Lex awakened with an "Ahh!" as Diamond lips went down on his morning hard-on.

"Mmm! Damn! That feels like sunshine!"

Weeks of sucking and fucking, billing and cooing passed. The two mismatched lugs grew even closer. Lex became a regular at Lucky's Lounge, watching his loverboy croon for the assembled jazz crowd. Each night, the Bentley would be parked near the back door for Diamond's exit. It became a routine for Fats to leave for a long leisurely smoke. It became the drill for the men to fuck between sets. Diamond seemed to sound better after a hot session with his stage door gangster. Sucking cock oiled his tonsils, and his pipes purred stronger after letting loose a wad up Lex's warm, tight, bushy asshole.

But, routines tend to get noticed, especially when a man's got enemies. Fats warned Lex. "I ain't one to interfere, but maybe you need to keep your eyes on the street. There's talk about the visit ya paid Juicy. Juicy don't like being punked in front of his boys. Word is, he's still sore and gunnin' for ya, so watch your back." Shortly after he said this, another Bentley, Juicy's Bentley, circled the block. "See what I mean? That fucker's demented!" The car drove away slowly. Very slowly.

Lex heard the warning, but it didn't mean anything. Someone was always gunning for him. It came with the chitlins dinner. Besides, there was this crazy, cuckoo beat in his heart—and Diamond Roundtree had put it there. Lex was a goner, a sap who'd fallen hard for some glamourpuss in a smoky dive.

When The Checker crashed, he bang, crashed, smashed, boomed, hard! So hard, he went a little crazy, impulsive, acting out and leading with fists. He went out of his way "protecting his own" and wasn't beyond lashing out whenever he felt threatened. One such threat was some fancy Colored writer who'd been shaking the branches of Diamond's tree. After a violent knock-down-drag-out, Lex made a hasty purchase, a little something to show his lover exactly where he stood.

The warm August night moved with the same smooth verve of the nights before, but Lex's Bentley wasn't waiting. Diamond lit a cig and basked in the neon afterglow of his performance. He was happy, content. In an instant, some lug jumped him from behind, and a chloroform-soaked rag dimmed his view of the lush life.

When he awakened, he found himself tied to a chair in a tiny room lit by a red light bulb. As the haze cleared, Earl recognized the butt-ugly mug looming over him. Oh, shit! It was Juicy Carlito, in the flesh! All those newspaper photos never quite caught him right: the eye patch, that one wandering eye, the long, vicious scar on his left cheek, his balding, sweat-drenched brow.

"Well lookie here. If it ain't Lex's little secret. Ya know, I ain't no fan of that shit you sing, but I been itchin' to meet ya!"

Diamond's heart thumped hard. He studied Carlito's powerful, yet jittery body. Juicy could pounce at any moment—he was crazy like that, a two-bit gangster with a rep and a hair-trigger temper.

"So, you fancy sissy! What I wanna know is, who dukes who in duh ass, huh?"

Earl didn't answer, not about to sing on his man. No way. He played the dope.

"Aw, c'mon! Tell me about you and Lex." Carlito insisted.

"Lex? Lex, who?" Diamond asked.

"Cut the bull! See, I know all about ya and ya punk-ass loverboy! Always thought Lex was sweet in the ass. Now I got proof, prettyboy. Oh! I love it. This shit'll ruin him in this town once and for all! If only he was still alive to care!"

Roundtree's confused brain began screaming, What? Still alive? But he didn't shout it.

"What do you want with me, Mr. Carlito? I'm just a musician. Don't bother nobody. I'm only small change to a man like you. Ain't you got bigger fish to fry, sir?"

"Don't eat fish. But I hear you eat meat," he taunted. Then he whipped his extra-thick dick out.

Carlito had one hell of a chunky, uncut prick, but Diamond was too scared to be impressed. Don't let 'em see you scared, he repeated to himself as he glared back.

"So, whose got the biggest one, huh? Me or Lex?"

Diamond glared at him. Sure, it was the thickest, fattest, meatiest prick he'd ever seen, but Lex's dick was longer, prettier, smelled better.

Carlito went for the kill, shaking his obese peter in Earl's face. "Why do ya think they call me Juicy, huh? Well, tonight, you're gonna find out!"

Carlito squeezed his fat shaft. A long gooey chain of jism hung from its wide head. He pushed the dick cap to Diamond's mouth and smeared his lips. Then, he picked up a nearby .45, emptied it of slugs, wiped it clean of prints with his shirt and smiled. His gold tooth gleamed as he thrust the gun into Diamond's right hand. "Grab it. Grab it, damn it!" he demanded.

Diamond obeyed him, gripping the trigger, wishing there was one more bullet.

"Good. Now, guess what, fancy boy. You just killed your lover!" Carlito laughed.

Horrified, Diamond dropped the gun. What has this sadistic motherfucker done?

"Checker was walking past my club tonight. You two had one of your little spats. You punks get so emotional! Well, ya saw him and flipped. In a fag's rage, you gunned him down!"

Diamond sat, speechless, hurt and lost in a shock too thick to fully absorb. Lex was dead? No! It wasn't true. It couldn't be. Lex was too smart to be set up. Diamond closed his eyes and flashed-back to earlier in the day, when Lex poured his heart out: "Why do you make me so crazy? Huh? I mean, I'm The Fuckin' Man! Gangsters Ain't No Sissies! I run things. People fear me! They respect me! Why? Cause, I'm The Checker! The Fuckin' Man! Damn it! Don't you understand that?"

"Well, I'm a man, too! I might suck your cock, but that don't mean you own me. You own a suit, a lid, a gun, a ride, a fuckin' radio! Not me, Lex! No one does!"

"But I don't wanna own ya. What if I...I really care about you, Earl! What if I said, if I could, if the world was different, I'd fuckin' want to marry your arrogant ass!"

"I'd say all that bad hooch must be fuckin' with your mind!"

"Don't say shit you don't mean! This here is serious business I'm talkin'! But, what I need to know is, how the hell do you feel about me? Huh? Well? Say something!"

Lex sweated out the silence as Earl looked into his eyes. Doesn't he already know? This crazy, maddening thing we share, this was it. Things don't get any more intense. But now, Lex needed to hear it.

"I dig you, Lex, you crazy, violent cat! I dig you just fine. You're swell. You're the bee's knees, when you're not busy being a fuckin' thug! All right? Happy, now?"

Lex touched Roundtree's face and pulled him closer, closing his eyes, kissing him.

Their cocks hardened inside their trousers. Lex removed his shoulder holster. He placed it on a table, fell to his knees, and slowly pulled Earl's stubborn tool forth and began sucking it passionately.

They retired to Diamond's tiny bed. Ripping their clothes away, they fell to the squeaking mattress. Earl sunk his cock deep inside Lex's ass and fucked him with earnest vigor. The pulsing inside Lex's butt was hot and beating, beating harder than it ever had before. It gripped his dick, nearly milking him bone-dry. The heat between them was enhanced by a quiet desperation that felt like love.

Afterward, Lex gave Earl a small box. Inside was a diamond ring, surrounded by a band of tiny rubies. This was not some gaudy rock. It was beautiful. It was the nicest thing anyone had ever given him.

"Read the inscription," Lex insisted, kissing the nape of Diamond's tan neck.

"Forever in Lex's Check." Earl grinned, repeating the phrase in amazement.

"We're married now. Fuck the world. Right here in this bed, we're married. Lemme put it on ya."

Lex's cock grew harder just watching the happiness playing on Diamond's face. His erection stood like a monument below the sheets. Diamond noticed. He couldn't help but notice.

Diamond played with Lex's elongating bone, rubbing it, running his fingers along its wide, juicing head. Why had I been so fearful of it? What would taking it up my ass mean? I'd still be a man. Is it about the pain? Just living was full of pain. This is just a dick. Yes, it's as big and thick and hard as Colored life in 1931. But it's connected to the man I love. As his fingers lingered along the blunt head, he turned and spread the seepage to his ass ring. The decision was made. He was going to give his cherry to Lex. His lover looked at this sight, this surrender, this silent message being sent to him. Lex's mouth fell open, and he asked, "You mean? You...you ready to give me some?"

"Yes. Yes! Do it! I want you to fuck me, Lex. Now, before I change my mind."

"Oh, damn it! Baby, I gotta go. You know I wouldn't leave if I didn't have to. I got a meeting with some fellas downtown. I'm already late. Don't worry. After the show, I want ya to pack all your stuff. I'm taking you away from this joint. Gonna set ya up in a nice place in Jersey. It'll be our getaway. Our joint. Our own little love nest. Got that, huh? Now plant a big wet one on me. Knock me one right here! C'mon, my li'l wifey," Lex teased.

"Sheeeeit! Wife, hell! I'll be the husband in this cuckoo relationship. Don't you forget it!"

They kissed strong, long, shamelessly, as Lex gripped the smooth mold of Diamond's booty.

"Man-oh-man! I got plans for you! Go do your show. And don't forget, have your bags packed! Tonight's our night," Lex said, winking as he dressed in a hurry.

He grabbed his coat, cocked his black fedora at a rakish tip, and disappeared through the door.

This was all earlier that evening. Before the show, before that smoke in the alley, before everything blurred into a dick—a big, hard, gruesome dick that was about to enter Earl's mouth.

Carlito was telling him Lex was dead. And Lex's mortal enemy was thrusting his wide, drool-spewing cock head against his cheek as a silent tear coated it.

The sadist kept slapping his big cock and sweaty balls against Diamond's stunned face. "Now, I'm gonna fuck dat pretty mouth like a fuckin' racehorse...an make ya scream MY name!"

But, something happened that scared Juicy, that sent that waiting come-load back to his burly nuts. Just then, the furious force of Fats Brown's big, brawny, titanic shoulder boomed like thunder, breaking down the door. He came stumbling in, and behind him stood Lex, looking better than a wet dream with his rod drawn, a bullet-hole in his cocked hat, and a Lucky between his lips.

"Thought I told you not to mess with other people's property! Step away from him, right now, you slimy motherfucker!"

"Lex? What duh fuck! I thought you was taken care of. Damn you! Damn you!"

"I was ready for you Carlito, wearing something special underneath my suit. You all right, baby? Did he hurt ya?"

"No. But I'll be washing my fucking mouth with soap for a week!" Diamond spat, wiping his lips.

"Juicy, your shit's history. You're about to be permanently checked! Fats, take this perv out and fit him for a pair cement shoes, size small! Me and Diamond, well, we got us an appointment."

In a tiny bungalow off the Jersey shore, as the Atlantic Ocean crawled the sand, Roundtree kissed the skin of the vest that saved his lover's life...and his own life. He whipped it away in a heated flourish and buried his grateful face in Lex's hairy chest. And then, those two crazy cuckoo newlyweds stripped naked. Lex was so fucking horny, his dick curved up like a hem. Once Diamond touched it, a deluge of cock honey slimed his fingertips. He used the crystal juice like lube, spreading it slow and deep up his puckered hole. Lex watched, licking his full lips. They kissed, Lex walking his lover backward to the waiting bed. Another flood of dick sap bubbled to his cock head, and he spread it inside Diamond's waiting prize. He dipped a slow finger within the pulsing pink chute and wiggled it as Diamond shivered. It was now or never. Fuck the world! thought Diamond. His hole, his never fucked hole was Lex's. The seam itself called out to Lex, willing his hard, impatient prick forth.

"You sure, baby?" Lex questioned.

"Y-yes. Do it. Now! Do it before I change my chickenshit mind!" Diamond implored.

Lex quickly mounted Earl's sweat-polished globes. As Lex slowly entered that steaming magenta fuck bud, it was, for Diamond, more than simply inserting a hard cock into a waiting orifice. A huge Colored dick was traveling past a place where fear, issues, "faggot" voices and taboos had lived coiled for 27 uptight years. There was a welling in Diamond's eyes, a swoon in his breath.

"It's OK, baby. I know, it's a little scary. But it'll be new for the both of us," Lex whispered.

The pulsing shaft plowed through tunnels of tightened skin. "Ho-o-o! Fuc-k-k-k!" Earl cried. 11 inches of dick felt bigger in his ass than it ever had in his mouth. He murmured into his pillow, his hole convulsing around the hard column. Lex kissed Earl's neck, assuring him he'd be gentle, but the feel of that tight fuck bud was too much.

Lex shuddered as he lunged and withdrew, lunging, withdrawing, his full throbbing cock exploring Earl's warm, cushy, uncharted cavern. Diamond's virginal man pussy was like some delectable feast. Its sphincter had a way, an urgent way of gripping tight to Lex's pole each time he withdrew. Lex pulled Diamond's long, sleek legs further apart and let his dick submerge deep in the pucker of that spastic ass-hole. He paused there, slowly drew back, and found a rhythm that suited them both. With short, tense strokes, he began to plow his oversized organ in and out as the tight, slippery rectum clutched each hammering thrust. With a grunt, Diamond found his tender butt-hole giving in, accommodating the enormous prick that was sound-ly embedded in it. What was misery, a second ago, was now a raw and unbridled lust for more! The ocean roared. A storm was brewing in Diamond Roundtree. His cock was weeping. His wild brain shouted, Yes! His fevered lips were screaming, Fuck me! Yes! O-o-oh! Oh, Lex!

F-u-u-uck me! F-u-u-uck me!

Lex moved his body over Diamond's, stroking the sides of his hips, kissing him the way men kiss when they really mean it. Roundtree wiggled and squirmed as his lover's dick bared down in slow, deep de-scents, sinking, pulling them both into a hot burning oblivion. Lex was losing himself in that firm, luscious grip, and Diamond was en-veloping some strange, big hunk of gangster love. Sounds of the ocean and slapping flesh filled their ears as Lex shivered with a pump-ing violence, and the kingpin shot his seed. A wild white-hot load ri-fled from his prick head, scorching the confines of Roundtree's gut. The vibration set off a charge in Diamond's being, and he detonated like a machine gun—a hail of bullets ratta-tat-tatting to the wet sheets beneath him.

"WHOA, babeee! Damn baby! Your ass is gold! Mmm! I mean that was, that was more than copacetic! Man-oh-man! We've had some night, huh?" Lex sighed, panting and satisfied.

"Y-yeah! Shit, yes! Some, fuckin' night, all right!" Diamond purred in concurrence.

But the tough guy competitor in Lex still had to know: "So, baby. You gotta tell me. Who's got the biggest gun, huh? Me or Carlito?"

Fade to sepia...and black.

Bringing Up Robbie
By Mark Caldwell

Robbie is my boy. Well, actually he's 28, and we are not related at all, but he is still my boy. And like a good boy, he calls me Daddy.

Today Robbie called me from the studio and said he had been a bad boy. I said nothing. I smoked the last few puffs of my cigarette and waited. I could hear Robbie squirm.

Robbie is a local newscaster in our palm tree-lined town. His job involves lots of public exposure and high pressure. In difficult situations with his fellow workers, Robbie often becomes cross or peevish. I don't care for this sort of attitude, and Robbie knows it. He also knows that he'd better call me right away and tell his daddy all about it.

So now I am waiting and smoking my cigarette. I don't need to ask Robbie what happened. Robbie will tell me. And as his words stutter and fall over each other, I can feel his blush heat up the wires between us. His voice is hushed and muffled as he explains some flippant abuse he perpetrated on a hapless PA.

He stops for long pauses, and I know it is because he is in a crowded room and cannot speak frankly or else the humiliating nature of his phone call will be disclosed. It's about 5:30, and he knows that he must be already made-up and dressed for the 6 p.m. live broadcast.

As Robbie's confession sighs to a finish, I stub out my cigarette in the black marble ashtray next to Robbie's bed and sit up slightly. "Robbie, you make people very unhappy and tense when you behave like a spoiled child."

Silence.

"There must be some way that I can firmly impress upon you how inappropriate your actions are."

Silence.

"Robbie, I want you to go to your office and open the third drawer down."

A strangled whimper.

"I want you to wear Jeffy tonight for the broadcast."

"No!" he blurts defiantly. It is the daring taunt of a young man vainly trying to usurp his father's power. All cocky and brave in the face of unbeatable odds.

I can feel the silence now between us as it erodes his nerves. I wait till I can hear the sweat form on his brow, and I burst into laughter.

"Robbie, I'm very comfortable here, and my dinner is almost ready, but don't think for even a moment that I wouldn't hesitate to put my clothes on and get in that BMW of yours—which, by the way, you still haven't put the plates on—and drive down to the studio to deal with you in person."

"No!"

The same word but as if from another language. A pleading, hoarse whine instead of a defiant bleat.

"Well, then, as I said, I want you to wear Jeffy tonight to help you remember to be a little more considerate of other people's feelings."

A wet sigh bubbles through the wires.

"And besides, Robbie, Daddy wants that little hole opened wide by the time you come home, so please don't take it out before you get here. I've got to go now. Terrence just called up that dinner is ready. Good-bye, Robbie."

I hang up without waiting for a response. He'd just be wasting my time anyway. He'd snivel and beg and use up all his time before the broadcast to evade his responsibilities. He's tried it before. A father has to be cleverer than his son at times. Brute force alone will not transform an errant lad into a fine young man.

As I sit in bed with my dinner tray, I reach for the remote control to the television. Fifteen minutes until the news. I picture Robbie hurrying down the tiled hallway to his office and rushing to lock the office door behind him. I wish I could see the look on his face. I called the maintenance department earlier today to have them remove the lock, "per Robert's orders." He must be panicked by now, knowing that he's got to be back upstairs in moments.

The phone rings. The house phone is on speed dial.

"Hello," I answer in a calm, measured voice.

Rather than words, an exasperated whimper bursts my ear. Then,

"God, oh, God, I've only got... How could you do this? How am I supposed to—"

I can't help but laugh. Then I remind Robbie that he'd better not waste his time sputtering as he has only seven minutes. Then I hang up.

I picture my boy now, sweat building on his handsome brow. I picture him stripping his pants down over his globular smooth cheeks—underwear and all in one swoop—and then yanking the third drawer open and pulling out the Jeff Stryker dildo and a large jar of Albolene. I can see him placing the dildo on the chair and then slathering his perfectly formed asshole with the goo.

Robbie must be checking his Raymond Weil watch now. But there's no time to get used to the imposing thickness. I see his classic good-looking Italian face contort as he squeezes himself down on it as fast as he can. I can hear the deep groan as he hits Jeffy's balls.

Normally my boy can take bigger and thicker than the Jeff Stryker dildo. Especially if he is at home with his dad and we're just having a little father-and-son roughhousing. But now, as his intercom comes on and the assistant director is yelling for him to come to the set right away, my boy is ripping off a length of gaffer's tape to secure the dildo and painfully pulling up his crisp white Jockey shorts and his navy gabardine slacks from Polo/ Ralph Lauren.

Grunting from the pain of adjusting to the intruder inside him, Robbie quickly and carefully tucks his shirt back into his slacks and straightens his navy, yellow, and maroon brocade tie. I bought him that tie at Selfridge's when we were in London last year. On his charge.

I smile as I imagine him having to run upstairs now to the soundstage, almost waddling with discomfort. I see him whisking past the crew, carefully tugging at the back of his navy blazer so that the bulge of Jeffy's balls doesn't show behind him.

One or two may raise a knowing eyebrow to each other. A couple of them have witnessed my chastisement of Robbie at the station. But Robbie is so good-looking and so good at delivering the news and his ratings are so high that the powers that be have chosen to ignore his little "family problems," as they are referred to.

I turn up the sound on the remote control just as the commercial is ending and the titles start for Robbie's show. And there he is. My boy. A son any father could be proud of. Robbie has the perfect white teeth and regular features of a classic news broadcaster. A masculine authority radiates from his warm brown eyes as he informs us of the day's events.

His well-timed responses and perfect pacing are absolutely irreproachable, very much in keeping with a confident, intelligent, and imperturbable man on his way to the top of his field. As the camera pulls back to include video graphics illustrating a rise in summer vandalism, one's eyes tend to stray from the graphics to Robbie's broad shoulders filling more than his fair share of the wood-toned desk space for the three newspeople.

One would hardly guess that a man so utterly masculine and self-assured had only moments before been ordered to stuff his ass with a grossly large dildo by someone he called Daddy.

But a good father knows what a boy needs, and Robbie needs to be reminded all the time that Daddy loves him and is thinking about him. And only a daddy can tell by the slight twitching movement in Robbie's right temple that the stuffed-full pain of the dildo is stripping his veneer.

A sleepy haze takes over after my dinner. The ringing phone wakes me, and I see that Entertainment Tonight is already on.

"Hello," I yawn into the phone.

Robbie groans. I hear static and street noises, which indicate he is on the car phone.

"Oh, Daddy, please let me take it out. It's been in too long. My ass is cramping. Oh, God, please—"

"Robbie, if you come home and that dildo is not in place, there will be hell to pay. Now stop wasting time blabbing to me about your troubles and get your ass back here. The sooner you get that sorry excuse for an ass home, the sooner Daddy can take Jeffy out."

I slam down the receiver.

God, I hate being awakened by the phone!

Over the years I've had to punish Robbie for a number of reasons. But Robbie is not being punished tonight. He is merely being disciplined. I believe in discipline.

Discipline is often loving but always firm. Punishment is very loving but quite a bit more serious.

Robbie knows that if he doesn't follow my orders, he will be punished, and so he always submits to my discipline. Well, most of the time anyway. Sometimes Robbie tests my limits. He tried tonight earlier with that defiant little "No."

Just as I light another cigarette, I hear the door bang open downstairs. I sip the coffee that Terrence has brought up to me as I hear Robbie bounding up the steps.

And indeed he's panting now and sweating like a horse. He practically backs into the room as he yanks his pants down around his tan thighs. Offering his ass to me, he whimpers, "Please, Daddy, please take it out!"

I puff on my cigarette and flip through the TV Guide. "No," I say in a deliberate imitation of his earlier refusal.

"Oh, God, Daddy, I'm sorry I said that earlier. Please, I'll do anything. Just take it out for a few minutes at least!"

Absentmindedly I pick at an edge of the gaffer's tape and rip it off his ass, pulling the dildo out with what must be for Robbie an embarrassing plop. Five pounds of lifelike latex bounces off the berber carpeting as Robbie yelps from the pain and pleasure of release and topples facedown on the bed in front of me.

"Hard day at the office, honey?"

I take in his form stretching before me. Long, well-built limbs and the spinal curve of a pubescent. His ass, even in its relaxed state, arches up into the air. I can still see the rosier pink stripes where the tape took off a light layer of skin. His very elastic asshole has already contracted but not exactly to its original pucker.

Robbie is finally able to relax now and remains stretched out like an offering. He is fully clothed with his torso bared. His face is turned toward me, and his eyes are closed. There is still a little glow of sweat on his forehead and upper lip, and his mouth is open. He is breathing deeply in preparation for sleep.

But my son will not sleep for a while yet. He still needs to be bathed, powdered, and tucked in. I smack him hard enough on his ass that a large red handprint appears immediately. Robbie is up like a shot, startled out of his near-sleep state.

"Into the bathroom, young man!"

Robbie is already clean as a whistle inside. I make sure of that each afternoon before he leaves for the studio. After all, the last thing you want to see when you watch the 6 o'clock news is an anchorman full of shit.

So now I have my baby boy in a tub full of bubbles with all his favorite toys: his rubber duck, of course; his styrofoam tugboat; his Nerf football; and my favorite, the panda scrub mitt. I like to sit on the edge of the tub and have a smoke while Robbie bathes, just to see that he doesn't get carried away while cleaning his genital area and to make sure that he thoroughly cleans the bathroom when he is finished.

Robbie is in a happy little mood now as he lies back in the tub, bubbles breaking cutely under his chin while he babbles on about his day at the studio. As he talks he is bouncing his Nerf football higher and higher off the tiled wall.

"Young man, watch it! We don't want any accidents in the bathroom, now, do we?"

Robbie uncharacteristically ignores me and continues talking about himself in the manner that young boys are wont to do, bouncing the ball higher and higher until he finally misses his catch and the ball splashes soundly in the tub, splattering water all over my silk pajamas.

One can hear a pin drop.

"Uh, I'm sorry. I didn't mean to—"

As I grab Robbie by the hair on his head and lift him up out of the tub to flop him on his hands and knees, the water lapping at his balls, he continues to sputter his pointless apology. But Robbie knows how I feel when he has purposely ignored my warnings. He has to pay the price.

His ass is raised out of the bubbles, and soapy water drips down his hairless crack. I still have a hold of his hair, and as I wind up for the pitch, I dunk his head under the water.

Spank, spank, spank, spank.

Glub, glub, glub, glub.

Then I let go of Robbie's head, and he comes up coughing and gasping for air. I let him get enough in his lungs for another round, then redunk him as I haul off and whack his upturned butt repeatedly. Water is splashing all around us, and my pj's are soaked.

There will be hell to pay.

His ass is good and red now, and he is flailing in the tub, trying to come up for air and avoid the connection of my hand to his ass at the same time. When I let him up this time, he is not only coughing and gasping for air, I'm afraid, he's also crying. Little Robbie was scared that Daddy wasn't going to let him up.

I am a strict father, but when my boy cries, I lose my resolve. I grab my boy to my chest even though he is all wet and hug him tightly to me. My cock is hard immediately in my wet silk pj's, and it bumps around between us.

"Daddy is sorry he had to be so mean, baby, but I told you to stop, and you didn't. Now, let's get you scrubbed up real good. Daddy will help."

Robbie sniffles and coos as I pull my pj's off and toss them into the corner. My cock stands up straight as I get into the warm soapy water and put on the panda scrub mitt.

Robbie's face starts to beam at me as I work up a lather. The combination of Robbie's neon smile, his black curly hair, his cheeks all pink from the hot water, and his eyes still brimming with tears is enough to melt the heart of Attila the Hun. As I scrub him all over briskly with the mitt, he holds on to my cock. His hands are slippery with soap, and he slides his fists up and down slightly, making it fairly hard to concentrate on my task.

All pink and scrubbed now.

I turn on the showerhead to rinse us both off as the tub water drains. Robbie is on his knees before me. The burst of water rains down on his head, and the suds rush off of my cock. Robbie leans forward slowly, as if waiting for my approval before his head glides in a swift motion to engulf my cock. As I wash the suds from my hair, then his, Robbie's head bobs up and down, his eyes tightly shut so as not to get water in them.

Robbie stands obediently with his arms raised, passively watching me as I dry him off, getting the towel into every little nook and cranny. A light dusting of baby powder, then a sparklingly white pair of Calvin Kleins and a white T-shirt finish the job.

I let Robbie off the hook tonight about cleaning up the bathroom, mostly because I still feel bad about scaring him. So when Terrence brings Robbie's dinner up on a tray, I ask him to attend to it. Terrence is a rather avuncular old man and has warmly fulfilled his duties for us for several years now. He is used to cleaning up the little messes we make and sometimes has had to assist me when Robbie's treatment has required punishment rather than simply discipline.

For instance, the time I came home and found Robbie blowing our gardener, Louis, in the foyer. Terrence was only too happy to take pictures of Robbie sucking Louis's hugely engorged cock as I whipped my boy's ass with a wet belt. Robbie, of course, thought that I would send the gardener away.

But I knew that Robbie had planned for me to catch him. So instead of blaming the gardener (and who could really blame him? Robbie has a mouth like an angel), I made Robbie continue and finish Louis off with a good hand job, spraying his load in Robbie's camera-perfect face.

Terrence took a great picture of it that I keep in an envelope addressed to the TV station as another means of discipline.

But there have been no major crimes tonight. Simply the naughty misdemeanors of a young boy who needs to know the boundaries of his father's patience. So we sit happily on the bed, Robbie tucked in and me spoon-feeding him supper.

When Terrence finishes in the bathroom, he stops by the bed and daintily suspends the Jeff Stryker dildo by his forefinger and thumb.

"Will you be wanting me to have this cleaned yet, sir?"

"No, Terrence, I don't think we are finished with that yet tonight. Please leave it here next to the bed."

I hand him Robbie's cleaned plate on the tray, and Terrence thanks me as he backs out of the room.

Robbie has a dumbfounded look on his face. He had forgotten completely about Jeffy, and I am sure that he thought he was moments away from being tucked in, all warm and snuggly. Robbie nervously reaches for his glass of milk on the table next to the bed, and as he jerks it to his face to drink, some spills down his front. He looks down at the white drops on his tan chest and then suddenly up at me to see if I will laugh or be angry.

I'm angry. I hate spilled milk in the bed, and Robbie is very aware of that.

"All right, young man, we have a method for dealing with boys who can't hold their milk."

Before he can react I have the dildo in one hand and Robbie dangling by his upper arm in the other.

Robbie is already yelping a little when I throw him down on the fluffy white rug in the bathroom. Out of the cabinet I grab a small white towel, two very large safety pins with blue plastic tops, and a tube of K-Y jelly. Robbie is watching this all through puppy eyes and a pouty mouth. He knows what is going to happen, so he just lies back on the rug and waits for Daddy to do it.

The full-length mirror on the bathroom wall reflects everything as I pull Robbie's pristine white shorts down and drag them over his puffy white socks. Robbie had already removed his white T-shirt after dinner, so all he has on is his great tan and a little chest hair.

I keep Robbie cleanly shaven so that I can see everything that goes on down there. A growing boy must be closely observed for any irregularities. And besides, the curve of his taut little stomach above his rather thick cock is so cute. It just makes me want to hug him and kiss him all over.

Robbie is lying on his back, staring up at the ceiling in a dream world, as I fold the towel carefully, then lift him by his legs to place the towel beneath him. I squeeze a large gob of K-Y into my hand and pack it up into his ass, slathering the rest around the general area of his pert hole. Then I put some more on the entire length of Jeffy, and as I place it at Robbie's hole, he closes his eyes, and his thumb distractedly grazes its way to his mouth.

I hardly notice my own cock stretched out in front of me as I concentrate on working the dildo up into my little newscaster's asshole. Robbie is panting and sucking at his thumb furiously, and his eyes are squinched shut. His free hand has strayed to his nipples, and it plucks and pulls on them alternately. Robbie's thick cock is rock-hard and bouncing on his stomach, and his shaved balls have tightened up to his body.

Once the dildo is in place, Robbie relaxes a bit, and I pull the flap end of the towel up tightly between his legs and secure the safety pins with the large baby-blue plastic heads at each side. Our diaper performs the task of holding Jeffy snuggly up my little boy's bottom. I can see the bulge of Robbie's cock throb in its confines.

"Robbie, into the bedroom."

As I stand in front of the deco armoire, I see Robbie crawling on all fours out of the bathroom, his right sock starting to slip off his foot. He stops in front of me and looks up into my eyes from his position on the floor. In the mirror on the armoire, I can see his diapered butt, the bulge of the dildo sticking out obscenely.

"Make your old man feel good, Robbie."

Robbie crawls up my legs with his wide hands, and on his knees in front of me he begins to lick my cock, which is arched out in front of him like a toy. In the mirror I see the back of his head perched on his long thick neck as it bends and swivels so he can lick all around my crotch.

I am much taller than Robbie, so even on his knees he has to reach up to tongue my balls.

As Robbie impales his head on my shaft, his hands busy themselves elsewhere: One is jammed down the front of his diaper, and the other alternates between his nipples and tugging and pushing at the large object lodged in his tight rectum.

I lean over and unpin the sides of Robbie's diaper, and it flops down at his strained flanks. Since he is in a squatting position in front of me, it naturally forces the thick dildo out, and as he sucks fast and wet on my cock, spit drooling from his lower lip, the plastic cock slips out of him until just the head is still in and the balls and base rest on the cream-colored carpet.

Putting my hands on his shoulders, I push firmly, grinding him back down onto it, and then I let go again to watch him rise up off of it.

Watching the impossibly thick shaft squeeze in and out of Robbie's hole turns me on so much, I have to jam my cock as far back as it will go in Robbie's clutching throat. He gags and sputters but makes no move to stop me.

The thought of his perfect white teeth raking over the head of my dick is too much, and I rest hard on his shoulders, pushing him all the way down to Jeffy's balls. I hear a muffled yelp from him, and that sends me over the top. Yanking my cock out, I squirt long streams of clotted white over his perfectly cut hair and watch in the armoire mirror as it drips down the hollow formed by the strong muscles on either side of his spine.

Robbie has to watch the 11 o'clock news. It's part of his job.

Tonight Robbie is watching it with Jeffy strapped into his mouth by his own diaper. He is facedown on the bed with his head propped up on a pillow so that he can see the news team on the TV. Robbie is snuffling air through his nose as fast as he can, and sometimes he tries to open his mouth around Jeffy and gasp for more.

He needs a lot of air because the pounding I'm giving his ass is using up a lot of energy. The whole bed is shaking and rocking.

Robbie's ass is twitching fast around my cock, and the way it looks, his strong thighs spread wide and the thick column of my cock sliding in and out, is hypnotic.

I haven't shaved for several days, and I can see red marks around Robbie's neck, and the tops of his shoulders have been rubbed raw. He's my boy, and I can mark him up any way I want to.

That thought alone is enough to send me over, and as the female news anchor signs off for the night, I slam home and feel jet after jet as it fills the condom around my cock. Robbie moans as he feels each throbbing salvo in his rectum.

Terrence turns off the bedroom light as he removes our dessert dishes.

I'm not quite asleep, but Robbie has just turned the TV off, and he gives his old man a long, wet tongue kiss before he pads off into the kitchen to get himself another glass of milk.

I struggle deliciously against sleep for a while, waiting for Robbie to come back to the warm bed so I can wrap my strong arms around him.

That's the only way I can really sleep, with my son safe and tucked in place.

In the darkened room I stare out the window next to my bed and see the moon reflected in the swimming pool. The garage and the gardener's apartment are both dark across the patio, but it seems there is a fleeting shadow out there.

Suddenly I see the lights come on in Louis's apartment and two silhouettes in his window.

There will be hell to pay for this. Robbie knows how I hate his blowing the gardener when he is supposed to be in bed with me.

Ripped Rasslers
By Bearmuffin

I was super ripped for the Mr. Olympia 2000. But I lost to Muhammud Belizar, a hot 24 year-old Ethiopian sporting 36 inch arms and a 15 inch cock.

I was disappointed but those were the breaks. After I had congratulated Mustafa with a friendly squeeze on his humpy butt, I went to the locker room to dress. I had just slipped on my jeans when Mr. Grant handed me a business card.

Grant worked for Don Wildfire, the biggest wrestling promoter in the business. If you played your cards right, Don would shoot you to the top.

"I'm always looking out for new talent," he said with a friendly grin. His eyes were running up and down my body. He licked his lips. "I know Mr. Wildfire could use a fine specimen like you."

"I'll think about it," I said. I finished dressing and drove back home.

I pondered Grant's offer. What the fuck? Lots of bodybuilders had gone into wrestling. Some had made big bucks. I figured I'd had my last shot at Mr. Olympia. So I called Grant. "Tell Wildfire I'll see him."

Grant was pleased. "You won't be sorry," he said. Then he gave me an address and hung up.

The next day I drove to a warehouse located in a seedy part of town. But I didn't worry about that. With my 6-foot-5 frame, 30-inch biceps, and tree trunk thighs, nobody was going to fuck with me.

I looked straight into the security camera as I rang the buzzer. Seconds later, the door opened. I climbed a long flight of stairs until I reached the loft on the top floor.

In the center was a huge wrestling ring where a pair of jockstrapped studs were grappling on the sweaty canvas. After I had taken in the astonishing sight of those two bronzed, muscular dudes glistening with sweat, I turned to see a big blond naked dude sitting on a rim chair.

It was Wildfire. He was in his late forties and in great shape with thick muscles and a hairy chest. He wore a huge black cowboy hat and black cowboy boots. And he was smoking a black cigar. He stroked his firm thick cock while a muscle-bound wrestler lay beneath him. The dude grunted like a pig as he sucked hard on Wildfire's sweaty asshole.

Wildfire ignored me for a few moments while he jacked off eagerly, keeping his big blue eyes on the two wrestlers. Then he glanced at me. He broke out in a huge grin. His eyes flew to my bulging crotch.

"Glad ya could make it, son," he drawled in a thick Texas accent.

I noticed his cock jerk up. A thick strand of pre-cum oozed from his piss-slit. It trickled down over his vein-etched cock. Wildfire licked his lips.

"Why don't you get comfortable?"

I quickly stripped to my jock and faced him, arms akimbo.

Wildfire's jaw dropped. "Whoa! Fuckin' hot bod! Grant sure as hell wasn't exaggerating when he described ya! His cock was bobbing up and down with excitement. His toothy grin had become a lecherous sneer. "How's about posing for me?"

I was always turned on by posing. Regardless of whom I was posing for, my bulge would get bigger and more defined as I posed. "Sure," I replied.

As I went through my standard posing routine, Wildfire ogled me. His thick lips were twisted in a lustful snarl. "Ohmigod, ohmigod," he kept on moaning, jacking himself off into a real frenzy. For a moment I thought he was about to topple from the rim chair and shoot his wad.

I capped off my routine with a little trick I'd learned from Mohammed. I bent over, grabbed my ankles, and spread my legs. My cheeks split wide open. Wildfire had a bird's-eye view of my asshole.

"Ah Fuck! Ah Holy Fuck!" Wildfire screamed as he shot a thick boiling come load that landed right on my butthole. Then he barked, "C'mon stud. Let me lick my cum off your fuckin' hot butt."

I pushed my ass against his eager face. I felt his thick, fat, sandpaper-rough tongue glide over my haunches. Then he stuck his snake-like licker right into my hole.

He began lightly circling my anus with his tongue tip. That really drove me crazy making my cock bolt straight into the air. I grabbed my crank and began fisting it. Wildfire was a champion rimmer. I was only to happy to let the fucker eat my hole until I popped my rocks.

But Wildfire had no intention of letting me cum. Not just yet. He slapped my butt and pushed me away. "Plenty of time for that later," he snorted. "I wanna see you wrestle!" He shot a look at the two studs who were still wrestling.

"Carlos!" he barked. "C'mere!"

Carlos dropped his opponent on the mat. When he saw me, he broke out in a lewd smile. He jumped out of the ring and sprinted over to us.

Wildfire's greedy eyes ran all over Carlos's gorgeous Brazilian bod. He was 6 foot 4 with barn-house shoulders, corded biceps, shelf-like pecs and the dick of death. The head was fat and wide. Ready to tear a hole right through his jockstrap.

Wildfire jerked a thumb toward me. "You're going to wrestle him," he said to Carlos.

Carlos grinned. "You're the boss." Then Carlos gave me the once over. His sexy green eyes glittered with lust. He grabbed his throbbing basket and winked at me. "Let's wrestle!"

The dude he'd been wrestling hopped out of the ring and kneeled in front of Wildfire. He began sucking his cock. The other wrestler continued to rim him. Wildfire lit up another stogie, leaned back, and shouted, "Start rasslin'!"

Carlos and I hopped into the ring. Carlos was a horny motherfucker. I knew he wanted to take me down so he could plow me with his Brazilian buttwhanger. As much as the thought of getting totally reamed by that bronzed beauty might have appealed to me, nobody was going to fuck me. No sir. I was a total top.

Carlos kept grabbing my cock and squeezing it. I whacked his butt a few times. Each time I did it, Carlos whimpered and moaned like a little boy. I figured he wouldn't mind me fucking his ass. I just hoped it would be as tight as it was hot. I like a dude's glute muscles to grip my cock and milk my cum out for all its worth!

I didn't know any wrestling holds apart from what I'd seen on TV. But it wasn't hard to get Carlos on his back. Within seconds I'd tossed Carlos on his face. His ass was wriggling in the air. So I stuck a finger inside it. His butthole rumbled like a volcano ready to erupt.

"Ay, si, papi," he moaned like a big pussy. "Chingame, papi, chingame bien!"

Wildfire bolted up. "He wants you to fuck him, son!" he said with a hoarse chuckle.

Wildfire pushed the cock sucking wrestler away from his thick upright cock. He snorted like a bull, obviously aroused by the scene. He tossed me a tube of lube, which I caught with one hand.

"Fuck him!" Wildfire frothed at the mouth. His eyes rolled up into their sockets. "Fuck that big Brazilian puto!"

Before you could say "butt fuck," I had squeezed a glop of lube on Carlos's anxiously twitching pucker. I placed the head of my cock flush against his anal ring. Then I rubbed my cock-head all along it. The friction made Carlos pant and squirm all the more.

"Please, papi, please fuck me!"

"Fuck him, Goddammit!" Wildfire roared as he plopped back on the rim chair. He grabbed the cock sucking wrestler by the hair and plunged his cock down his throat.

I slam-dunked my cock right inside Carlos's ass. Carlos was medium tight so my cock was able to snap right past his tight anal ring. Smoothly it glided down until the root of my cock struck his fat balls.

"Ay...ay...ay..." Carlos whimpered.

He reached down between his legs and began whacking off. I started to slowly hump him. Carlos was a real hot piece of ass. His butt muscles sucked around my pumping cock like a greedy mouth. I felt like leaving my cock inside his hole and letting him massage it with his talented sphincter, but I knew Wildfire expected a good show and so I gave it to him. I pumped away slowly at first, gradually building up a steady rhythm until you could hear my balls slapping against hot sweaty butt.

"Dios mio!" Carlos gasped.

Meanwhile Wildfire was screaming at us to get it on. "Fuck him, fuck him, fuck him, fuck him!" Wildfire screamed while he yanked on his tits. He was still being serviced by his two wrestling slaves. One eating his ass and the other sucking his cock.

I plowed full steam ahead. I was whipping my head back and forth. Hot sizzling sweat flew off my hair.

"Give him the works!" Wildfire bellowed.

I boldly grabbed Carlos' firm waist for support as I fucked the holy shit out of his steaming Brazilian ass.

"Ay, ay! I'm coming, amigo! I'm coming!"

Carlos suddenly slammed back against me as he shot his wad on the canvas. His ass muscles gripped my cock so hard I thought it'd snap right off. I was ready to cum inside Carlos but Don had something else in mind. He leapt from the rim chair screaming. "No, no, no! Give it to me. Shoot your load at me!"

Wildfire rushed to the ring. I yanked my cock from Carlos's butt and aimed it right at Wildfire. He grabbed the ropes and opened his mouth. I shot a huge fuckin' come shot at him. It flew right over his head.

"Oh, God, no, fuck no!" Wildfire screamed in agony. Luckily, the second come shot hit him square in the kisser.

"Yargh!"

Wildfire's tongue flew out from between his sweaty lips. He ate my cum like a greedy cum pig. He grabbed his crank, jacked it a few times, and out spooged his hot stinking load. I splattered him with a third, fourth, and fifth come shot. I shot all my cum until Wildfire was drenched in hot steaming jism.

Wildfire ordered the two slaves to lick my cum from his body. Then he turned to me. "Goddamn, son. You're hired! Carlos will show the ropes, won't ya boy?"

Carlos looked up. He had a shit-eating grin on his thick, sensuous lips. "We're going to be good friends, amigo!" He reached up to squeeze my cock.

"Yeah," I said. "Real good!"

The Porn Writer
By Bob Vickery

I run into my neighbor Mark in the apartment-house lobby on my way out. "Yo, Bob," he says, smiling. "Where you off to so early?" We walk out the front entrance together.

"I'm having breakfast with a friend," I say. "It's kind of a Saturday-morning ritual."

There's a moving van pulled up to the entrance, and the movers are in the process of hoisting a grand piano up to a fourth-story window. We watch their progress for a minute. Mark turns to me again. "How's the porn-writing business? Still cranking out the smut?"

"Yeah," I say. "I'm writing a story where I'm the hero."

Mark laughs. "Are you serious?"

"Yeah," I say. "Why? You think it's a bad idea?"

Mark shakes his head. "Jeez, Bob. What an exercise in vanity that would be." His eyes sweep up and down my body. "And besides," he says grinning, "you're a nice guy but hardly jack-off material. You'd have to do some major embellishing."

I smile. "Really?" I say. There's a sharp snapping sound of a rope breaking, the whistling of air, and a sudden shadow on the sidewalk growing rapidly bigger. Mark looks up. "Holy shit!" he screams. He flings himself to the left just as the piano comes crashing to the sidewalk.

Mark climbs unsteadily to his feet, shaken but unharmed. He looks down at the pile of kindling that was once a piano. He looks at me again. "You know, Bob," he says slowly, his voice trembling. "I don't think it's such a bad idea after all, your writing a stroke story where you're the hero." He attempts a smile. "A hot stud like you... Hell, it would be criminal if you didn't put yourself into one of your stories. Maybe a whole anthology."

"Stop, Mark," I say, smiling. "You're too kind."

Mark smiles and leaves. When he's half a block away, he breaks into a fast run. He must have a pressing engagement somewhere.

I get into my car and drive to my breakfast date with Eddie. Because he lives in the East Bay and I live in San Francisco, we compromise by meeting in a diner in Berkeley. When I get there I see Eddie with someone I don't know, sitting in a booth by the plate-glass window that overlooks the street. Eddie sees me at the door and waves me over.

"Hey, Bob," he says, grinning. "How ya doing?"

"I'm doing all right," I say. I look over at the guy sitting next to Eddie. Eddie catches my glance. "This is my friend Jack," Eddie says. "I ran into him outside and asked him to join us." Jack's face is well-scrubbed and smooth, with cheeks that are pink and cherubic and a mouth that reminds me of a moist keyhole. "Jack just got a novel published," Eddie goes on. "I thought you two might hit it off." Eddie's eyes shift over to Jack. "Jack, this is Bob Vickery. He's a writer too."

I shake Jack's hand. "Congratulations," I say. "Your first book?"

Jack gives a polite smile. "Actually, my fourth."

There's a pause. I notice that Jack doesn't ask me about my writing. Eddie also seems to notice this.

"Bob's been published a lot too," he says.

Jack peers at me over his wire-rimmed glasses. "Oh, really?" he asks. "What's your genre?"

I give him back his polite smile. "Short stories. Mostly erotica."

"Oh," Jack says. "Porn."

"Yeah," I say. "I guess you could call it that."

Jack picks up a knife and uses it to clean under a fingernail. He looks bored. "That's nice," he says.

Eddie sits up. He glances at me and then back at Jack. "Hey," he says, "a lot of talented writers are writing porn nowadays."

Jack gives him a tolerant smile. "Look, I'm not trying to be rude to your friend here, Eddie, but give me a break. There's writing, and then there's hack work." He looks toward me. "No offense, but I think we all know which category porn fits in."

"Wait a second—" Eddie says.

I cut him off with a gesture. "Let it drop, Eddie," I say. "The man's entitled to his opinion."

Jack glances at his watch. "Oh, jeez, it's late. I have to run." He finishes his coffee and climbs out of the booth. "See you around, Eddie." He turns toward me. "Nice meeting you, Bob. I hope I didn't hurt your feelings."

I give a self-deprecatory wave of my hand. "Not at all," I say. I hold out my hand. "Good luck with your book."

Jack shakes my hand and leaves. Eddie gives me a long level stare. "You took that very graciously."

I shrug. "It's no big deal. He's probably right. I never claimed to be Dostoyevsky."

Jack is outside standing on the curb and waiting for a break in the traffic. There's a lull in our conversation, and Eddie and I watch him from our booth. Jack steps off the curb and starts a mad dash across the street. He miscalculates. A diesel truck comes tearing down the road and hits him. Jack's body flies 20 or so feet into the air and lands in the other lane with a sickening splat that can be heard even through the quarter-inch of plate glass. A cement mixer coming the other way runs over his body and then roars off. What's left in the road is gruesome and stomach-wrenching. Suddenly a pack of dogs comes racing around a corner and descends on the bloody pulp. They run off, carrying in their slavering jaws various bloody bones with tatters of flesh attached.

Eddie slowly turns and looks at me. I smile. "It seems that Jack has had an accident," I say.

Eddie doesn't say anything for a long time. He swallows and tries to speak. Nothing comes out. He swallows again. "You know, Bob," he finally says, "have I told you how talented a writer I think you are?"

"No," I say thoughtfully, "I don't think you have. It's nice to hear you finally say it."

Eddie swallows again. "I-I'm sorry. I think you're a wonderful writer. One of the best."

I raise an eyebrow. "One of the best?"

"Th-the best," Eddie says hurriedly.

"Eddie, please," I say, smiling indulgently. "You go too far."

Eddie glances at his watch. "I-I have to go now, Bob." He looks at me, his eyes pleading. We can faintly hear dogs howling off in the distance. "That is, if it's all right with you."

I laugh. "Of course it's all right. You don't need my permission, Eddie, you big jerk. It's not like you're my slave or anything." Eddie climbs out of the booth. "Oh, and Eddie," I say, "I'm tired of crossing the Bay Bridge for breakfast. Next Saturday let's eat somewhere in San Francisco, OK?"

"Sure, Bob," Eddie says. He beats a hasty retreat. I look back at the red stain on the road. "Poor Jack," I say, shaking my head.

That night I go to the Stud for a drink. I lean against the wall, sipping my beer, watching the men dancing.

"Can I buy you a drink?"

I turn and see some guy standing to my left, his eyes trained on me. My eyes sweep down his body, taking in the broad shoulders, the chest muscles straining against the tight T-shirt, the pumped-up biceps, the narrow hips, the conspicuous bulge in the too-tight jeans. I look back at his face, noting the flawless set of his features. I stifle a yawn and smile politely, holding up my beer. "Thanks," I say, "but I'm not done with the one I have."

He looks crestfallen. I turn and go back to watching the men on the dance floor. I can see him out of the corner of my eye as he shifts his weight from one foot to the other. The song comes to an end. There's a brief period of silence.

The guy puts his hand on my shoulder. I look at him, frowning. His eyes are wide and a startlingly clear blue. His mouth is finely molded, his jaw line strong. Of course there's a cleft in his chin. "I'm not trying to be pushy," he says, "but when I saw you across the room, I had to speak to you. You have this sort of aura—I can't put it into words..."

Here we go again, I think. "A sort of brooding masculinity?" I ask.

"Yeah," he says excitedly, "that's it!"

"A quiet steady calm that hints of smoldering sexual fires?" I ask.

"Yeah," he says, "you got it exactly!" He smiles, flashing teeth that are even and dazzling white.

I look at him more closely. "You look familiar."

He coughs modestly in his hand. "Perhaps you know me through my work. I'm in gay porn." He grins boyishly and sticks out his hand. "The name's Butch. Butch O'Horrigan."

"Yeah, I recognize you now," I say. I shake his hand. "I'm Bob." He looks at me expectantly. Oh, well, I think, it won't hurt to at least talk with the guy. "Do you live here in San Francisco?" I ask.

Butch shakes his head. "Naw, I live in L.A. I'm just up here to shoot a flick." He takes a drink from his Evian bottle. "I've spent the entire day today having sex in front of a camera with some of the hottest guys in gay porn. Men who look like fuckin' gods. But when I saw you just a few minutes ago, I realized that next to you they were dreck. I could tell that you're something special. I don't give a shit that your hairline is receding or that you've got a slight paunch or that you're on the rainy side of 40 or that—"

"I think you made your point," I say.

"I gotta ask you," Butch goes on, "what do you do for a living? Are you a fighter pilot? A race car driver? A Hollywood stunt man?"

I smile. "Well, since you ask, I'm in the porn business myself. I write it. My name's Bob Vickery."

Butch stares at me. "Oh, my God," he whispers.

I raise my eyebrows. "You've heard of me?"

Butch nods. "Are you really Bob Vickery?"

I shrug my shoulders modestly. "In the flesh."

"I can't believe it, " Butch says, his voice choked. He takes my hand in both of his. "You are like an idol to me!" He shakes his head in amazement. "This is fuckin' incredible—I'm actually talking to Bob Vickery!"

"Please, stop," I say, laughing modestly.

"Hold on," Butch says. He pulls a beat-up magazine out of his back pocket. "This has your latest story in it. I always carry it around with me. Do you think you could autograph it for me?"

"Sure," I say good-naturedly. I take the magazine from him and page through it. I look at him. "You've ripped out all the pictures of the naked guys," I say.

Butch gives a gesture of dismissal. "Aw, they just got in the way," he says. "I just buy the magazines to read your stories."

I pull out a pen from my shirt pocket and sign my autograph across the front page of my story, "Subway Studs." "Here you go," I say pleasantly, handing the magazine back to Butch.

Butch takes it, his eyes brimming. "I will keep this with me forever. The only way anybody will take this from me is if they pry it from my cold, dead fingers."

"Butch, please," I say, embarrassed by his flattery.

Butch gives me a searching look. "Listen, Bob, I know I'm just a porn star and that all I have to offer you is my muscles, my face, and my nine-inch dick, but would you consider having sex with me tonight?"

"Butch," I say, "you seem like a nice guy—"

"Pl-e-e-ease!" Butch begs.

I sigh. "All right. If it means so much to you, I'm willing to go along."

"All right!" Butch says. His eyes are bright with excitement. "I've heard about how good porn writers are in bed. This should be a night to remember for the rest of my life."

I give a self-deprecating smile. "I'll try my best."

Another man approaches us. "Hi," he says to me, ignoring Butch. "I don't know if you recognize me, but I'm a Calvin Klein underwear model. I just happened to see you from across the room and thought you might want a little company—"

"Fuck off," Butch snarls as he ushers me away.

I lead Butch out to my Porsche. Butch gives a low whistle. "Nice wheels," he says. "Is it new?"

"I just bought it last week," I say. "You wouldn't believe how much money I make writing porn. It comes in faster than I can spend it."

"Whatever they pay you, I'm sure it's not enough," Butch says, his eyes glistening with hero worship.

I reach over and squeeze his thigh. It feels like granite. "You're a sweet guy," I say. "But you really have got to stop giving me all this praise. I'm very modest by nature." We drive off.

We don't take three steps inside my apartment before Butch pins me to the wall, his body pressed against mine, his tongue deep down my throat, his bulging crotch rubbing against mine in slow, grinding circles. I reach back and cup his ass with my hands, pushing his hips even harder against me. "I want you so bad, baby," Butch gasps. He begins pulling off my clothes.

"Easy, baby, easy," I murmur. I gently push him away. "We've got all night."

Butch is panting, and his eyes have a wild, almost crazed look to them. We just barely make it to the bedroom before he's on me again. He pushes me onto the bed and fumbles with my belt. He's so excited, he can't get the buckle undone. He gives a frustrated whimper. I push his hands away and unbuckle my belt for him. I slowly pull down my zipper. "Yeah, that's right," Butch growls. "Get naked." He yanks my jeans down past my hips, hooks his thumbs under the elastic waistband of my boxers, and pulls them down too. His jaw drops in amazement. "Holy shit!" he says. He looks up at me, his eyes wide. "Are all porn writers so well-hung?"

I smile. "Only when they get to write the story."

Butch quickly strips and jumps into bed with me. He straddles my hips, wrapping his hand around both our dicks, squeezing them together. He slowly strokes them, sliding his hand up and down the twin meaty shafts. Butch's dick is thick and long and red, the head poking out of the foreskin like some animal climbing out of its burrow. My dick, however, is even thicker and longer. I slide my hands up his torso, feeling the play of muscles, which are like hard rubber under velvet. I flick both his nipples lightly with my thumbs, then pinch them. Butch groans. "Oh, baby, that feels so good," he moans. I slide my hands over his biceps. They feel like cannon balls.

Butch slides down and buries his face in my balls. I feel his tongue lap over my sac, tasting it, teasing it, sucking on it. I lean my head against the pillow and let myself sink into the sensations. Butch's hot, wet tongue slides up my dick shaft, slowly, lovingly, until it reaches the head. Butch squeezes my dick, first gently, then with increasing pressure. My cock head deepens in color, from pink to angry red to purple. Butch loosens his grip and presses his lips against it, taking the head into his mouth. He slides his mouth down my fuck pole, his lips nibbling gently, his tongue writhing against it. He has to stop before he's even halfway down, but damned if Butch doesn't shift the angle of his head and forge on down. He makes it three quarters of the way down but has to stop again, his mouth pulled back wide by the thickness of my shaft. He's breathing heavily through his nose, the air whistling in and out. Butch shifts again, and, impossibly, he continues on down until his nose is mashed against my pubes. No one has ever been able to do that before, though many have certainly tried. As Butch's hot mouth slides back up the fleshy pole again, the shaft of my dick reappears, inch by slow inch, like a rabbit Butch is pulling out of a hat. Butch finally pulls away, panting.

"Incredible," I murmur, impressed.

Butch grins. "I once spent the weekend with a sword swallower from a traveling circus. He taught me all sorts of tricks." Butch wraps his hand around my dick again and starts stroking. After a couple of beats, he resumes sucking on it.

"Turn around," I growl. "Let's get a little sixty-nine action going."

Butch pivots his massively muscular body around, and in no time we're both chowing down on each other's dicks like a couple of sex-crazed cannibals. I look across at Butch and pull his cock out of my mouth. "You having a good time?" I ask.

Butch is sucking on my scrotum. "I'm having a ball," he says. He slides his tongue up the shaft of my giant schlong and starts sucking on it again. His technique is truly masterful, and it takes only a couple of minutes of his skillful mouth before I have to pull out.

"Easy," I pant. "I don't want to come just yet." I look over at Butch. "I'd love to fuck your ass right now. That is, if you think you can handle my throbbing, gargantuan fuck muscle."

Butch shakes his head and grins. "I just love the way you porn writers talk!" he says. He looks dubiously at my dick. "Well...I'm willing to give it a try. But you have to go slow."

"I promise," I promise.

I open the drawer to the bedside night table and pull out a condom package and jar of lube. Butch watches with wide eyes. "I never saw a condom so big!" he says as I pull it out of the package.

"I have to have them made especially for me," I shrug as I roll it down my dick shaft. "The fuckers cost me a bundle, but none of the commercial brands will fit me."

I sling Butch's legs over my shoulders and guide my sheathed cock into the crack of his ass. With infinite patience I slowly, lovingly push into his bung hole. Butch grunts, and a sheen of sweat breaks out on his forehead, but he takes it like a trouper. I pause when I'm halfway in. "Are you OK?" I ask with concern. He just nods his head without saying anything, his eyebrows knitted together. I ease a couple of more inches in. Butch groans, and I count to ten before the next long thrust. When I'm finally all the way in, I lie next to Butch, not moving, just letting him get used to the feeling of my monstrous dong up his ass. After a couple of minutes of this, I start pumping my hips, slowly at first, but then with greater tempo. My eyes are locked onto Butch's face, ready to quit any time he gives me the signal, but he's silent, apparently in bliss. After a while he starts moving his hips in synch with mine, pushing forward to meet each of my thrusts inside him. He rolls over on top of me, and it doesn't take long before we're enthusiastically boinking, our bouncing bodies making the bedsprings creak.

I wrap a lube-smeared hand around Butch's dick and start stroking him, timing my strokes with each thrust of my hips. Butch groans piteously. "Oh, that feels so good!" he moans. He bends down and kisses me, thrusting his tongue deep down my throat. His body squirms against mine, slick with sweat, and I can feel the muscles of his torso ripple against my flesh.

Butch pins down my arms, his teeth bared, his eyes burning with a fierce light. He wiggles his hips and squeezes his ass muscles tight. I groan loudly. "Damn, that's nice!" I exclaim.

Butch just grins. I wrap my legs around him and with a quick upward thrust twist our bodies around, pivoting him onto his back. "OK, baby," I snarl. "Get ready for the plowing of your life!" I push my hips forward, sliding my dick full up Butch's ass. Butch's eyes turn up in their sockets, and he gasps. For a moment I'm afraid I've ruptured the poor guy, and I start to pull out.

"Oh, God," Butch cries out. "Don't stop! Please!"

That's all the encouragement I need. I plant a hand on each of his shoulders and start giving this guy a truly serious fucking, thrusting my Brobdingnagian wand of love repeatedly in and out of his tight, tight ass. Butch groans loudly, pushing his hips up to meet me, tightening his velvet ass muscles around my meaty schlong, squeezing hard. My body shudders from the sudden stab of pleasure, and soon my groans are mingled with Butch's. We wrestle and tussle in bed, snarling and spitting, me plowing ass, my lube-greased hand wrapped around Butch's cock, each thrust of my hips and stroke of my hand ratcheting the two of us up to another level of pleasure.

One final long, hard push is all I need to topple me over the edge.

I cry out as my body begins to spasm.

"Pull out, quick!" Butch gasps. "I want to watch you squirt your load!"

I pull my dick out of his ass and rip the condom off. The first volley of spunk arcs across space and slams onto Butch's face. His head snaps back and hits against the wall behind the bed. "More, more..." he groans. He doesn't have to beg; my one-eyed Komodo dragon is spitting out a steady torrent of jizz. Soon Butch's face and chest look like they're crawling with banana slugs. Butch slides his hand across his face and makes a feeble effort to wipe off the mask of spunk that drips thickly over his cheeks and chin. He wraps his come-slimed hand around his dick and starts beating off with short, quick strokes. It takes only a few seconds before he gives a long trailing groan, his back arches, and his own load splatters out from his dick head onto his chest and chin, the higher drops mingling with my own joy juice. He collapses back onto the bed, gasping, his eyes closed. After a while I begin to feel uneasy. The last guy I fucked had an orgasm so intense he passed out and had to be carted off to the local intensive care unit. (The next day he was on my doorstep, begging for more. I had to call the cops.)

I put my hand on Butch's shoulder and gently shake him. "You OK?" I ask.

Butch slowly opens his eyes. He looks completely stunned. "I...I had no idea sex could be that good!" he whispers.

I relax. He's OK. "Yeah," I say, "I hear that a lot."

Butch wants to spend the night so that I can fuck him again first thing tomorrow. I have to gently but firmly get him dressed and escort him to the door. I have a busy day tomorrow, and I don't want my sleep disrupted by a sex-crazed porn star begging for more.

As I start getting ready for bed, I notice that I'm out of dental floss. How annoying, I think. Fortunately there's an all-night drugstore on the corner of my block. I get dressed again and walk out of my apartment. On the street I pass the neighborhood café. The evening is warm, and people are sitting at the outside tables. Four men are seated at the table closest to the sidewalk. I can't help noticing the bulge of muscles under their tight T-shirts. As I walk past, one of them reaches out and lightly touches me on the arm.

"Excuse me," he says. "Me and my buddies are members of the U.S. Olympics gymnastics team. We were just talking about Gore Vidal's line that everyone is essentially bisexual. Although none of us have ever had sex with a man before, we decided we'd like to put that statement to the test. Could we please go up to your apartment and have sex with you like crazed weasels?"

I glance at my watch. "Gee, guys, it's pretty late," I say. I sigh. "Well, what the hell."

"All right!" the guy says, grinning. The four young gods get up from their seats and join me on the sidewalk.

Damn! I think, as we walk into my bedroom and start to strip. The life of a porn writer can sure be exhausting!

Looking for Mr. Right
By Michael Cavanaugh

"Honestly, Michael, I can't take much more of this." My room-mate stood over the sofa looking down at me, his fists clenched. "This has been going on entirely too long. You've got to pull yourself together—and the sooner, the better."

"You're right, Cal. You're absolutely right." I sat up and pushed my hair out of my eyes. "It just isn't worth it." I glanced over at the clock. I had been moping about Carlos for almost half an hour—far longer than he deserved. I flashed a weak grin at Cal, then stood up and stretched. "I think I'll go to the gym. It'll do me good."

"There, that's better." Cal beamed at me sunnily, then flopped down on the sofa I had just vacated. "Now maybe I can watch Oprah without having to listen to your pissing and groaning all afternoon long."

"You could be a little more sensitive, Cal. I really thought Carlos was the one."

"The one what?"

"The love of my life, Cal. Mr. Right. The man I could spend my life with."

"Michael, you say that about every man you go to bed with. How many does that make in the past five months—two dozen, at least?"

"Certainly not!" I was scandalized by the very idea. "I can't think of anyone other than Carlos."

"What about Tim? And Joe? Then there was Bill, Tom, Anthony, Rich, Dave, Steve—"

"Stop it! Stop that shit right now!" Roommates can be so unkind, so unfair. "I sincerely believed that my relationship with Carlos was serious."

"Come on, Michael. Give me a break. How could you take a man like that seriously?"

"He was very romantic, Cal. I really thought—"

Cal interrupted me with a rude snort. "Romantic? Your first date was when he fucked you in the steam room at the gym. You call that romantic?"

"That isn't the way it happened," I protested hotly. "Not exactly, anyway."

"Is too. Everybody at the gym knows about it."

"Only because some asshole started that revolting rumor."

"Only because you let him fuck you right there in front of anybody who happened to wander into the steamer. You're just lucky you didn't get your gym membership revoked." Cal grabbed the remote from the coffee table and flipped on the TV.

I glared at him, then stalked off to my bedroom to gather up my gym clothes.

Cal obviously didn't understand relationships the way I did. OK, so maybe Carlos and I did meet in the steam room, but Cal had the dynamics all wrong. It wasn't sex...well, it wasn't just sex. It was... Anyway, you had to have been there to understand the nature of the attraction between us.

The day I met Carlos, I'd had a really great workout, and I was pumped to the max and looking damned good, if I do say so myself. I only went into the steam room that afternoon because the showers were full, and I had to do something.

Carlos was sitting on an upper bench in the far corner, his olive skin glistening with sweat. The skin was stretched over an awesome array of muscles, so naturally I looked over at him and smiled. He smiled back and waved me over to him.

"Hi," I said brightly, going over and standing in front of him. He was built like a brick shithouse.

"Hey, dude," he said, shifting on the bench and flexing his pecs. He had a dynamite chest. "I saw you working out today. Looking good."

"Thanks."

"You gotta have the hottest fucking ass in this entire gym, man. I mean it."

"Thanks again." He really was sweet. Observant too.

"Why don't you turn around and give me a good look at it?"

How could I say no to such a reasonable request? I turned around and flexed my cheeks. He grunted; then I felt one of his big hands on my ass. Next thing I knew, he'd plunged a finger into me up to the second knuckle.

"Damn, man," he breathed. "Nice, tight hole. Look what I got here for you."

"Oh!" I looked over my shoulder. He spread his powerful thighs, and this absolutely enormous hard-on rose up and pointed right at me, the fat cap flaring out like a helmet. I'm usually the shy type, but the sight of all that hard cock (we're talking in excess of ten inches here), not to mention the huge, hairy balls that hung down over the edge of the bench, really got me going. I clenched my hole playfully around his invading digit and took a step back.

"Ugh!" Before I realized it, he had picked me up, pulled me onto his lap, and crammed about half of his immense schlong up my un-lubricated butt hole. "Spit on it!" I squealed. "It's too fucking big! You're splitting me in half!"

"Yeah, baby. That's the way I like it." He thrust his hips forward and buried several more inches of man meat up my chute. I wriggled and squirmed, but that only drove him in deeper. If his fat knob had-n't punched me in the prostate at that instant, I don't know what I would've done. As it was, I grunted and bucked, then settled back against his hard, sweaty torso, ready to ride.

Carlos was the masterful type, that was clear from the beginning. He slapped my belly hard enough to leave a perfect imprint of his hand on my skin and started pinching my sensitive tits while he packed my ass with a vengeance. I looked down at my chest, watch-ing in amazement as my nipples were stretched a good inch beyond the rise of my perfectly sculpted pecs. They'd never been pulled that hard before, and I only hoped they wouldn't be permanently stretched. I didn't think they'd look good dangling.

"Ride my fucking cock, man. Tighten up that hole. That's it. Squeeze it hard! Fuck!"

I was crouching on the lower bench, ass thrust back, every muscle tensed, getting the fuck of destiny. My own dick was hard now, arching up against my belly, twitching and throbbing as Carlos continued to plow my aching hole. His big balls had stopped swinging up and slap-ping against mine and were now knotted at the base of his prick, punch-ing against my ass ring with every gut-wrenching thrust of his meat.

"Bounce on it, dick pig!" He was biting my neck now, snorting and grunting, the sweat pouring off of him in rivers. His prick felt as if it had doubled in size since he first shoved it up into me, and I half expected to feel it battering against my tonsils any second. My tits were numb, but my hole was feeling every hard, veiny inch of him as he plowed in and out, in and out, reaming me as if this were the last fuck in the civilized world.

"Here it comes, fucker! Take my hot load! Oh, yeah!" He jammed his dick in deep, and I could feel the heat as he let fly, pumping my hole full of his juice. I tensed up and popped my rocks as well, hitting the man sitting across from us right in the face. To be honest, I hadn't even heard the door to the steam room open and was totally surprised when I opened my eyes and saw the man with the come on his face, not to mention the 20 other guys who were crowded around, watching me get my ass packed. I doubt if any of them thought anything about it until that rumor got started about me a couple of days later.

Anyway, my relationship with Carlos blossomed after our first meeting. He was always horny, and we must have screwed at least four times a day.

I was at the point of letting Cal know that I was moving out when disaster struck. I showed up at Carlos's place one afternoon, about an hour earlier than usual, only to find the jerk in bed, packing his dick up the ass of some anonymous blond who just happened to have bigger biceps than I did. On the other hand, the blond didn't have nearly as nice an ass as mine, and his legs were embarrassingly skinny. Obviously, the taste Carlos displayed when he got together with me had been a fluke.

I shot Carlos this totally contemptuous look, then walked right into the bathroom, where I retrieved my toothbrush and the expensive soap I had bought for him the week before.

"You are a total jerk," I snapped on my way back through the bedroom.

"Hey, man, it ain't what it looks like," Carlos panted, not even slowing down. The blond had his face buried in the pillows and wasn't in any condition to say anything.

"So, Carlos, what is it? A proctological exam?"

He just stared blankly. He obviously didn't get it.

"We are officially finished."

"Fuck you, buddy," Carlos snapped, flipping me off.

"In your dreams," I replied with as much sarcasm as I could muster, walking out on him, my head held high.

Afterward I had come back home and practically suffered a nervous breakdown until Cal brought me back to my senses. He was right—Carlos hadn't been the one. Definitely not.

I got to the gym before the evening rush and put on my new workout gear. It was a white spandex unitard, as tight as a second skin. I had bought a size small instead of a medium, and the fit was perfect. The front was cut to below the navel, and the thin straps left my pecs totally bare. I walked over to the mirror and took a good look. All of my assets were highlighted, leaving nothing to the imagination. I mean, you could practically tell that I shaved my balls. I struck a pose, then, satisfied with the results, headed out to warm up.

I was working on my biceps when I first noticed him. He was just my type: tall, dark-haired, handsome, and built like a Greek god. He was at the bench press, doing 275 pounds. Every time he pumped out a rep, his pecs bulged out like big boulders, and his arms got absolutely huge. When he was finished he stood up, and I could see the thick veins that cabled his hairy forearms and snaked up over his gorgeous biceps. He had dark beard stubble and beautiful green eyes with long lashes. I checked out his basket and could tell that he was really hung, even under his baggy old shorts. Lumps that size don't stay hidden—not that they're all that important. Not really.

He saw me looking at him and flashed me a smile. I smiled back and started pumping reps like crazy, determined to add more bulk to my arms. He soon moved on to work on his legs, and I followed along. I figured my thighs could use a little toning, not to mention the fact that it gave me a chance to keep an eye on the dark-haired man.

He was concentrating on his calves, which didn't really need any additional development. I love a man with good legs, and this guy's were really superior. Every time he rose up on his toes, his calves would twitch and swell, every individual muscle showing clearly beneath the dark, glossy hairs that coated his long legs. I stood beside him, doing my best to duplicate his moves even though I was using only half the weight. I had to quit when my right calf started cramping, but he went on and on until I thought his muscles would burst right out of his skin.

I tailored my workout to coincide with his, noticing how he kept looking over at me from time to time. Obviously he was pretty interested, although he didn't say anything. The strong, silent type—better yet. When he finally finished up and headed back to the locker room, I limped along after him, wishing I had done about a dozen fewer squats. My thighs really hurt.

When I got to the shower, he was there, soaping his magnificent body. He really was incredible: huge, sculpted chest; a perfect six-pack of abs; narrow hips; tiny waist; cute furry butt; arms to die for; and, of course, those amazing legs. I beelined for the shower jet next to him, oblivious to the two guys who had seen it come available at about the same instant I did. I ignored their muttered remarks and turned on the water full blast.

I took a quick, discreet peek at his crotch. Below a dense tangle of dark pubes, his dick hung down, thick and heavy, the fat glans hitting him about mid-thigh. It curved over a pair of big balls that sagged down to the tip of his prick, the left riding on top of the right. His dick had the coolest blue vein running up the middle of the back. It branched about halfway along the shaft, wrapping around it like tiny blue fingers. Short hairs sprouted for a couple of inches along the base of his meat. I couldn't help thinking how they'd tickle a guy's lips if he managed to swallow it that far.

"Great workout," I said, hoping to spark a conversation.

"Light one today," the man replied. "Have to give the old bod a rest once in a while."

"Uh...yeah. Me too." I wondered what a heavy workout would be for this dude. Wow!

"I'm Michael."

"Dane." He was a man of few words. I tried to think of something else to say, but before I could get started Dane had turned all of his attention to washing his left armpit.

I soaped myself up as well, turning so that the big guy could steal a look at my ass if he felt the urge. I kept peeking over my shoulder at him and finally caught him staring at my twin globes of muscled flesh. I grinned at him, and he raised his eyebrows, then turned toward the shower jets to rinse himself off. When he turned off the water, I did the same and followed him into the locker room.

His locker was across from mine, so I got dressed in a hurry, then went out to the lobby to wait for him. Casually, of course.

When he came out he saw me and raised his eyebrows again.

"Waiting for someone?"

"Yeah. You." He chuckled at that and shrugged his thickly developed shoulders.

"What the hell? I've got a couple of hours to kill, and you look hot enough to melt paint. Let's go." The words weren't exactly romantic, but I could tell by the way he said them that he was a good deal more excited than he was letting on. I grabbed my bag and followed him out to the parking lot.

Dane lived in a big house in a nice section of the city. I trotted after him across a huge lawn with expensive landscaping. It looked pretty great already, but I figured I'd probably put in a bunch of red petunias after I moved in. I think petunias always add class to a front yard.

Dane showed me into the kitchen and offered me a Coke, then went off to change his clothes. I stood at the sink, looking out over the back. He actually had a swimming pool and a hot tub. The man was obviously a class act. Cal would simply piss green ink when I invited him over for a barbecue after I got settled in.

"You ready?"

I turned and looked at Dane. He was naked except for a leather strap cinched around his cock and balls. It was doing its job, and his cock was already at least two inches longer than when I'd seen it at the gym, although it wasn't anywhere near hard yet.

"I sure—whoops!"

He'd put his hands on my shoulders and pushed me to my knees. Before I could say another word, he grabbed my hair and tilted my head back, then began stuffing his cock down my throat. It was a huge cock and nearly cut off my air supply, not that I was going to complain. It tasted really hot, a blend of sweat, soap, and piss that got me revved up in a hurry.

After he'd ridden my face for a couple of minutes, bouncing his big balls off my chin, he pulled back, and I started nursing his fat piece of meat in earnest. I kissed the swollen fist-size knob perched on the end, teasing at the gaping piss hole with the tip of my tongue. I heard Dane growl and saw his balls try to rise. They rolled up a little, then sagged back down, way too heavy to climb the cords this early in the game.

Once I'd gotten the head all worked over, I went after the sexy vein, tracing it up into his bush, then back down to where it branched. I was licking his big cock, kissing it and slobbering all over it, when Dane grabbed my hair again, pulled my head back, and started slapping my face with his meat. He was getting really hard, and he popped me a couple of good ones that really stung. After about the fifth whack, he started leaking profusely, and hot lube juice began splattering across my forehead and cheeks.

I was just about to see stars when he grabbed me by the neck and hauled me to my feet. I was going to say something clever and witty and maybe even give him a big kiss, but he spun me around and bent me over the island counter in the middle of the kitchen. My head accidentally bumped against the tiled surface, and I saw stars for real.

I reached out and grabbed the edge of the counter at about the same instant that I felt the head of his cock bump my ass pucker. It was hard and hot and sticky, and I forgot whatever it was I'd been planning to say.

His cock slid up and down along my crack until his knob hit me about mid-spine, then slid back and butted my hole again. I heard him hawk a wad of spit and felt it land on my bull's-eye. He wedged his knees between my legs and splayed them wide apart, leaving me totally defenseless. I waited breathlessly for his next move, my dick rigid, my heart pounding.

"Aie-e-e!" He skewered me on his prong, punching it into me up to the hairy hilt. His balls crashed against mine, shooting sparks of pain and lust throughout my frame.

"Hold on tight, Steve."

"Michael," I corrected him.

"Whatever," Dane whispered, grinding his hips and stirring his massive cock around in my straining chute. "You are about to get your lights fucked out."

I felt his dick withdraw all the way, leaving me gaping. Then he slammed forward, driving his gigantic hard-on back in to the limit again.

He kept it up, all the way out, all the way in, leaving me clawing at the counter and gasping for air. Every time he thrust, he hit my prostate hard, soon reducing me to a whimpering mass of horny nerve endings. I could feel the hairs on his thighs against the backs of my legs, shooting little sparks right up to my belly, where they exploded in mind-numbing rushes of lust.

He was going at me like a pile driver when I heard voices in the hall. I opened my eyes and saw two men step into the kitchen, then stop and stare at the scene being played out in front of them on the counter.

"Hey, guys," Dane said casually, not even slowing down. "I'm getting this hot little piece all warmed up. There's a hole up front going to waste. Come and join me."

I thought that was rather presumptuous, his not asking me or anything, but before I could protest, the men began shedding their clothes, and I decided to keep quiet.

They both obviously subscribed to Dane's brand of working out. We're talking major muscles here, one set dusted with copper fur, the other totally hairless even at crotch level. They walked over to the side of the counter my head was hanging over and started smacking me in the face with their swelling dicks. I was going to get major bruises if I wasn't careful.

Once they both got hard, they started to fuck my face, taking turns at first, then cramming both of their bloated hard-ons down my throat at the same time. They both had fat, tasty pricks, and I wouldn't have complained even if I could have at that point.

Dane was still fucking my ass like wild, his belly slapping my ass cheeks, his big balls battering my aching nuts like hairy hammers. Then one of his buddies reached back and stuffed a finger up my ass alongside Dane's huge, pistoning prick. The other one got into the act as well, and pretty soon I had more fingers shoved up my ass than

I cared to count. The thing was, it felt good. Dane really liked it too, judging by the way he was fucking me, which was so hard, it made the counter creak.

All of a sudden one of the guys up front yelled and popped his cock out of my mouth. He started pumping it and blew his wad. I felt it splattering down across my shoulders, hot and pungent. The guy still in my mouth grabbed my ears and really went for it, fucking my face like a wild man. I could feel his dick getting stiffer and bigger, and then he started shooting his load down my throat. I sucked and swallowed, eating every drop of his white-hot come.

He went over to stand by his buddy while Dane rode me into the homestretch. He bucked and thrust, pounding my ass royally. I heard him groan, then felt his cock flex. He stopped pumping, and the heat began to gush out of him, flooding my ass channel. He shot again and again, filling me up till the come was running down over my balls and dripping down my legs. When he pulled out of me, I slid off the counter and onto the floor.

Dane would've helped me get off, I'm sure, but the phone rang, and he had to answer it. I jerked myself off into a kitchen towel, then lay back on the cool linoleum, too dazed to move.

It turned out that Dane and his buddies had to go out to dinner at someone's house, so we couldn't sit and talk as long as he would've wanted to. Hell, he didn't even have time to give me a lift home. It was a long walk, but I didn't mind. It wasn't really raining all that hard.

"You look like you got beaten up," Cal remarked when I trudged through the living room on my way to the bathroom to take a shower. "Who ran over you?"

"I met a very nice man, smarty," I retorted, smiling smugly. "I think this one is serious. He even introduced me to a couple of his friends."

"Right." Cal looked at me and shook his head. "What happened to your face, Michael? It looks like somebody pistol-whipped you with a Polish sausage."

"Mind your own business, Cal," I snapped back at him. "If the phone rings, it'll probably be Dane." I had scrawled my telephone number on the message pad on his refrigerator before I left. I was sure he would find it. "I'm going to take a shower."

"Good. You smell like a sperm bank."

"Up yours, Cal." I stuck my head out of the bathroom door. "You're just jealous. I've got a feeling this is the one I've been waiting for. We really clicked. I may be moving in with him by the end of the month."

"Right, Michael. I'll put an ad in the paper for a new roommate." He picked up the remote and pointed it at the TV. "Try soaking your head in cold water, Michael. It'll help with that swelling."

"Cal, why don't—" I decided to shut my mouth and closed the door. He just didn't get it. Either you're a romantic or you're not. There are no two ways about it. Dane would understand; I just know he would.

Pig
By Phillip Mackenzie Jr.

When I get home from the gym, Alex is in the kitchen, looking like he's just rolled out of bed. It's 10 p.m.

"Hey, man," I say as I drop my bag and head for the refrigerator for water.

He grunts something at me and turns away. I hear him shuffling back down the hall.

Not that I expect anything else. Whatever I say or do is always met with the same slightly quizzical stare.

"As always," I say aloud, "good to see you. Nice chatting with you. But I know you're busy, so don't let me keep you."

Alex has a way of making me feel not just inconsequential but slightly ridiculous. He looks at me as if I'm a laboratory chimpanzee, as if he's amazed that words come out of my mouth despite my being a lesser life form.

At first I mistook his behavior for poor social skills, until one day when I asked him if he was shy when he was a kid too. With little more than a look, he insinuated that he could talk to me but simply didn't find it worth the effort.

Believe me, I've tried. I talked about my job—until he made it clear that what I did was a drain on society. I talked about music—until he accused me of contributing to the downfall of culture. I tried to talk about books, but that seemed to cause him physical pain.

Sighing heavily, I drop myself onto the kitchen chair and kick my shoes off.

I hate having a roommate. The second bedroom made a great office—and a great place to store all the crap that wouldn't fit anywhere else, like the bike I barely rode anymore, the extra stereo I'd refused in a fit of immature vindictiveness to let my ex take when we split up, and the weight bench that served as a place to put the boxes of books my brother dumped on me when he moved to Montana with his girlfriend two years ago.

But I really needed that membership at Crunch, and the trip to Florence was too good to pass up. And don't get me started on the rigorous demands of appropriate attire and hair as well as the combined introduction of the new Macs and DVD. Well, all of it put my credit card through a too-vigorous workout. Which was all OK, until the record company folded one morning, and after three weeks I was forced to take a job as a personal assistant to a B-list producer who inevitably took it out on me when no one returned his calls—which no one ever did.

Which explains my roommate, Alex. An assistant professor of anthropology, he is actually poorer than I am, but that doesn't stop him from assuming an air of superiority, which is now primarily manifested through a steadfast refusal to interact with me—or even to engage in rudimentary conversation.

I have a fairly realistic estimation of myself and a very good idea of my place on the food chain, but I also know I'm not stupid, can be fairly witty, and can embark on a superficial discourse on current events, which is pretty much all that is asked of you in L.A.

And when I finally realized I needed a roommate, I imagined something along the lines of Three's Company, a set of fun-loving misfortunates sitting cross-legged on each other's beds, bemoaning our love lives and cooking up pasta primavera in our little kitchen. Instead I got Apartment Zero.

It's amazing how exhausting this is. And frustrating. Is it any wonder then, given the beating my ego takes on a daily basis—combined with the double whammy of the drought in my dating life and spike in my libido—that I've begun spending more time and money than I should in computer chat rooms?

Fuck it, though. The thing is, in there I can be anything I want. I'm not some beaten-down, beaten-up walking advertisement for early-21st-century ennui. I'm an out-of-control, uninhibited, radical, streetwalking, turn-me-upside-down-and-fuck-me-sideways alley cat of a sex monkey.

I can walk through the door, strip out of my clothes, and slide my ass down over the thick hard shaft of some straight frat boy sitting alone in his room and let him ride my tight hole until he shoots his sticky load into my guts, and then I can get up and walk away while he's dribbling into his pubes. I love that. Who cares if it's actually some fat middle-aged Judy Garland queen tickling his pecker with one hand and the keyboard with the other. Who the hell knows what he's fantasizing about either?

Not that I'm hard on the eyes in the real world. Despite my current financial restraints, I've never given up my gym membership, which has succeeded in not only relieving the stress of my current state of affairs but also resulted in a physique that demands display in a Dolce and Gabbana black silk tank top. My abdominal muscles are visible without flexing even when I stand at the end of the hallway from the full-length mirror on the bathroom door.

Yes, I'm bragging. I've earned the right. At least I'm not like Alex, still waiting for that gamine starving-artist look to come into vogue.

I feel my dick starting to uncoil inside my jock, and I slip a hand inside my shorts to encourage it when I realize Alex might make another foray into the kitchen and find me sitting here playing with myself, giving him one more thing to feel superior about.

That's another thing about having a roommate. If you can't walk around naked, you sure as hell can't jerk off in the kitchen.

Alex's door is directly across from mine, so I always have to make sure mine is closed firmly if I'm going to get it on with myself. I hear it click when I close it, but I give it an extra nudge just to be sure. Then I walk over and turn on my computer.

As I'm slipping my shirt over my head, I hear that I have mail.

My mother, read later. My ex, discard now. Frank, well let's see what he has to say.

"I have tix to Jeff Stryker in Doing Hard Time. Tonight, 8 p.m. Wanna go?"

I'm glad I didn't check my E-mail until now. What's with these porn stars doing theater? We want to see your dick or your ass or both. We want to watch you come. In closeup. That's it. Period. We don't want you to do anything else. Ever. And we sure don't want to hear you talk. Got it? Good.

I plop my ass down on the chair and head straight into Man2Man. First I check out the supposedly live guys. One guy is fingering his asshole, but the digitization makes it look like he's breaking his finger. Another guy has just come and is starting to go limp. Damn, missed the show. But looking at his still-oozing slit restarts my cock, so I head for a chat room.

Darkman is there, and so is AssCrazy. They always are.

"Hey Toybox" (that's me...OK, I know...but I was under pressure when I came up with it).

"Hey, guys. Anything up?"

"Me," says AssCrazy, " I just got back from that Jeff Stryker show."

"Jesus, she is so tired," says Darkman.

"Maybe, but that pole makes my loins ache," AssCrazy responds.

Hung4U pipes in: "I saw Ryan Idol in Making Porn, and I'd take him over Stryker any day."

I am wondering again if AssCrazy was really Frank, when Rdy4Bear logs on and almost immediately heads for a private room with Darkman.

Hung4U and AssCrazy are still debating the finer points of porn-star appendages when someone new logs in. NickName. That's actually kind of funny.

"Hi," the instant message pops up on my screen.

"Hi," I shoot back.

"Toybox, huh?"

"Yeah, Nick: Toybox. What of it?" OK, so I'm a little crabby still.

"It isn't any lamer than the other ones," NickName says, seemingly trying to tone things down.

"Thanks."

"Wanna get outta here?" he asks.

"Sure," I say. I like the direct approach. It cuts through the bullshit, acknowledges why we are all here, and saves time. We click to a private room.

"Take off your clothes," he says.

I slip my shorts down to my ankles and slide a finger along the edge of my jock, feeling the sweaty dampness of my curly cock thatch. I'm wondering what this one is into, as I massage my crotch. I'm cool with being ordered around in here.

"Tell me," he says.

"My shirt is off. I'm rubbing my hands over my chest. I just worked out, so I'm a little sweaty."

"Smell your pits," he insists.

I turn my head and sniff. It's a little gamey but not bad.

"Tell me."

I'm a little thrown. What am I supposed to say now? "I stink," I type back tentatively.

"You fucking pig."

My terminal almost snarls and my dick twitches hard. Oh, yeah. Oh, yeah, baby. This is gonna be hot. "I am. I am a pig. I'm a filthy fucking pig," I type back hurriedly.

"Show me your little pig pecker."

I slip my jock down around my thighs, and my dick rises up, pulsing from its nest of brown curls. I slide my hand down under my balls, squeezing them, rolling them around inside the sac.

"DON'T TOUCH IT!" his words scream back at me.

"I'm sorry."

"You don't do anything unless I tell you to."

"OK," I start to type and then erase it and type, "Yes, sir."

"DON'T CALL ME 'SIR'!" he screams back.

Shit. Maybe I should have typed "Yes, Daddy." Crap. Who is this guy anyway? Peppermint Patty? Fuck it, it's Saturday night, and of course I don't have a date, so if it was going to be a little daddy-boy scene, I could get into that.

It's certainly different. I hadn't done that scene yet. I don't really think it's something I'd get into out in the real world, but in here, like I said, you can be anything you want for 20 minutes.

"Get down on your knees," he tells me.

I assume this is figurative, but just in case, I push the chair back and kneel down.

"I'm on my knees," I let him know

"Do you want my cock?"

"Yes, please," I type, praying it's the right thing to say.

"Beg for it," comes his response.

All right. This is a little much. But OK, my dick is bouncing happily away down there, so what the hell: "Please show me your cock. I need your cock. I really need it. Please give it to me."

"I don't think so."

What the fuck is going on here? I reach down and palm the head of my dick, slicking it with ooze. Screw this guy. I'd touch myself if

I wanted to. I start typing again: "Please. I really want to see your big cock. I want to touch it. I want to suck it."

"Can you suck it good?"

"Yeah. I can make it feel real good," I tell him.

"Can you take it all the way down? Can I fuck your tonsils?"

"Yeah. Oh, yeah, I can take it. Let me show you," I play along.

"Are you gonna make it hard enough to fuck your little toybox?"

"Yeah, it's gonna be so hard. It's gonna rip right into my hot tight ass."

"OK. You can touch it," he allows me.

Finally! Jesus Christ.

I run my hand down my dick in a long, slow shuddering stroke and then slip my fingers down under my balls, which are tightened up around the base of my shaft. My middle finger finds the tight knot of my asshole, and I start rubbing in tiny circles.

"I'm taking it out now," I type one-handed. "I'm unzipping your pants and slipping my hand inside. Oh, God, it feels so good."

"TAKE YOUR FUCKING HAND OFF YOUR PITIFUL LIT-TLE PRICK RIGHT NOW!"

My dick bounces, and I actually gasp as I jerk my hand away. Fucker. What a dick. But I had to admit, this little game had its hot side. I'm harder than I could remember being in a long time. Hmm. Maybe there is something to this, after all.

"I'm sorry," I type back lamely.

"If you want my cock, you give it the attention it deserves. Do you understand me, pig?"

"Yes."

"That means both hands. Now open your mouth."

I actually do this! What am I thinking?

"I'm just gonna give you the head because you didn't listen," he teases.

But his efforts are working. I feel it. The slick rubbery head of a monster shaft rubbing my lips and leaving them slick with precome. I can smell the heated funk and taste the salty tang of cock. The head of my dick is purple with frustration, weeping golden liquid, begging for attention.

"Your mouth is sweet, little pig."

My fingers are no longer on the keyboard. They're buried in wiry curls of hair, full of wrinkled ball flesh, my mouth stretched by cock, my tongue aching sweetly from pressure and friction as he pumps my face.

I reach up to type: "God! God! God! Yeah, fuck my face! Fuck it! Fuck my throat!"

"OH, YEAH!" the words hit my screen—and at the same moment I hear it. I mean really hear it. From across the hall.

What the hell? I'm thinking. "Alex?" I type and then erase it.

My heart is pounding in my throat, and my dick rapidly deflates.

"Take that cock. You cock pig," flashes across my screen.

Oh, sure. Snotty, rimless-glasses-wearing, intellectually pretentious Alex as über daddy? Right.

No way. I settle back down on my knees and start typing again, my cock swelling as I fall back into the mood. I give him what I hope will thrill him more: "Yeah, it feels so good. You taste so good. God, I love your cock!"

"Stand up," he says.

I stand, my cock jutting out and dripping on my keyboard. I swipe the sticky drop with my finger and put it my mouth.

"Bend over," comes his next order.

I lean forward placing both hands on my desk.

"Ask me to eat your ass."

With one hand I begin typing: "Please. Please eat out my tight hole. Stick your tongue up my asshole. Make it nice and wet."

"Oh, your ass tastes sweet. Nice and sweaty." At least I get a compliment from him.

He has me back in that mode. "Oh, God, yeah," I say, "tongue my hole. Jesus, you're so good. God!" I am feeling it again, the sandpaper roughness of a man's face between my cheeks, the rasp of a tongue against my puckered crack, the nip of teeth, the blast of hot breath. Fuck this guy is hot! God damn he's hot!

"You think you can take this big cock up that tight little hole?"

"Yeah. Fuck yeah," I assure him.

"You want me to plant a big load right up there, don't you?"

Oh, Christ. I almost come. My untouched prong jerks, and my balls spasm, ready to spew their contents all over my screen. I grit my teeth and clamp a hand around the base of my shaft to keep from shooting, and then jerk it away guiltily. I get back to the keyboard: "Yes, I want your load. I want to feel your hot cum inside me."

I feel hard thighs against the back of my legs, hands pulling my ass cheeks apart, a thick finger sliding into me—and then another. I feel a long, hot, thick pole of flesh against my back and low-hanging hairy balls against the smooth flesh of my butt.

"I'm ready. Fuck me now, please," I type jerkily.

"I'll fuck you when I'm good and ready, pig," he says, clearly not willing to relinquish his control.

"I'm sorry," I type almost wearily. Jesus H. Christ—this could get old.

"Don't you tell me when to fuck you. I oughta leave your ass right here for that."

"Please don't. Please, don't leave. I just love your cock so much, I got carried away," I work to give him a plea.

"I was gonna be gentle because you were a good little pig, but now I think I'm gonna rip you apart."

"Please. Yes! Fuck your little pig as hard as you want."

"Yeah, your little pig hole feels nice and tight."

I'm past caring. Call me a pig, swear at me, treat me lower than whale spit on the bottom of the ocean. I don't care at this point. Just give me a cock up my ass.

"TAKE THAT COCK!" he screams at me as I feel a huge mass of male muscle breach my chute and slam into my guts like a red-hot poker.

"YEAH!" I scream back

"FUCK!" he howls.

And again...I hear it. From across the hall.

I fly backward from my computer, my dick swinging crazily as I leap at the door. Cracking it open, all I can see is a light coming from under Alex's door. I tiptoe across the hall, and press my ear to the door. I hear the clicking of keystrokes, that's all.

As I scurry into my room, I pause, ready to click the door shut. Heart pounding crazily, I slowly swing it back open. My unhandled rod is jumping and jerking, and sweat trickles down between my pecs.

It is Alex. Alex who fucked my throat and slapped his balls against my chin. Alex's shaggy bush I had buried my nose in. Alex's tongue that had wormed up inside me, setting me on fire and making me beg for the monster cock he crammed into me a few seconds later.

"You love my big dick, don't you, dick pig?" he had typed during my frenzied foray across the hall.

"Oh, yeah, your cock feels so good. God, fuck me harder!" I type back frantically, pulling my desk and chair away from the wall so I can sit in full view of the door.

What if he opens the door? It's Alex. Wierd, dark, cynical, mean Alex. Skinny, punky, freaky Alex.

Who would have thought it? I try to imagine Alex's thin lips saying the words "dick pig." My hard-on throbs, leaks, and jumps untouched. My balls are like rocks. My ass is aching, imagining those lips against my quaking hole.

And his cock, thick and slick with my juices, burying itself deep inside me, then sliding out to the crown before slamming back into me, turning every inch of my chute into raw nerve endings. Alex's cock. Alex's cock?

"You like me pounding your tight pig pussy?" his words flash at me.

Yeah. I love it. Alex. God damn it. Not Alex. Fuck, why did it have to be Alex? I hate that fucker for doing this to me, but...Jesus...just keep doing it.

"I fucking love it!" I scream out loud. And keep screaming, "Yeah, fuck me harder, Alex! Fuck me harder!"

The screen stays blank. Then footsteps in Alex's room. I turn toward the door legs spread, dick standing straight and proud, my hands dangling by my sides.

His door flies open. The first thing I notice is the tattoo. A snake stretches from his cock over his chest and coils around his left pec, its mouth open over his nipple. Its sinuous body accents his own lithe muscularity. Long flat planes of muscle stretch over his chest and stomach, sinewy cables over his arms and legs. A patch of dark hair nests between his tits, narrows to a thin, dark line over his belly before spreading out again into a dense patch of black curls between his legs. Following this trail, my eyes are riveted on the pole of flesh pointed almost straight up, curving slightly to the right at the head. His hand grasps it along with his heavy, hairy balls, pointing them directly at me. Without saying a word, he turns back to his computer, his hard ass flexing as he walks.

With his eyes locked on mine, one hand gripping his cock, slowly massaging it, his other hand types, "Show me your asshole."

Silently I lift my legs and spread them, scooting down in my chair until I feel the cool air of the room against my throbbing pucker.

Alex types more: "Stick your finger in."

I put my index finger in my mouth and suck it slowly. A thin strand of saliva stretches and breaks as I lower it between my legs and rub it against my fuck hole, slipping a tiny bit in, and then with a quick twitch I push it all the way in.

I can't believe I'm doing this. That I want to do this. That I'm looking at Alex, pale and hard, staring at me with those reflectionless dark eyes, his hand stroking himself as he watches me finger fucking myself.

"You want me to fuck you?" he asks aloud.

Not trusting my voice, I type, "Please!"

He spits into his palm and slicks it over the length of his twitching cock. "I'm fucking you," he says as if he were telling me the weather.

Dry-mouthed, I watch his hand travel the length of his dick, pulling the skin tight as he drives toward his bush. My finger matches his slow rhythm. Adding a second finger as he picks up speed, I drive into my hot center, finding the hard knob of my prostate.

He spits again, pounding at his prick, as his balls pull up, jerking inside their sac.

"You like my thick cock, pig?" he asks conversationally.

"Jesus, Alex." I gasp. I want him inside me. To fuck me for two days and then shoot gallons of Alex spunk all over me. I want to swallow his cock and massage it with my throat until he fills me with come.

"Are you my little fuck pig?" his voice hitches slightly.

"Yes." I breath, transfixed on the blur of his hand on his swelling muscle, the purple head looks primed and ready to blow.

I drive another finger into my hole, and my body spasms as if hit by 10,000 volts of electricity.

"You gonna take my hot load?" his eyes bore into me, impaling me.

"Fuck. Oh, fuck, Alex, I'm gonna come. Oh, God, Alex please let me come."

His hand stops, and his toes curls. Then his legs shoot out, and every muscle in his lean body pops as his cock fires a white stream that hits him in the throat.

I'm frozen, my fingers pressed tight against the throbbing knob at my center as jet after jet of sperm flies from the flaming crown of his shaft, abstractly painting his abdomen, as his body jerks and a sound like grinding machinery fights out of his clenched teeth. I imagine it shooting into me, burning my guts, filling me until I overflow, and it pours out of me.

I lose it. I can't stop to save my life. My ass ring clamps down on my fingers, the velvety muscles inside clench, and the room disapears in blackness. The first blast never hits my body at all but I feel it coursing up the length of my cock, ripping the hole open and flying into space. My balls seize and release, and a flood of come pours out of my cock, burning my skin and bringing a scream from my throat that I had never heard before.

I come back into my body, shivering and trembling, the funk of jism in my nostrils, the cooling slickness of it covering me from nuts to neck.

Alex rises from his chair, his own load running in rivulets into his dark bush and walks toward me. He stops, and the corner of his mouth jerks upward in a half smile.

"Pig," he says, and then with one foot kicks the door shut.

Assume the Position
By Jay Starre

It was rough—four weeks of hell had just ended, although it was only for a weekend, then back we'd be at army training camp. I was sick of it and happy to get away for a couple of days. Thing was, I didn't know a soul in the godforsaken Midwestern state where our base was located.

"Want to go to Chicago? We can share a room." I heard a tentative voice asking.

I turned and confronted one of my fellow soldiers. Aaron Stacy stood there with an enthusiastic grin plastered all over his handsome face. The redheaded stud looked like an eager puppy. I didn't have the heart to say no. Later, I was very glad I had agreed.

We took the train and arrived in the evening, ready to hit the bars. The Windy City proved to be an alcoholic heaven: We were plastered before 11 p.m. We managed to find a seedy little hotel room that had only one small double bed. We had been sleeping in creaky bunks, so it looked like heaven.

I collapsed on the bed and gazed up at Aaron. He was standing there, uncertain, weaving on his feet, staring down at me with the weirdest expression on his face. "You don't mind us sleeping in the same bed?" he finally asked, his voice trembling.

I laughed. "You can sleep on the floor, soldier!" I barked out, mimicking our drill sergeant's gruff voice.

"Yes, sir!" Aaron snapped to attention and saluted, his body erect, although still weaving.

I looked at him and laughed again. His eyes were on the wall. What the hell was the matter with him? I had been joking. Then I happened to glance down and realized Aaron had a distinct bulge in the front of his khakis. I sat up and stared. He had a boner!

I looked back up at him with more interest. I had been spending every minute for the past month with other men, sweating, grunting, fighting, showering naked, sleeping in a crowded bunker. Men with hard bodies, with dicks and balls and asses. I was horny, I had to admit it. Now I was alone with this young stud, a short body thick with muscle, standing there at attention but drunk and vulnerable and with a big damn hard-on to boot. What was I to do?

"Get undressed, soldier! Snap to it, fucker!" My voice whipped out in the small room. I watched him, wondering if he would laugh it off or what. To my amazement, he obeyed with alacrity.

"Sir, yes, sir! All of my clothes, sir?" he snapped back. He was already tearing off his shirt.

"You can leave on your boots and tags!" I practically yelled. Why the hell I was yelling, I didn't know. I was drunk, but there was more to it. I had a lot of pent-up emotions boiling in me, and suddenly they were coming out.

Whatever Aaron was thinking, he was sure quick to strip. I watched him with keen interest. His naked chest was taut, two big pecs with no hair, two dark nipples that looked stiff and hard. His skin was alabaster-pale, smooth, and thick with muscle. He jumped around awkwardly as he stripped off his pants over his boots, but managed without falling, which was a near-miracle in his drunken state. Then he skinned down his army-green boxers and stood back to attention.

A big, hard dick stuck right out from his crotch. It was thick and fat, suiting his stocky body. A pair of plump nads hung down below that dick, nestled between two very hefty thighs. A patch of flaming-red hair surrounded the base of his hard pole; otherwise he didn't have so much as another hair on his smooth, fleshy body. He was expressionless as he stood there, although his entire body was trembling. His dick throbbed, jerking in time to the trembling of his limbs.

I took a deep breath to keep myself from shaking too. I moved around behind him in the small room, my own body only inches from his but not quite touching it. I shouted in his ear. "Assume the position!"

He snapped to, lifting up his arms and flexing them behind his neck, spreading his thick thighs and planting his booted feet wide apart. I almost laughed again—I had no idea of what I had meant for him to do, but what he did was just fine with me. I was wondering how far I could go with this bullshit—and smirking secretly behind Aaron's back as my mind raced ahead to a number of exciting scenarios.

But I had to catch my breath again as I surveyed the hunk standing before me. What a body! His broad shoulders bulged as he held up his crossed arms, the brawny biceps heavy with muscle. The V of his back descended toward a narrow waist, then curved back out in the swell of his ass cheeks. I stared down at them, round and full, so white and hairless they didn't look real. He had the most perfect skin I had ever seen. He was standing at attention, but he was shaking violently, and those two big butt mounds were quaking in erratic spasms that had me gasping with lust.

I wanted nothing more than to reach out and grab hold of those plump ass cheeks and squeeze and squeeze before pulling them apart and shoving something in the deep crevice between them—my fingers, my face, or my hard dick straining at the fly of my khakis.

"Assume the position!" I barked again, although I didn't know why the hell I did. I was drunk, but I was not quite drunk enough to grab Aaron's ass and do what I wanted to it. So I yelled instead.

What Aaron was drunk enough to do was another matter. My mouth actually fell open when he responded to my shouted order. He yelled back "Yes, sir!" and leaped forward. Jumping on top of the small bed, he landed on his hands and knees, pressing his head down into the mattress.

There he was splayed out on all fours, with his beautiful naked ass in the air, his face down, and his big ball sac dangling down between his hairless thighs. I guessed that was the position he assumed I meant.

What could I do? I stripped so fast I fell down. While he remained on all fours on the bed, his plump white ass quivering, I sprawled on the floor, ripping off my pants and shirt and underwear. I kept my eyes on that butt, getting a good look at the spread crack and a small crinkled opening peeking out between those white cheeks. I crawled forward when I had managed to get my clothes off and got up behind him, on my knees at the edge of the bed. His big ass was level with my face.

I had my eyeballs fastened on that puckered hole as I reached out, grasped one big butt cheek with each hand and dove into Aaron's crack. Right on target, my mouth connected with his ass slot, opening wide and smothering the hole with my lips and wet tongue.

"Sir, lick my ass, sir!" Aaron shouted out.

I had to stifle a hysterical burst of laughter. Aaron was really into this game! I was really into licking his smooth ass crack. There was only one thing on my mind at that moment—the silky smooth flesh that was burning my tongue and lips as I swiped and licked and tongued up and down that hairless crack. I slobbered on the puckered rim of his butt hole, jabbing my tongue at the opening, which quivered and convulsed in response. That sweet hole opened up to my tongue, and I was entering the tight confines beyond. I tasted male funk, inhaled musky soldier butt and crotch odor, and jabbed deeper with my tongue.

"Sir, please, sir, yes, sir, tongue my slot, get in there deep, sir!" Aaron was shouting out, although his voice was breaking and his breath was coming in gasps.

I spit all over his crack, moving one of my hands in to add it to my mouth. I slid a finger into his quivering anus alongside my tongue, jabbing past the first knuckle. He squealed, and his thighs splayed wider. "Sir!" he shouted. I rammed that finger as deep as I could, the slippery saliva I was gobbing all over his hole easing the entrance. His fuck hole was a tight channel, viselike around my digging finger. I worked it around, trying to stretch him out, but he remained tight as a drum. I came up for air, staring down at my finger buried up his butt hole, spit glistening all over his hairless crack.

His butt was up in the air, squirming around in circles as my finger frigged in and out of that tight little hole. His head was on his folded arms, his face turned to the side. I could see his expression, his mouth open and drool in the corners. His eyes screwed shut in concentration, beads of sweat on his forehead.

"I'm going to fuck your poor butt hole, soldier! You are going to have to open up that tight slot for my big, hard dick! Understand?" I barked out. I had no idea of what I was going to say beforehand. The words just came out.

"Sir, fuck my tight hole! Open me up with your big dick. I can take it, sir!" He replied, wiggling his plump white butt as my finger twisted deep in his guts.

"Assume the position, fuck boy!" I yelled out crazily. My finger up his clamping asshole was driving me nuts. It was incredibly hot and exciting—I was almost ready to shoot just from that alone.

I wondered what he would do this time. I found out. He squirmed around onto his back, reached down and clasped his legs behind the knees, then pulled them back to his chest. My finger remained up his chute all the while. He must have known what he was doing: His asshole opened up just a bit in that position, with his thighs pulled wide and his ass up in the air.

I stared down at that tempting target. I stood up, pulling my finger out of his clamping fuck channel. The small ring of muscle gaped open for a second, then clamped back down, drool oozing out of the tight lips. I spit back down on his crack while I massaged my hard pole and spit on it too. I pointed it down into his parted cheeks and shoved it up against that hot hole. The ass lips pulsed around my dick head.

I was gasping, the intensity of my own lust nearly too much. My dick looked huge next to that small slot. I am well over six feet tall, with long limbs and an equally long dick. The head of my rod was beet-red, contrasting sharply with the pale flesh of Aaron's hairless butt. The thing would never fit inside that tight channel.

"Sir, fuck my poor butt hole with your big dick! Stick it up me, sir!" Aaron grunted out, his face as red as my dick head.

Oh, well, what was I to do? I spit down on my dick and rubbed it into the head and his tight hole. I grasped the shaft with one hand, spread his cheeks with the other hand, and began to shove. Goddamn, it was so tight! But the spongy flesh began to stretch apart so that the tapered head began to go inside him.

"YES! SIR!" he shrieked. He shoved upward with his hips, impaling himself on the entire head of my dick.

"FUCK YOU, SOLDIER!" I shrieked back. The clamping vise around my dick head throbbed with painful force. I drove my hips forward and crammed half my dick inside Aaron's straining guts. I used both hands and pulled apart his ass cheeks. Then I shoved again, and my balls were nestled up against his spit-coated butt.

Aaron was whimpering, his face rolling from side to side, his mouth open and his eyes clamped shut. "Look at me, soldier!" I yelled.

He did. His eyes opened, the look of agony in them easy to read. "Open up that butt hole, soldier! Work that tight ass around my dick like you love it!" I ordered, my voice steely.

It worked. He looked up into my eyes, his soft green orbs melting as he began to writhe his hips up and down over my dick. I felt his tight channel caress my pole with its confining walls, and I held my dick still to let him get used to it. He began to loosen up.

I looked down, tearing my eyes from his. The tight ass lips were swollen and puckered around my shaft, stretched and straining as he worked his ass up and down. My dick went in and out like the steady pumping of a piston.

"That's it, soldier, work that tight ass over my big soldier dick!" I grunted.

"Yes sir, yes sir, yes sir!" he was moaning. I caught his eyes again, which seemed to help. He began to writhe around in circles, working his hole over my dick with quicker strokes. I looked down and saw his own dick was ramrod-hard on his belly, as red as mine. It was oozing a steady stream of precome. His fat balls were swollen huge, and I reached out and took hold of them, rolling them and squeezing them in my hands.

"You gotta unload these big fuckers, soldier! You gotta fuck yourself over my hard pole so hard that your poor nuts ain't got no choice but to juice themselves." I said, my voice lower, but the steel in it harsher as I rolled and squeezed his fat balls.

He groaned, his thighs quivering wider, his hips rising up into my hands and at the same time impaling his spit-slick ass channel over the entire length of my dick. He was huffing and grunting so loud, he couldn't reply.

"Soldier! Answer me!" I growled, squeezing his sac and jabbing at his hole with my dick.

He squealed. "Sir! Yes, sir! Make me unload my balls! Fuck the jizz out of me!"

I grinned. Then I let myself go crazy. With his big body sprawled out naked and wide open, his asshole snug around my dick, his balls in my hands, I gritted my teeth and went for it. "I'm gonna fuck your poor soldier butt hole to a squishy, slutty mash! I'm gonna fuck you till you come!" I shouted.

I pounded into him. He writhed and squirmed and mewled beneath me. I rammed my soldier pole in and out of his fuck cave, stretching it open with every violent thrust. He punctuated each stab with a shouted "Yes, sir!" His whole body went limp eventually, his previously snug butt hole gaping open as he lay there and took it. I squeezed and yanked on his nut sac with every shove.

It was more than I could take. Sweat flew off my face and ran down into my eyes. The mewling soldier beneath me was the victor as I couldn't hold back and felt my own balls roil, my guts clench, and my dick begin to spurt. I yanked my pistoning meat out of his spitty asshole and shot white cream all over his sweaty, pink butt cheeks.

"Sir! Come all over my butt!" Aaron shouted out. I was gasping, unable to reply as I looked up into his eyes. He was grinning, the fucker!

Then he shot his own load. His ass lifted up off the bed, his asshole clenched and convulsed, his balls pulled up tight against the base of his dick, and come spurted out of the purple head all over his white hairless belly. I collapsed on top of him, out of breath and suddenly remembering how drunk I was. His big, warm body felt terrific in my arms. He smelled like sweat and sex and come. I was shaking.

Then I looked into his eyes again. The green irises were sparkling. He was laughing. Then he grasped my head between his hands and shouted in my face.

"Assume the position!"

So I got fucked. What a weekend. Can't wait till next time.

He

By Lee Alan Ramsay

The man rolled over in the otherwise empty king-size bed. He was a man, and both he and the bed were big and empty. August desert heat infused the dark room, and though the windows were open, no breeze moved into the solid block of temple-pounding swelter. The man's temples were not the only aboriginal drums banging out rhythms in unison with his heart, the man's brow was not all that was moist with pungent male sweat.

He rolled his head toward the night stand and focused on the blue-green digital readout: 11:02. The ':' blinked incessantly to prove electronically that this was the proper hour. He wanted to sleep. But the blinking, blinking, blinking of the ':' added to the thunder of skin-and hide-covered drums. He did not have to move his huge hand down to his naked groin to confirm the major voice in the percussion section.

He teetered a moment longer on the cusp and he knew what he wanted. It would come to him in the smoke of dreams if he just willed himself to sleep. But that was only mind satisfaction; like masturbation, its fulfillment, its banking of the real fires would only be ephemeral, momentary, no actual cool water on the seething embers.

He came to full wakefulness, and it was time for him to get up off the white sheets. He pulled his great hairy bulk from the starched linen to the shower. Hot water from the polished tap overhead spilled and pressed the dark hair downward over the scalp and bulging sinews. He opened his mouth to the flushing stream and bathed himself, beginning and ending with the ritualistic cleansing of his engorged genitals.

He stepped from behind the plastic veils, pulled aside on clattering metal hooks, and dried his swarthy skin with fluffy towels, he was pink and gray and brown. He pulled on tight jeans, the worn pocket behind the zipper automatically shifted him to dress left. He slammed the door on the leather closet and chose a black T-shirt from the top dresser drawer. They that want leather will find it in my eyes, he thought sardonically.

He put on work boots and descended a staircase to garage level. Ah, the garage. Only half of it contained his Porsche. He mounted and pressed the proper buttons; the first opened the huge door to the street. How much of life is dictated by the pressing of buttons.

Shifting gears expertly he descended the planted hills in the roaring machine to the neon-flashing playground at the foot of the hills, hills shielded by expertly planted pines, pines and yucca around his affluently blinded home. Wielding the stick in his right hand he descended.

There was a bar. All people know bars, places where moods are altered and the folk either go wild with lies or tell the absolute truth. He had always been able to tell the difference. He parked and walked through the door like a new sheriff with a shiny star at his breast.

The store was smoky and yellow. There was pool and drinking. The scents of stale beer, misbegotten incense and sawdust flowed into his nostrils. Sawdust caved under his boot heels and the walls were decorated in cowboy memorabilia, harnesses, tracings, sickles, and horse hobbles. These mule skinners are delicate in their ways.

He walked to the bar and looked at the bartender; that was all that was needed to put a cold amber bottle in front of him. Then He looked about the room and He wanted to spend as little time as possible in this misbegotten marketplace. He was ultimately miffed that so few of his "peers" realized the difference between the talking and the doing of it.

In a few minutes a bulging Tide-bleached T-shirt slipped into position beside the He. "Can I buy you a beer, Sir?"

"Just bought one."

"Then maybe there's something else I can do for you tonight. That black hanky looks real."

"It's real."

The two males facing each other relaxed just a bit from their "OK Corral" posturing. The younger man in his white T-shirt moved a little closer. He lowered his tawny curled head, perhaps to draw in the scent of his potential mentor's breast. "I'm a little new at this," he whispered. "Please teach me."

"What would you like to learn?" asked the Master, as any Gypsy would explore a cold reading. He felt the fluids in his groin begin to move.

The man/boy looked up into the eyes of his protector, fawnish, innocent, vulnerable. "I'd like to belong."

"The breathtaking outrage of non-involvement," rumbled He. "So what have you read? What have you looked at on tape? What sort of dirty work do I have to undo?"

"It's all crap," said the boy. "I want the real thing."

"Do you, now?" He crossed his massive arms across his chest; the gesture was much louder than the murmured words.

"Is it OK if I'm afraid a little bit?"

"You'd better be afraid. Otherwise I'd have some questions about your sanity for openers." He began conjuring the great vortex, the grand imaginary tornado that sucked in the other man, the massive low pressure area that pulled the other soul into his sphere like inevitable isobars on a weather map. He breathed in and out, making sure the puffs of his mighty nostrils went directly into the shiny desert-colored curls below his face.

"Take a good look into the old brown eyes."

The young man raised his hairless, squarely masculine face and looked deep into the huge trickster god before him. After a tender moment the boy sighed. "It can't be faked and it can't be hidden, can it?"

"Nope."

After another eon of seconds, another sigh. "Teach me, Sir. I want to know your pain."

"What makes you think I'm going to hurt you?" huffed He.

The younger man did not hesitate. "Anything that's worth having hurts. Ask any mother."

He released a long low "Ooooo" sound from between his textured lips. Then He leaned into the young man's face and sealed the bargain with a moist kiss. For a moment the tongues played with each other like mating snails bringing their shells together. He disengaged. "Follow me."

He walked across the smoky room, not really caring whether the boy was indeed following. Then He heard the boy's shoes on the sawdusted boards, and a moment later on the sidewalk cement behind him. He unlocked the passenger door of the green sheet-metal bubble and opened the door to the boy. The boy folded his long Midwestern legs into the car like a praying mantis. He slid into the driver's cockpit and checked his blind spots through mirrors. The car cleared its throat.

The midnight traffic was sparkling and sluggish. He wielded the stick shift like a knight would manage a mace. "It'll take about ten minutes to get to my place. You'd better be naked by the time my garage door opens."

The boy leisurely untied his beige work boots and pulled them off. He was in no apparent hurry since the mentor had given him the full ten minutes. "Should I tease you, Sir?"

"Wouldn't be advisable."

With that the boy raised his butt off the car seat and slid off his tight jeans. A second gear shift appeared, long and throbbing, stiff and veined, assuming about the same angle as the one coming out of the floor of the German vehicle. The young man peeled off his socks and pulled the T-shirt over his head.

He glanced over at the lad, taking in the smooth tanned skin, the rather well-defined chest, not vulgar, not pumped, just defined precisely. He made sure the car was progressing safely and glanced again, this time taking in the tight waistline, firm abs and thick smooth thighs spread as wide as the confines of the passenger seat would allow. The boy's face and eyes remained locked forward. Again He mentally attended to the progress of the car, again He glanced back, this time at the center of the boy, his manhood, a wispy swatch of red-blond pubic hair visible momentarily in the glare of a flashing-past streetlight, and the shaft of flesh emerging from the nest, emerging and demanding in its hardness, casting moving shadows in the moving quartz halogen light. He reached over for the second gear shift and pumped it a few times. The boy went into small quivering spasms of pleasure, squirming, slightly squirming.

The Master snorted. "Pretty. Very pretty. Now, am I going to be able to get both you and the ego into the dungeon? Door's a little narrow."

The boy thought a moment. "Left the ego in the bar, Sir. I'll collect it on the way home...if I need it any more."

He snorted again, convinced now that He had made a rather spectacular choice.

The car made its way back up into the hills, back up to the camouflaged aerie in the planted hills. He pressed the button on the black box on the dash to open the garage door and the green Porsche slid silently into its niche. The machinery overhead hummed, and the door closed with a mighty thud, as if to punctuate the young man's state of being trapped.

He dismounted and spoke through the open driver's side door. "Out."

The boy scrambled out and gently shoved the door closed. Immediately the lad came to his teacher and went directly to his knees in front of the bear-like man. The boy buried his face in the bulging crotch and wrapped his arms almost desperately around the sturdy legs.

"Anyone tell you to do all that?" rumbled the He.

"No," mumbled the boy still in his Master's groin. "Maybe I should be punished."

"You think it's that easy, huh?" intoned the He. "What if I told you I don't need a reason to do what I do?"

The boy looked up with a weird amalgam of confusion and wonderment. "Teach me," the lad said in barely a whisper.

The He raised the boy to his feet by one wrist and with the other hand opened a door next to the driver's side window of the Porsche. The door led into an oblong room. He flipped a light switch and three very small amber bulbs lit up, barely revealing the black interior of the chamber. At one end of the room there was a jail cell; dominating the other end was a rack suspended on four square floor-to-ceiling pillars. Chains hung from the ceiling about the room and the walls were festooned with all manner of equipment: lashes, crops, weights, stretchers, paddles—the textured walls were solid with the toys of grown kinky men.

It took a moment for the boy to absorb the magnitude of the room he had just entered. Then the lad's eyes rolled back into his head and he gave out a long energized sigh. "I'm home," the boy pronounced almost tearfully.

With no wasted motion the He positioned the boy between two of the hanging chains and raised each arm to the height He wanted. He folded the boy's fingers around the chain where He wanted them and then He glared directly into the boy's eyes. The He said nothing, but the fixed and frowning stare said everything. He was certain now that the boy's hands would not release the chains even if the building caught fire. The boy was in bondage until the He released him with word or gesture. He positioned the boy's bony feet in the same manner, spread wide.

The boy gave out only one brief glance of bewilderment, then it was obvious from the resigned expression that the bondage was real. The boy strained slightly against the chains in his fists.

He stepped around the boy, his palm coursing over the smooth naked skin, flawless tanned skin stretched over powerful young muscles, the artist's canvas, blank and waiting for the Master's mark; blank paper for the Master to write his incantations. The boy's penis was still stiff; it had not relaxed in all the time the two had been together so far. The He reached for the organ and pumped it a few times as He had done in the car, but this time He could give full attention to his work. He rubbed the livid engorged head and the boy went into trembling spasms. He grabbed each cheek muscle in turn, holding on, squeezing it. Then He gathered up the testicles in his palm and massaged the sac, pulling until the lad winced slightly.

"Now then," said He, disengaging from the boy, stepping back in mock contemplation with his hand cupping his own chin. "What am I going to do with this naked young man I find in my chains tonight?" As if He had just chanced on the boy there, the He spoke. He licked his thumbs and began stroking the boy's dark nipples, rubbing them gently at first, gently but insistently with the moist thumbs.

The boy pushed his chest out within the limits of his tethers and groaned as the pressure on his nipples increased.

The He teased the boy's nipples, now stroking with moist thumbs, now pinching lightly, now pinching not so lightly, and all the time He gazed directly into the boy's eyes, gauging, watching, discerning the slightest change in the boy's demeanor, playing the lad like a well-tuned instrument, pushing, backing off, watching and playing.

If anything, the boy's male organ grew stiffer. As the boy squirmed lightly, the member flailed the holy air. The low-hung testicles jiggled about in their wrinkled sac, freed by well-parted thighs; the balls swayed and juggled. The boy pushed himself toward the He, pushed out, chest and body and mind, pushed toward the man before him, hungry for the man before him, hungry for the hands and the thumbs.

He disengaged his fingers from the lad's nipples and then slapped each pec lightly, then not so lightly. The cracking sounds of palm on naked flesh split the air. The boy began to slowly undulate in his chains like shafts of wheat before a prairie breeze. Swaying, the boy also moaned, long guttural moans of something akin to a thrilling death rattle. The boy's head rolled around slowly on his neck and the breeze over his vocal cords rattled louder as each slap grew louder and harder and louder, now not only on the pecs but on the belly—"Thy belly is like a pile of wheat...." And the louder and louder slaps continued, mounting slowly and slowly. Now to the spread-wide thighs and on the back, now to the juggling cheek meat, firm but lightly jiggling cheeks. And between the slaps the He drew his palm over the flesh, skin the color of honey and ripe wheat.

The boy's utter submission and continuing absolute submission began to surge into the He's being, little by little the scent of the boy's clean, smooth body began to invade his nostrils like pure amyl; slowly and slowly the He began to intoxicate himself on the boy's utter compliance, the lad's instinctive ability to sexify everything the He hurled at him. His breathing began to change the same as the boy's. He began to drool and breathe heavily and between the now-vicious slaps the He snailed his tongue over the flesh, skin the color of honey and ripe wheat. Now He savored the musky sweetness of the skin with his wide flowing tongue. He licked the pecs, He licked the naked spread-wide thighs, He licked the nests of hair in the pits of the arms and the boy went insane, thrashing in his chains, moaning louder than from the slaps.

The slaps continued, more on the belly, more on the cheeks, jiggling loaves of cheek meat. And the licking continued, from the secret place where the scrotum joins a man's body, the secret place in his groin where he joins his manhood, the snail tongue coursed its way slowly up the line where the leg joins the torso, up the crease where a man stands on his mobility, up the side of his belly. And the lad's moaning became monumental, the thrashing and hopeless quivering grew. The boy's body went taut and strained and the vocal cords tightened into strained silence for a moment, and then the boy thrashed and squealed. Riding the squeal like the perfect wave, the He drew the boy's penis into his mouth and drove it deep into his throat.

The boy went utterly mad. His young bony pelvis came helplessly forward, the low-pressure area sucked him helplessly forward, and the boy bellowed some trashy reference to the Almighty with his head back as far as his neck muscles would let it drop.

He knew the boy was his now. He felt the great shift in power, the monumental demonstration of who was Master and why. The He stood to his full height before the trembling and sweating lad, and the absence of any stimulation eventually got the boy's attention. The boy looked at his Master through watery eyes, through drooping lids, through a thin smile of admiration and respect.

The He pulled his T-shirt over his head revealing the thick bear-like body, bulging pec mounds, and the massive forests of black hair covering the bas-relief map. The boy's eyes rolled back into his head and he moaned anew. The boy pushed himself forward to be with the bulging Master, straining forward, the boy pushed himself toward skin-to-skin contact. The He drew back by centimeters just to remain teasingly out of reach and the boy begged with watery eyes.

Once the Master made it clear that contact would be on his terms, the He moved closer and the chests, one bulging and hairy, one smooth and defined, came together and the He pressed another kiss into the boy's mouth. The He's firm steady bulk stopped the boy's uncontrolled trembling, stopped the swaying and undulating. His mouth stopped the sighing. He sucked the boy's breath out of him; sucking on the boy's tongue, the He quieted the noise...for the moment.

He detached himself from the boy and without looking, without taking his eyes from the gaze contact with the boy's eyes, He reached out with his right hand, the right biceps bulging and bulging. The hand came back and in the gnarled, hairy, mighty fist was the handle of a cat, a cat with 20 strands the length of a man's forearm and the thick round handle slightly shorter.

The lad's eyes closed briefly, partly in dread, partly in resignation, partly in the same expression of being home that he had expressed the second he entered the room.

He drew the strands of the cat very slowly forward over the boy's shoulder and let the exciting tips trickle down the boy's chest, black trickling traces flowing down; these mule skinners are delicate in their ways. The He repeated the act on the other shoulder, this time the boy stretched his lips over and kissed the black rawhide, with a slow lick and a quick peck as the whip flowed slowly off his shoulder like black quicksilver flowing down.

The He stepped back, and then He made a very slow circle about the lad, like a spider spinning a devious web, spinning and circling, moving slowly and deliberately about the boy. Choosing the back first, the strands of his cat started pelting like a spring rain, softly but insistently. Stroking and pelting, getting the earth loosened up and ready for the agrarian's mighty plow, slowly and carefully getting the sod ready.

The He grew in bulk, grew in stature, grew in strength. Fed by the vital contact with the boy, the He grew. No one but the perfect Top knows the delicious thrill of the growing, the boldness, the strength and audacity that the perfect bottom hands his tormentor. No one but the perfect Top knows the thrill of perfect trust, and how that perfect trust can be used to send two men to S/M Nirvana. No one but the perfect Top can know how close to God two men can approach.

The He reached for his belt buckle and unfastened it. Then, with a vicious tormenting smirk He drew his fingers and palm down over the boy's face as one would close the eyes of a fresh corpse. The lad thrashed in his chains and bellowed. "No! Please don't blindfold me. Please! I'll do anything if you let me see you. Please." The boy was pleading and crying.

"You'll do anything, regardless," stated He, whispered forcefully into the boy's ear.

The whimpering subsided slowly. "Please let me see you...."

For the boy there was no time left, no time before the commencement of his catharsis, the great aboriginal awakening the boy had begged for in the bar, the bar covered with aboriginal wrought iron memorabilia from the prairie and the floor covered with sawdust. With tightly closed eyes, the boy braced his body like a young draft animal might do on his first day in the field.

The He took his jeans off, knowing the sounds of the tinkling belt buckle and the rush of denim on skin was exciting the boy beyond the lad's limits to contain himself. Yet He knew the boy would not open his eyes under any circumstances. The warm moist air engulfed the He's naked countenance, bulging hairy thighs and semi-engorged plantain-sized penis, the penis would slowly engorge itself the rest of the way as the next two hours unfolded. He pressed his naked body against the smooth tanned boy skin, unblemished, unmarked skin like a blank slate waiting for the shaman's incantations to be carefully and meticulously written.

The boy would feel it now; what had gone before was preamble, now the real poem. The lash strands sailed high into the holy air with a mighty whoosh and came down together into the small of the boy's back, and the boy went high into his tethers on trembling biceps, shrieking and sighing; his stiffened body went high and came down slowly before the next stroke.

The He never left skin-to-skin contact. He either kept his bulging hairy body pressed against the boy's skin or He kept his palm locked about some large muscle mass for contact, always contact; He never left the boy. Indeed it was through this contact that He not only read what was happening within the boy's quaking body, but it was also the means to take the journey with the lad, not send him on ahead, but go along with the boy. The galvanic signals sent through the lad's muscles and skin went directly into the cells of the He, and it was the happiest game of all.

The lash went on high again and came down again on the stretched skin of the boy's naked back. The lad stiffened and sucked in a quick harsh breath. The He could feel the boy's muscles stiffen and then relax.

He drew close and teased the boy's earlobe with the hot breath of his voice, whispered puffs of voice into the ear. "This is what you wanted, wasn't it?"

"Oh, yes, Daddy. Yes, Sir!" The boy spoke in quick gasps. "Please don't stop, Sir. Please."

"Do you trust me?"

"Yes, Sir. Yes, Sir."

"Daddy's gonna take you on a little trip. You ready for liftoff?"

The boy simply nodded his head quickly. Maybe it was the boy who suggested with his silence that not much more be said for the next stack of hours and indeed there was not much more said.

He began the long, slow pummeling of the boy's body. There was no rush to complete the act nor was there any need to exchange the cat in his hand for another of a different length and weight. The He simply adjusted the blows to the boy's skin with his arm, with his mind, with his heart.

And still He kept himself close to the boy, skin to skin, spirit to spirit. The lash had no rhythm to it—the He stroked when He felt like it, to no other man's drum beat than the demented one in his own psyche. The blows rained down on the boy's skin intermittently, when He felt like it, and in between there was caressing and skin rubbing skin and licking. The He's tongue coursed and snailed its way up the naked bony backbone and the boy reacted the same way as he had reacted moments earlier when the strands of the lash had caressed the same line of bone. The boy stiffened and heaved out great sighs of quivering delight. Pleasure and pain were bleeding into one; the He knew that because it happened all the time in this room, all the time.

With each thundering lash stroke the link between Daddy and boy grew stronger and more intense. The flash of energy exchange between the two intensified. Slowly, ever so slowly, the two souls were becoming one, linked and locked in the dynamic surge of sexual energy the He was unlocking from both of them. He had the mystical key that unlocked and unfettered the powers of the cosmos, the magic unfolded since the dawn of man in the ritual caves, in the jungles, and in the hearts and minds and groins of all those who went before us. He was the mighty shaman who could make the fiery magic happen, and He did it all with pain!

Stroke on top of lash stroke mounted on the boy's reddening skin. Now the chest, and the boy, still with his eyes tightly closed, pushed his boy pecs out to the father, out to receive the delicious ecstasy of his initiation into the mysteries of the Brotherhood. Naked and trembling and probably still a little afraid, the lad pushed himself out with every ounce of energy he could muster, an energy pool that was waning as the lash strokes took their slow but mighty and inexorable toll on even the boy's reserve of youthful energy.

Now the cheeks, and the boy would shift his thrust backward, backward into the lash behind him. The whirring lash left its scarlet marks on the boy's cheeks, criss-crossed cheeks with red.

And now the back again. The back bone, the place that held the lad upright, the bones that had evolved over eons of time to be straight, now seemed to be turning to sponge because the boy was showing signs of not being able to stand upright that which was his birthright. The He was taking it away; little by agonizing little, the boy was weakening. And yet, the lad's fists clung to the overhead chains as if his life depended on the grip, and perhaps it did.

Harder now came the strokes, harder, and then a space of feather light taps and more caressing and licking and sucking, loving, slow and loving cock sucking, to drive the boy mad with the available spectrum of notes on the He's musical scale, to drive the boy on toward the incredible plateaus of S/M Nirvana, the places of intensity unknown to the timid, the ignorant, the intolerant. To drive the boy mad and bring the He along on the same surge toward utter madness.

At times He clung to the boy, his breathing changed as well as the boy's, his sweat mingled with the boy's and the two bodies at times writhed in unison to the pain and the pleasure and the agony and the relief. The lines between labeled and cubbyholed concepts were beginning to fuzz, to lose their powers to distinguish, just as the lines between the two dancing figures were beginning to fuzz. He grabbed the boy's tawny curls and pulled the head back for a kiss, a kiss delivered from behind with the He's massive hairy body pressed against the boy's back, their tongues traded places and massive noise pounded in both brains, temple against pounding sweaty temple the kiss was given by both.

The lash was raised again to surge on with its deadly work, on high the lash went again. And again it came down on the boy's skin, skin now afire with the welts of the black lash. No blood, the He didn't draw blood, that was not the meaning of the game. But the boy's skin was becoming hot to the touch, most of it raised and welted like some misbegotten living waffle iron.

The Master's rite surged on to its thundering conclusion. Blow after savage blow mounted on the boy's body, blow after blow, quickening now to staccato rhythms. The drums were quickening now, just as the boy's mind was quickening to the savage rites, just as the boy had quickened once before, long ago, encased in a watery womb, the boy had quickened for his mother—now he quickened for his father, and both mother and father felt the same twitching and quickening.

The He clenched his teeth for the finale, the last acts on the boy's body that would drive him to the point of unconsciousness, to the point of the keenest and most reverent awareness the boy would ever experience, the edge of the known world, the rim of the cosmos. The boy would know with a new kind of awareness how utterly huge the world he lived in really was, and He was there beside him sweating and straining and glowing just as the boy was fired and glowing.

The lash finished its divine tasks. Now leaving deep red marks with each mighty stroke, the lash and the Master's heavy arm bashed the lad onto one final plateau of ecstasy. The He knew there were none higher for the boy, not tonight. The lad slumped in his tethers, sobbing uncontrollably, yet not one syllable of stop came through the clenched teeth and the quivering lips, lips parched from shouting. The boy slumped sobbing but still the lad did not let go of the chains. He was fast to the chains as if the metal and his skin were one.

The He lifted the boy to standing and held him there; the He was sobbing too. The He held the boy close and the two breathed heavily for a long moment. The boy sobbed anew and perhaps the He sobbed anew, too. The moment of the loss of innocence is a sobbing moment, and maybe, just maybe, when father and uncles dragged a boy away from his mother and, in the savage aboriginal caves of our species' past, frightened the lad to turn him into a hunter, maybe, just maybe, father and uncles wore ugly masks not just to scare the boy, but to hide the tears.

The He released the boy's hands and feet with prying gestures, prying the boy's fingers off the chains and away from the imaginary shackles that had held the boy's ankles fast, ankles that had not moved from where the He had put them two hours earlier. The He scooped up the limp, tired lad and carried him through the dungeon door, through the garage, through the yellow kitchen of the house and up the stairs to the Master's bedroom. Though the lad's limbs were free, the He had not opened the boy's eyes, yet. The boy kept his eyes obediently shut and saw not garage, kitchen, stairs, or bedroom, not yet.

The He spread the boy out on the still-tortured bed clothing and stretched out beside the lad and held him in the huge arms. The boy, now breathing again, snuggled and purred against the hairy chest.

"Sir," came the pleading whisper from between the mighty pecs. "Sir, can I please look at you?"

The He reached into the drawer of the night stand and pulled out a wrapped condom. He put the packet into the boy's palm and then spoke. "Now, open your eyes and put that on me."

The boy's eyes popped open and it took only a fleeting moment for the lad to absorb the magnitude of the man he was with. The boy threw his arms around his benefactor, strong arms, yet arms dwarfed by the He's bulk. The boy set to his task and tore the packet open with his teeth, then carefully rolled the condom down the length of the Master's engorged shaft. Worshipping the organ, the boy sheathed it in rubber, worshipping and sighing, knowing what was about to happen.

When the organ was covered, the He gently pushed the boy onto his back and raised the boy's legs. This time the boy closed his eyes on his own. The youthful head deep in the pillow with closed eyes, perhaps because he would feel all he needed to feel without seeing.

The He reached into the night stand drawer for the tube of lubricant and liberally applied it to man and boy.

The He was already feeling the great pulse of ownership, the monumental surge of energy from one man to another as only men can know it. He would have the boy, and the boy would not mount one minuscule effort in resistance. The He pressed his body down on the lad gently, slowly, but inexorably.

The mighty organ entered the boy's body, and the boy went insane with the combination of pain and pleasure his benefactor had just taught him. The He did not know if this was a virgin or a veteran; it didn't matter, the boy belonged to him. He sank deep into the boy, and as the boy engulfed him, the He went into his own form of madness, the uncontrolled, flowing, smothering madness of ownership.

As He began to stroke, His body and mind centered and centered again. He did not lose sight of the boy, but the boy became a receptacle. The boy was real, human, but the boy was property as well. Owned. The He sank deeper into the lad's body and sank deeper into his uncontrolled chain reaction. Only the lead rods of orgasm would slow the reaction and that was moments off—until then the He would enjoy the slowly building rite of ownership.

The boy pushed himself up toward the Master, pushed his pelvis up and sank his bony knuckles into the soft pillows around him, grabbing handfuls of white sheet and squealing out his infinite delight of being owned.

There were no more words exchanged between the two, just a stack of long, sweaty moments, man in boy, boy engulfing man with equal desperation.

The He felt the mounting tickle in his groin, the signal that He was about to explode. He tried to drag the moment out more, to prolong the delicious mutual agony for man and boy out a little longer. He lost control and the gargantuan orgasm rent the air of the bedroom with searing explosive pleasure. The He quaked and pumped, pumped the last of his male juices into the boy, pumping and quaking until He slumped exhausted onto the boy's body and there, over the next few minutes, oriented himself to breathe again.

At length the He rolled to one side, withdrew his organ from the boy, peeled off the rubber and, after a quick toweling from a swaddling cloth of terry cloth in the night stand drawer, the He positioned the two for sleep. He embraced the lad, already sighing from sleepiness, and the two slept. Deep, satisfied sleep came to the He, and He was certain the boy was greeted in the realms of Morpheus equally well.

They slept.

In the morning the He stirred first. He looked down and the boy's mouth was pressed out of shape in the Black Forest of the He's chest hair. It was then the boy stirred too, perhaps sensing the changing of the breathing chest he was against. The pale blue eyes opened slowly, and over a thrilling moment the boy reconstructed where he was, and who he was. He looked up into the face of his mentor, the He, and whispered ever so reverently: "How do you like your eggs?"

Shelter
By Barry Alexander

Brodie fought the rain for a couple more miles, but the sky opened and dumped half a ton of water on his head. His breath fogged the visor of his helmet, making the gray, drizzly afternoon even grayer. He knew he was going to have to pull over or risk running his bike up the ass end of a semi. Cars still roared past, making no concession to the heavy rain or decreased visibility. Hell, some of them didn't even have their lights on. The wash from a semi splattered his windshield, temporarily blinding him. He fought to steady the big Harley Softail as the suction from the semis threatened to pull him in.

Once Brodie got the big hog stabilized, he started looking for a place to pull off the interstate. The last town was twenty miles back. He knew he should have stopped, but he was so close now, he'd wanted to ride straight through.

There was no sign of shelter. If there were farmhouses, it was getting too dark to see them. Stubbled fields of corn, the last of the winter's snow frozen to the broken stalks, alternated with huge expanses of yellow brown pasture. Muddy water swamped the ditches. Mud— the first sign of Iowa spring, Brodie thought with a grin.

When he saw the exit sign, he slowed and watched for the overpass. At least it would give him some cover from the cold rain. He finally saw the slash of concrete across the horizon and rolled down the throttle. The revs died down and he glided up to a controlled stop on the shoulder. Silence roared in his ears like it always did for the first few minutes after he shut the engine down. He swung his leg over, kicked out the stand, and leaned the heavy bike. His balls still tingled from the heavy vibrations of the V-twin engine. Straddling the big hog always gave him a huge hard-on. He grabbed his heavy shaft and squeezed gently. Might as well take care of it while he waited out the rain.

Brodie took off his helmet and ran his fingers through his short brown hair. It still felt strange, having so much hair again. He kept it cropped for the last three years, but hell, he had to let it grow again if he wanted anyone at home to recognize him. His mom would have a heart attack if she saw what he'd looked like out in San Francisco—cropped hair, queer radical T-shirt, pierced nipple and ears. She'd never see the tats or the piercings, he thought with a grin, then sobered as he remembered what brought him home.

He sat down on the concrete spillway and leaned against the slope. It wasn't the most comfortable place to jerk off, but at least no one could see him. Brodie dug out his swollen cock and stoked it while he looked around. There wasn't much to see. A row of concrete columns separated him from the edge of the interstate. Late afternoon had slid into evening; it was so dark now he couldn't make out the opposite side of the divided highway. Rain gurgled down the gutters and sluiced down the edges of the cement slope. The curtain of rain falling from each side of the overpass concealed him from the oncoming traffic. The hollow rumble of cars passing overhead and the growing darkness made him feel like he was in a cave. Brodie jumped when he heard something move. He looked up and saw a row of bedraggled pigeons fluttering between the ridged beams. Nothing like a little company on a cold, wet night. Well, it sure as hell didn't look like it was going to let up any time soon. He might as well get comfortable. Brodie resigned himself to spending one more cold, lonely night on the road.

He left his dick hanging while he unpacked his bedroll and spread it out. It was still tumescent but no longer as hard as it was. He worked it for several minutes after he got settled, but he just couldn't get into it. Maybe he was too keyed up from thinking about how close he was to home. It felt weird going home again. It was hard to believe that only five years ago, he'd traveled this same road, in the opposite direction, to California. Even the name had seemed a golden promise of paradise. California—sun and sand and unbridled sex. A place where he could be openly gay for the first time in his life.

The freedom went to his head. Too many parties, too many drug-hazed days. Three years had passed in a blur of pleasure, then he'd met Scott. If it hadn't been for Scott, he might still be there, an endless party of dope and sex. The parties stopped when Scott got sick. He still felt guilty that Scott had been the one to get sick—Scott wouldn't even try drugs and hated anonymous sex. Brodie hadn't gotten him into bed until their fourth date.

Sitting by Scott's bed, Brodie had had a lot of time to think. Scott's mother didn't even go to the funeral. She couldn't bring herself to accept a gay son. Maybe if she had seen what a sweet guy Scott was, that he had made something of his life. Maybe, if there had been time, they could have made up. Scott had tried, but she just wouldn't listen. "I gave her a chance," he said sadly.

Standing at Scott's grave two months later, Brodie knew it was time to go home. Without Scott, there was nothing to keep him in California. He'd never even tried explaining things to his own parents. When they yelled and ranted, he'd walked away and never looked back.

A semi roared past, blaring its horn. Its lights flashed on something bright on the other side of the highway. Had to be another biker, Brodie decided. A car wouldn't have that much chrome. He decided to introduce himself instead of waiting to find a visitor stealing his wallet while he slept. Most bikers were decent sorts, but Brodie liked to play it safe.

Brodie tucked his neglected cock into his jeans. He crossed the road, his boots thudding on the wet concrete. He caught another flash of chrome, as he got closer, and grinned. The bike was bristling with polished aluminum and chrome. The guy must have decked it out with every piece of chrome he could find. It glittered like a diamond necklace, reflecting the red taillights of the receding truck.

Just as he was about to say hello, so he didn't startle the guy, he banged his shins into something, pitched forward, and landed in something prickly. "Damn it to hell!" he roared. He'd forgotten the metal guard rail. He wriggled around, trying to get out of what turned out to be the dried up carcass of a Christmas tree

"Who's there?" The voice sounded young, but Brodie couldn't see much more than a vague silhouette in the darkness.

But there was nothing young about the 12" inch hunting knife in the hand of the guy standing over him. Brodie hadn't seen a knife that big since he'd watched Crocodile Dundee. It looked like a movie prop, but he had a sinking feeling it was very real. He stopped thrashing about and lay very still.

Light flickered from the polished blade, and Brodie realized the hand holding the knife was shaking. The realization did not reassure him. A scared kid with a knife was more likely to act first and think later.

"Take it easy, man," Brodie said in his friendliest tone. Cautiously, he started to sit up.

"You hold it right there, mister." The kid's voice was shaking as badly as his knife, and his accent sounded like a very bad John Wayne imitation, but Brodie didn't feel like laughing—not until he got rid of that damn knife.

"Hey, come on. At least, let me get out of this damn tree—the needles are poking me right in the balls."

"First, you tell me what the hell you're doing here." Brodie thought he detected a slight relaxation in his tone.

"Same thing as you. Raining too damn hard to be scooting. I saw your wheels and came over to check it out."

"What are you riding? I've got a 96 Bad Boy with 13" ape bars, full floating rotors and a bad set of pipes. Wait until you hear it. Man, those porkers sing."

Brodie grinned and stood up. Worked every time—ask a man about his ride and he'd fall all over himself telling you.

The next thing he knew he felt the knife whip past his ear. "I didn't say you could get up yet."

Brodie had enough. Before the guy could recover from the near miss, Brodie slammed the guy in the right shoulder, snaked his hand up his arm, and grabbed his wrist. Brodie then kneed him in the crotch. When he doubled over, Brodie hooked his leg around the guy's ankle and followed him down. His breath went out of him with an oof and Brodie wrenched the knife away when the guy's grip loosened.

Brodie straddled the guy, pinning him to the ground. It was too dark to see much, but he could feel the slender body trembling under him. The man was also wet—Brodie could feel the dampness from the guy's jeans soaking into his.

"What are you going to do?" the guy panted.

A little scare might teach him some manners, Brodie thought. "I could do anything I wanted," he snarled, leaning close to the pale blur of the guy's face. "And there's not a damn thing you could do to stop me." He paused a moment to let that sink in. The guy squirmed underneath him and Brodie was startled to feel a new hardness between them. The guy was getting a boner!

Brodie felt an answering surge of blood in his own cock. He was tempted to do something about it right there. To reach down and touch that stiff cock poking into his balls. To lean in and taste the lips so close. To explore the slender body trembling under him. It had been months since he'd been with another man. Even before Scott died, he'd been too sick to be interested. There'd only been that one night—when Brodie had been so horny, he had called an escort service for simple relief.

"Are you going to hurt me, mister?" He sounded very young and very afraid.

Brodie pulled himself together. He got up and pulled the guy to his feet. "No, of course not. I just wanted you to remember this. You could really get hurt trying something like that. Never pull a knife on a guy unless you know how to use it. Understand?"

"Sure. I'm sorry mister. I didn't mean nothing."

"What's your name, kid? I'm Brodie."

"My name is Chris, and I'm not a kid, damn it, I'm twenty."

"You're soaked. Don't you have any rain gear?"

"Didn't think I'd need much where I'm going. I'm heading out to California. San...Fran...Cisco! He said it as proudly as Lancelot announcing his search for the Grail.

"What about blankets or towels?"

"I've got a sleeping bag. Don't need much else. I'm traveling light."

"How long you been on the road?" Brodie asked dryly.

"All day. Started out from Galena. That's in Illinois," the boy added helpfully.

"Look," Brodie said, "I've got some dry stuff on my bike you can use. It's too cold to sleep wet. Grab your sleeping bag and come over. I think I can even promise you a cup of hot coffee."

There was a long silence.

"If I'd have wanted to try something; I'd have done it when your boner was poking me in the crotch," Brodie said quietly.

"I was hoping you wouldn't notice."

"It's a little hard not to notice something like that, especially when it's not so little."

"You really think so? You're not mad are you? Because I'm..."

"Gay? It's OK to say the word, Chris. No, I'm not mad. I've been on the same trip you're on."

"You've been to San Francisco? Wow. So what are you doing back here?"

"Come on, let's get that coffee and get you dried off."

Brodie picked up the Christmas tree and dragged it behind him as they crossed the interstate. The overpass had kept it mostly dry. He broke off several branches and started a small fire. The dry needles caught quickly. He filled the small kettle from his canteen and set it on the fire.

"The fire won't last the night, best get out of those wet clothes while you can."

Brodie couldn't see much as Chris got undressed. Chris stood carefully out of the firelight, his body hidden by the deep shadows. But Brodie could hear. The creak of the leather jacket. The metallic jingle as Chris loosened his belt. The snap as he opened his jeans. The slow, ratchety scritch of his zipper sliding down. The wet drag of fabric over bare skin. He was glad Chris couldn't see his own arousal. Probably scare the kid out of his wits, he thought with a grin.

He caught occasional glimpses of bare skin as a car or truck would pass, their headlights briefly strobing on Chris' slim body and long legs. But before he could focus on what he wanted to see, the vehicles were past, their taillights casting red spears on the wet pavement.

He handed Chris the soft towel he kept for polishing his bike. Their hands touched for a moment, and Brodie thought he felt the cold fingers tremble.

"I can't wait to get out there and get out of this hick state." Chris' voice bubbled over with enthusiasm as he dried himself. "I've heard about San Francisco ever since I can remember: Castro Street, The Eagle, the bars, the baths... Imagine, you can actually walk down the street with your arm around another guy, or kiss him, and nobody thinks anything of it. I can't wait".

"You have to pick your street. Do that on the wrong street and you can get the shit beat out of you in San Francisco just as well as in Red Neck City."

"I'd love to get in one of those videos, you know? Everyone says I have a great body. What do you think?"

"It's a little hard to tell in the dark," Brodie said, dryly.

"You can touch me if you want."

Brodie hesitated, not sure how much more Chris was asking for. He wanted to touch him very much. But Chris' earlier modesty left Brodie a little unsure—no point in getting himself all excited if he was going to back away. He ran his hands over Chris' shoulders and across his chest. His fingertips touched a small tight nipple, and he felt Chris suck in his breath. He drew his hands back before they were tempted to reach lower.

"Yeah, you have a nice chest." Brodie's voice was unexpectedly hoarse. He draped a blanket around Chris' shoulders. You'd best put this on so you don't freeze."

"What's it like?" Chris asked, as they sat on the sleeping bag and waited for the coffee to heat. "San Francisco must be just packed with porn stars, at least according to the magazines. You could be just walking down the street and run into Joey Stefano."

"Joey Stefano is dead, Chris."

"Yeah, but what a great life—getting paid to have sex! Can you imagine? You ever meet one?"

Brodie couldn't resist a little name dropping. "Just one. Joe Star. We went out once."

"Oh my god! You dated a porn star! I would just die. Tell me," he asked, his voice low with hushed awe, "What was he like? Was he really as gorgeous as in the videos or was it just makeup and lighting?"

Brodie knew what he wanted to hear. "Just what you'd expect—totally gorgeous. Hot and hung and hunky." And it wasn't a lie. Joe was all of those things. "Actually, he was kind of sweet." He was also strangely shy and very unsure of himself, except for his sexual prowess.

"I knew it," Chris said in a tone of satisfaction. "Did you, ah...make it with him?"

"Yeah."

"So-o-o? How was he?"

"Very talented." Chris wasn't about to tell him the rest of it—about calling the escort service and getting the surprise of his life when Joe Star came to the door. Or the guilt he felt after having sex on the bed Scott would probably never come home to. Afterwards, Joe had just sat there and held Brodie while he cried—and didn't even charge him for the extra hour.

"God, you're so lucky! I'd love to have that gorgeous cock up my ass."

Brodie just let him babble. He didn't tell him that it was his own ordinary 6 inch cock that had plowed Joe's backfield. It was the least he could do for Joe—help him keep his carefully nurtured image.

Chris looked at him differently. Brodie could almost feel the speculation in his eyes.

"Brodie, you wouldn't want to ah...that is..."

Brodie reached out and pulled Chris in, covering his mouth with his own. His tongue plunged down Chris' throat. He was startled by his own hunger. Chris didn't mind. He rolled on top of Brodie and ground himself against the hard ridge in Brodie's jeans.

Brodie pushed the blanket off Chris' shoulders. His hands slid down the smooth muscles of his back to cup the small globes of his butt. He cupped them, his fingers sinking into the fleshy mounds as he pulled Chris closer to his aching cock. His fingertips brushed the back of Chris' scrotum and the boy groaned as he tried to climb inside Brodie's skin.

Chris practically ripped off Brodie's shirt in his eagerness. Brodie pulled it the rest of the way off and tossed it over the Harley. Chris' mouth sucked its way down Brodie's throat, licking and lapping and tasting. He nuzzled through the thick mat of chest hair and whimpered like a puppy when he finally found what he was looking for. His lips tightened around the distended peak and his tongue played with the little bar that pierced Brodie's left nipple, pushing it back and forth and making the nipple harden even more. He caught it in his teeth and tugged. Brodie groaned. He loved it when guys did that.

Chris opened Brodie's jeans and burrowed his hand inside. His fist closed around the base of Brodie's cock and squeezed. Another dollop of precome oozed out of Brodie's cock and soaked into his damp briefs. He took his hands off Chris' rump long enough to force his jeans over his thighs. Chris abandoned his nipple. His hot mouth moved down Brodie's torso. Then Brodie remembered.

"I don't have anything," he warned. "How about you?"

"A whole box on my bike."

Brodie groaned and stood up to pull up his jeans. "I'd better go get them. You're not exactly dressed for a trip across the street."

Chris caught Brodie's hips to stop him. "I also have a handful in my jacket pocket. I'm going to San Francisco, remember? I'm damned well going to be prepared. But we don't need them yet. I've got something else in mind."

Chris rubbed Brodie's shaft over his face and took a deep hit of Brodie's ball scent. His tongue reached out and touched the base of the sac. Brodie shivered as the warm tongue lapped upwards. He loved having his balls worked. He was beginning to think Chris was a lot more experienced than he had thought. He felt Chris' lips press against his furry pouch for a second, then the lips parted and Chris sucked in one fat ball. Brodie had to grab his shoulders for support.

He slid his hands over Chris' shoulders and caressed the smooth, taut skin on his chest. He brushed his fingertips over the flat nipples and felt Chris' gasp tickle his balls. He squeezed the tiny points gently, and Chris began to suck furiously, his tongue lashing over the captured ball. Chris kept his hands busy, his fingers stroking the sensitive area behind Brodie's balls. Brodie's cock swung back and forth, bumping against Chris' forehead and leaking copious amounts of precome in his hair.

Chris' finger slipped up the moist crack and gently circled the closed ring of Brodie's anus. "I can't believe Joe Star's cock was up here." Brodie was going to correct him, then thought, Why bother? Let him enjoy his fantasy.

"You are so lucky, man. It must have been fantastic."

Brodie wasn't surprised when Chris asked him to lean over the bike. He'd half expected it. He hadn't anticipated the intensity of Chris' reaction—the almost reverent way he gently parted Brodie's cheeks, the hesitant, shy little licks along the sides of the deep divide as he prepared to rim Brodie, to worship at the shrine anointed with Joe's seminal offering. He acted as if Brodie's ass was a kind of reliquary, precious because of its former contents.

Brodie felt his tongue drive deep inside, searching for...what?

Some trace of Joe's phantom presence? The secrets of the universe? Brodie had never expected his ass to be such an object of worship. Maybe he thinks there's a trace of ectoplasmic semen up there that emanated even through latex, Brodie thought.

Then he stopped thinking. The hot, wet tongue scouring his inner walls was driving him out of his mind with pleasure. Brodie braced his forearms on the leather saddle of the Harley and widened his legs. Chris' chin ground into his ball sac as he tried to drive his tongue even deeper inside. Brodie squirmed with pleasure. He'd never had a rim job like this.

"If you want to do anything else, you better do it fast. I'm just about ready."

Chris pulled his mouth away. "Can I...you mean you'll let me?" he panted, his warm breath huffing against Brodie's damp skin.

"Sure, but hurry up—it feels awfully empty up there."

Chris scrambled to find his jacket. Brodie heard him rip open a packet and shivered in anticipation. In seconds, Chris was back, his hands on Brodie's hips as his cock pushed against the ready hole. Brodie reached back and ran his fingers gently over the shaft, then across Chris' hip. He felt the thin layer of latex and relaxed. He'd learned long ago to always check.

The fat head pushed easily into the well-lubricated opening, but Brodie still felt a twinge of pain as his passage widened. He hadn't been on the receiving end for a long time. Chris didn't give him long to get used to it; he was too eager to get inside. He pushed hard and lodged half of his dick inside. A couple more hard thrusts and Brodie knew he had every inch. Chris' bush scraped his cheeks, but the warmth of his groin felt wonderful in the cool night air.

Chris humped and pumped and pounded as enthusiastically as if he were trying out for a porn video. And he just might be pretty good at it, Brodie decided, as his fat cock plunged again and again inside him. He didn't seem to tire; his hips slammed against Brodie's butt, power-driving every hard inch. What he lacked in style, he more than made up for in speed and stamina. Brodie's cock swung enthusiastically in tempo with the rhythmic thrusts. Brodie wanted to pump it, but he needed both hands on the seat to keep his balance. Chris was pounding him so hard he was in danger of knocking bike and man over. He knew he was leaking precome over his Harley, but he didn't care.

Chris leaned closer, his bare chest warm against Brodie's naked back. He reached under and caught Brodie's swaying cock. Brodie moaned as the fist wrapped around him and started pumping. He bucked forward to drive more of his cock into the fist, then back again to get more of Chris' hard meat inside him.

He was getting damned close, when Chris let go. Brodie was about to protest, but Chris grabbed both his hips and started jack hammering him. A torrent of oh, shits and fuck yeahs escaped from Chris' mouth. In seconds, Chris was there. His hips stopped and his body shuddered as he pumped his load into Brodie's ass.

Brodie was afraid Chris was going to leave him hanging. He pulled out and whipped off the used condom. He dropped to his knees so fast it must have hurt. He plugged Brodie's empty hole with his hot tongue. Brodie was wide open and Chris was able to get deeper inside him than anyone ever had. He had to have had the longest tongue Brodie had ever felt. When he felt the hot tongue flicking inside him, Brodie let go. Torrents of hot come splashed all over his Harley. Waves of pleasure rippled through his body. Chris plunged his tongue all the way inside, and Brodie felt his guts clamp around it. He didn't think he was ever going to stop. They were both gasping when it was finally over.

They squeezed into the same sleeping bag, but they didn't get much sleep. Chris had a hell of a lot of stamina. Brodie couldn't remember when he fell asleep, but soon enough, it was morning. The rain had stopped. Chris' body was pressed tightly to his in the sleeping bag. Every muscle in Brodie's body ached from sleeping on the hard surface, but he didn't want to get up. He wanted to savor the heat and touch of the young body next to his for just a few more minutes. He knew he didn't dare. It was still dark, but already it was clearing to the east. Already he could make out the shape of the Harley sitting beside them, waiting. In a little while, drivers would be able to see them. He didn't fancy spending his first day home in jail on a morals charge. It was time to get up.

He nudged Chris awake. Whatever had drawn them together was gone. Chris was eager to get on his way. He looked very young and very vulnerable in the morning light. Brodie thought of all the things he'd like to warn him about—the dangers of too-easy sex and too-easy drugs. But he remembered how he had been at that age. And he knew he couldn't tell Chris a damned thing.

In minutes, they were both dressed. Chris hugged him briefly, then dashed across the interstate, ignoring the semi that blared its horn at him. He quickly started his bike and revved the engine several times so Brodie could hear the staccato thunder of the bike's song.

Brodie waved and straddled his own machine. For a moment, he was tempted to swing the bike around and head west again. Going home seemed like the scariest thing he had ever done. But he knew he had to try. Brodie glanced in the rearview mirror. Chris and his bike receded into the distance, blending into the landscape Brodie had left behind.

Brodie blipped the gas, and the Harley roared into life between his thighs. He paused to wipe the wetness from his eyes, then settled the helmet on his head. Damned morning sun always did hurt.

In-Tents Encounter
By Christopher Morgan

Jack's hand was busy doing something that couldn't be mistaken for anything else. It pumped up and down in a steady long rhythm, and the length of each movement made me understand that the young man was hung the way only a Midwestern-raised football-playing giant can be. I sat there and watched, entranced, despite the light rain.

Though wet and chilled, I was reluctant to leave the vision of masculine perfection that lay stretched out in his own perfectly pitched tent, an ever-helpful lantern swinging inside. That lantern afforded me a perfect view of the goings-on: of Jack stripping down, reclining on a pile of packs and his bedroll, and then starting to work his huge cock.

I hate camping, but my friends had all implored me to get out of my apartment, out of the city. I ask you, Why on earth did I move to the city if I didn't want to get away from the damn woods? I was raised in Mississippi—and that state's got enough woods, swamps, meadows, and lakes to shake a stick at. If stick shaking is your kind of thing. Me, I prefer shaking martinis and double mocha lattes.

But I was tired of the bars and the dance clubs, meeting one glossy gym boy after another—hard pecs, firm abs, and empty skull. One-night stands were becoming too much of a hassle—I'd enjoy fucking them but couldn't stand to have breakfast with them too. I kept having wet dreams about the kind of fellows I knew at home—strong and quiet and shy, with shaggy hair and strong bodies that were tanned by the sun, not by lamps.

So gradually my friends convinced me to head off to this gay campground. They eagerly loaded me down with a borrowed tent and sleeping bag and a battered knapsack full of essential camping things. I personally provided myself a cooler full of beer—I knew what was essential to me! I also brought along condoms and lube.

But the camping trip didn't get off to a sexy—or happy—start. I tromped around getting lost for about two hours and then spent another two hours trying to figure out how to pitch the "easy to use" tent. I finally pitched it, all right—I pitched the fucking mess into the woods with a string of curses.

I was starting to repack all my supplies when I heard someone approaching through the trees. I looked up in time to see a huge guy. The man who stepped into my little clearing was the stud of my wet dreams. Easily six and a half feet of hard-workin', load-liftin' muscle, well-dressed in the kind of layered sensible clothing I really should have brought instead of my chic designer pseudo-country getup. His feet were laced into strong leather hiking boots, and his long hairy legs were strong and firm and deeply tanned. A baseball cap was tilted back on his forehead over a shock of almost-white blond hair.

He was holding a crumpled pile of green canvas: my tent. "Did you lose this?" he asked. My heart melted, and my cock hardened. "I found it back in those trees. Is it ripped or something? I've got a patch kit in my pack; you can borrow it."

I managed to figure out how to talk after a moment or two of just admiring him. "Um," I said brilliantly. "I was—it's not torn, it's defective!"

"Oh?"

"Yeah. It won't stand up by itself," I said quickly. And I almost blushed, because it must have been obvious that other things in my campsite did not share that problem!

But he ignored my clearly defined hard-on. "Well, maybe I can give you a hand," he suggested. And without a single bit of help from me, damned if he didn't toss that stupid thing down, tie a few knots, and flip a few sticks into position, and—boom—there it was: my home away from home.

I was very impressed—and anxious to keep this guy around. We exchanged introductions, and I found out that his name was Jack, he was 22 years old (my 30-year-old body experienced a huge pang of guilt and longing), and he was from Virginia.

Then he asked, "I was wondering if you'd mind if I pitched my tent over there?" He pointed to a clear spot directly across from my tent.

Mind?

I shook out my borrowed sleeping bag, wondering if it smelled too funky for a guest, and then decided that he wouldn't mind once I was sucking his cock. While he set up camp, I scarfed down some gourmet freeze-dried camping food. How, I wondered, do the ad copywriters sleep at night, knowing their prose sells such a wretched product?

By the time night fell, I could smell something delicious in the campsite across from mine and knew that the man of my dreams also cooked. Grabbing two cans of beer from my six-pack, I took them over as an offering.

But after I'd filled myself on his scrumptious grilled chicken and beans and we'd finished the beers, I was no closer to fucking him than before. All my polished lines fell flat, and all my innuendo seemed to go straight over this young man's head.

Wondering if he had a steady boyfriend back home, I gave up and slunk back to my tent. My cock was as stiff as a log and twice as ready for action as ever before. And as I snuffed out my lantern and rolled over in the darkness, I saw Jack's clearly outlined form against the side wall of his tent!

I hadn't realized that these canvas homes away from home could so clearly show what was going on inside them. But the minute I turned off my light, I could see every inch of Jack's outline, from his broad chest to his shock of hair to the jutting salami that extended from his body.

Oh, yeah, Jack was well-hung.

I watched, fascinated, as he rubbed his cock and ran a hand over his nipples. I scooted onto my side so I could drag my cock out of my jeans—it had been too cold to undress all the way. My cock fell into my hand with a heavy slap, and I knew the chances of my lasting as long as Jack were slim. I fisted my cock and stifled a groan as I felt the familiar heat of my own hand. But I had to do something— it was jerk off or cream right in my pants.

So I watched as Jack took a good long time to play with himself. I tried to follow all the movements as well as I could. That hunching movement must mean he was cupping his balls. My hand felt warm and rough over my own balls, and as I gave them a gentle squeeze, I had a sudden image of sucking Jack's heavy sac into my mouth and tugging on the twin orbs until he had to stuff his big fat cock back into my mouth.

But it was when he got up on his knees and turned away—making a large dark lump in the tent—that I realized that Jack was showing me his hot and hairy ass, spread wide and humping up and down as he fucked his own fist! I gasped and shot a load of jism straight onto my tent wall and almost screamed with pleasure. Just the thought of the crack of Jack's ass made me want to run over there and pounce!

But I didn't. I shoved my wet cock back into my pants and watched him until he shot his load as well. Then he finally snuffed his lantern, and I was alone in the complete and silent darkness. I fell asleep almost immediately, despite my frustration.

I was dreaming about large ferocious bears romping through the forest when I felt something furry pass my nose. I jerked away in panic, thinking, Oh, my God, I am gonna be eaten by a bear!—and then I opened my eyes. What was before my face was not some woodland creature but a carnivore that was bred in my neck of the woods!

It was my neighbor, Jack, and he was lying down next to me! I decided I was still dreaming.

"I can't sleep," he said, his voice low and urgent. "Wanna get it on with me for a while? It always helps me relax, you know?"

Yes, it had to be a dream. But I wasn't one to waste any dream as sweet as that one, so I reached out for him, forgetting that I was wrapped in layers of polyester and cotton. He chuckled and unzipped me, one zipper at a time.

By the time he got to my jeans, I had my mouth on his mouth and my hands in his fine light hair. He tasted like ginger and mint. I breathed him in as he grasped hold of my cock, and then I realized that this was no dream. Jack was really right there with me in my tent! I fumbled for my lantern and snapped it on. I was right—he was real!

"I've wanted you since the first time I saw you," I whispered, groping for his clothes. To my surprise and delight, he was wearing only a light pair of shorts. I ran my fingers through his luxurious chest hair and nibbled on his neck. "You're so hot!"

"You're the hot one," he murmured back. "I want to see you out of these jeans!"

We obliged by stripping down completely and exploring each other's bodies, hands entwined sometimes, legs wrapped around one another. Wet kisses seemed especially loud in the mountain air, and we shared a lot of them, making obscene sucking noises that must have scared every critter for miles.

Somehow I managed to grab a strip of condoms, and I tore one open while I was sucking on one of his nipples. But as soon as I had it in my hand, I dived for his huge cock and slurped around it, sucking the head into my mouth with the slow, deliberate movements I'd promised myself earlier.

But that wasn't enough for him—he moved and shifted so that I was on my back and then turned around so that he could take my cock into his mouth! I remembered seeing that he liked to come belly-down and moaned around the thick cock head. I felt the pressure of the rubber as it slid over my cock and then the sheer ecstasy of his hot, wet mouth following it.

We devoured each other for what seemed like hours, and for once I was grateful that we'd both jerked off earlier. I was able to hold back, even when his sucking mouth smacked off my cock and started nuzzling my nuts. I just did the same, and we played follow-the-leader on our crotches.

Soon we had to roll over so I was on top, and the pleasure of sliding my cock into his willing mouth became too much to bear. He was making little desperate sounds as I sucked him now, and I knew that he was eager to be on his hands and knees again, so I pulled up sharply and drew my cock out of his throat.

"Your ass," I hissed, slathering his spit all over the length of my cock. "I'm gonna come in your ass!"

"Oh, yeah!" he cried, twisting up onto his knees. "Drive it into me hard! Make me feel it!"

His hairy butt hole was exactly the way I'd imagined it except even more inviting than I could have believed. One quick thrust, and I was sliding through him like an oiled ear of corn through a tight fist. And as I sank deep, he squirmed and panted and started to push back at me, taking me all the way to the root.

"Fuck me, man, fuck me," he chanted, slamming back at me with every word. I didn't have to move—I could let him do all the fucking. The pressure in my nuts was building and building until I was ready to explode, so I grabbed on to his hips and began to slam back at him.

"Take my cock," I growled, shaking with need and desire. "And shoot your scum all over the fucking ground! Show me how much you like it!"

"Oh, yeah, oh, yeah," he whined, wiggling and fucking. "You got it, you got it!" He gave a short shout of almost anguish, and then I felt his butt muscles clenching at my cock, drawing the come out by the gallon! I shot into him like a fucking cannon, even as his cock exploded into the condom that had slipped almost halfway off.

I found the sight of it, dripping with my spit and full of his spunk, very erotic.

I gathered him in my arms, and we sank down into the smelly sleeping bag.

Somewhat belatedly I remembered to turn off my flashlight. I should have remembered sooner. From not too far away came the unmistakable sound of two men applauding. I think I blushed until dawn!

Working Up a Sweat
By Thom Wolf

I knew it was going to be a good night when as I walked through the doors to the club an old Kylie Minogue track was brewing up a storm on the dance floor. Fucking excellent, pure-glad-to-be-alive pop. The dance floor was already packed. The club was sweating. Dry ice blasted over the crowd. I breathed in deeply—the best fucking smell in the world. I was high. Ready for anything.

I was looking pretty good too. I was wearing my favorite trousers—black, tight across the butt and thighs, and a cool new top—white, tight and sleeveless. My limbs were tanned and firm and I was showing off my latest tattoo; a black tribal band around my right biceps. I didn't walk around the club, I prowled.

I was feeling pleasantly drunk. I'd had a couple of very strong vodka martinis at home while I was getting dressed and I had been to three other bars before hitting the club. I don't do drugs theses days apart from the occasional spliff. Hard drugs don't agree with me, they make me do very silly things. Things (men) I'd rather forget about.

I went straight up to the balcony so I could have a good look at the club before I went into action. I bought a drink at the upstairs bar, vodka martini again, only this time it was a ready to drink bottle. Not as nice nor as strong as my own cocktails, but good enough to have the desired effects.

The balcony was just as packed as the rest of the club. The full length of the rail was thronged with men, most of them half-naked—posing, dancing, cruising. I shoved my way in next to a couple of young bunnies dressed in tight disco-wedgie-hotpants and not much else. Cute, but a bit too cute for me.

I leaned over the rail and gazed out over the floor beneath me. There had to be about 500 people gyrating against each other down there. I scanned the crowd with keen eyes searching for a face—the right face. I knew what I was looking for. He had to be tall and strong and over 25. Handsome but not pretty. A little bit mean, a little bit dangerous. I wouldn't make do with anything less than what I was used to.

After five minutes I finally found him.

He was dancing at the edge of the floor. Alone. He was wearing blue jeans and a black shirt that was stretched tight across his broad chest. His hair was bleached blond, almost white, and cut very short. His face was angular, square cut. I couldn't put an exact age on him from this distance but he was somewhere in his thirties.

I watched him pull a bottle of poppers out of his pocket. He unscrewed the cap and raised the bottle, inhaling through both nostrils. A sudden blast of dry ice enveloped him.

It was time to go down for a closer look.

I finished my drink and dumped the empty bottle at the bar before heading downstairs to the dance floor. It took me a couple of minutes to find him again. The place was so busy that it was a real struggle to fight my way through the sweaty crowd. A couple of guys made a grab for me as I hurried past them. I shot them both a glance that said get out of my way and pushed onward in search of my potential sex partner. Luckily for me he hadn't moved.

He was still there at the edge of the floor, dancing alone.

I stood back for a moment before making a move, just to be certain that I did want to make the effort with this one.

It didn't take long to make that decision. This guy was fucking gorgeous.

I guessed his age to somewhere around 35. Up close he was a big bastard with an immense set of shoulders, but his broad chest tapered down over his stomach to a very compact waist. His face was moody, almost hard looking, but there was no denying that he was a handsome fucker.

Any lingering qualms evaporated.

I was going to have him.

He didn't even see me coming. One moment he was all on his own, dancing away quite happily to a Tina Cousins remix and the next I was right there with him. I slipped through the throng of sweaty arms and torsos to take up my place in front of him. I raised my arms above my head gave myself over to the music.

He couldn't take his eyes off me. He was hooked. I ground my hips and my torso, swaying nearer and nearer to him until we were less than a foot apart. My eyes held contact with his steely blue gaze. I licked a film of sweat off my top lip. He smiled. His mouth was long and wide. There was a sexy little gap between his two front teeth.

I spun around and moved my tight ass back and forth in front of his crotch. My butt grazed against his bulge. He was hard.

I turned back around and arched my back to the powerful track, thrusting my hips even nearer to him. Rubbing my hard bulge against his own.

He dug the poppers out of his jeans and unscrewed the top, offering the bottle to me. I took it from him and held it up to my nose, inhaling the contents slowly through each nostril. The chemical fumes had an instant effect. I felt the music more deeply and my desire to fuck this guy increased a hundredfold. I gave him back the bottle and he sniffed from it again before stuffing it back into his jeans.

We moved closer, both of us seduced by the music and each other. He leaned in toward my ear.

"Who are you?" he shouted over the noise of the dance floor.

"I'm the guy you're having sex with tonight," I shouted back.

He laughed. "I'm Jack."

"Thom."

I slid my hands around his waist. It was tight and trim. I swayed my body against him, rubbing my hips against his. Our cocks brushed, kept apart by a few layers of clothing. We were both rock hard.

I felt his huge hand in the small of my back and he drew me tight against his wide chest. I leant into his embrace and found his lips. We kissed passionately. Our lips yielded to the pressure. His tongue slipped into my mouth. I pressed against it with my own, forcing it between his teeth and into his mouth. I tasted the smoke and booze on his breath and throbbed even harder.

His hands slid down my back and over the curve of my ass. He held it in both hands, lifting me even closer. I could feel his raw strength. I grabbed hold of his ass. It was tight and firm, just the way I like 'em. I shoved a hand down the back of his jeans. He murmured something into my mouth. He wasn't wearing any underwear. His butt was hot and sweaty. I felt his cock swell against my hips as I kneaded the taut muscle.

My fingers slipped into the tight crack. The cleft was wet. I had a sudden urge to tear his jeans down around his calves and get my face stuck right into the crack, to lick out all of that fresh, funky sweat. But I resisted. I didn't wanted to get thrown out just as the two of us were starting to get going.

My fingers quickly located his hole. It was smooth and wet and when I pressed the tip of my finger against it, it opened effortlessly. I pressed in right up to the knuckle. Jack started kissing me with even greater passion. His ass lips fluttered around my finger.

I slipped my free hand round to the front of his jeans to get a feel of what he had down there. Wow. I wasn't disappointed. He had a good, solid piece of throbbing meat. I squeezed the thick shaft and traced the outline, trying to get an indication of size. There was a good eight inches there, at least.

That was enough fooling around. It was time to get serious with this guy.

I slowly removed my finger from his ass and withdrew it from the rear of his jeans. I raised it to my nose and inhaled his scent. It was soft and savory and very fucking horny. The smell heightened my arousal.

"Come on," I said, taking his hand in mine. I lead him off the dance floor.

Though this club wasn't my regular haunt, I knew it well enough. I knew all the dark spots, all the lovers corners and hiding places. On the ground floor there was a good spot by the fire exit. It was hidden away around a corner, out of sight of the main club. It was a popular location for casual sex. There were already two guys there getting a blow job from a third as I led Jack into the corner. I ignored the other men. For the moment, I had enough to be getting on with.

I shoved Jack up against the brick wall. Though he was bigger than me, surprise gave me the upper hand. He tried to kiss me again but I avoided his lips and dropped down to my knees in front of him. My hands worked quickly. In no time at all I had his belt unbuckled and had ripped open the fly of his jeans. His cock leapt to freedom.

My God. My eyes widened. After so many years and so many forgettable cocks it's always nice to be surprised. This was a beauty. I had been right in my estimation, the shaft was about eight inches long. But it was the shear girth of the piece that really impressed me. It was like a can of beer. My fingers could not close around it. He had a foreskin, too, which is an all too rare delight, and a cute Prince Albert crowning his piss slit. His balls were big and low hanging in their smooth sack. I realized that Jack was completely shaved; pubes, balls, ass crack—the lot.

I wrapped my hand round the shaft as best I could and started to jerk him off slowly. I was never quite sure how to handle pierced guys so I started to lick his head and piss slit, taking extra care around the steel sleeper. There was no way I would ever get his shaft into my mouth so I would just have to make do polishing off his head for him.

There was already a good stream of precome drooling out of his slit, and the flow increased considerably when I tightened my grip on the shaft and jerked him harder. It tasted strong and salty, as strong as some other guys' full load. I gently poked his piercing with my tongue. That caused him to sigh.

"Does it hurt?" I asked.

"I'd tell you if it did," he replied.

I guess he knew what he was talking about so I nipped the sleeper between my teeth and tugged at it gently. The big man groaned.

Jack reached down, stuck his hands under my arms and yanked me to my feet. He had the advantage of strength; there was no use fighting him so I just let him do what he wanted. He spun me around and shoved my face against the cold brick wall. I realized that a crowd of five or six guys had gathered to watch us.

His hands slid round my waist. He unfastened my trousers and dragged them all the way down to my ankles. I wasn't wearing underwear either. My ass was bare for anyone to see.

"Nice ass," Jack growled giving it a hard slap. "Bend over and give us all a look at it."

The crowd around us had moved in closer. Their faces were pretty indistinguishable to my sex-crazed brain.

I spread my legs as far as my tight trousers would allow and bent over, sticking out my ass. Though my pubes are trimmed into a tidy bush, my ass is as smooth and shaven as Jack's. I spread my crack with both hands and pouted my ass lips for the benefit of my audience.

"Nice," Jack said shoving a finger straight into me. He curved his finger rounded the bend and found my prostate. My cock leapt as he stroked it. A big gob of precome oozed over my cock head. I moved my ass, forcing it back onto his hand. He knew what I was hungry for.

He pulled out his finger.

"You got a rubber?"

"In my pocket," I said, my face still pressed up against the cold brick wall.

Jack searched through the pockets of my trousers and quickly found what he was looking for. I never leave the house without at least three condoms and a couple of sachets of lube.

He tore open the lube and smeared it all around my expectant hole. My asshole grabbed at his fingers as he greased it up. He stuffed some of it inside me, making sure that I was well lubricated. I guess he knew from experience that guys needed a lot of lube to get his big prick into them.

He gave me his bottle of poppers. "Here. You'll probably need these."

I didn't argue. I unscrewed the top while he sheathed himself up. Then his big blunt tip slipped into the crack of my ass and pushed against my hole. This was it. I steadied my legs and took a big sniff from the little brown bottle. Jack pressed forward. My asshole stretched, it burned. Thank God for amyl. The big crown popped the resistance of my sphincter and he was in me. He pushed all the way in until his smooth balls pressed against the cheeks of my ass.

I had both hands pressed against the wall to steady myself.

The guys who were watching us moved in even closer.

Jack began to fuck me with long, hard strokes. After another sniff of amyl I was suddenly fuck-crazed. I wanted it as hard and as fast as he could give it. This was the real thing. In those moments it meant more to me than anything else in life.

He grabbed my hips and dragged my ass back onto his cock while he fucked it mercilessly. The rhythm was frantic. His hips slapped loudly against my wet buttocks. I tightened my hole, gripping him as though my life depended on it.

Through half lidded eyes I saw that a couple of the other guys had started to jerk off. Jack seemed to notice this at the same time. Without losing a beat he pulled me away from the wall and spun me around in their direction.

The two guys didn't have to be told what to do. They stepped forward and held their cocks out toward me. I took one in my mouth and the other in my right hand. The guy in my mouth was young, early twenties, the skin on his cock was naturally very smooth with an almost sweet flavor. The other man was older, mid-forties, and his dick was thick and hairy. After sucking off the kid for a few moments I alternated between the two of them, deep throating them in turn.

Watching me suck cock seemed to really get Jack going. He was fucking my ass like a madman. My insides seemed to shift around him.

Something wet hit me across the back of my neck. Someone out of sight had just shot his load over me. The hot liquid trickled over my skin.

Jack's hips bucked. His cock swelled and I knew from the irregularity of his strokes that he was coming. I swallowed the older guys cock while Jack emptied his nuts into me. He pulled out when he was finished.

My ass suddenly felt deserted. Somebody else was quick to take Jack's place. I didn't see his face or know who he was, but another cock slipped into my fuck-hungry ass. This guy was not as big as Jack but that didn't matter. It was a cock and that was all I wanted. He immediately picked up a fast rhythm.

Jack was standing beside me now, watching. He pulled the spunk heavy condom off his cock and tossed it down on the floor at my feet.

The older guy suddenly swelled inside my mouth. He quickly whipped his cock out of me. I finished him off with a few short hand strokes. His cock jerked and the first spurt landed right across my left cheeks. He blasted one white ropy strand after another splattering my face with his load. He wiped his cock across my face, smearing his load all over me before stepping aside.

I still had a tight grip on the younger man's cock. I pulled him forward and slipped his dick into the far recesses of my throat. He jerked his hips, fucking my face. I grabbed hold of his lean thighs to steady myself as I took a hard pounding from in front and behind. My own dick was slapping hard against my belly as my body rocked between these two men.

There was more wetness as one of the other guys out there shot his load all over my back and into my hair.

The two men inside seemed ready to come together. They both pulled out. The man who was fucking me ripped off his condom and blasted his load all over the sweaty cheeks of my ass. I could feel the warm wet trickle all the way down the back of my thighs. The younger man erupted in my face, covering me in even more strong smelling spunk.

Jack grabbed hold of me and helped me to stand up.

"It's your turn now," he said, holding me against his broad chest.

He grabbed my cock and slipped his fist quickly up and down the shaft, palming the head. It was fucking exquisite. I erupted in his hand. My load bubbled over the top of my head and dribbled down the back of Jack's hand and onto the floor. It was almost too much pleasure to bare.

I didn't even get to see who the other man was who had fucked me. When I opened my eyes he was gone. A couple of new men had started fucking in the corner and they were now the focus of everyone's attention.

I ran my hand through my hair. It was soaked with sweat and come.

"I think I need to clean myself up," I said pulling up my trousers.

Jack smiled and kissed me on the mouth. "Go to the bathroom and sort yourself out. And then meet me at the bar," he said. "I want to buy you a drink after all that."

I didn't usually socialize with men after I had finished fucking them. I told him so.

"But this is different," Jack said.

"How?"

"Because we haven't finished fucking yet!"

Plaza del Sol
By Sean Wolfe

Ihad been in Guadalajara, Mexico, for nine months. I had a good job teaching English at a private school. Made lots of money, had lots of friends, gotten lots of sun. Being 25 years old, with blond hair and blue eyes made me more than a little popular with the cute Mexican boys down there and, to my horror, even with the girls. I did my best to put the girls off as much as possible—and to get it on with as many of the cute boys as possible. It wasn't hard. I never dated a student of mine, but once I was no longer their teacher, it was open territory, and never a shortage of volunteers. The clubs there were always packed with lines way out the doors, and I never went home alone unless I wanted to.

Not that it was all about sex. I did make a lot of really good friends. Coworkers, straight and gay friends from the theater and dance groups I went to see often, friends from clubs.

But after nine months I began to become a little bored. That, and I was a little homesick. I worked 10 hours a day during the week and five on Saturdays. Though I loved my job, I was getting a little burned-out and started thinking about returning to the States.

We had two-hour lunch breaks at the school. There were a number of fast-food restaurants right around the school that I visited every once in a while. But I usually went to a little family-owned restaurant located in Plaza del Sol, a shopping mall three blocks from the school. Every day they had three homemade meals you could choose from as entrées. They were all cheap, delicious, and served with fresh homemade tortillas and endless glasses of "agua frescas," delicious drinks made with water and fresh fruits. After eating lunch I would take a book and sit in the open courtyard and read for an hour or so until it was time to return to the school.

I was always so engrossed in my books that I never realized the intense cruising that went on in that open-air mall. On this sweltering day in July, however, I finished my book very early after lunch and contented myself with watching the action and scenery around me. Sitting on one of the park benches that surrounded a fountain at the main crossroad in the mall, I was given a fantastic view of the goings-on around me. Mall employees rushing back to or leaving leisurely from work; high school kids and working moms getting in some shopping; little old ladies sipping lemonade.

And then there were "the boys." It amazed me how many young men, anywhere from 15 or so to about 30, roamed aimlessly up and down the sidewalk, staring each other down. There was nothing subtle about their movements at all. They nodded their heads at one another, raised their eyebrows, licked their lips, and groped their crotches. Several of them cruised me very openly, some of them even daring to sit at one of the benches next to mine and flirt with me there. I was amused but had no place to take them, since I lived quite a ways from the mall, so I pretty much ignored most of them. I watched with fascination, as they performed their mating rituals in front of me, and thought about returning to San Francisco.

Then Javier sat down right next to me. I'd seen him a couple of times before, eating lunch at the same little restaurant. He was always wearing a name tag that tattled he was a sales clerk at Suburbia, a Mexican equivalent to Montgomery Wards. He was tall and very solidly built, with straight black hair and hazel eyes accented by long curly eyelashes. Twin dimples pierced each cheek that was braced by a strong jaw line and a clefted chin. He was young, probably about 19 or 20, and adorable. I'd stared shamelessly at him when I saw him, trying to get his attention, but whenever I looked at him he was either not looking at me or he'd look away suddenly. I never pursued it more than that.

But now here he was, sitting right next to me. He was reading a book and finishing his lemonade. I nodded at him as he sat down, and he nodded back before he began reading. No smile, no licking of the lips or groping of the groin. So I went back to my people-watching, trying hard not to think about Javier.

I wasn't very successful. I kept sneaking a peek at him through the corners of my eyes. I could smell his sweet cologne, and after a while I swear I could distinguish his body heat from the 98-degree humid heat of Mexican summer. I'd sat there for about 15 minutes when I suddenly felt his knee brush mine. The first time, it was just a quick brush, and he pretended to reposition his feet. The next time, he let it rest there for a few minutes before moving it. The third time, it rested against mine for a moment and then began applying pressure against my leg.

I looked over at him. He continued reading his book as his leg pushed harder against mine. I looked away quickly and kinda gave my head a quick little shake. I looked back at Javier, and this time he looked me right in the eyes and smiled. His beautiful pink lips parted to reveal perfect, pearl-white teeth and those drop-dead gorgeous dimples. My heart did a triple beat, and I quickly looked away. With just the batting of his eyelashes and the dimple display, he was causing my dick to stir in my jeans.

When I looked back at him, he marked his place in the book he was reading and closed it as he got up to leave. I panicked. My heart dropped to my stomach, I stopped breathing, and I felt my face flush hotly. Where was he going? Why didn't I talk to him when I had the chance? Why couldn't I live much closer?

He brushed my leg again as he deliberately walked in front of me rather than going around his side of the bench. I watched him leave, and saw that after a few steps he turned back around to look at me. He smiled that lethal smile again and nodded for me to follow him.

I couldn't breathe. This was one of the most gorgeous men I'd seen while in Mexico. He seemed shy and sweet and sexy and mysterious, all at once. And now he was motioning for me to follow him. I turned to see which direction he was heading. He stopped right outside a door marking the men's room, made sure I saw where he'd gone, and then disappeared into the door.

I stood up slowly and took a couple of deep breaths before forcing my feet to move one in front of the other. When I reached the rest room door, I saw it was a stairway that went up a narrow hallway, winding around one corner before opening up into the rest room. I took the steps two at a time and walked into the rest room before I could chicken out. Once inside, I had to stop and catch my breath. It was a fairly large bathroom: eight urinals on either side of the room at the far end, with six stalls between the door, and the beginning of the urinal section on one side and a bank of sinks and paper towel dispensers across from them.

The doors to each of the stalls were locked, and I could hear slurping noises coming from behind them. Javier stood alone at the wall of urinals on one side, and two young guys stood next to each other on the other side. They'd moved their hands back to their own tools when I walked in, but it took them only a few seconds to size me up and move back to jerking each other off in their urinals.

Javier smiled when he saw me walk in, and then moved the shy smile down to his cock. He was standing a few inches from the urinal, showing me his cock. It was still soft but already long and thick, with a soft sheath of foreskin covering its head. He watched it himself as he shook it a couple of times and then looked up at me, still smiling, as he began moving his foreskin slowly back and forth over the shaft.

He nodded at me to take the urinal next to him. I gulped deeply as I noticed his cock hardening in front of my eyes, then walked dazedly to the pisser next to him. I pulled out my half hard dick and pointed it into the urinal, looking straight ahead and pretending to pee.

Javier gave a quiet "psst," and when I looked up he winked at me and motioned his eyebrows toward his cock. I ventured a look down there, and my knees almost buckled beneath me. His cock was fully hard now, and a drop of precome hung loosely at the head. It was long, maybe nine inches or so, and very thick. When he pulled the foreskin back I saw a long throbbing vein run the length of the top of his dick. My mouth was dry as cotton, and I forced my eyes back to the wall in front of me.

I heard some of the stall doors open, and their occupants began to meander out one by one. I was getting nervous and started to put my cock back into my jeans when I heard Javier cough conspicuously. I looked over at him, and he shook his head no and nodded toward my dick. Another man, about 40, came into the rest room and took the last urinal on our side of the room. He peed quietly as I leaned as far as I could into the urinal so he couldn't see my shriveling dick. Javier didn't seem to care one way or the other and remained where he was. The older man finished relieving himself and left the rest room along with the last of the stall occupants.

The two boys behind us were still there. The shorter of the two was on his knees sucking his friend, who was leaning against the stall next to him. The sucker kept darting his eyes toward the door, watching out for anyone coming in. They apparently did not think of Javier or myself as a threat.

Javier turned away from me and, with his dick still hard and sticking out of his jeans, walked to the rest room door. He pulled a piece of paper from his back pocket and used a piece of gum from his mouth to stick it to the door. Then he shut the door and stuck the chair which was occupied by a lavatory attendant except during lunch under the handle.

I watched this with stunned silence and listened to my heart pounding in my chest as Javier walked smoothly back toward me, his huge, uncut dick leading the way. When he reached me, he put his hands on either of my shoulders and slowly pushed me back until I was leaning against the wall.

My cock was fully hard now and throbbing uncontrollably in front of me. Javier looked me directly in the eyes, smiled, and leaned forward to kiss me. His lips were soft and warm. I parted my lips slowly as he licked them and slid his tongue into my mouth. The room grew very hot, and I felt a little dizzy as he kissed me passionately. I don't usually precome, but I felt a drop slithering out of my cock head. I was afraid I'd come just from Javier's kiss, but he broke it before I did.

The two kids behind us were moaning and groaning, and Javier and I looked over at them. The kid on his knees was shooting his load onto the floor as he continued to suck his friend furiously. The taller guy let out a loud grunt and pulled his dick out of the shorter guy's mouth. He yanked on it twice, and we saw him shoot a huge load onto his friend's face. Spurt after spurt of thick, white come covered the kid's face. He turned his face away after three or four sprays, and the jism shot past his ear and onto the floor.

Watching this turned Javier on more than I could ever have imagined, and before I knew what was happening, Javier pushed my shoulders down, forcing me to the floor. Before I could stand back up or figure out what was going on, I felt a shot of hot sticky come land between my nose and my mouth. I looked up at Javier's dick. He wasn't even touching it at all, yet it was shooting a load almost equal to the tall guy across from us, all onto my face. He moaned loudly and just let it shoot onto me without touching his dick. I didn't turn my head away; I loved the feel of the hot wet come as it hit my face.

Javier hooked his hands under my arms and pulled me up to my feet again. He kissed me on the lips, licking his own come from my face and sliding his tongue covered with his cooling jizz back into my mouth. I sucked on his tongue hungrily, swallowing his come and making my own cock throb spastically.

The two guys who'd shot their loads just a minute earlier walked over to us and began undressing us both. I looked around nervously, and the younger and shorter of the two boys took my chin in his hand and kissed me strongly, letting me know we were safe and wouldn't be bothered. When we were completely naked, our two new friends dropped to their knees and began sucking us at the same time.

I can't vouch for the kid sucking on Javier's huge dick, but the one with his lips wrapped around mine must have had a Ph.D. in cock sucking. He swallowed my thick cock in one move and somehow had eight or 10 tongues licking the head, the shaft, the balls, all while he moved his mouth up and down the length of it.

Javier leaned over and kissed me while we fucked the boys' mouths in front of us. It didn't take long before I felt the come boiling in my balls. I moaned softly and sucked harder on Javier's tongue as the kid on his knees in front of me sucked and swallowed my dick like it had never been sucked before. Javier sensed that I was close and broke our kiss as he pulled the young guy off my dick and onto his feet.

He turned me around so that my back was to him and pushed me gently up against the wall. He told our friends to do the same, and they did as they were told; the older and taller boy against the wall as the younger guy moved behind him. He and Javier bent down and played follow-the-leader.

Javier began kissing behind my right knee, nibbling and licking his way up the back of my legs until he got to my ass. He kissed and licked my ass cheeks one by one, then gently spread them apart. I was so hot by then, I could barely breathe. I wanted him to fuck me so badly, but when I pushed my ass closer to his face, he just licked it again and blew a cool breath on the exposed hole.

I looked over and saw the short kid was playing the same cat-and-mouse game with his partner, who was as delirious as I was. His eyes were closed, and he was moaning loudly as he pushed his tight, smooth ass closer to his partner's teasing mouth.

Javier reached between my legs and pulled gently on my hard cock as his fingers spread my ass cheeks and teased my hole. I grunted my delight, and he finally decided to reward me with what I wanted. I felt his nose press against the small of my back and a second later felt his hot tongue tickling the outside ring of my sphincter. I almost shot my load right then, but tensed up my body and counted to 10 to avoid it. Javier moved his left hand from my cock so he could use both hands to keep my cheeks spread open. He slowly worked his tongue around the outside of my ass for a couple of minutes, and then slid it very slowly inside, snaking it in, then out, then back in a little deeper each time. I was going nuts, and noticed the guy next to me was too.

The younger of our new friends was really getting into licking his friend's ass. I looked down and saw his cock was rock-hard and dancing wildly between his legs. He had a nice cock, about my size, but uncut. Huge amounts of precome dripped from the head of his dick, enough to make me wonder if he'd come again.

Javier and his counterpart stood up simultaneously. They must have had some secret code, because they moved together as one from the moment Javier turned me around. The younger kid turned his partner around just as Javier did the same to me and directed me and my counterpart to kiss. We did, very deeply and passionately, as Javier and our other friend dug through their jeans pockets for condoms. As we kissed, the guy in front of me reached for my hand and placed it on his cock. It was huge, almost as large as Javier's. I wrapped my hand around his dick and began sliding his foreskin up and down his thick pole.

He moaned and gyrated his hips, grinding his cock into and out of my fist. His dick was hot and throbbing strongly. My mouth watered with desire. I wanted to suck him so badly, I could almost taste him in my mouth, even as my hand pumped him gently closer to orgasm.

Javier leaned forward across my back and kissed my ear.

"Que quieres, papi?" he whispered huskily in my ear. He had his nerve—asking me what I wanted as he gently pressed his huge dick against my ass.

I shuddered as my response and pressed my ass harder against his hot cock. He gave me a tiny laugh and bit my ear softly to let me know he'd gotten the message. Then he moved his head back down to my ass and licked the hole some more, lubing it up to take his mammoth dick. As he stood up again and positioned the huge head of his cock against my twitching hole, he bent me over, indicating he wanted me to suck the guy next to me.

Never one to argue with authority, I leaned over and licked the head of the cock of the guy next to me. It was covered with precome as well, salty and sweet at the same time, and slick as silk. I'd never been with anyone in the States who precame very much at all, but decided at that very moment I was quite fond of the sweet, sticky stuff. I licked the guy's head until it was clean from stickiness, then took a deep breath as I swallowed his cock all the way to his balls.

On my second time swallowing the giant cock I felt Javier shove the head of his big dick just inside my ass. I tensed up and knew the boys in front of me were doing exactly the same thing, by the deep animal groan escaping my suckee's throat. It took me a moment to relax with Javier's throbbing pole up my ass, but I finally did, and resumed the task of sucking my new friend dry.

I think it may have been a little awkward for the kid fucking the guy next to me, since my guy had to stand up straight so I could suck and swallow his dick. The kid fucking him kept pulling out of his ass and trying to find better positions to fuck him in. He must have signaled Javier, because after only a couple of minutes Javier pulled me into a standing position. He had absolutely no problem whatsoever staying inside me. My ass wrapped itself around his long, thick pole and sucked it further inside. He slid into me in long, slow strides, as the shorter guy to my side smiled gratefully and bent his friend down toward my cock.

I closed my eyes as I felt Javier's cock slide into my hungry ass and a hot, wet mouth envelop my dick. I'd never been fucked and sucked at the same time, but it took no time whatsoever to realize it was my new favorite position. The kid getting fucked while sucking me was every bit the expert cock sucker his friend was. He and Javier found their rhythm with me almost instantly: Javier's thick cock sliding into my ass just as the guy sucking me slid off my cock.

I looked over at the guy with his dick inside my cock sucker's ass. He was pumping wildly, sweat dripping from his brow. He closed his eyes and moaned loudly, just as Javier was doing. I could tell they were both close. I was too, and trying desperately to hold back my orgasm.

I was up to about eight in my silent counting game when the guy fucking my cock sucker pulled out suddenly. He ripped the condom from his cock and pointed it at his friend's back. The first shot rushed past his friend's head and landed on Javier's chest. Javier grunted loudly, and I felt his cock grow unbelievably thicker inside my ass. It started contracting wildly inside me, and I knew that he was shooting a huge load into my ass as the kid across from me shot his hot load all over his friend's back and ass.

Javier kept his cock inside my ass as he came. That, and seeing the other kid shoot, was all it took for me. I pulled my cock from the other guy's reluctant mouth, shooting my own load in every direction. Some of it landed on the guy's face, some on the floor, some in the air, and some even on the kid fucking my cock sucker. I'd never shot such a large, wild load, and I laughed a little as it just kept pouring out of my dick. When I laughed, my ass muscles squeezed Javier's cock and sent shocks of pleasant pain up my ass and back.

The guy who had been sucking my dick suddenly stood up and tensed his entire body. He cried out loudly as wave after wave of thick white come shot out of his dick and splattered against the wall in front of him. We all just watched in amazement as it kept coming and coming. It seemed there was enough to fill a glass.

I started laughing first, which caused me so much pain, I had to pull Javier's cock out of my ass. Unbelievably, he was still hard. Then the others started laughing as well. We all leaned against a wall or sink and caught our breath. There was come everywhere; on the wall, the floor, a sink, all of us. The air smelled strongly of it. Pity the next people who came in here to actually use the rest room!

Javier removed his condom carefully and laid it on the sink next to the paper towel holder. It was almost completely filled with his load, and as he laid it on the sink, a good amount spilled out onto the counter. All four of us looked at it and began to giggle again as we got dressed.

We all kissed one another and walked out the door together. As I passed through the door I pulled off the note Javier had placed there earlier. I wanted a memento of the best fuck of my life. I stuck it in my pocket and watched as Javier ran back to his work and the other two friends departed in separate directions. I started walking back to school and pulled the paper out to read it on my way.

Temporarily out of service

I smiled to myself, doubting the rest room had seen that much service in quite a while.

Now and Then
By Dale Chase

I don't understand the time warp, I just enjoy it. The professor tells me to stay the hell out of it, but he says this while he's got his dick up my ass, and anything said during a fuck doesn't count, at least not to me. So I indulge myself, so to speak, because there are things I like better about then as opposed to now although then and now sort of lose their context on these particular trips.

It's really more place than time, these voyages, even though I know time alters place. The result is always an unfamiliarity that in itself finally becomes familiar. I awaken from a state just this side of sleep to find myself somewhere so far beyond beyond that I feel a kind of weightlessness, then a gradual settling, like coming back down to earth when I've never left. And then I take in the sights, which are always remarkable.

I've learned not to ask exactly when I've landed and if where isn't apparent I don't ask that either. Questions are a giveaway, at least those kinds of questions, so I just try to blend in.

I've taken maybe a dozen time trips, and the professor knows it—how I'm not sure. I wonder if I'm leaving some kind of snail-trail or maybe come-trail because, you see, I'm travelling strictly for the fucks.

"If you'd gather a bit of scientific data," the professor says during one of his tirades, "I wouldn't mind so much. But all you're doing is coming in another millennium. It's such a waste."

"They don't think so."

He shakes his head and huffs, almost endearing with his genius pout. I sidle up behind him and grope his crotch, and he doesn't stop me. "And I won't have you fucking in three different millennia," he says, pushing into my hand. "There have to be limits!" I unzip his fly and fish out his dick, and he goes quiet. He always does.

I won't call all this a problem because I'm having too much fun. Situation is more accurate because I genuinely adore the professor, this 50-year-old scientist-stud who took a mere lab techie under his wing and into his bed. I already had a crush on him so everything was quite welcome and he's a great fuck, don't get me wrong. It's just that when I tried out the time warp in his absence things got complicated and now there's this issue between us. Come spread out over three millennia. What a kick.

"You're too bright for your own good," the professor says as I suck his dick. We're in the lab, me just back from my latest jaunt, ass full of future-come, and the professor starts thrusting into my mouth. I suck his long shaft, tongue cradling him until he's fully primed. He's talking the whole time, telling me it's not real out there, that I have to remember it's a warp, that I haven't really gone anywhere. I keep sucking. Listening and sucking.

"You'll have to give me a full report," he says as I pull back to play with his fat knob. The professor is well endowed, mind and body, and I like to handle his big cock as much as he likes to stick it up my ass. "I hope you made at least some scientific observations this time," he adds. And then he pulls out and slips on a condom—he carries them in his lab coat—while I strip. He mounts me from behind as I grip a table, and I savor the feel of that hose snaking up into my rectum.

The professor is never urgent. As with his scientific inquiries, he fucks methodically and I enjoy the ride. My own cock is just the opposite, and I last about three strokes before squirting cream all over the table. The professor pauses, peers over my shoulder, and murmurs his approval. He always saves my jism. I don't know what he does with it, but I like the idea.

He resumes his fuck and we settle into an easy rhythm, and then he says, "Tell me about your trip." As much as he dislikes my little runaway adventures, he still gets charged at the idea of future fucking.

"I'm not sure they're people," I tell him. "But then I've run into that before. Maybe by the fourth millennium human beings have superseded themselves. Anyway, they look human, of course, only better. It was the same as always about where, a lab but empty looking, as if they don't need devices. I didn't ask—"

"But you should!" the professor shouts, ramming his dick into my ass for emphasis. "One or two questions could bring me so much."

I give it a second and he resumes his stroke, hands on my hips, cock steadily thrusting. I continue; I'm getting to be an expert at giving reports while taking a prick up the backside. "So I'm in this lab alone but I don't hang around. Outside it's beautiful, there's a kind of serenity in the air, almost like it's part of the air, like the air has been drugged. Some kind of natural high."

The professor starts fucking madly at this, over-excited at such a discovery. He's squealing now, and I know he wants information as much as he wants to come. He gets off on all kinds of things. "I keep taking these deep breaths," I continue, "because the air is so sweet but not in a scented kind of way. It's what it does to you, and I realize I'm getting a hard-on from just breathing. Just from air. And then I wonder if it does this to everyone, if they're all walking around with stiff dicks or is it just us newcomers who are overwhelmed." I start laughing now because I've made a pun. The professor isn't interested, he's almost there now, but I won't give up. "Newcomer!" I say. "Get it?"

He doesn't acknowledge my attempt at humor. The fuck has taken him over and he's very unprofessorlike as his dick squirts its load. "Fucking shit!" he cries. "Oh, fuck it, oh God, yes, fuck it! Fuck! Fuck! Fuck!"

I grip the table as he slams into me, stopping my narrative to listen. I love it when he gets dirty. "Fuck! Fuck! Fuck!" he shouts, and I know each fuck is a pulse of come. I savor the idea of his highly educated dick spewing cream like us commoners, never mind science or millennia or anything. "Fuck," he says one final time before slumping against me. I squeeze my muscle and he groans. "You don't need the future do you, Jason?"

"Need? No, of course not. I have everything here." I nuzzle back into him, give it a second, then add, "But the lure of adventure is very powerful."

He yanks his dick out of me and storms to the bathroom, wounded yet again. I've reminded him so many times that I'm faithful in this world, but that never seems enough for him. It's become a sore point and yet I can usually get around it. Geniuses are such babies about life and sex and all the good stuff.

I purposely don't put on my pants because I know he'll want to hear the full narrative of my journey and also that he likes it best when I stretch out on the corner sofa and play with my dick as I tell it. I settle there now and wait.

He ignores me at first, acting professorlike, capital P-h-fucking-D, acting as if he's never stuck his cock up a techie's ass or any ass for that matter. I ignore him back and he glances at me as if I'm just some kid masturbating in a corner but after a few minutes at his desk he settles into the old leather armchair opposite me. He adjusts his cock and says, "Tell me more." He's got a notepad on the arm of the chair; he writes down the non-sex parts, eager for clues about the future in the crumbs I bring him. I keep telling him he should go, but I think he's afraid of what he's found.

"The atmosphere," he prompts. "How did it affect you as time passed, aside from the hard-on?"

"I don't think time passes there. It all seemed stopped in some way, like maybe they found the right moment and just kept it. But maybe not. It was just a feeling I got."

The professor gives me an exaggerated sigh. "You've got to be more observant, Jason. If you're going to keep sneaking into the warp without permission, without guidance, the least you can do is maintain a minimal level of scientific inquiry."

I go silent and look down at my prick instead of him. It's starting to fill and I wag and squeeze until he says, very softly, "Go on."

"So I've got this hard-on and it feels urgent, like I might just come with no hands any second, and...oh, wait, did I mention I'm naked? Sorry, didn't mean to leave that out, but it was so natural. So it's all very smooth outside, clear, fresh, with that great air. No buildings even though I was just in one, but I've learned things like that happen, things come and go. Oh, man, another pun, get it? Come and go?"

The professor frowns. My dick is hard now because it knows where we're headed. "Go on," the professor says.

"So there are trees and lawns, everything soft. No concrete, no streets or sidewalks, and then I see this kind of meadow, and there they are, these people if that is what they really are. And I just walk right in among them because I look like them or them me. I mean we're all naked, we're all blond, and we've all got major boners."

"Jason," the professor snaps and I look up at a scowl. "You're not making this up, are you? It's a bit much."

"It's the fucking future!" I say, ticked off that he doesn't believe me, which makes me work my dick even harder. Juice starts running out my slot and down my hand. "And maybe they're not so uptight," I add, mustering all the indignance possible with a cock in my hand.

He considers this, then says, "I just don't want to be manipulated. If this is simply one of your little masturbation plays please tell me as I have better things to do."

He doesn't, of course, at least not in my book. Science will always lose out to a good dickoff. "It's real," I say. "Honest to God."

"Very well."

I close my eyes and stroke my cock as I continue. "At first I think there's really no difference between them and me. They don't say anything but hands are all over me, warm hands, too warm. That's the first clue, like they're artificially heated and it's a notch too high. One is pulling my cock—did I say they're all gorgeous, young, firm, smooth, tanned?—and the rest are watching. It's like it's all kind of ceremonial, like they know I'm from somewhere else, but boy it feels a lot more than that and I'm still sucking in that drugged air and it's starting to feel like it's going into my prick and my ass, and then it's like I'm sort of oozing, my whole body about to dissolve into a pool of come. And they know it. They smile and this guy playing with my dick starts fondling my balls and then another is behind me sticking a finger up my ass and it feels sweet, there's no other way to describe it, not a tasting kind of sweet but still sweet. Honest to God. And I feel some kind of lube, warm and so smooth, and God I love even that, and then, when I'm so ready I'm about to scream, the crowd parts and up steps this guy who must be the king or something because his cock is about a foot long and they're all kind of bowing to it. I just stare at it and suddenly I can feel it in my mouth even though he's 10 feet away. He's aimed at me and he's like this Greek god, so handsome, curly blond hair, perfect features, incredible blue eyes, red mouth, and pecs I want to climb on and down below a bush of yellow silk and then that missile. And I want him to fuck me so bad I start to wiggle because there is still a finger up my ass and the guy is still playing with my cock.

"The Greek god smiles as if he gets the message and they lower me to this thick lawn and it's cool and warm all at once. I'm on my back now and I don't have to do anything. They pull my legs up so my ass is positioned perfectly, sort of hanging there, and a guy even pulls open my cheeks and I feel this kind of air-enema go up me, as if they're blowing the channel clean, and that feels good, everything does. And then...."

I couldn't go on. I was working my prick and about to come, and I looked over at the professor who had his hand at his crotch, rubbing himself as he watched me. His look was a sort of scolding lust that I'd seen before. And then I'm going over, juice shooting up onto my belly as I pump my meat. I'm thinking of the Greek god and what he's going to do to me, and it makes the climax keep on going, as if part of him is still in me. When I'm finally done, breathing hard, limp dick in hand, the professor simply says, "And?"

"Gimme a second," I say, knowing I have to lie here with come all over me because he'll want to harvest it, as he says. But first the future.

"All right," I say finally and as I picture it, it starts to feel real and it doesn't matter that I've just emptied my balls. My cock twitches and my nuts start to swell. I take a deep breath and continue. "So I'm sort of hanging there in their arms, ass up, and he's there at my hole which has been cleaned and I know he's clean as well, it's like he's telling me in some way, and then he sticks his dick in me."

I stop the narrative for the initial few strokes because they are truly other-worldly and the professor clears his throat because he doesn't want me going off so totally. Going off, all right. My prick is getting hard again. I can't believe this.

"So the guy, the Greek god," I say, "fucks me." I'm afraid to tell much more because I don't want to hurt the professor and yet I know he wants to know while at the same time he hates it. But never mind all that because my ass feels like the whole other world is going up into my bowels, so warm it feels like a creature all its own, so sweet I think I'm salivating. Jesus, I am. I swallow and I have to grab my dick because I'm so ready, so already ready. I'd call it an out-of-body experience if it wasn't so in-body.

"Tell me what you're feeling right now, Jason," the professor says. "You're turning a shade of pink that's a bit beyond human."

I hadn't noticed but now I look down. I'm a sort of magenta color, hot pink without the hot, cool looking except underneath I'm saturated with heat. And all the while I can feel the Greek god's cock up my rectum and come is boiling in my balls and those balls are straining my sac. "Tell me," the professor says, leaning toward me now. His look is something between sexually excited and scientifically excited, which is so very much the professor, the only guy who could mix the two and enjoy it. "Tell me about the fuck," he says. "I know he's doing you right now so give me details, please. It appears this particular fuck has transcended the time warp and we haven't experienced that before."

I'm looking at my genius mentor, my teacher, employer, the man I admire more than any on earth, and as I do I'm feeling that dick pumping in and out of me and I can't really find words. My mouth is open, my eyes are fixed, sort of lost to the moment. I see the Greek god instead of the professor; I stare at his hard nipples and wish I could suck on one. I'm stroking my prick while all this plays inside me and outside me, and then I feel the Greek god start to come. He doesn't go frantic like we do and he doesn't make a sound; his cock just sort of does things on its own, contracting and shooting stream after stream, recoiling inside me like a repeating rifle. The come is hot and it goes up me in gushers, in waves, and I feel myself filling. There's an urgency now, I'm reaching capacity, and it gives the fuck a kind of sweet agony that pushes me over and I come like never before. As cream pulses out my slot I wonder if it's even mine, there is so much, and when I finally stop, which seems like minutes later, my stomach is awash in jism. The professor runs a finger through it because it's a gorgeous sky blue and has a scent—not a smell. He sniffs it, runs a fingerful by my nose. "Remarkable," he says. "You've brought me quite a treat. Our first sample from the future." He leans over and kisses my cheek. "You don't have to tell me any more."

I lie still while he scoops all the blue come into a beaker. My skin is now its usual human pale pink and I'm having trouble remembering the Greek god or his fuck. I can feel it getting away and it scares me. I tell this to the professor.

"The fourth millennium seems to have control over the warp," he says, all professorial now which is what I want, "and I suspect the inhabitants might not appreciate our intrusion. They've allowed you a bit of recall as a sort of consolation, but they essentially want you to forget them. A privacy issue, most likely." He comes over and sits beside me and fondles my tired prick.

"Why won't you tell the world that you've discovered a time warp?" I ask him for what must be the hundredth time. He's never answered me before, but he does now. "They'd all want to go," he says a bit sadly. "Who could resist such freedom?" His hand gently traces my cock head. "Promise me you'll stay here from now on. No more warp trips."

"I promise."

He kisses me and my tongue meets his; I feel his breath against my own. And then he takes his beaker of blue come to his worktable and begins to prepare slides. I think about the promise I've made him and how I make it after each trip. He knows it won't be kept.

The Training Session
By Grant Foster

"Sam Stanton?"

The man nodded. "Lew Drake."

My father strode across the big, mirror-lined room, hand outstretched. I lingered near the door, seriously considering making a break for it. I wanted nothing to do with this Stanton character or with anything he had to offer. I was perfectly happy—well, resigned anyway—with the way I was. My father, however, was of a different opinion. So, here I stood, like a lamb led to the slaughter.

"What can I do for you, sir?" Stanton looked like an ex-marine—broad shoulders, flat gut, ramrod posture, buzz-cut hair, rugged features, hawk-like stare. His lips were set in a tight, straight line, too Spartan for smiling. His expression as he looked at me gave away nothing.

"Joe! Come over here, son." I approached them warily, hands stuffed into my pockets. "I want you to make a man out of him."

"Pardon?" Stanton looked at my father curiously.

"Oh, I know, he looks like a man, but he's a wimp. He's all nerves and moods and mysterious silences. It's all his mother's damned fault."

"Dad."

"Don't interrupt, son," he snapped. I flinched. Stanton's gaze shifted from my father to me, then back again. "She always spoiled him rotten. You know, kept him in the house with her, away from other kids. Never even let him get dirty, for chrissakes."

"I see." Stanton looked my way. His gaze was intense. It felt almost like he was touching me. I quickly averted my eyes.

"Joe, take off your shirt so this man can see what he's got to work with." I felt my cheeks get hot, but obeyed. "Stand up straight, son. That's better."

"There's certainly nothing wrong with your son's body, Mr.

Drake." I glanced at Stanton again. He was staring at my bare torso like he was trying to memorize it. The tip of his tongue skittered, left to right, across his upper lip. My heart jerked hard against my rib cage.

"Physically my son's a fine specimen." Dad sounded like he was talking about a prize show dog. "He's built solid as a rock. Make a muscle, Joe." I hesitated. "Show the man your damned arms!" I flexed. "Look at that. Eighteen years old and he looks like that. He should be out winning medals with that body."

"Impressive," Stanton said softly. "Very impressive."

"Unfortunately, he's afraid of his own shadow. He could have any girl in the senior class, but he won't even talk to them. He could be on the football team, the wrestling team, the...hell, pick a team. Instead, he spends all his time hiding up in his room, pumping weights and reading books...and jerking off constantly."

I stared doggedly at the floor, twisting my T-shirt nervously. Of course I jerked off. It's the most popular indoor sport for guys my age. I wasn't interested in team sports, and I had my own reasons for not wanting to wrestle. As for the girls—why couldn't he just leave me alone?

"Your ad said you train and motivate young men." Stanton nodded. "I guess I just want you to train some damned spine into him. Teach him how to act like a man."

"I'd like to talk to your son before I agree to take him on as a client. Privately." Stanton turned to me. "Joe?" I dared to look into his eyes again. I felt like I was falling into their emerald depths. I nodded, cheeks flushing scarlet.

"You do exactly what Mr. Stanton tells you to do, son. I'm paying good money for this." With that command, my father turned on his heel and stalked out, leaving me alone with the man.

"Well," Stanton mused as he circled the spot where I was standing, "your father seems to think you're entirely too timid." He stopped directly in front of me. "Do you think that's your problem, Joe?" Stanton's voice was soft, intimate. He was very handsome.

"I...I guess so." The truth was, I was too aggressive—or wanted to be. If only he knew what I dreamed of doing to the men who populated my dreams. I only held myself in check because I was afraid of what would happen if I let myself do what I really wanted to do.

Stanton folded his arms over his chest and rocked back on his heels. "I think I might be able to help you, Joe. Before we start, though, I want you to take off all your clothes." I looked at him like he'd lost his mind. He just smiled and began to unbutton his shirt. "Opening up lines of communication with your physical side is part of your training, Joe." He tossed the shirt aside and began to un-buckle his belt. He had a dynamite body—well-defined furry chest, sculpted abs, thick, meaty forearms and bulbous biceps. The man was right out of my hottest dreams. I could feel the tingling in my crotch as I took off my own pants. This was going to be a disaster.

"There now, Joe, that's not so bad, is it?" He took off his briefs and tossed them aside. I did the same. His hairy legs were solidly mus-cled, especially his calves. Very hot. "Being naked with other people is perfectly natural. Nothing fundamentally frightening about seeing me naked, is there?" Oh, but there was. Naked, he was terrifying! I couldn't help staring at his crotch. His cock was long and thick, curv-ing out over a pair of fat, hairy balls.

"You've got a terrific body, Joe." He was looking me up and down, a feral glint in his eyes. "Skin like silk. Pumped muscles. Nice cock, too. I can't figure why you'd be timid around any guy you might hap-pen to meet. You're not afraid of me, are you?"

"I don't...I'm not...I guess I'm not afraid of you. I guess I really just don't like to be touched, Mr. Stanton," I improvised, frantic to avoid this conversation. "And...and I don't like touching other people. That's it." That most definitely wasn't it.

"Really, Joe?" Stanton obviously didn't believe me. Neither did I. He approached me, his cock swinging from side to side, smacking against his thighs. When he stopped, he was so close I could feel his body heat. I started to step back, but he gripped my waist. His thumbs pressed against my lower belly, pointing towards my crotch. His fingers curved against the slope of my butt, burning hot.

"I think maybe you've just never been touched properly, Joe." Stanton's hands slid up my sides, thumbs riding over the ridges of my abs, my ribs, up to the full curve of my pecs. I looked down, watched his thumbs rotate around my tits, then press against the thick, ten-der points of flesh.

My prick got hard almost instantly, rising till it was trapped between Stanton's legs. I felt his hairy balls against the shaft, felt his cock, still limp, rubbing it as well. I started to pull away but he held me, his hands like steel clamps against my sides.

"Touch me," he murmured. I obeyed, tentatively at first, then more avidly as I was overwhelmed by the pleasure of it. The feel of his fur against my palms was incredible. I rubbed my hands back and forth over his thick pecs. They were rock-solid, radiating heat and power. I touched his fat nipples and his muscles flexed, pressing the thick points harder against my fingers.

"Pinch them," he whispered. Again, I obeyed. His eyes fluttered shut and I felt his dick begin to press against my thigh. I rubbed my hands down his belly, tangled my fingers in his coarse, curly pubes, brushed them against the swelling shaft of his cock.

"Play with it, Joe." He had one hand on my butt, the other on my prick, stroking it, pumping up and down. I let my fingers curl around his rubbery thickness. I felt it pulse and jerk against my

hand. I pulled my fist up, let the hot cylinder slide against my palm, growing harder and thicker by the second. The head of it was silky soft, moist with sweat and piss, the slit in the tip gaping.

"Put my prick against your belly, Joe. Now, put your cock against mine. Good. Now, put your hands on top of your head and hump." I followed his instructions, grinding my hips against him, my thighs tight against his thighs, my belly against his, our cocks trapped, side by side, between us.

His hands were on my ass and he was hunching his hips as well, sliding his big hard-on up and down my gut, slow and easy. He winked at me, kissed my elbow, then began licking a line down the inside of my arm to my armpit. He nuzzled in the mossy fuzz there, sniffing and licking at me. His tongue trailed over the curve of my left pec, and I felt his lips against the tender point of my tit.

He kissed it, nipped at it with his teeth, began sucking on it, shooting a stream of fire down to my belly that roared up the shaft of my cock. I could feel the hairs on my balls prickle as the two fat orbs drew up tight between my legs. His hairy legs were rubbing against my smooth ones, tickling me unbearably. I pressed closer to him, feeling like I wanted to crawl inside his skin. The shaft of his cock rubbing against mine was creating a dangerous level of friction.

"I'm going to come!" I cried, writhing against him now. I threw my arms around him, held him as my groin muscles began contracting, spraying hot jism between us, making our bellies slippery as glass. I seemed to shoot forever, every nerve in my body on fire, all wide open to the sensation of his touch. I humped until the last shock wave of pleasure had coursed through me, then leaned against him.

He held me tight, still pumping his narrow hips. I braced my feet against the floor, pushed against him, pawed at him, his chest and shoulders, his ass and back, wanting to touch him everywhere, all at once. He shuddered, then went rigid, the veins in his neck and arms standing out like cables. I felt his cock flexing against my belly, then the heat of his jism as it spurted up my torso to my neck. He shuddered again and another spout of his seed pumped out onto my belly.

"Not bad for your very first session," Sam—he told me to call him Sam—had said after we were showered and dressed. "I think I'll tell your father that we need to meet regularly for at least the next few months." He chuckled softly. "There really are quite a few areas where you could use a lot more training."

"Thanks, Sam. I'll be here. You can count on it."

"Oh, Joe—I'd also recommend that you take what you've learned here today and start applying it in your daily life. You might even want to reconsider wrestling. Your father would be pleased—and he probably won't be the only one."

"Yeah?" I was intrigued.

"You don't want to break training, right?"

"No way!" I shook my head vehemently.

Sam smacked me on the butt as he escorted me to the door. "Once you master a few basic techniques, I've got the feeling you'll be unstoppable." I left him and headed over to school to talk to Coach Watson about maybe getting a spot on the wrestling team. After today's session, I was more than ready to get fully in touch with my physical side—not to mention the physical side of any other hot guys within reach—as fast as I possibly could.

Chain Male
By Scott Pomfret

A cluster of Gargoyles guards the door to the club. They are dressed all in black. They have leather holsters to carry their bellies. They are beefy and bald and their eyes glitter. They check IDs and take no shit and wear muscle shirts that say, Obey Me.

Behind a velvet rope, we wait in line outside the club like a line of supplicants at the castle walls. After they accept the price of admission, the club is revealed. It is a revelry, one of a dozen carnivals that litter the night, like a Medieval fair on a wide plain beneath a walled city, open to wanderers, crusaders, and errant knights. The club woos the lonely traveler with electronic spectacle and siren promises and raw flesh. It is softness after the hard road.

But that false sense of chivalry is a deceit. Bandits without honor wait inside. Pockets of men stand in clusters like tents, keeping their secrets— though for a price they'll display the wonders they have looted from far-off worlds.

Languid men droop into place on the long sofas, but I never lose my guard. I wander among the pretty patrons, sampling the merchandise. I never give up my name, as if it is a secret that has the power to undo me, in the hands of the person to whom I revealed it.

The bar is a wizard's lair, where the skinny black boy in a Hawaiian print shirt takes drink orders and remembers them forever. He mixes weird potions and watches out for the bandits who drop unintended roofies in unattended cups. The old dragons who do not dance shovel crumpled dollars on the bar and ogle the younger crowd and demand more grog and breathe fire and remember when they used to turn heads. Their clawed hands find my back pocket as I lean over the bar to order another drink.

The virgin comes into the Club much later than I did. He is perhaps 19, maybe 20. He has been lurking outside gathering courage, waiting for the moment of elevation from squire to knight, waiting for the time to be right. I watch him in the mirror over the bar. As he passes the gauntlet of drinkers and dancers, he acts as if he does not have to choose. His strides are long.

The dance floor seethes like a witch's cauldron. It is a frothing, lawless place, where the flesh parades under a confetti of flashing light. Princesses in spectacular drag flutter softly. At the margin, timid boys like pretty maidens fan themselves against the heat.

The virgin slows, stops, turns infinitely slowly, as if he is being sirened. He understands instinctively that this is his destiny. He turns his sweet ass to me, and he stares. He maintains a careful habit of rocking from heel to toe. He has never seen men coupled in dance; he has never watched a man kiss another man. He thinks: Is this allowed? Should I be here?

He concludes, I am safe.

Fanlike nervous gestures emanate from his hands and spread all over his body, seeking loose ends. He produces a couple of glow sticks. He has obviously been saving them up for tonight. He breaks them with a quick, short violence that is erotic, and out of the violence fire grows in his hand, flutters, breaths, expands, flutters some more. The fire becomes two quick butterflies mating around his head. And then the music takes control, nets and captures them, and trains the boy's movement to its own ends.

His ramrod posture dissolves into liquid. The movement draws me to the rail that skirts the dance floor. I take a place next to the predators, who survey the fresh meat from the raised dais, the highest point, the castle's turret. Their rapacious gazes are boiling oil poured down on the dancers below.

A pouting, shirtless boy with perfect pecs flits his eyes at me. They cross me, hold me, the disco ball turns in them, and then they go dead. A gargoyle passes close to check the marked hands of an underage kid who carries a drink he should not have. The gargoyle is a dark shadow, a cold mist off a Scottish loch. When he is gone, the heat rises again, shrouding the virgin in the snarl of flailing limbs. I am patient; I wait for him to struggle free, to come out.

The virgin flinches at the first hand that touches him. His avoidance is graceful, like a vine twisting its way up a trellis pole. He is light, agile, seemingly oblivious. Yet concentrated in his body is complete self-awareness, wielded like a weapon, powerful and pulsing, as if he is standing outside of himself, next to me on the dais, and also watching himself dance.

Next to him wrestle two short boys of identical build who are identically dressed in baggy Structure x-pants and oversized white T-shirts, cut narrow beneath the tight latissimus. Chains glint at their necks. They maul each other. Their hair is cut short and clean. Their foreheads glisten.

Watching them, the virgin surrenders to the hands that want him. Someone approaches him from behind, and grinds his groin against the virgin's ass. His hands flutter along the virgin's shoulder, under his whirling glow-stick arms, to his chest. In front of the virgin, a worn 40-year-old in the clothes of someone half his age twists to his knees. (He will regret it tomorrow.) He presses his face against the boy's crotch, miming fellatio to the techno beat. His eyes are half-closed in a pose of ecstasy.

It is a joy to be wanted, the virgin thinks. It is the very first time. He has never before been wanted, physically, intensely, never like this. The floor beneath him explodes with light. Other men sense that he is available and close in.

I feel no jealousy. I get off on the old men wanting him, as he gets off on being wanted. I have no fear of losing him to the trolls because on some deep, mystical level I have always known he is like me, a comrade-in-arms, a brother, a warrior, of the same generation and tribe, a squire, a page, a knight-in-training. He is me a short two years ago.

I trail him to the basement below the dance floor. It is a dungeon; the walls are painted black. Teeth and eyes have purple magic in the ultraviolet light. The men's room reeks of ass. In one stall, a four-legged beast, trapped, heaves and groans in its cage. A frantic boy has dropped his pants and totters about the room, bound at the ankles, laughing, offering himself to whomever will take him. The Gargoyles come for him, cover him, and carry him out.

Boys come in, boys go out. Money passes, then one of the old dragons from the bar is on his knees. He has become a groom, a valet, a faithful servant, servicing the boy-knight who took the money. Friends block the Gargoyles further entry. The dragon grips the boy's pale ass until it bruises, taking the whole cock in as if he were a starving serf scavenging bread cast off from a carriage into the road, the leavings of young kings.

The virgin is wide-eyed at the urinal; he cannot pee; he cannot look away. The dragon gets lower, opens wider, his mouth is a cave into which the boy's nuts disappear. The dragon rolls them around like a set of dice, strokes the hard hidden shaft all the way to the ass, slicks his finger, presses, the boy gives off an obligatory moan and no one can tell if it's real. The court jester, a short ugly Jewish boy in Buddy Holly glasses, cracks jokes about the old man's health, his heart rate, and the likelihood that anyone would be willing to give him CPR.

I ambush the virgin outside the men's room door. Thrust him against the wall, kiss him hard. His chest strains up against me, his heart seems to come out and flog me, he defends himself as best he can. Then, at the moment I was going to release him, he nearly pokes my eye out, grabbing the back of my head, and thrusting his tongue into the open wound in my face that is my mouth. I bite gently. I drop slowly. I am in the barnyard of his armpit, nipping the cherry-pit nipple through the shirt. He groans. The groan is quite real. His sweat is the froth from a cauldron. His hips are handles.

Then the DJ's voice summons us to battle. He announces the contests, the challenges, the jousts, the will of some unseen king.

The virgin considers the invitation. By that time, he has been in the Club an hour or more. He knows what he wants; he has sloughed off the old men like a dead skin. There is a moment of brief fear as he wavers; it hasn't occurred to me that he might turn me down.

He does not turn me down. He has seen something in me. Some intimation of the destiny I felt earlier. He trusts something in me, wants something in me. His eyes do not leave me. They have not strayed over my shoulder to someone prettier. They have fixed on me, they have appointed me a worthy opponent. They have booked me for the night. It is a matter of ripeness. It is an appointment arranged by the gods.

The music is louder and faster, the lights are brighter and more urgent. On one side of us, the short, muscled, white T-shirt boys are sucking face. The pretty pouting disdainful boy has found a better match; he is dancing, he is complete. His eyes flicker over me, stopping proudly to demonstrate the partner he has found to show me that he has settled for nothing but the best. I forgive his arrogance; it is erotic and necessary; it is no longer against me, as when he had nothing but still rejected me; it is with me, in solidarity, it says: We all find what we need. He pays tribute, nodding at the virgin, who is at my side and very hot.

The exchange of glances is a gauntlet thrown down. The virgin peels off his own shirt. His wrists become bound over his head, until it seems he is suspended by his arms, or a set of thumb screws. He matches the pouting boy pec for pec, nipple for nipple, 6-pack for 6-pack. His ribs are a basket, his belly a loaf of fresh bread into which I drive my thumbs to release the steam. My touch dissolves him in laughter, and he leans against me, momentarily legless. His cock stabs me.

Then he loops the shirt around my neck like a noose or a garland, and leaves it there. He runs his hands over his own body, touches his shoulder, his nipple, passes over the rippled belly, plays at the band of his boxers. His eyes are on me, watching me watch him, as if he is taking instruction. There are a hundred hands now. His chest heaves and that breath also seems a hand, kneading and plumping him, filling the flesh. The sweat that runs from the V of his neck between the pecs and into the belly is also a hand. The lights play all over him. And then my hand is there too, unbidden, on the collar bone, cupping the shoulder as if it were a breast, inexorably dropping, dropping, dropping. To the waistband, a line of hair, a dew of sweat. Shaping him, transforming him, effecting a change.

There is no laughter this time. He presses against me, he trembles, he does not own his hips. My hands work around his back, under his boxers, on the two cheeks that move with the music. They bunch, escape me, and then come back. My eyes meet his eyes, and his do not drop. They enter me, wound me, dodge, feint, then strike again, eye to eye, blow for blow, strength matched to strength. And at our side the white T-shirts cling to one another, and the proud boy undulates like a long slow river, and the heat rises, and voices crow, and the pulse pounds my heart into something new and impervious, impregnable and hard, a shield, a mighty weapon.

All dancers are warriors. Gay warriors. Battle-tested, synchronized, born to watch one another's backs. To stand tall, to hurl lances, to slay beasts, to sing poetry that makes the sky weep. We are indestructible. The world quakes at our coming. The virgin will soon be in our ranks.

It is easy to believe. The dance pit is a jousting ring. The warriors are deep in the fray. Young, strong, pretty, proud. Bellies that are a tangle of writhing snakes; hair dyed to the color of electricity; hands and wrists armored in a chain mail of silver thumb rings and hammered bracelets; defined, hard, in mutual contest, straining one against the other, heaving against one another and yet on the same side, the same team, all at battle peak.

When last call sounds, would that there were some challenge for the virgin to accept with his brothers, some gauntlet to take up, some grail to find. But there is none of these. The enemy is flitting and elusive, so we fight among ourselves, practicing our martial arts, because we are dimly aware, even here, even under the protective pulse of this safe haven, this bounded arena, that we must toughen for the long haul, questing, alone, out in the hostile world.

Afterward, we spill out of the club and ransack the streets. There is a party. The boy comes willingly, without fear, without coercion, hungry and cocksure. His pride is his greatest weapon. He thinks he knows all there is to know. He thinks he is already one of us. That his training is done.

This time, we have left the timid behind. There are none but warriors at this roundtable, none but the young and proud, with stiff cocks and raging blood. The virgin's eyes consume the sumptuous feast. Clothes are shed, strewn to the side like armor. We resort to purer, Grecian contests, the greater tests of manhood, the barest, rawest, most basic contests of man on man, with neither accouterment nor shield, but only the natural armor of our own hearts.

I lie back and instruct him to sit on my face. He crouches. I slide my finger into his ass and spread it. I touch, taste, lick. Eat him out ferociously, lapping like a dog, biting, thrusting, sucking, teasing with the tip of my tongue until his stink is spread all over my cheeks.

When I'm done, he vows, "I can't do that to you."

I pet his shoulder as if I understand. His arms are rubbery.

"I could never do that," he insists.

I make him take it back. I instruct him that he should never shrink from a challenge. I remind him how sacred are a warrior's vows. I give him the battle skills that he needs. And the minor props he should carry: lube, latex, and a sense of abandon, a sense that finally he is among his own people. And in a moment, I am proud: His face is deep in my buttocks, and he performs like a champion.

I am on all fours, still teaching, always teaching. The virgin abandons my ass and steps around in front of me. He kneels solemnly. My mouth closes over his mushroom tip. His hands close around the back of my head. Behind me, another warrior has taken the virgin's place. His hand finds and plumbs my ass, testing my depth, my resilience. A breath relaxes me, both cocks enter me, one on each end. I am infinitely capacious; I believe I could take in a world of cocks and each one make me stronger.

"Fuck that ass. Fuck that ass," the boy says without jealousy to the warrior behind me. The boy's hard stare enters me as the cock behind enters me. The boy bends, his belly wrinkles, my head bobs, his lips brush my ear. Something runs down my neck, from my ear down the knobs of my spine over the bubble ass, runs a message down to the cock that enters there, that frays my ass-lip, and jostles my kidneys.

Warrior, the messenger says, we have battles ahead.

Hackles raised, goose bumps pricked, the boy is harder, is arched, is straining, is willing himself not to be defeated. My hand closes under his package. His sack is like a leather pouch in which a shaman keeps his secrets. My finger finds his ass again, returning thrust for thrust. The virgin's nut draws up as he approaches his climax. The virgin pulls his cock free from where it's buried to the hilt in my mouth. He issues a cry of triumph.

"How much do you want it?" he asks. "Tell me how much you want it."

Spit or swallow is a metaphor for life. You can treat everything as bitter, but then you'll go hungry. You've got to force yourself to like hot jizz, force yourself to put your tongue in places your old self would not have dreamed; you force yourself until the gesture is no longer forced, but part of you. It becomes an appetite, and then you are strong. And so the virgin becomes a warrior, thus so he is dubbed a knight, blooded, daubed with the thick chrism that comes from cock.

My orgasm obliterates the world. There is nothing but a bare moor left, no watch kept in the castle's dark tower, the fires have burned low, breezes rush around in the corners, stirring and collecting shadow and running home again.

I wake much later in a pile of bare limbs. I am the first to stand among the bodies of my naked comrades. The dream is intact; the warriors are fallen. I kiss the virgin, who is now a knight. I take a shaky step, alone, into a sharp, new morning. I will never be defeated.

Side Effect
By R.W. Clinger

Let us sit back and critique this subject for a moment. Do not rub anything more than the side of your head in deep thought. Keep your analogies and subject matter as straight as possible. Focus now and listen...

I'm very good at critiquing, because I have to be. I teach freshman composition at an all-musky male school, and I'm forced to use a red pen to correct vital errors, produce young and charming writing spirits out of unessential, moderately unbound boy-minds. My victims are usually 18 or 19 years old. I prey on them, adore them, feed off their errors with ease. I stay up late-late into darkening, emotionless hours and read their every fiery written passion. I'm a wordy slave, if the truth be known: Professor Lethargic. No kidding.

This story isn't about now, though; it's about a young man who was adorably Black in every sense of the word, was not very keen on word usage, and came to me for help. And this story is about critiquing. The beginning starts about five years ago, when springtime caught up to the end of the semester, when young men began to run around shirtless and nipple-hard on campus. They wore those skimpy see-all shorts that were about as snug as the African-male lovemaking gods, Nika and Sulu, who can be found pressed together in the warming, come-covered jungles.

The young gent that I speak of was named Emanuel Faulk. A delicious and supine creature with intimate, caring blue eyes. Manny, as I reluctantly named him, was not the genius or carver of great words. He was only 17 when we first met and when he spawned interest in passing my class, since he had a solid D. The D, of course, meant determination to succeed in my vast, worldly mind—or delectable, dainty, and distinct.

Our visits were utterly too short, but dreamy for me. I had spotted him at the beginning of the semester. My thoughts craved the need to touch his dark skin within my brown dancing fingers. I wanted to suckle a virgin nipple on him, press his young head into my splendid crop of Kenya fineness, and have Manny gobble up every inch and morsel of Professor Lethargic's immaculate beauty. But this never occurred. Yes, all throughout the heated semester Manny left me perplexed and disgruntled as I sat with my balls tightly pressed inside sweaty inner thighs, clamping my eight-inch erection against my solid, lined, cocoa-colored chest, listening to his words of hope and need to pass my so-called excruciating(!) class.

Our last visit came just before school let out. He sat bare-chested across from my reddish-brown desk. A football rested in a firm hand. His pecs were wide and solid, slick with glazed, edible sweat. I counted his abs with meticulous care. Our glances clung together for a few seconds. Then he directed his view at my...own chest, maybe looking at my tie, maybe comprehending that Professor Lethargic had a woody building inside his Jockeys. I pulled my glance away, desiring immediately to pinch his nips with teacher's ease. He had been running, and his flat chest rose and fell, rose and fell, like the visions of our bodies clinging in my shameful mind.

I couldn't bare to see him struggle with words, I confess now. I wanted to be unbiased and give the dashing God something wholesome, a real chance to (plunge his long, red, slithery man-tongue into the back of my bookish throat?) survive.

"I'll pass you, dear thing," I uttered with simple enchantment, one hand pressed against my sweaty, frivolous brow. I felt his blue mesmerizing eyes tickle the base of my nervous spine and workable buttocks. I felt his smile against the nape of my back—large and beaming-white, thin-lipped and kissable—making a professional like me...succumb to grace him with a generous C.

"Thank you," he uttered, smiling, pressing his firm, football-tossing, breast-holding hand into mine. Manny naïvely said, "I'll repay you some day. I promise."

As he left, I wondered if I would see him again. He would never make it in college. The world was tough. Not everyone was generous like P. Lethargic. I hoped he wouldn't get eaten up. And if anyone was going to eat him up, devour him, I wished it were me.

"Good-bye, Manny." I found it easy to blow a gentle kiss in his direction, but he was already gone.

Let's critique for a second.

There are four rules in teaching young, hot guys:

1. Be fair.
2. Never look a stud(ent) directly in the eyes.
3. Do not be touched by a stud(ent).
4. Do not touch a stud(ent).

I was fair with Manny, I think. I broke rule number 2 with ease, though, because I looked him in the eyes on that last united day, leaving me want to slip over his 10-inch of coal-colored niceness and have him squeeze some of his ivory-white student juice into my...

And, of course, I broke rules number 3 and 4 too.

Shame on me!

B-a-a-ad Mr. Lethargic!

Listen more...

Three summers had passed rapidly. I woke one early morning from a dream about Manny Faulk sucking my cock head dry, repeating with come spilling out of the corners of his mouth, "C, C , C, C, C, C, C." I ran that dream off, enjoying a fine sweat on my well-toned biceps and dark chest. Naked, I swam privately in my pool, long strokes, continuously for hours, having my dangling brown balls glide with me underneath a watery world. Usually those wet moments of slick aloneness made me grow hard and harder, enticing a teacher like me to come into the pool with chlorine-colored explosion, but that didn't happen on this day. It seemed as if I wanted to carry the dream out (like foreshadowing in a composition paper). I wanted to save my precious white, hot spew for a certain time later—and a certain handsome someone.

By evening I ate alone and drank a single glass of red wine underneath the June, July, August stars that I had named after all of my most handsome, exuberant male students: Marco, Lamont, Tanglo. Manny was one of those stars too. I became the silent professor, diligent in my quiet. I was happy and unchanged by time...until another visit aspired with Emanuel Faulk.

It was unintended, this second visit. I did not search the now 21-

year-old boy-man down, investigating his every intricate move. I did not stalk Manny, hunt him down, threaten him with my lined cock dangling before his shivering mouth. What transpired was spontaneous—out of the African god's hands, even. Simple actions in a perhaps needy sexually frigid time. It occurred a few evenings after I had dreamed of Manny and his delicious cock. It had happened...

There is this larger-than-large bookstore across town that I frequent often. Barnie's Books. It's made up of three levels (of course, constructed in an old, refurbished barn). The third level is designed with narrow, book-lined passageways and is a dusty tomb of male-on-male books and had the privacy to match. While visiting up there, if you are lucky, you may retrieve a pretty boy's phone number or smile. These narrow passageways permit one to glide a richly masculine back against that of a stranger's. Elbows could bump in some type of literal dance. Lips may sometimes caress luxurious, brilliant skin, like a shoulder or cheek or neck. It's not a dirty place, but rather romantically kind to the silent fag or peaceful queen.

Yes, I was involved in the pages of a delicious piece of fiction inside the attic room. James Baldwin was tucked away up there inside my craving hands, and I was totally immersed with a charming, ancient copy of Giovanni's Room.

Usually I stand still, consumed by the literature around me. After reviewing titles and copies of some unpopular, naughty fiction and gay-toned classics, I pick a book off the shelf, browse through it, see its worth, become interrupted by a moving, handsome body beside me (about six inches away from me), and say hello to the six-foot African god. I maybe wink at him or allow his nice hands to travel up and down one of my muscularly built shoulder blades. We share generous hellos, and then I pass along with wanted purchases, happily.

I was hooked into Room when I heard Manny's familiar voice beside me, looked up, and saw his dark, unchanged, and splendid face again. He simply said, "Professor Lethargic, is that you?"

I blushed. Of course, blushing on a dark man isn't that easy to see, but I did blush, and I think Manny knew I turned a different, beautiful shade of cocoa.

It was the last place I believed to run into him. I couldn't possibly imagine how a football-playing hunk was interested in literature. These thoughts became easily erased, though, because my inquisitive eyes began to scan Manny. He was still delectable, dainty, and distinct. Manny's smile was broad and all teeth; I've always liked men with large smiles. His caring blue eyes twinkled like the night stars that I had named. His chin was dotted with the familiar dimple that I had so wanted to press my tongue into and utter chants like something out of Mali in Africa. His shoulders were broad and massive-looking, tucked nicely into a skin-tight white T-shirt. My eyes passed over every bump and line on his well-formed chest. I counted his abs again, like only months before; unintentionally licked my lips. My eyes darted quickly down to the man's massive lower torso. Manny's blue shorts were too tight, sporting a well-defined package that allowed me to think for a brief moment: He pushes some kind of side effect into me.

I was at first surprised to see him in the upstairs part of Barnie's Books, but that willowy sort of feeling vanished easily. "What brings you here, Manny?" I asked.

I wanted him to say "man sex," "cock-craving," or "rim job." I wanted Manny to become dirty and intentionally undignified. I wanted to watch him strip off all his sexy, needed-no-more clothes, and dance meticulously with our chests pressed together in Brotherly fineness. I wanted him to push me against one of the bookshelves, facefirst, and have my moistened, tender lips drag across a well-used, tiny paperback called Do Me More Favors as Manny did his man-job from behind me with every scheme to hurt and please P. Lethargic.

The side effect offered dribbles of saliva to caress the edges of my lips. I licked the upper one first, then the lower. I listened to Manny's delicious answer: "Rumor has it that a boy like me can find something fun up here."

He was making my solitary place dirty...but I didn't mind. Manny just corrupted a sweet, pleasant place in an upstairs attic room with slim books and passageways. I answered softly, closing Room, "And what kind of fun did you have in mind, Manny?"

I should have never asked that question for two reasons. One: I was still his former teacher and easily stepped over my boundaries as a professional. And two: Manny, I realized for a brief moment, was too pretty for me, too model-perfect. His eyes connected with mine, but that was the only connection I believed or told myself that we would share. Granted, I worked out. I had the chiseled-perfect chest and biceps. I looked good for my educated age. But Manny...he was divine in every way. He was richly masculine in all the right places, destined to bed the hottest brown dudes in the world. He was out of the teacher's league, I figured. And I was OK with that.

"Don't I owe you something?" Manny whispered, blinked.

Side effect-ness again. I felt woozy. I felt as if I could lean into him, because I would eventually fall and strap my thin arms around his cord-lined neck, plunge my tongue down his red throat and suck face with Manny for the next half hour. Instead I swallowed Lethargic juice, sighed heavily, smiled back, kept my eyes tucked away into some kind of boy-man or student-teacher package with him. I simply answered, despite feeling completely flushed and out of place-out of mind, in a pompous, arrogant, rather domineering tone, "You owe me everything, Manny."

Then...he smiled back, giggled slightly. I didn't think he would have ever giggled like that with a female companion. I didn't think that sissy-slippery giggle would have exited his fine lips with his foot-ball-tossing pals. It was a teacher-student giggle that uttered playful need all through it. Lethargic need.

After that smile and questioning giggle was shared, rule number 3 got broken. Manny quickly moved forward, tilted his head slightly, dove for the arch of my neck, and placed one firm, intended kiss to the fragile nape. His right hand clamped on to my left hip as he whispered, "I followed you here, Lethargic. Keeping my eyes on you. I always keep my promises."

He dashed away before I could say anything. I still felt his untamable lips on my neck. I felt his breath inside my ear, teasing me. My legs wobbled, and it was then, immediately after I watched his large, splayed back vanish into the day, that I fell into one of the shelves of books. I sat with my legs spread apart on the floor. One knee bumped a book called Ready for You Now. Shaking all over, breathing in a quick shift of motion, I thought how appropriate the title of the book was. Maybe I was willed to lead Manny into a sense of being dirty with me. Maybe I was ready for Manny to cash in his promise. I breathed quietly, and patiently I waited for him to return and to begin a long, enchanting process of African queer love, with Manny Faulk sucking on my hard, popping knob in my vulnerable khakis.

I had other errands to run. I didn't return home until later that evening. It was too hot, sticky, and unclean. Every inch of my colored skin was limp and malleable. I thought of Manny all afternoon, that sudden, heart-pulling kiss. It was probably one of the better kisses I have ever shared with a man. Manny seemed so innocent but so experienced at the same time; that's what that single, delectable kiss produced in my stimulated mind.

Once at home, tucked away from the city, I put Black Jazz on the stereo, showered, shaved again. Tucked away in a summer robe, evening allowed me to reach for a single wine glass, and evening also allowed me to spot something large and beautifully Black floating in my outside pool. I snatched up two wine glasses instead of one and walked out to greet Manny Faulk.

Of course, he was naked. I saw his long stems, his flat stomach and chest. I noticed (almost immediately) his long cock, which was stiff and looked generous. I listened to him add to the sensual, sexual scene, "I've been watching you for a long time."

I wanted to tell him that he didn't have to talk, that I was all ready for his payback. I was no longer soft and malleable. Every muscle on my body was tense and hard. My heart pounded within my chest with unstable nervousness.

"Bring the wine, come in, and join me."

A dream come true. I listened, dropped the robe to the side of the pool. He said I was handsome and looked ready to handle a student like he. I poured two glasses of wine, carried them into the pool, handed him one. He gulped it down quickly, kissed my lips before I could even touch them to the glass I was holding. He pulled at one of my nipples with his free hand and chanted, "Why don't I show you some of the literature I know?"

I didn't argue with him, breaking rule number 4.

The wine glasses were somewhere. My robe was lost. We stood in aqua-blue pool water up to our waists. Manny shoved his tongue down into my throat, pulled on nipples, cupped my luscious balls in his hands. He whispered, "This is what I owe you, isn't it?"

I said "Yes" because he did owe me.

"I won't stop until you get enough."

I pulled away, felt dizzy from the wine or Manny's intrusive touching. I whispered with a lethargic, beaded smile, "I hope you don't." Then I touched his countable abs and nips, sucked on Manny flesh with the greatest potential. I felt my hard rod slip against his. I felt the two of them dance and linger for the longest moments, gliding together with warm, summery water wrapped around their extended, fleshy bodies.

"Follow me."

I did. I wasn't about to argue or contemplate or meander in deep thought about right or wrong. All the rules for teaching had been broken with this singular, divine student. Everything from that moment on was going to be nasty and dirty, completely unprofessional...but fine too.

We waded through the water to the edge of the pool. As Manny collected protection, I sat on the side of the pool with a rock-hard cock touching the top of my naval. I peered restlessly into the glimmering, dreamy pool and thought: Manny's a legal drug.

He came back to my side, kissed both nipples, touched the head of my mushroom-shaped man probe and whispered, "Time to be dirty, professor."

I thought: Time to be dirty, roll around, back pressing against concrete and swimmer's towel...time to Ready for You Now and Do Me More Favors and tongue down my throat again, something finding my nips and my own delicious abs, my mind splitting into two equal halves as my dark ass splits into two halves with the same tongue that was just down my throat...time to dance to Black Jazz, have Manny's fingers inside me, spreading Prof. Me wider and wider and wider...

His words: "Breathe now...one big breath."

Our eyes snagged onto each other's.

I thought: He's between my legs, and I can see his fine body above me, willing itself to enter me. Manny is a god that I have adored. He is every man that I have loved, swept up into one body. He is my stalker, my student, my lover, my friend, my new companion. He whispered for me to close my eyes and listen to him, move with him, feel his hot steel rod enter me, leaving me in deep, penetrating thoughts, critiquing this direct moment in masculine time:

The African god, Tika, has bumped into Me, cock inside hole, international literature being accomplished here, promises being kept by the summer pool, nipples touching, swollen hearts and cocks beating, men doing one of those naughty-dirty tribe dances together, push and grind, all the Black Gods in Africa dancing together, Tribesmen of the jungles in love, Baldwin witch doctors, Giovanni's Wet-Dew-Come-Covered Room, lost in Africa, inside Africa, red, yellow, green...

"Please," Manny moaned from atop his own plateau of gay erotica, pumping and pushing inside literary me.

I opened my eyes and watched glistening sweat dribble down his perfect cheeks and defined chest. I listened to Manny huff and pump and grunt like some unknown jungle animal along the Senegal River in French west Africa. I felt Manny blasting into me, pushing student meat into me, holding my thighs apart and then touching my slick, moistened, erect jism rod with both hands.

As he spread me apart, I whispered in delight, "I should have given you an A in my class."

He chanted back in his methodical, reassuring measure, "I'm the teacher now...you'll pay for errors," pushing harder, willing my cock with his free hands, spreading Professor Lethargic apart.

Then, both of us dizzy and confused, he pulled out of me, ripped the condom off and tossed it aside. Manny leaned into me further, pressed his slick ass stabber against my shaft. Kissing African cocks. With his right hand, he grabbed my left hand and placed the two hands against the two kissing cocks. Pump, rush, pump; hips moved uncontrollably and 10 fingers mixed with the flesh of the student-teacher cocks.

I imagined we were in the jungle again. I saw tropical plants with unfamiliar names. I saw tribesmen naked and surrounding us. It was one giant, Black circle jerk. All of us were coming together, stroking and chanting, jungle music playing, drums and wood being beaten by worthy hands, pounding and pushing, a tribesmen orgy in my mind. I thought of one of the books I might have found in Barnie's attic, Witch doctor's Circle, and couldn't hold back anymore, couldn't keep my eyes open anymore, couldn't help from pumping and thrusting my body into Manny's hand.

"Comi," I thought he whispered, some African word that I didn't understand, but it was really "come" that he said. Again I listened, feeling African rain splatter over my fingers and on my chest as Manny chanted in his ancestral manner, spewing on me, spewing with me, covering my dark skin with white bubbles of majestic tribal ooze. Dancing together. We arched backs and thrust one last time together. Spew flowed like white, creamy rivers in my mind that I had imagined. We pumped jism wildly, allowing it to mix over our hands and in our dark pubic hair. We huffed and flinched, pumped and moaned. Man love. Divinity. Sex-end.

With promises kept and shared, all the rules of the teacher broken, I was exhausted and spent. I watched Manny write his tribal name on my chest with our mixed spew: tika. He kissed my lips and my neck and whispered, "Will you swim with me now?"

As he backstroked out into the pool, I sat up with international, white come dripping over fingers, stomach, chest, and stiff rod, feeling compassionate and dizzy, bonded to him. I felt out of my pink mind and perfectly content. Softly I whispered, watching him, adoring my Black Tika and young scholar, "Absolutely," as I slipped into summery water.

The Hot Nine at 9:00
By Derek Kemp

Iknew it was him the moment I heard his voice. I was dialing through stations on my car radio when, out of nowhere, there he was. He said, "Let me hear you beg for it," and that was enough for me. It was like something out of a dream, like déjà vu. My cheeks suddenly flashed hot, and my cock started to swell in my pants. I closed my eyes and tried to focus on his demand: Let me hear you beg for it. I sucked my tongue and tasted a plea forming there but didn't put voice to it. I knew he couldn't hear me.

Almost immediately a young girl took up his request. She whined "Please, Max," and I instantly hated her. Her voice was high-pitched and annoying, her plea pathetic. I thought she should have had to work harder to win whatever prize Max was giving away, but Max let her off easy. "Please what?" he gently teased her. She started whimpering, "Please, Max, I'd do anything to win those concert tickets." She put extra emphasis on the word anything, but I didn't think she had a clue what that might mean to a guy like Max. "Oh, really?" Max purred suggestively. "Are you sure about that? Anything?" The heavy hint of sex in his voice gave me the vapors, but the girl seemed utterly insulted by his dallying. "Yes, anything," she defiantly declared; she wanted those tickets no matter what it cost her. Fortunately for her, Max was smart enough not to test her limits. "Well, don't sweat," he said. "This one's easy. All you have to do is tell me what station is your choice for the hottest hits." Like a cheerleader, the girl suddenly perked up. "Ninety-nine, K-POW," she said enthusiastically, with the station's call letters coming out at as one word. Kapow! Like in a comic book. Biff! Thwack! Kapow! Her fizzy answer was immediately followed by a sharp crack of thunder, then a canned station-ID tag. Kinda gimmicky, I thought, but also easy to remember.

As Max went on to introduce the next song, I picked up my new cell phone (a freebie from my latest employer) and dialed the number for local information. When the operator came on, I turned down the volume on the radio and asked her for K-POW's number. She gave me two options: the station's office number or its request line. I figured it would be easier to reach Max on the request line, so I chose that one. But every time I tried the number during the next few minutes, I got a busy signal. It was exasperating. I started wondering if I should have asked for the station's office number as well when I noticed a gas station's glowing neon sign about a quarter mile up the road. Surely they would have a phone book I could borrow, I thought, but when I got there the kid sulking behind the counter said, "Sorry, somebody stole our phone book."

I was briefly disappointed by such a ludicrous theft, then it hit me: The kid behind the counter was drumming his fingers to the beat of a familiar song. It was the song Max had started playing when I first pulled into the gas station's lot. So I asked the kid, "Is this K-POW you're listening to?"

He nodded his head eagerly: "I listen to it all the time." Even better, when I told him I was trying to find the station, he said, "That's easy. I know how to get there. It's not far from here, maybe 20 minutes or so." I quickly scribbled down the directions on the back of a paper bag, then hastily left to resume my quest.

When I got back to the car, Max was on the air plugging the Hot Nine at 9:00, K-POW's nightly countdown show. "There's not much time left," he warned his listeners. "If you want to hear your favorite song tonight, you've got to call me and get your request in." I looked at the clock. The digital readout said 8:27. "Yeah, right," I mumbled to myself, "like anybody could get through." Still, I picked up the cell phone and hit redial again. To my surprise the line started ringing, but Max didn't answer right away. He left me hanging for a good 20 minutes—plenty of time to think back to the night we first met.

That was at least 10 years ago. I was 18 years old at the time; Max was about 30, maybe 35. We met one weekend night at a roadside rest area on the highway between the state university and my parents' house. A college freshman, I was on my way home to visit Mom and Dad when the urge to take a piss suddenly came over me. I stopped at the rest area with nothing more than relieving my bladder in mind. I was naive then; I had no idea how cruisy rest areas can be. As a matter of fact, I didn't even know then what the word cruising meant, but Max clearly did. From the moment I walked through the door, he had his eyes on me. When I first noticed him he was standing in front of the state highway map and had this screwed-up look on his face like, Can you help me, man? I'm lost. But I couldn't stop; my bladder felt like it was going to burst. I quickly scanned the room to see if there was anyone else who could help him. The place appeared to be deserted. I was the only other person there, so I tilted my head at him and gave him a signal to follow me into the bathroom. I figured I could give him directions while I was standing there peeing. Nice, huh? Completely innocent? Little did I know, he had something other than directions in mind.

Almost from the moment I pulled my dick out, I felt him standing uncomfortably close to me, just behind me. For a brief, panicky moment, I thought, Oh shit, he's got a gun. He's going to mug me. But then I turned around. Instead of a gun he had his dick in his hand, and it was huge. He tugged on it slowly and pointed its dribbling eye at me. For a long moment I just stood there, slack-jawed, staring at it, thinking, My God. But then reality sank in. I realized we were in a public building. This was insane. I didn't want to get caught by someone or possibly even arrested, so I turned my back to him and tried to focus on peeing. Just do it, I tried to tell myself, just piss and then run for your life. But I couldn't piss. I was too nervous and deliriously scared.

Sensing my distress, the man finally spoke. "Looks like you've got a problem there," he said, his voice low and gravelly.

I shook my head stupidly and stammered "N-n-no." I almost wished I could crawl down the urinal drain and disappear.

Then he smiled at me; I could feel it, warm and kind, against the back of my neck. He said, "Just relax, pal," and his voice was so friendly, so soothing; it felt like fingertips pressing against my spine. Then he started humming, or murmuring, really: "Hmm...mmm." I closed my eyes and concentrated on the slow cadence of his breathing, those subtle mmms, then my dick twitched, and suddenly I was pissing. It came out in a torrent, hot and seemingly unending. When it finally stopped, my shoulders slumped; I felt weakened. The man behind me whistled. "Holy shit, kid," he said. "You been holding that back for days?"

Again I slumped and leaned back a little. The man put a hand up to steady me, and the heat of that first touch dissolved any further reluctance I had to turn around and face him again. He was handsome, I thought, in a rugged, older-man sort of way. He was tall and well built, with dark hair and scruffy stubble. Our eyes locked—his wet, gray eyes were utterly mesmerizing—and he lured my gaze down to his dick, which was enormous. I'm not kidding. It was at least nine inches and obscenely thick—a work of art. He gave it a few proud strokes, then asked, "You ever seen a dick like this?" My mouth watered; I shook my head. His stroking—long, languorous squeezes from base to tip—made me think of a cake decorator squeezing a tube of frosting, which in turn reminded me of my father, a closet cake decorator himself. How many times had he let me eat the frosting right out of the tubes? It was our little secret. My father would always warn me, "Don't let your mother know I let you do that." My mother didn't approve of him indulging me with sugary treats, but that never held my father back, and I absolutely loved him for it. My father was the first man I ever fell in love with—not sexually, just the idea of him, a generous man. After him there was Mr. Thompson, my ninth-grade gym teacher. Then a long string of muscular high school jocks. But over the years I'd never acted on any of those desires. I'd been too frightened. I was still a virgin.

My stranger—that's what I called him for 10 years, until I heard the girl on the radio call him Max—asked me, "You ever sucked dick before?" I thought about how I'd only thought about it, and gulped: "No." His question frightened me, so I took a small, reflexive step backward. "Well, there's always a first time," he said and stepped forward, pursuing me. Again I stepped back—one, two, three steps—and bumped into a stall. I looked back to see what I'd run into. "Not here," my stranger said. "Somebody might come in." As if I'd been trying to find us cover! I opened my mouth to protest, but he put a finger to my lips and pushed it in a little. I licked the tip and tasted the saltiness of him. Then he pulled it out and said, "Follow me." He reached down and stuffed his dick back in his pants, then walked out the door.

For a moment I was gripped by panic. Don't do it, the reasonable side of my brain tried to tell me, just run to your car and head for home. But the taste of his finger lingered tantalizingly on my tongue. It tasted like a promise of more where that came from. And my dick was hard; I didn't even notice until I had to struggle to push it back in my pants. I knew I was starving for some kind of experience, some lightning-rod moment that would change my life and push me out of the closet. This had to be it. I took a deep breath and zipped up my pants. Then I walked through the door and followed him outside.

I half-expected my stranger to lure me into his car, to drive me somewhere private, like his apartment or a motel, but instead he walked across the parking lot and waded into a small, lushly wooded area that lay on the other side. He disappeared into the brush like a phantom, so I quickened my pace and honed in on the spot where he'd vanished. Although it was dark, I had no trouble finding him. A narrow, well-worn path guided me through the foliage to a large open space where my stranger stood waiting for me. He seemed to know the place well.

Shaking with nerves, I tried to be funny. "You come here often?"

"Often enough," he responded. "Now, why don't you get on your knees." For a brief moment I didn't know what to do. My throat tingled, and I lost my sense of equilibrium. I couldn't help wondering, Is it safe for me to be here with this man? But it suddenly hit me: I wasn't scared of him; his anonymity was actually a turn-on. The only fear I had was of getting caught.

"Shh," I whispered, admonishing him. "Someone's going to hear us." I got down on my knees.

He seemed startled by my silly rebuke, but didn't pay it much mind. He just stared at me, then slowly his scowl softened into a dirty smirk. He stepped in front of me, his crotch in my face. "You want this?" he asked. "You want this dick?"

That close to him, I could smell the saltiness of his flesh. "Yes," I hungrily moaned, my voice husky with desire. I leaned forward and nipped at the fabric of his jeans, then licked it and felt the thick pulse of life pounding beneath.

He tilted my head back. "Let me hear you beg for it."

Almost choking on my own desire, I managed to sputter, "P-p-please."

Playfully, he stepped back a few paces and crooked a finger at me. He wanted me to come after him.

Like a baby going for its bottle, I started crawling. "Let me suck it," I moaned. "Please. Let me suck that cock." I licked my lips and started growling. I felt like an animal driven by instinctual lust.

After a few more steps back, he stopped and sighed. "Fine," he said, feigning reluctance. He was a masterful tease. "Maybe just a taste."

With my lips just inches away from him, he pulled down his zipper. Oh, how I remember that sound, the staccato chatter of metal teeth. He pulled out his dick and rubbed my face with it, and that surprised me. My cheeks tingled, and I could feel the blush. My entire body erupted with gooseflesh. I stuck my tongue out to catch a taste of his dick, and when it finally skidded across my tongue, it was not enough. My taste buds sprang to attention, demanding more. I chased his dick, struggling to get my lips around it. When I caught it in my mouth, I started sucking. I worked my tongue over and under it but refused to let it go. I was afraid he wouldn't let me have it back. I tongued the shaft and tickled the head, tasted his precome. I swallowed and drooled and gave my stranger the best blow job I could muster.

When he suddenly came I was reminded of my pissing. His load seemed unending, bloating my gut. I swallowed every drop, but still it wasn't enough. I wanted more. I wanted him to fuck me. My asshole twitched with need. But it wasn't to be.

Out of the blue we heard a sudden squawk, a cop car's siren-a highway patrolman. He must have seen our cars in the rest area's parking lot and gotten suspicious when he didn't find anybody inside.

In a panic I jumped up and worried aloud, "Oh shit. What do we do?" I pictured myself in a police station trying to explain things to my parents. But my stranger was calm. "Don't worry," he said, and casually zipped up. Then I heard the crackle and honk of a nearby walkie-talkie. The cop was coming up the path. Frantic, I looked at the trees around us, trying to find some place to run, but my stranger put a hand on my shoulder. "Be quiet," he whispered. "Don't say a word." Then he reached into his jacket pocket and pulled out a length of chain. Just as the cop discovered our hiding place, my stranger started making kissing noises. Smooch, smooch, "Here, Dolly," he called and crouched down, as if he were calling a dog.

The cop sneered in disbelief. "You fellas lost?"

My stranger shook his head. "Just my dog, officer. This guy here was helping me try to find her."

The cop rolled his eyes at us. "That so?"

"Yep," my stranger confirmed, then turned back to the trees and clapped his hands. "C'mon, Dolly," he whined, "I haven't got all night."

To, I think, everyone's surprise, there was a sudden jingling noise and a rustle of leaves, then a tiny yip. A moment later a small puppy came charging out of the bushes. "Dolly!" my stranger said, beaming as he scooped up the dog in his arms. "You bad dog," he baby-talked to her as he scratched her under the chin. "Daddy better not get a ticket for you being off your leash."

The "daddy" part set me off. I started laughing; I couldn't help it. A trained dog? Both the cop and my stranger looked at me. My stranger looked panicked; the cop just looked amused. He smiled at me, "Looks like you're off the hook." But I didn't take his hint. I just stood there looking dumb. Then, a bit more forcefully, he insisted, "You can be on your way now." In other words, dismissed. I knew from the look on his face he had something other than a simple slap on the wrist in mind for my stranger, but I felt powerless to help. "Thanks," I said, wishing I could come up with something to get my stranger out of there, but my mind was a blank. Finally I turned around and skulked off, but before I was out of earshot I called over my shoulder, "I'm glad you found your dog, mister." I didn't know his name. What a fucking shame. "Thanks, kid," he called back, and that was it. A legend was born. My sexual die was cast.

Needless to say, I spent the next several years making many unnecessary trips home to visit my parents. Every time I did I stopped at that rest area and walked down that same well-worn path, hoping that maybe I might find my stranger waiting there to fuck me. But I never did. I finally gave up looking for him after a few years. I graduated from college and moved away, ran through a series of jobs, then I got the call for a job in Max's hometown. Again, it required a move to a new state, a new place I didn't know, but I didn't mind. I've planted very few roots in my life; I'm not a sentimental guy. But that man—my stranger, Max—is one of the few things I've ever regretted leaving behind.

"Ninety-nine, K-POW," a voice said from the receiver.

Bolting up, I pressed the cell phone to my ear. "Max?" I asked, just to make sure; I hadn't been listening closely. Was it him?

"Yeah, this is Max," he said, a little impatiently. "Do you want to make a request?"

I didn't hesitate. "Yeah, Max, I want you to fuck me."

"Uh—" he started to say, then paused.

"I'll even beg for it."

Finally he said, "Listen, I don't know who you are—"

"How's Dolly?" I interrupted.

"What?" he asked. "Who?"

"Dolly," I said, "your dog. Is she still alive? I haven't seen her in ten years."

For a long moment the man was silent. I started worrying that he might hang up on me. What if it wasn't him? What if I'd made a mistake? Then he asked, "Who is this? Do I know you?"

As casually as possible, I answered him, "You'll see. I'm an old friend." Then I hung up. A quarter mile ahead of me the aerial warning lights on K-POW's transmitting tower blinked like a Morse-code beacon. It seemed to be saying, Come and get it. I hit the gas.

Max remembered me right away when he opened the station's door to let me inside. "You're the guy I almost got caught with by that cop," he said without prompting, and I was heartened by his remembering that night. Still feeling bold, I quickly asked him, "Are we alone?"

Max looked over his shoulder, as if to make sure there wasn't anyone there, then nodded confidently. "No cops tonight."

"Good," I said, and lunged forward to kiss him. He hadn't changed much over the years, aside from getting a little grayer, which actually turned me on. He was still a model of pure masculinity—muscular and strong, butch and fit. He was so completely a man, it drove me wild.

To my delight he met my kiss with equal fervor, then steered me back into his studio control booth. When we finally came up for air, he put a finger up to his lips and instructed me to be quiet, then flicked on his microphone and introduced a song. While he did that I scanned the machinery, marvelling at the multitude of knobs, switches and flashing meters. I looked at the walls, which were covered with promotional posters and glossy photographs. On the back of the door there was a collage of Polaroids, all identified with hand-markered captions. Most showed K-POW staffers with touring musicians, but in the middle was a shot of Max with his dog. The caption read "Max and Dalí—Partners in Crime," and that made me laugh.

Max came up behind me and embraced me around my waist. "What's so funny?" he asked, pulling me close. I pointed at the photograph: "Dalí's a he?" Over the dog's white nose was a dramatic Daliesque wisp of black mustache; the name made sense. Max nuzzled against the back of my neck and growled, "Mm-hmm." I was instantly reminded of the night we first met, when he stood behind me at that urinal, murmuring "Mmm" to help me pee.

"I thought it was Dolly," I said, and arched my back against his hard body, "like Dolly Parton." Max chuckled. He pushed away from me and said, "Oh, man, you're cute. I want to fuck you right now, but I have to work." I pouted suggestively and that seemed to inspire him.

In a blur of motion he set to work, utterly amazing me with his technical prowess. From the moment I knocked on the door to K-POW's studios to the start of the Hot Nine at 9:00, Max had about five minutes to get everything carted up and ready for broadcast. In that brief window of time, he gathered up the top nine CDs and stacked them in descending order, then went back to the phones and recorded various listeners announcing each song. By the time he shoved the cartridge in for number nine and pressed play, I already had his fat dick in my mouth.

Max leaned back in his battered vinyl swivel chair, the soundboard controls an arm's length away. I was kneeling on the floor between his legs, almost hidden beneath the soundboard desk. It seemed like I was hiding, trying to conceal myself and the sexual act I was performing, and that only helped to make the experience seem more naughty, more furtive, like our first adventure in the woods—except that this time there wasn't much chance of our being caught.

Still, my heart was beating like stuttering drumbeat. I felt so wicked. A tear on the arm of Max's swivel chair was held together with a shiny bumper sticker, and the logo read 5in. it took me a moment to equate 5in with "sin." Ah, yes, I thought, feeling debauched. No doubt about it. I inhaled deeply, and the fragrance of Max's sweaty pubic hair filled my nostrils. The salty taste of his flesh overwhelmed my senses until I felt light-headed, my brain popping fizzily like a freshly opened bottle of champagne. I couldn't get enough of Max, of his cock. I gorged myself on it as if it were a long-lost family recipe, found now, years later. It tasted sensational.

Then Max leaned forward an inch or two and pushed in the cartridge for number 8. I heard a teenager recite the song's title, then Max pressed play. A swollen drumbeat thudded around the room and seemed to fill it. I felt compressed by it, felt Max's abdomen pushing down on the top of my head as he slowly turned down the volume a bit, but I never let his cock fall out of my mouth. It was a prize, all mine. I didn't want to let it go.

Max leaned back and put his hard, strong hands on my head. He guided me down, down, down. I sucked and swallowed, and let him control me like a maestro conducting an orchestra. He twined his fingers in my hair and pulled me up. "Lick my balls," he instructed, and for once I felt no anxiety in letting his cock go. I obeyed him, basting his ball sac with saliva. A moment or two later, he let go of my hair with one hand and turned his chair a bit; I followed. He reached out and strained to shove in the cartridge introducing number 7. Again a teenager's voice filled the air, but I paid no attention to it; it sounded like white noise to me. The number 7 song followed, then, a few minutes later, a prerecorded string of commercial breaks, followed by number 6. Max managed each cartridge and CD like a magician, with a minimum of motion—sleight of hand. He stayed put, letting me do what I was clearly meant to do, and only lifted his hips once when I reached up to pull his jeans off. Then Max spread his legs and arched his ass up so I could have easier access to his humid asshole.

For this, I got off my knees. I crouched down so my butt rested on my heels. I held onto the chair with one hand and used the other to probe Max's hole. Each time I pulled a finger out, I sucked on it greedily, then I leaned forward and wiggled my tongue deep inside of him. Max groaned with satisfaction and writhed in his chair. He had to struggle to pop in the cartridge introducing number 5.

As the song waned and Max leaned forward to segue into number 4, I stood up to shuck off my clothes. I pulled my shirt over my head and Max let out another satisfied murmur. I looked at him as I slowly kicked off my shoes and stepped out of my chinos. Max was leaning back in his swivel chair again, naked from the waist down, his dick standing up, hard in his lap. He gave it a few lascivious strokes, then reached up to slowly thumb open the buttons on his shirt. He pulled it off, and I felt myself suddenly grow harder watching the muscles in his shoulders and arms flex as he dropped it to the floor. Then he leaned back again and motioned me forward. He pointed at the digital timer on the number 4 CD. "I've got two minutes and 37 seconds before I have to introduce the next batch of commercials," he said. "Get over here so I can get a quick taste of that dick of yours."

I quickly obeyed. I stepped up beside Max and he leaned over the arm of his chair and instantly swallowed my dick—every inch of it. I lifted my hips forward, then shifted back on my heels. I slowly fucked his mouth, even though there were only seconds left before he had to say, "And now a word from our sponsors." His tongue and cheeks languorously caressed the shaft of my dick like a warm, gentle sleeve, and my whole body shook from the pleasure of it. It was a struggle for me to say on my feet.

Then it was over. Max suddenly let go of my dick and pulled his microphone toward him. He flicked a switch and babbled in DJ-speak. I didn't hear a word of it. I kept my eyes closed and let my imagination keep going. Then his hands were on me, exploring every inch of my skin. He tweaked my nipples and felt the taut musculature of my neck. His fingers roamed down my back, as he counted aloud, backwards—"Nine, eight, seven, six, five, four, three, two, one"—and then his fingers were digging between my ass cheeks. I bent forward and let him explore the throbbing heart of me. I don't know when he did it; somewhere along the line Max reached back and popped in the cartridge for number 3, then he was back in my ass, digging and stretching, moaning huskily, "Yeah, what a nice, tight hole. I can't wait to get inside of you."

I felt my heart lodge itself in my throat. I would have begged him, "Now, now," but Max was already a step ahead of me. Reaching back again, he popped in the cartridge for number 2, then grabbed me by the hips and guided me down onto his lap. He pulled me back so we were facing the same way. As his cock head nudged its way between the twin mounds of my ass checks, I felt my asshole clench tight in protest, then suddenly give way. Max blew out hot puffs of air as I slowly slid down the length of his massive dick; I felt his warm breath pelting my back as if he were trying to melt my spine and turn my body into jelly, a more accommodating fit for his massive cock. Then it was done; I had him inside of me, all nine inches. I started to ride him, slowly, eagerly, up and down like a horny carousel horse.

The swivel chair squeaked under us and groaned in protest. It rolled on its casters—back, back, back—until Max put his feet down and inched us forward again. Number 1 was coming up, and we were too far away from the desk. Then it was time. Max stood up, moving me with him. His cock never fell out. He bent me over the desk and pulled the mike toward him.

"OK, folks," he said. "You've been waiting for it, now here it is." And then he pushed in the final cartridge. Another giddy teenager announced the number 1 song, a sweeping love ballad from the current box-office champ, and then Max started the CD. Over the opening strains of the song, Max said, "And after that, stay tuned to K-POW for Dr. Sex." I let out a guffaw; Max's body tensed. "Thanks for listening," he blurted. "This is Max Bundy. I'll see you tomorrow night." Then he flicked off the microphone and playfully swatted me on the ass. "You little brat," he chided me.

I laughed again. "Dr. Sex?"

"It's a national call-in show," he said, "for sex advice. Maybe we should call him and see what he says about sexual partners who don't take sex seriously."

I stood up and reached back to cradle his head in my hands. I turned my head so he could suck on my tongue, then when our lips parted, I said, "I seriously want you to fuck me."

Max needed no other prodding. Placing a palm against my back, he bent me over again, then started pummeling my ass. I watched the little lights on his console blink and imagined them as seismographic meters measuring his powerful thrusts into my ass. My tender hole felt raw and utterly used; his cock was like a rigid piston. The light meters were all blinking maniacally now, so I reached out and turned up the volume knob I'd seen him turn down only minutes before. The ballad was now in full swing, its orchestral swells and dramatic vocals filling the room. I closed my eyes and constructed a mental picture of the music, an animated crescendo, vividly colorful and luridly throbbing, and as it reached its climax, Max did as well.

Pulling out of me, he hosed my thighs with thick blasts of come, then I came too. I pointed my dick down and heard the splatter of liquid as it rained down on the floor.

Max slumped back in his chair and pulled me down in his lap again, this time so we could face each other. He kissed me hard, tugging on my tongue and chewing on my lips, then he suddenly pulled back and said, "Hey, you didn't tell me your name."

"No, I didn't," I said, grinning at him impishly, "just think of me as your stranger." And I left it at that.

Revelations
By Dante Williams

Today is the day the world ends. I crawl out of the rubble, not knowing how I survived. The building I used to work in is a pile of jagged stones. I push away the last pieces of debris and stand, expecting to see the sun. Instead, the sky is a reddish black. Before me, Wilshire Boulevard is a torn-up memory. In the middle of it, a grungy Labrador gnaws lazily at the arm of a dying woman. I stumble forward and chase the scavenger away only moments before the charred woman takes her last gasp of air. The city is the image of hell. My skin feels hot. My stomach hurts like I've had too much to drink. I wander out into the chaos. Los Angeles is a maelstrom of rubble and fire.

I remember yesterday or the day before that. I can't quite tell. I was at a sex party in Venice. There were almost thirty guys there. Nine of them were on the bed with me. I was on my hands and knees getting fucked, pressed against another guy getting fucked. Some guy's nuts were in my face. He pushed his cock in my mouth. Men were all around me getting fucked or fucking or sucking cock. We were drunk. A little stoned. I remember having one of those moments of clarity. I remember thinking, briefly, in the space of time between one guy shooting into a rubber up my ass and another guy suiting up to take his place, that I was what one would call a sinner, a true sinner, not the kind of sinner that people think they are because they can't be perfect, but a true, unapologetic sinner. I lived for sin, for sex, for drugs, for whatever kind of vice I could find to help me forget the daily tortures in my life. I was ungrateful, unrelenting. I was the kind of man that populated Sodom, and now the world has been made brimstone. I can't help but think that it is all my fault.

As I walk westward, toward the beach, I feel a sense of elation. I grin and laugh. It's euphoric. I'm alive. I'm walking. I'm intact. Everything has been destroyed, and I'm still here. Endorphins rush through me. I expect to feel despair, but I don't. Being human is such a strange thing. Even in the midst of desolation, I feel joy. I keep walking in the shadow of scarred and burning hills, and it isn't long before the feeling fades, letting loneliness set in.

At a recent brunch with some friends, we talked about the state of the world, about whether or not our conflicts in the East would result in war. I remember how jovial my hosts were. They were an older couple living in Hancock Park. Their flat was beautiful, and now it's probably leveled, their collection of paintings destroyed, their adopted daughter Patricia incinerated like everyone in that part of town.

I look at my bruised and slightly reddened skin, at my dirty and torn clothing, and imagine that I should be grateful that the weapons of our enemies are not as powerful as our own. I can't be grateful. I had known Doug and Randy since I first moved out here to go to college. They were my friends. They were kind. They introduced me to people, to things, showed me all the best things that a homosexual could be.

I have a hard-on and I don't know why. Narrow survival does something strange to the system. I picture a man on his knees, sucking my cock. I walk, thinking about the millions of tiny bumps on his tongue and the way they feel when experienced as one collective surface sending messages through the nerves in my dick to my glands, to my prostate, to a place in the center of my brain, my hypothalamus, my cerebral cortex, up in the front, the region responsible for the way things are. I picture the man, his young face, his golden, blond, no, maybe auburn hair. It falls in his face. I twist my fingers in it, clinch it in my fist. I twisted my fingers in it. It was another time. I fucked his mouth, felt the back of his throat, shot a load on his face, and he let me, jacking his own cock until his spunk covered the floor. Where was that? When was that? It's all gone. I can't believe it's even happened yet.

I walk for hours. Somewhere in Santa Monica, I see an old man pacing slowly around a black patch of land that was probably once his lawn. He looks everywhere for something that he knows is gone. Behind him, the burning remains of his home lie scattered and mixed with the remains of other homes. He looks to me. His eyes are sad, reflecting loss. My eyes must look the same. There's a depth to his eyes, a fathomless depth the likes of which I've only seen on television. "David," he says weakly, not to me, just, "David," again into the vile air. I figure it out. This is where his son once lived. I feel it. Everywhere there is an overriding sense of pain. It comes from him, from me, from all of the unlucky ones left wandering around this wasteland. I feel the pain inside as if we are all crying, and my eyes stay locked on the old man's misery as I walk past, but I don't stop for him. I keep walking and he keeps crying, "David," because we both know that we cannot help each other. Our bodies sense it—the inevitable—and I have my peace to find, and he has his.

I really tried to have a boyfriend once, but it didn't work. I didn't really try. He was caring, fun, handsome, perfect...even sexy. I always wanted something new. Now, I imagine that I can't complain. There isn't anyone that I can feel loss for. I have no name to give to God, no name to cry out into the emptiness. I remember the last night we slept together. It was about two weeks before we officially broke up. I coupled with him slowly, because I really did love him. I entered him from behind, his entire body pressed into the mattress, his thighs slightly open, his ass slightly raised. My whole body slid against his as I pushed into him, my left hand cupped around his chest, my right hand trapped under his hips, wrapped around his dick. I fucked him romantically, biting gently into his neck. He came in my fist and I released my semen into the latex between us. When I fell next to him after cleaning him with a towel, I looked into his eyes, said "I love you so much," and realized that I could never live that way. He never said, 'I love you,' back. He knew. I knew. Neither of us knew where we would be in just two weeks.

Eventually, I cross what used to be a park and climb down the rubble of the ramp that leads down to a shattered Highway 1. Like all the roads I've seen, cars are piled up and bodies are everywhere. Roaches crawl across charred skin. I move through the wreckage and reach the beach. Patches of sand have fused and look like impure glass. I walk carefully and see dead fish, sea lions, even dolphins littering the shore. I think I see the sun behind the sludge-like sky. It must be 3: 00 or 4: 00. I look around. The human bodies here are really cooked, having been totally exposed when the warhead hit.

I was here a few weeks ago, enjoying the sun—not here exactly, somewhere further north, the gay section at Will Rogers, near the Friendship. Ginger Rogers; we called it Ginger Rogers. The boys were beautiful. It made me proud to be gay. I'd lie in the sun—one perfect boy in a sea of perfect boys—and, on occasion, I'd sit up, look around, and think, Dear God, I never want to be anything else.

I sit on the beach. To my left, a great black skeleton still burns. It used to be the pier. My best friend's mother used to bring us here when we were kids. His name was Chris. We used to boogie board together. It was so crowded then—so noisy. There used to be so many radios playing so many different songs and so many children screaming as waves hit them that all I ever heard, when I came here, was noise. It's quiet now, deathly quiet. So much so that the pun, the cliché seems unimportant. All I have here is the quiet, the waves, regrets, the surprising vision of someone walking down the beach.

Shortly before she died, my grandmother said to me, "Looking back, I only regret the things I didn't do." She was right, even though she was not the one who first coined the phrase.

I stand and walk toward the advancing man. As he gets closer, I recognize him. I don't know his name, but I've seen him before. This city once held ten million people, and it always amazed me how much like a small town it was, if you were lucky enough to be gay. He gets closer and I can see the dirt on his clothes, his face, bruises, despair in his eyes. We keep walking toward each other, and instead of stopping in front of me, he keeps going as if he were a ghost, oblivious to matter. His arms close around my waist. His head touches my shoulder. I hold him. He cries.

I dream about him, holding him with my eyes closed. I could kiss him, take off his clothes, my clothes, lower him to the sand, kissing him, holding him, fucking him as if this were our last day on Earth. It would be like that movie, The Living End, concluding on a beach, one guy with a gun down his throat fucking the other, raping the other because they had AIDS and no future. When he came, he pulled the trigger, but the bullets were gone. Their story ended without freedom or hope. This scene is even bleaker. At least he had a gun and the never-to-be-fulfilled fantasy of coming with a bullet in his head.

I hold my stranger and watch the sun drift down, the ocean looking red and murky like the dome above. "It doesn't hurt..." he says after awhile, "...anymore." "I know," I say. "We're going to die," he says, "aren't we?" "Yes," I say. I move his blond bangs aside and kiss his forehead. "You're thinking about sex," he says. "Of course," I say. "Aren't you?" "Why?" he says. I kiss his forehead again. "Because," I say, "it's the only good that I have left."

I think about all the guys I fucked. All the parties I went to. All the nights out. All the orgies. All the drugs. I wonder if it was worth it. I wonder if it still means anything. At those times, I told myself that the memories would last forever. Now, I'm not so sure. The memories seem so distant, and I haven't even died yet. Maybe it's because there's no longer any reason to hold onto them.

We sit down next to each other on the sand. The waves creep closer as we stare forward. I think about the last guy I dated. His name was Damien. I look out at the destruction of the world. The irony amuses me. I used to jokingly call him Satan's kid. Once, we even played "Omen" in bed. He was the Anti-Christ, and I was his naive and innocent cousin, like the kid in the second movie, only older. He tempted me, made me sin, made my soul his, forever. It was a fun game. I remember being on my knees while he fucked my mouth. He said such evil things. I really felt possessed. It all seems so sad now. Next to him, it would have been a blessing to die in bed. Now I regret not making things last for just two more weeks.

I look out at the ocean. So much of it is dead. I wonder where the Beast is. I look for him. I wait for him to rise out of the ocean with his seven heads. I look for the Dragon. I look and wait. I look and wait, thinking that they're supposed to show up here.

The boy next to me kisses me and pushes me down by rolling on top of my body. His breath is strong and pungent, like my own. He kisses me with a passion I've never felt. He kisses me and opens my shirt. His hand brushes a bruised rib. It hurts like hell, but not in the way I'm used to feeling pain. It hurts, but the pain is distant. It's like the feeling is there, but I'm incapable of interpreting the feeling as being unpleasant. This new pain feels good, and I kiss him back, pulling off his clothes. "I have to have you," he says, straddling my chest. When I open his fly, his hard cock juts out toward my mouth. I lick it, smell it. The scent is strong like his armpits, like my whole body. I suck his cock, smelling the sweat and the grime. It makes me feel driven. I fill my throat with his cock and I lick at the head and swallow the whole thing again, getting a good whiff of his nuts.

At a party just a month ago, some guy was talking about pheromones, about how some link between the human hypothalamus and receptors in the nose. His obsession seemed strange. At the time, I called it just a leather thing. At the time...

It's just a leather thing.

My stranger stands and takes off the rest of his clothes. I pull off my shirt, shoes and pants, feeling the warm, wet sand beneath my feet and ass. He kneels in front of me and swallows my cock. It's already hard for him, and he pushes his mouth down until his lips touch my pubes. "Smells strong, doesn't it?" I say. I run my hand along his spine until I find a bruised scar just above his ass. I caress it with my middle finger, and he moans around my cock, pulling off to let out a deep cry. He looks up at me and I touch the scar again. He tenses and gasps. His body shakes. I can see the precome leaking from his cock. I kiss a bruise on his neck. He moans. "God, I love you," he says. I look into his eyes. "God...I love you, too." He smiles, straddles me, and sits quickly on my cock. I gasp as his warm bowels wrap tightly around my skin.

I've never fucked a guy without a condom. I was born to that generation which only knew how to fuck latex. I'd never felt a direct connection. It feels warmer, slimier, more intense. I can feel more of the body heat, more of the soft, giving flesh. He fills his body with my cock and I think about how truly deep inside of him I am. What we do now is so forbidden. We learned never to do this out of respect for life. Now, as his ass rides my cock, I have more respect for his life than I have ever had for anyone else's. He is such a magnificently beautiful creature. His body is like a statue, his mind containing depths that no other living being could ever see. It is like he is an elaborately carved box with a golden padlock and no key. Everyone in the world could marvel at his beauty and still never know what secrets he contains. And he is mine. I am the one inside his body, giving him one of the few gifts that makes being human worth the pain.

I think that I love him. He is all I have left that can be loved.

He lifts off my cock and kneels between my thighs, gripping my ankles and lifting my legs until my asshole is exposed. He spits on his cock, spits on my hole, and plunges into my depths. It hurts but doesn't hurt. He starts fucking me immediately. He pounds into my ass, saying, "I've never fucked anyone as beautiful as you."

My head spins. No. More like swoons. It's like I've been doing poppers. My body tingles as he fucks me. I close my eyes, letting euphoria wash through me as if the ocean carried pleasure inside its foamy waves. He fucks me, and I lie back feeling the wet sand on my back. The ocean splashes against my ass, his ass, his feet. I taste salt in my mouth, on my upper lip. I wipe my hand beneath my nose and look at my fingers to see the blood. "Dude..." he says. "Don't..." I say. "Keep fucking me!" He does. It's good, I think. He understands what's going on.

He fucks me harder and harder, small, warm waves advancing up the beach, between his legs and into my ass every time his cock pushes deep inside. "Fuck me!" I shout, and I picture two-thirds of the world pounding inside my ass. "Fuck me!" I shout again, and he keeps thrusting like a wild horse. "Cum in my fucking ass," I command. "I want to feel your fucking spunk shoot inside my ass!" He thrusts and pistons and erupts, grunting, filling me with warm jizz, his whole body becoming one rigid flesh machine buried in my bowels.

"Oh fuck," he pants, letting his cock gush out of my hole. I feel the come spilling out only to be washed away. "Sit on my cock!" I say, and he straddles me again. His hole slips around my cock as he sits down. I look at my feet, his toes digging into the sand. He bounces up and down and my cock begins to tingle more and more. I feel dizzier and dizzier, and another soft wave slaps my nuts and hole, and that's enough to make my cock erupt, spitting out millions of sperm, each of them carrying my tragic DNA, my only true potential in this world.

He collapses on top of me, breathing heavily. I hold him as he pants, his warm chest heaving against mine. I hold him until our hearts return to normal. I feel my semen dripping out of his ass onto my crotch. The ocean washes it away. He rolls down onto the sand next to me, still clinging to my body. "Maybe we should get up and get dressed," I say. "Maybe we can find food." He opens his eyes and looks at me before giving me a kiss. "I'm not hungry," he says. My head still swims. "I want to go to sleep," he says. "But, what about the tide?" I say. "Make sure the dogs don't get me," he mumbles. I hold him and listen to him gently breathe.

I regret the things I didn't do.

I feel the tide against my legs and sides. It somehow seems less cold. The sun fades, but I can't see stars. I close my eyes and listen to the waves. It feels so peaceful. "What's your name?" I ask. "I want to know your name so I can find you in the afterlife." He doesn't answer. My limbs feel numb. I notice that he seems much heavier. I no longer feel the rising and falling of his chest. I try to pull him tighter against me, but my arms don't respond. My hand rests quietly on his shoulder. I think the waves have reached my neck. I open my eyes. It takes forever. The sky is dim. The sun is gone. I can only see a few stars through the haze, but they suddenly seem so bright. I hear something. Helicopters. They're getting closer. I can almost feel the sand swirling up around me. I can almost feel it, the sand, the wind. Almost. The world. The whole, beautiful, insignificant world.

Karma
By R.J. March

Micah sipped his coffee; the heat of it hurt his tongue, which he'd apparently injured the night before while eating out Kelly's ass. He could see Kelly now, facedown, legs spread. Kelly had a smooth little fanny that appealed to Micah, a young man's rear end: blemish-free, peach-fuzzy. His balls spread out between his thighs like something spilled, easily slurped up and rolled about in Micah's mouth—but only one at a time because of the size of the things. Nothing boyish about them or his prick, with its horselike dimensions. Pink and straight, with a network of blue veins coursing under its surface, it had a downward point, a beautiful helmet.

"Mikey," Dick Jones barked, startling him and causing him to spill some coffee. Dick laughed; Micah didn't.

"You had this dreamy look on your face," Jones said. "You know how the Gland is about that."

"The Gland is playing golf with some du Pont." A brown stain spread across a report Micah had just finished. This, oddly enough, wasn't his day. Despite the awesome ass-licking, butt-fucking time he'd had the night before, this day was shaping up miserably. It was pouring when he went out to start his car that morning, only to find it wouldn't.

"Not the wrestling lover, I hope," Jones said.

"She might like wrestling," Micah responded. "I didn't receive a profile."

"I didn't know you had a brother," Jones said, pulling tissues from a box on Micah's desk and dropping them on the spill.

"I don't have a brother," Micah muttered.

Dick's mouth squirmed to fight a greasy smile, his hand going inside his gray flannel vest. His white shirtsleeves were rolled to the middle of each forearm. He had the upper body of someone who crewed the Delaware. Micah glanced away from the oar-hardened wrists and sneezed.

"Getting a cold?" Jones said. "Out in the rain without your rubbers?"

Micah looked up, making his features dull, feigning incomprehension. Jones sighed.

"Oh, Mikey. No ear for irony."

"I told you about that 'Mikey' shit, didn't I?" Micah said, blotting up the rest of the coffee.

Jones rolled his eyes. They were that strange contact-lens blue, but natural, his own. He looked through glasses that looked borrowed from someone named Fritz. His blond hair was cut short to combat a natural kink and underplay a slightly receding hairline, which Micah secretly found attractive.

"So who was your celestial twin?" he wanted to know from Micah. "I seriously thought he looked like your brother."

"My ride this morning?" Micah said. "Friend of mine." He waved the report to dry it, giving himself the air of a coquette with a fan. Dick grabbed the fluttering papers.

"Sometimes I think I don't know you very well at all," he said. "Print up another copy of this, Micah, that's all you have to do."

"What do you mean?"

"I mean, open up the appropriate file and click on the print icon, for Christ's sake."

"No, I mean about not knowing me very well."

Jones looked at his watch.

"I've got a lunch meeting in fifteen," he said. "What are you doing after work?"

Fucking, I hope, Micah thought, his mind running through his "good excuses" file and coming up with a wake for a dead aunt—why, he didn't know. Easier than explaining Kelly, he figured.

Jones regarded him drolly, looking very close to shaking his head admonishingly.

Micah had met Kelly at the gym. Kelly was the chiropractor's assistant on duty when Micah turned his head sharply to check out a wagging bob in someone's shorts. He was all but crippled immediately. Instant karma, he thought, carrying his head crookedly to the back of the gym. "Pinched nerve," he grimaced, pointing to the back of his neck.

Kelly jumped out of his swiveling office chair and bounded over to Micah like he was a code-blue emergency. He led Micah gently to one of the rooms in which the doctor manipulated bones.

"I'm not licensed to do anything but give you ice," Kelly said, his voice deep. He wore spandex shorts and a cropped T-shirt—typical gym gear for someone in as good a shape as he was. But can I trust him with ice? Micah wondered, trying to check out the boy's basket. His damned nerve throbbed, preventing inspection.

"Dr. Glenn will be back soon," Kelly said. He wore a name tag that made his T-shirt swing, its sleeves long gone, his pesky, pert nipple popping into view every now and then. "Would you like to lie down?" Kelly asked. His red hair was combed back with gel, just long enough to flip up in back. There were freckles running across his arms, his shoulders. Is his dick freckled too? Micah wanted to learn.

"I've got two or three fused vertebrae," Micah said, pointing again to his neck.

Kelly brought an ice pack and placed it with care on Micah's neck and came around, squatting before his patient. "Does it help?" he wanted to know. His legs were spread, and the heavy wad in his skintight shorts became Micah's focal point.

Micah nodded as best he could.

He left the gym with the ice pack and Kelly's number, feeling like a smooth operator despite the odd tilt to his head and the shooting pain that made him see stars.

He dialed Dick's extension.
"Yallo," he answered.
"My car's not done yet."
"Can't your, um, friend drive you?"
"He's at work," Micah told him. "Never mind. I'll call a cab."
"What about your aunt's wake?"
"Canceled," Micah said.
"Canceled? They canceled a wake?"
"Hang up, I'm calling a cab," Micah said.
"Like hell you will."

There was an accident on 176, and traffic was stopped dead. Dick put the car in neutral and popped in the latest Dave Matthews Band CD. "This guy's gay, isn't he? I think he's gay."

"How the hell would I know?" Micah snapped. He hadn't any plans for his evening, but he never thought he'd be stuck in a car with Dick Jones. He wouldn't be so obnoxious with his mouth closed, Micah thought, or biting a pillow.

"So why'd you lie to me this morning?" Jones asked. "Don't you like me anymore?"

Micah looked at his clasped hands in his lap. "Look, I'm sorry," he said, unable to come up with anything suitable to follow that up with.

Jones shrugged. "I'm callused, buddy, don't worry. No feelings to worry about since that nerve-ending removal. Hurt like hell for a little bit, and then—nothing. Haven't felt a thing since. Just ask my wife."

"How is Candace?" Micah asked, putting his shoulder to the window.

"Gone," Dick said, taking his hands off the wheel. He laughed. "Our first anniversary is next week."

"Jeez, I'm sorry," Micah said, feeling like an ass, and for some reason he remembered a dream he'd had that morning in which the roof of his house was gone and it was raining like hell. It started to rain in real life, drumming the roof of the car like anxious fingers. Jones switched on the wipers, but there was nowhere to go and nothing to see. He turned off the engine. "I'm low on fuel," he said, and then, "So who's the guy?"

"This morning?" Micah stumbled. He was not comfortable talking about his personal life at work—those were two worlds he did not like to overlap.

"And last night," Dick said. "It's none of my business. I'm just interested lately in people who are enjoying a healthy sex life. I'm simply making idle conversation."

"We're no longer idling," Micah said.

"That is subject to debate," Dick said, then added, "So what's he like?"

"Are you sure you want to know? Why do you want to know? When did you suddenly become bi-curious?"

"I've always been curious. I watch the Learning Channel."

"His name's Kelly. He collects grenades."

"Hand grenades?"

Micah nodded. "They're nicely displayed, though."

"No doubt," Dick answered. He sat quietly for a while regarding the view through the rain-streaked window.

"What happened at home?" Micah asked.

"Are you sure you want to know?" Dick said, turning, fixing his blue eyes on the knot of Micah's tie. He shrugged. "The usual, I guess. Candace collects grudges. She remembers every shitty little thing anyone's ever done to her."

Micah said nothing, keeping his ill opinion of Jones's wife to himself. "You all right?"

"Oh, I'm just fine," Dick answered him with a fake smile.

They picked up a six-pack close to Micah's house. "Just wasn't working," Dick said, scratching himself. His shoes were off, and his tie undone. Micah sat across from him trying to be a good listener, trying to maintain eye contact. His gaze tended to drop down the stretched-out length of the man before him, though, and he'd find himself unaware of what Dick had been saying.

"You know what I mean?" Dick said, breaking Micah's concentration.

Micah nodded slowly.

"You're a good friend," Dick said, leaning forward, obscuring his crotch.

No, I'm not, Micah thought, I'm a fucking pig, so lean back again, because it makes your crotch look like a mountain in those trousers.

Micah held up his empty bottle. "Another?" he asked.

Jones made an iffy face. "What about your plans?"

"No definite plans," Micah said. "I'll call him later. Anyway, he's working."

"What's he do?"

"He works," Micah said, stalling, "in a gym."

Dick nodded. "I thought I saw deltoids this morning."

"He's a chiropractor's assistant."

"Is that anything like a dental hygienist?"

"He's really sweet," Micah said.

"Again, no doubt," Dick said, rolling his blue eyes.

Dick looked at his watch, then looked up at Micah. "Hungry?" he asked. Micah shook his head. "Me neither."

The beer was gone, and they opened a bottle of gin somebody had given Micah for Christmas. "Mixers?" Dick asked.

"Diet Coke?" Micah offered.

Dick shook his head.

Micah found some reconstituted lemon juice, so they drank the gin on ice with squirts from the plastic lemon.

"You should change," Dick said.

"I thought you liked me the way I am."

"Your clothes, I mean," Dick said, not impatiently. "I like you fine the way you are."

"I like you fine," Micah returned.

"You should get out of your work clothes, though. You look like you're at work."

"I wore these to work today," Micah said.

"Go change or something," Dick said.

"OK, all right," Micah said, getting up and making his way down the hall to his bedroom. He was feeling more than a little buzzed—he'd skipped lunch and now dinner, and the alcohol was feeding on him. He stripped down to his T-shirt and boxers, humming the Dave Matthews song he'd heard in the car. He stood in front of his bureau opening drawers and looking into them. He had no idea what to put on.

Dick was standing in the doorway. Micah saw him there and said, "I don't know what to wear."

"Have I ever seen your legs before?" Dick asked him. "You have big legs. Is that what your boyfriend is doing for you? Making your legs big? Lots of squats?"

"He's not my boyfriend. I don't even know his middle name."

"You know mine, though," Jones said, and Micah nodded. "And I know yours."

"You do?" Micah asked.

"Yup," he said.

They both stopped talking, but the voice in Micah's head was loud and rambling and wary. Not a good thing, it said. But look at him, his compact form there in the doorway, framed and backlit, the blond fuzz of his head, his 31-inch waist—each a siren song to Micah. But he's married, came the voice of reason, and straight and a coworker. He's disconsolate and kind of drunk and probably just horny. To take advantage of him now would be like raping a paraplegic, wouldn't it?

Micah blinked, and Jones was suddenly standing very close to him, his juniper-berried breath like cologne to Micah's nose.

"You're thinking way too much," Dick said. He put his big hands on Micah's chest; they were warm and moist through his T-shirt. "Jesus, you've got pecs too," he whispered.

"They were on sale."

Jones's left hand trailed down Micah's torso, stopping at his polka-dotted shorts. "I had you pegged for a white Calvins kind of guy," he said, swirling a finger into the fly.

"These were on sale too," Micah said. "Are you sure—" he started but stopped when he felt Jones's finger poking his soft prick into a doughy semierect state. Dick went to his knees, pushing his face against the front of Micah's shorts, mouthing the burgeoning head of Micah's prick.

"I'm not sure if this is a great idea," Micah continued, palming the back of Dick's head and forcing it harder against his groin. "I mean, what will we say to each other tomorrow? Are you going to talk to me at all?" Jones pushed up Micah's T-shirt, exposing his crunched abdominals, the smooth six-pack that was his glory—they were like leather-covered rock—and Jones exhumed his face from Micah's crotch.

"Jesus," he exclaimed. "You've been hiding all this!"

"I didn't think you'd be interested," Micah replied. His cock had become engorged and pressed itself insistently against the front of his boxers. Dick dragged the garish shorts down, unveiling the quivering rod. He stabbed his tongue at the hardened, goosefleshed conduit, licking up to the bulbous head that had always seemed to Micah a little odd, a little overboard, and so unlike all the other aerodynamic, arrowheaded cock heads he'd seen in his lifetime. He'd always felt strapped with a tom-tom. Odd or not, though, Jones was not averse to licking it up and down and handling it like a drumstick and sticking it all into his mouth.

"It's better than I thought it was going to be," Dick said.

"That's good to hear," Micah returned.

"I was always bugging Candace to buy bananas and zucchini and cucumbers. Was I sending some heavy subliminals, or what?" He unshouldered his suspenders and unknotted his tie. He looked up from what he was doing. "You OK? You look a little sick."

Micah nodded—he was feeling anything but sick. His cock tingled, needing to be touched more and more. He thought about the next day at the office. This was totally fucked-up, he decided, looking down at his shiny, rosy knob not eight inches from Dick Jones's mouth.

Dick talked as he undressed, about Candace, his lack of sex experience ("You know, with guys, I mean!"), even about some account they were working on. "Talked to Joe about that media plan for Westways. He thinks they're going to go with it." He got himself down to his T-shirt, trousers, and dark socks. He wasn't lean, and he wasn't fat, but he hovered somewhere in between, which was perfection as far as Micah was concerned. Jones wrinkled his brow, looking up at Micah, taking a deep breath. Standing, he unlatched his slacks. He himself was wearing the white Calvins, their pouch filled with a lot of flaccid dick. He gripped himself, pulling on his soft package.

"Guess I'm more nervous than I thought," he said, making a sheepish face. He let go of himself and grabbed hold of Micah. He got down on his knees again and took the man's prick into his mouth. He played his tongue along the underside when he went down and used it to lash the sensitive head when he drew back, his teeth lightly dragging and causing Micah to gasp. He was able, despite his inexperience, to bring Micah closer than he wanted to be to shooting. Micah pulled on Dick's meaty earlobes, pushing into his tight-lipped mouth and hitting the back of his throat, liking the muffled sounds the man made. His balls were bathed in drool that leaked from Dick's sucking mouth.

"Enough," Micah said, tugging on Dick's ears. Dick sat back, his fanny resting on his dark-socked heels. The pouch of his briefs had doubled in size. His plumped dick rode downward along his balls.

His crotch was camera-ready, picture-perfect. He had the look of an underwear ad.

"Take off the rest," Micah said, and Dick pulled off his T-shirt. He was covered with golden brown hair. His pecs were fat and accented with small brown nipples that were pointed and widely spaced. He put his thumbs into his shorts.

"This is a pretty definitive moment," Dick said.

Micah laughed, his cock bobbing. "I think you had your definitive moment a while ago, pal, right before you started giving me head."

"Guess you're right," Dick said.

"We can stop here," Micah said. "We don't have to do anything else. We can forget this ever happened."

"No way," Dick said, shaking his head. "No fucking way."

The shorts came down.

Dick Jones had the kind of cock that Micah dreamed about: fat-shafted and topped with a tiny gumdrop of a head that pointed up and out.

"Jeez," Micah breathed.

They waltzed to the bed and wrestled across the mattress, kicking off pillows and bedsheets, seeking a flat and uncluttered surface on which to fuck. Micah had already decided that it would be a nice gesture to let Dick fuck him. He got himself down on all fours in front of the man and started licking the perfect pecker. Little pearls seeped out and were tongued away. He chewed on Dick's fuzzy bag, bringing the whole tight thing into his mouth, sucking and snorting like a pig at a buffet.

"Mikey," Dick said softly, touching the side of the man's face, and Micah came off the bag, dragging his mouth up the sweet, curving shaft, up to that little point of a head. He went down hard, swallowing Dick's dick and breathing hotly into his bush.

When Micah crawled up Dick's torso and sat down on his cock, Dick said, "No way."

"You don't want to?" Micah asked.

"No. I mean, yeah, I want to, I just can't believe it, that's all. I read my horoscope this morning, and it didn't say anything about fucking you."

"You want to, though?" Micah asked, wanting to be sure.

"Abso-fucking-lutely," Dick said, pushing up with his hips and stabbing into the hole. It was an easy slide in; the sweet, pointy prick was perfect for fucking, although it thickened quickly and felt like a fire plug once it was all the way in.

"Shit," Dick said, cupping Micah's ass. "This is nice, man."

Micah squatted on the cock, playing with the brown points of Dick's nipples. He maneuvered his rear end so that his prostate bore the brunt of Dick's sharp-headed cock. His own dick bobbed happily and untouched, tapping away on Dick's stomach and leaving sticky dots.

"Am I doing it right?" Dick asked, and Micah laughed. "It doesn't take a rocket scientist, I guess," Dick said. "But are you enjoying yourself? Does it hurt? Am I equipped with a monster cock that is eviscerating you as I speak?"

"I'm in fucking heaven," Micah said.

"You look like an angel, man," Dick said, thrusting up sharply, making Micah gasp. He reached up and grabbed the back of Micah's head, pulling him down for a full kiss that made Micah's head swirl. He felt compelled suddenly to reach down between their bellies and start pulling on his cock.

"Shit," Dick whispered, his mouth full of Micah's tongue. "I'm—" He struggled to unpin himself, but Micah rode him out, taking the full blast of Dick's load up his ass. Then Micah sat up straight, his hand on his bone, and aimed for his coworker's face.

When it was all over, Micah unseated himself and stretched out beside Dick.

"I'm sorry, man," Dick said.

"What for?"

"Coming early."

"You were right on time, as far as I'm concerned."

"It's just that I haven't had sex in 32 days."

"Not at all? Not even jacking off?"

Dick turned to look at Micah. "You consider that having sex?"

"Well, yeah. Kind of. It's pretty much the same, isn't it? The end result, I mean."

"Well, then, I haven't had sex, according to your standards, since this morning in the men's room at work after I left your office," Dick said.

"That's so sweet," Micah said, putting his head close to Dick's.

"Yeah," he said. "So tell me, buddy, do you really know my middle name?"

Micah made a face. "Sure, I do. Sure," he said, trying to think of it. He was sure he'd seen it somewhere, on some interdepartmental mail or something. It began with a *j* or an *m,* he thought, or maybe an *s.*

"It's John," he said.

"Nope."

"Jacob."

"Jacob?"

"Not Jacob," Micah said. "So what's mine, then, smart-ass?"

"Jacob?"

"Nice try, asshole," Micah said.

"Steven," Dick tried.

"Close enough," Micah said, licking a running drip of come from Dick's chin.

Almost Better Than Sex
By Simon Sheppard

I'd just been stood up by another liar from AOL. Well, maybe "liar" is too strong a word...

I'd just been stood up by another tweaked-out, game-playing ass-hole shitbag from AOL. It was 1 AM and I was horny, itching to go out and pound some butt. So when the guy who said he would phone me after I signed off didn't phone me, when the number he'd given me turned out to be a recorded message about transit informa-tion, I was pissed off. Pissed off with a hard-on. The first few months I'd been online, I'd taken this sort of thing personally—or at least as evidence of the general decline of truth and morality in late capital-ist culture. Now I realized it was just the ways things were. But it was damned annoying nonetheless.

I signed back on. At 1 AM on a week night, the online communi-ty, such as it is, consists largely of the sexually desperate, the chemi-cally stimulated, and guppies in pajamas brushing their teeth in an-ticipation of another day of designing software, the better to keep their Grand Cherokees purring on down the freeway. It's the time of night when hope springs eternal, only to bang its head against the virtual wall. I'd already opened Netscape and moseyed on over to my favorite porn Web site, anticipating a quick, half-hearted wank into a paper towel, to be followed by a deep and dreamless sleep.

I was, though, also still parked in one of the M4M chat rooms, hoping my affair with some porn star's GIFs would be interrupted by the chime of an Instant Message. It was: "Hello Sir."

My cruising profile instructs boys to call me "Sir." OK, like any minor perversion, it probably seems silly to guys who aren't into it, but I like it. And boys do too.

His screen name was unfamiliar and utterly cryptic. I opened the Get Profile window, typed his name in, and clicked. His profile was nondescript, as well.

"Sir?"

"I'm here, boy," I typed. "Age?" I wasn't about to get busted for in-advertently chatting with jailbait.

"18," he returned.

Well, close to jailbait.

"And what are you into?"

The answer came up in the little window: "Following orders."

My dick, which had been half deflated from frustration, sprang smartly to attention. "You looking to play now?" I typed out.

"Yes."

"You looking to go out or stay in?"

"I'm in Hoboken."

New Jersey was a mere 3,000 miles away.

"I want you to tell me," he continued, "what to do, and I'll do it and send pictures of it to you while we chat."

I didn't have one of those CU-SeeMe setups that makes it possible to send blurry, jerky video from one computer to another, so that suited me just fine. "Yes," I typed, somewhat dubious. "OK."

"You've got mail," his next message read.

The E-mail consisted of a photo divided into four smaller pictures. The first two shots were of his dick. In one pic half-hard; in the other, fully erect and tied off with a piece of cord around the base. it was a nice dick. Now I know that just what constitutes a "nice dick" is pretty much indefinable, but let's face it, we all know one when we see one. He'd clipped his body hair really short and shaved around his cock and balls. Not my favorite look, but on him it looked good.

The lower left photo featured a neatly laid-out array of sex toys: three dildos of varying size, two flesh-colored, one bright red; a cock ring; a bunch of clothespins; several cords; and most suggestive of all, a disposable diaper. And the bottom right picture was even more well-arranged—nine small numbered panels, each containing a different style of underwear: briefs, boxers, jockstraps, a dance belt. I had to hand it to the kid; he was organized.

"So tell me what you want me to do."

I spit in my hand and started stroking. I was more than ready to be a nasty motherfucker, but if there's one thing I've learned about sex, it's that pacing is important. I decided to start slow. "Put on number six," I commanded.

"Yes, Sir." There was a longish pause.

You've got mail, my computer notified me.

I opened the message he'd sent and downloaded the file: a nice-looking torso wearing translucent white briefs that just barely hid a prominent erection.

"Nice," I typed. "Now wet them down." I figured the picture with briefs could have been anyone and come from anywhere. But if he sent me a picture on command, he was on the level.

"With piss, Sir?" he asked.

"Yes." While I waited, I spit on my hand again and massaged my hard-on.

You've got mail.

He'd wet his briefs, all right. A damp stain, spreading from his cock head, rendered the cloth transparent. This was getting good. I thought so, and my dick thought so too.

"Take off the briefs and show me your dick, boy."

In a minute, a picture of his hard-on, lazing stiffly against his thigh, appeared on my screen. Not a huge dick, which was fine with me. Just handsome and juicy-looking and ready to be shoved around.

"Take a cord and tie up your dick and balls."

In less than a minute I could see that he had. He'd done a so-so job of dick-bondage; I could have done better, made it prettier, but his shaft was bulging now, and his hairless ball sac was nicely stretched out.

"Show me your hole."

You've got mail. A shot from behind, his fingertips spreading his hole wide. It was one of those Biology 101 shots, the kind where you can see past the sphincter to the red wetness inside. Way back in my youth, when I first saw split beaver shots in straight porn magazines, I thought they were gross. Now, staring up into a boy's vulnerable insides, I almost came.

"Put a dildo in there."

"Which one, Sir?"

"Start with the small one, the red one."

The pacing of all this was immaculate. A command, a minute of jacking-off while I waited to be obeyed, then the results appearing on my screen.

New picture: his ass from behind again. His butt was hairy, but he'd shaved around the crack, and in the middle of the naked flesh, he was pressing the dildo into himself. The base was red jelly against his smooth young flesh—like a really perverted Gummi Bear. I had to take my hand off my dick; coming now was unthinkable. Not when I had more to command him to do, limits to push.

The doorbell rang. It was two in the fucking morning. Who the fuck could it be, a neighborhood drunk? I wondered. Fuck it, whoever it was would just have to go away. I just hoped it wasn't an emergency. Whatever. I wasn't going to call a halt to this, not even if the house was burning down.

"You still playing with the dildo?" I asked the boy.

"Yes, Sir, is that OK?"

"Take it out and suck it clean. Let me see it in your mouth."

He typed back, "I can't show you my face."

"Just your mouth. Now."

"Yes, Sir."

A profile from chin to nostrils appeared on my screen. Nice mouth, face just a bit fleshy, apparently. Pretty lips, wrapped around a dirty dildo. I didn't have to touch myself to stay hard. I'd found myself a kinky boy. Or, rather, he'd found me.

"Now show me your pussy again," I told him.

Seconds later the boy's shaved ass reappeared on the screen, a little the worse for wear. His hole was stretched wide open and wasn't altogether clean. This is incredible, I thought, I should write a story about it.

I gave my dick a tug, squeezed at the tip till I sent myself to the brink of orgasm, then backed off.

"Are enjoying this, you sick pig?"

"Yes, Daddy."

"Good boy. Now I want you to..." I typed, and the computer crashed.

Damn, damn, damn! My Mac had frozen, and I had to do a hard restart, wait for the extensions to load, launch AOL, sign on...talk about coitus interruptus!

Finally back online, I brought up an Instant Message window, typed out "Sorry, crashed," and clicked on Send.

An AOL window brought the bad news: "Member is not currently online."

Fuck! He probably figured I'd flaked, and gone off to clean up and jack off. Oh well, at least he wasn't playing online with somebody else. He might be a perverted, exhibitionistic pussyboy, but at least he wasn't a slut.

My computer chimed at me. An Instant Message window appeared. "Sorry, Sir, I got bumped." Par for the online course, but now we were back in business.

I was in the mood to have him hurt a bit for me.

"Those clothespins?" I asked.

"Yes, Daddy?"

"I want you to use them."

"Yes, Daddy."

"Put one on each tit and show me."

His chest was well-built, not quite lean, with close-trimmed hair. Perfect. A clothespin was fastened to each nipple, jutting outward. I was imagining what he was feeling, all the way across the country, as the wooden clothespins chomped down into his tender flesh, initial discomfort changing to more focused pain, then intense, searing sensation, then something else.

"Now your dick. Put clothespins on your dick. Start with your ball sac."

"Yes, Sir."

There was a longer pause than usual. I guess he was adjusting the clothespins over the stretched flesh of his sac. Then a message, not a pic: "Daddy?"

"Yes?"

"Where on my dick?"

I told him to put a clothespin where the base of his dick met his sac, then start fastening more up the underside of his cock, stretching out the delicate flesh, clamping the pins down. I loved this; it was delicious.

Eventually the next GIF came: a nice angle, him lying back, shot from below. At the top of the frame, the clothespins were still on his tits. Below closer up, on his dick and balls, he'd clamped three clothespins on the sac, four more running up the shaft. What a fine lad.

"It hurts, Daddy."

"I know. Have you done this before?"

"No," he said. I almost came.

I looked at the little clock on the upper right of the screen. It was getting late. But I was unwilling to give this up. Somewhere across the continent, in frozen moments of time, a boy was, somehow, giving himself to me. One of the things I usually like about amateur porn is the giveaway detail: the glimpse of work stacked up on a computer table; an unfortunate choice of carpets or drapes; even, in some precious instances, a bookshelf, the exhibitionist's choice of reading matter open to analysis. This boy's photos, though, were tightly cropped. There was no world outside the frame, nothing but the electronic sheen of flesh—although turned bluish by my monitor, delectable nonetheless. Naked flesh offered up to me.

"Daddy? Sir?" he said, bringing me out of my thoughts.

"Yes?"

"Are you still there?"

"Sorry, yes."

"What do you want me to do next?"

"Show me your face."

A pause, a hesitation. Then a polite refusal. And I realized he'd made the right choice, even if for the wrong reasons. Maybe all he wanted was the safety of anonymity, but that anonymity was a gift for me. As long as he remained faceless, featureless, he could be damn near anyone, and that meant he could be everyone, everyone I'd ever desired or come on to or fucked. He was, in some utterly cyber-erotic fashion, the embodiment of desire, only he surely didn't know that, and if I'd told him, he might have laughed at my pretentiousness and offered to stick the dildo back up his ass.

"Stick a dildo back up your ass."

"Which dildo?"

"The big one."

The next picture that appeared on my screen showed his shaved asshole stretched around a larger, flesh-colored toy. His dick, still covered by clothespins, stood straight up. Nice.

"Nice," I let him know.

"Now what?"

Now what, indeed. If this were the Real World, we might have come by now. We'd be wiping up, making small talk...about computers probably. If he was like too many young guys, he might be heading out to the back porch for a cigarette. Instead, we each were in ultimate control of our own lusts. There would be no surprise touch of his hand on my dick, a touch that would send me spiraling over the brink of orgasm. There would be no post-coital moment when our eyes accidentally meet. Here in electronic space, despite his apparent surrender of control, despite my losing my head over him—or rather over the pixels that defined his presence—we each had only to flick a button for the whole thing to end.

And it was getting very, very late.

I thought about it, then typed out, "I want you to come."

"But Sir, can't we do this longer?"

"Come."

"Please?"

"Now. And show me."

I planned to make myself spurt the moment I saw the pic of jizz on his belly. I stroked gently, delaying the release. And then the bedroom door opened. My boyfriend, his voice as bleary as his eyes, stuck his head through the living room door. "You still up?" he asked.

"Yeah. I'll come to bed soon."

He glanced down at my hand...my dick. "Slut." He smiled and tottered off to the bathroom for a pee.

When he was safely back in bed, I checked my mailbox, opened the E-mail titled "Last One," clicked DOWNLOAD NOW, grabbed the paper towel I'd left beside the mousepad, and watched as his picture opened. He'd taken the clothespins off his dick but added two to his balls—a fan of five. His hand was still on his dick, obscuring most of the shaft, leaving the head visible. And just slightly out of focus, come was splashed across his torso, all the way up to one of his clothespinned nipples. I imagined the ocean smell, the way his juice was viscously dripping down over his bare flesh. And I shot off, hard and long, into Bounty, the quicker picker-upper.

"Thanks," I typed out, adding a little smiley-face: :-)

"No, thank you, Sir."

"What's your name?"

"Jason," he typed. Maybe it was, and maybe it wasn't.

"I'm Simon. I'll add you to my Buddy List."

"And you're on mine," he said.

"Gotta get to bed," I told him. "Thanks again."

"No problem. My pleasure. Bye."

"Bye." And I signed off, the computer saying Good-bye to me, as well.

I finished wiping off my dick and used my right hand, the clean one, to click the mouse to shut down.

The base-level directory on my hard disk was still corrupted. I would be short of sleep the next day. Somewhere on the East Coast, a boy was wiping up and cleaning off his toys, and I would never see his face. The hard disk purred to a stop. The computer went silent. The screen went dark.

I threw the power switch on the surge protector and headed off to a deep and dreamless sleep.

For Real
By Dominic Santi

"No script?"

"Do whatever you want, Zak—whatever a couple of famous porn stars do together that everybody else only dreams about."

"That's not real specific." I drank the last of my soda and sighed—loudly. Marco was a good director. I liked working with him. But his brainstorms weren't always easy to understand when he was frustrated. At the moment, we were taking a break from filming a standard fuck flick. Marco was pacing a hole in the carpet, thwapping his clipboard against his thigh and complaining about his inability to cast The Right Couple for his next creative masterpiece. I was letting my dick rest and trying to figure out what the hell he was talking about.

In between his mutterings about "no fucking chemistry between them," I figured out that he'd been taping wannabe actors who'd answered his cattle call for "long-term couples willing to 'bare it all' living out their sexual fantasies for the camera." Apparently, the results had been less than stellar. Now, Marco was out of time. In fact, he was desperate enough that he was offering my partner and me a percentage, on top of our usual rates, if—big emphasis on the "if"—we could do a scene together hot enough for him to ditch the other footage he'd already shot.

The whole deal sounded too good to be true, which made me suspicious. Not that I didn't trust Marco. But I'd worked with him enough to know he always had a hidden agenda. I rolled the empty can in my hands until he finally slowed down enough for me to get a word in. Then I said, "I don't get it."

He stopped pacing and quirked an eyebrow at me.

"There's no script. We just have sex the way we do at home. If we do the scene hot enough, you pay us a bundle. What's the catch?"

"No catch, pal!" Marco grinned as he walked up next to me and slapped me on the back. "I film you and Jeff getting it on—you know, real porn stars having real sex." He winked at me. "It's the ultimate voyeuristic fantasy! If you make the scenes really hot—bump up sales enough to justify the startup costs—I can use this as the pilot to open up a whole new line of candid videos. Your audience gets to jerk off watching, you get one helluva bonus, the studio gets rich. Everybody's happy."

Suddenly, Marco grabbed my shoulder and turned me around, narrowing his eyes as he looked at my butt. "What the fuck is this? Did that asshole give you a hickey just before a shoot? I'll kill him!"

"It's a bruise. The makeup must have worn off." I pulled away, batting my eyes innocently. "I got it when Jeff and I fell out of bed, fucking. Does that make you feel better?"

"Ouch. Kinky, though." He smirked, then his eyebrows narrowed. "You guys do that often?"

I could almost hear the wheels turning, and I did not want to go down that road. I tossed my empty can in the trash.

"Every day," I smiled. I didn't have the heart to tell Marco that after a long day of fucking for money, my boyfriend and I liked to relax at home. We read, worked out together, watched movies with plots—slept! Our private lives did not revolve around a social whirl of orgies and anonymous tricks in the bars of West Hollywood.

Not that Marco would have believed that. He snickered, turning away as he waved the gaffer over to him. "We'll talk more when we're done today." He paused. "But give me a teaser. What would John Doe on the street need to do to have a sex life as hot as yours?"

"Marry Jeff Evans," I grumbled. I grabbed my dick and started stroking, ignoring Marco's laughter as I walked out of the room to get ready for my next scene.

Jeff was due home from his latest European shoot in two weeks. I knew I'd be horny as hell for him by then. But I wasn't looking forward to Marco's little project. Even though I was half of an "internationally famous" pornstar couple, I relished my private time alone with my lover. To my way of thinking, we didn't get enough of it.

Other than the one-take "you-suck-me-I'll-suck-you" jail scene where we'd met, Jeff and I hadn't done any movies together. I worked mostly in the U.S. Popularizing cock sucking with condoms was my claim to fame. Jeff worked more overseas. Having a thick, uncut, country cock—and being able to speak Czech as fluently as his never-adjusted-to-Omaha mother—gave him an instant in with American companies who were capitalizing on the burgeoning East European markets. Jeff looked Slavic. He could talk to his co-stars as well as to the director. And he had one fucking gorgeous body.

OK, so I'm biased. After five years together, Jeff's smile can still make my dick drool. Anybody watching a video of his can see how much he's enjoying himself. This is no straight man pretending to be gay. Jeff loves fucking ass. His beautifully tapered nine inches are thick as a beer can, and he's always hard. So, he's always cast as a top—even though he's so big it's sometimes difficult to find bottoms for his fuck scenes.

We get asked, often, what keeps us together. "You're both tops. Isn't it, you know, kind of pointless?"

Jeff's stock answer is "I married him for his mind." At which time he grabs my crotch and winks at our interrogators. His squeezing always has the expected result. It's a good thing I like being hard in public.

What he doesn't say is that when it's just the two of us, we bottom to each other. I'm as long as he is, though not as wide, and I'm cut. Directors love the way my wide-rimmed mushroom head looks popping in and out of lips and assholes. The definition stays clear even when I'm inside the rubber. The PR folks say that complements what they call my "chiseled Greek looks." I have to admit, my dick does look good—even more so on a wide-screen TV.

Jeff loves working that rim with his tongue. He gives a mean blow job. I shoot geysers when he's doing me. OK, so I'm also in love with the guy. He's well-read, intelligent, prone to pulling practical jokes, and I've gotten used to sleeping with his prong poking me in the kidney all night. Besides, I love playing with his dick. His come tastes great, and he's got enough foreskin for the both of us.

That's what was going to be hard to explain to Marco—the skin part. At work, everyone we suck or fuck is always sheathed in latex. Jeff and I have both eroticized condoms to the point that just hearing a wrapper being torn open makes us stiff. But at home, we're body-fluid monogamous. A couple of years ago, after another round of negative tests, we'd decided that as long as we used latex with everyone else, every time—and as long as there were no accidents—we'd go skin to skin with each other.

I didn't know how that was going to fit into Marco's grand marketing plans. He was adamant that he wanted to film us on Jeff's first night back from Europe—before we'd had a chance to fuck. After several long and very expensive phone calls, Jeff and I decided ol' Marco was going to get exactly what he'd asked for. We'd burn that bed up with the hottest action our illustrious director had ever seen. And for our troubles, Jeff and I were going to walk away with the money we needed for the balloon payment on our condo.

On the day of the shoot, Marco was in his usual rush. "What kind of props do you need?"

Jeff snickered and rubbed his crotch, the sizable erection tenting the front of his robe. Despite his jetlag, after three weeks apart, we'd have been happy humping on the carpet.

"A couple towels, three or four pillows, some coconut massage oil," I answered, shrugging.

"I want a second sheet and a blanket at the bottom of the bed."

I raised my eyebrows at my hot and horny partner's requests, but Jeff just smiled and kept rubbing his crotch. I reached over to help him.

"You got it." The ever-efficient Marco snapped his fingers and somebody was on it. His crews are always good. "Condoms, lube, the standard kit will be on the nightstand."

Jeff and I sat on the edge of the bed, ignoring him and the flurry of activity around us as we turned our concentration to necking and stroking the erections poking out through each other's robes.

"Zak, Jeff...*now*, please!"

We came up for air, gasping as we made a pretense of composing ourselves. I kept my hand in Jeff's lap, though. I couldn't quite bring myself to let go of him. I'd missed him.

Marco grabbed a fresh cup of coffee from his latest twinkie assistant and kept right on talking, like he actually thought we were listening to him. "Do whatever you want—fuck, suck, jack off. Just make it hot. And stay on the bed so we don't have to screw around with the lights."

He looked away, wincing as he sipped the steaming liquid. "We'll do the voice-overs later, as well as specific questions about your relationship and so forth, based on the action. Don't worry about that now." He stopped and looked at us over the edge of his cup. "Unless you have questions, we'll start in 15 minutes."

When Jeff and I both shook our heads, Marco turned his attention back to the crew, and Jeff and I went off to finish getting ready. Marco assigned us each a minder, though, to ensure we didn't sneak off for a quickie somewhere. He wasn't going to let anybody disrupt his grand plans.

"Leave them alone! I will personally shoot anyone who interferes with what I expect to be record come shots!"

Jeff and I knelt on the bed, facing each other, and handed our robes to the disappointed fluffers.

"Places everyone. Make me proud." Marco launched into his standard routine, and we were rolling. Jeff winked at me, giving my thigh a quick prod with that monster cock of his. I wiggled my eyebrows back at him. Then we took each other's hands and I let the techies' discussions fade away into the background. Just knowing they were there was all the encouragement my exhibitionist streak needed.

I was almost too worked up, though. I backed off until just my fingertips were touching Jeff's. Getting used to him again. Letting down my defenses. Letting him in. We didn't talk. Marco could damn well dub in music later.

Eventually, Jeff pulled my hand to his lips and sucked on my index finger, running the edges of his teeth sharply over my skin. When I shivered, he bit.

I don't know which of us moved first. One minute his mouth was hot and wet on my finger, the next we were kissing. I fell or he pushed me back on the bed—probably a little of both. Then we were rolling around on the sheets, groping blindly for each other, our dicks pressed together between us. I opened my mouth to breathe and sucked in his tongue.

"Damn, I missed you, Zak."

I shivered as he licked over my teeth.

"You are the hottest man on the face of this fucking earth!"

"Shut up and kiss me," I growled, shoving my tongue down his throat.

We were too turned on for refinements. When Jeff started licking my ear, I twisted around and latched onto a nipple. That had the expected result. My country boy threw me flat on my back and straddled me—his fat, juicy cock snuggling right up against my lips. He turned around and positioned himself over me, on his knees and elbows, his legs widespread so he could lower himself onto my face. Then Jeff pulled my legs up and back so he had access to everything he wanted. Marco always liked 69-ing. He was damn well going to get it today.

About two seconds later, I decided Marco was an idiot for not letting us come at least once before the cameras started rolling. My skin felt like it was reaching towards Jeff everywhere we touched. I fought not to shoot as he rubbed his face against my crotch. I gasped, wiggling as Jeff kissed the head of my dick. It was almost more than I could stand.

I tugged on his balls, trying to distract myself by licking his scent from them. It didn't help. It only made me want him more. His velvety shaft brushed against my cheek, teasing me. I opened my mouth. Using just my lips, I tugged his foreskin down over the slippery head. A drop of tangy juice oozed onto my tongue.

"Mmm. You taste good," I whispered, carefully licking the sticky precome into my waiting mouth.

As my tongue swiped over his piss slit, Jeff cried out, bucking and gasping against me. In his next breath, with no warning at all, he sucked me deep into his throat.

I didn't expect it. I jerked back as my whole body convulsed. "Stop!" I gasped. "NOW! Fuck, man, I'm gonna shoot!"

"Camera 3, you better be getting this!"

Jeff froze, and I panted—ignoring Marco's comment and his muttering that we definitely hadn't given him enough footage yet. I clenched the muscles in my arms, concentrating on the details of the condo mortgage, on how nice Marco's clipboard would look shoved up his ass, trying to will myself back under control.

"Give me a second," I whispered.

"Whatever you say, lover." Jeff had taken his mouth off my dick, but he couldn't seem to quit touching me. Pretty soon, his hand moved to my perineum. He started stroking, gently at first, then more firmly, gradually moving down, touching, rubbing. He drooled spit onto me—lubing the way for his fingers. By the time I finally got my breathing halfway under control, Jeff was playing with my asshole. He kept my legs spread wide, so the cameras could catch the way he was stroking me—the slow, lazy, slippery circles.

When he slipped the tip of his finger into me, I moaned and gave it up. I knew right then how the rest of the scene was going to go. Jeff's fingers were talking directly to my asshole. I opened my mouth and took the tip of his cock between my lips—kissing him, working the soft, warm hood over the glistening head, tugging gently on his smooth, heavy balls. We were too far gone to go slowly. If Marco wanted more cinematic build-up, he could damn well edit it in later. Jeff lifted up, sliding his finger down my thigh. "Roll over, Zak."

I did. When I was on all fours over him, Jeff stuffed a pillow under his head. I spread my legs wide and dropped down until just the tip of my cock rested on his lips. I hoped the cameras were getting everything they needed, because I wasn't about to budge for anyone but Jeff. And he had me right where he wanted me. He put his hands on my hips and pulled me down towards him. Then his hands were on my ass cheeks, massaging them, spreading them wider. My cock fell forward onto his neck as I felt the feather light touch of his breath caressing my asshole.

"Mmm. This pretty pink pucker looks good, Zak. Real good."

I groaned, jumping at the first touch of his tongue. It was hot, it always is. He licked the edge of my crack, wetting skin that usually doesn't see daylight, especially not in my movies.

I nuzzled my cheek against his cock, kissing him, inhaling his scent. I wanted to let him know how much I appreciated his touch. Then I rested my face on his thigh, facing Camera 2, and focused all my attention on my asshole, just the way I knew Jeff wanted me to.

I didn't try to control my reactions. I'm not dignified in bed. Not in real life. I moaned as Jeff rimmed me. He licked up and down my crack. I gasped the way I always did when the tip of his tongue flicked over my asshole. I knew what was coming. I wiggled my ass at him, asking for it—begging. Loud and slutty. I didn't care who saw me. I hoped the cameras were catching every whorish grind for posterity.

Jeff stuffed spit up my hole. His fingers held me wide open, stretching my sphincter. Each touch of his tongue let him slip that much further in. My ass lips fluttered, reaching back for him as he kissed and sucked. He licked further into me, caressing the inner skin, way inside, where the smooth surface was usually puckered tightly closed. With each step, he stretched me wider.

"You ready, babe?"

"Uh, huh," I gasped. I didn't care who heard the great porn star's boyfriend calling him "babe." My ass was hungry.

"You know what I'm going to do." He sucked, hard, on the outside of my hole. "You ready?"

I shuddered, nodding against his cock, unable to speak.

"You taste so good, babe." He kissed my asshole. "Here it comes."

I yelled when his tongue sank into me. I mean, Jeff dug his hot, nasty tongue into my ass and he ate me. He tongue-fucked my hole until I was almost screaming. Harder, deeper, hotter, he spread my cheeks so far apart it felt like my skin was splitting. I pushed back against him, grunting, bearing down, opening my asshole to him as he slurped. I didn't care what I looked like. My ass lips kissed his tongue like it was his cock.

I cried out as he pulled away. He pushed me over onto my back, still 69-ing, pressing his cock against my lips. I sucked him greedily into my mouth, inhaling the slippery, salty tang where the precome leaked out of his bunched foreskin.

"That's it, lover," he growled, thrusting into my mouth. His cock got longer, growing against my tongue. "Get it hard and get it wet. You know where it's going."

He was already like a rock, but I sucked, opening my jaw wider as his shaft thickened and stretched even further. His bared head was completely out of the foreskin now, the sensitive crown pressing against my tonsils, his cock filling my mouth. I breathed in through my nose, and as my lungs filled, Jeff thrust, gently, against the back of my throat. I tipped my head and opened to him, gagging as he slipped in deep. It was like trying to swallow a baseball bat. He shook—I love feeling him quiver, even when I'm suffocating. Then he pulled up and settled against me, his breath ragged, his cock resting above my mouth where I could play with it at my leisure—where the camera could catch every wet lick of me working the folds of his skin, sticking my tongue in his piss slit, sucking his low-hanging, smooth balls until they were pink and slippery.

In spite of his shivers, Jeff pulled my legs up and back. He braced his elbows on the bed, his biceps against the backs of my thighs. It was a perfect ass shot. I was spread wide and my hole was open. Virgin ground for Marco's cameras. I heard the click of the bottle cap, smelled the coconut. Then Jeff's oiled hands glided over my cheeks. He smoothed the side of his hand up and down my open crack, brushing over my hole, gradually concentrating on rubbing my hungry grasping sphincter. His fingers started stretching me.

"I want you nice and loose," he purred. "Show me how your boy pussy opens up for me."

"But Zak's a top!" Someone protested loudly in the background.

"Not today," Jeff snickered as he put one hand on each cheek. His index and middle fingers pulled me open. With each stroke, his fingers reached in further. He kept pulling, stretching me wider, until my whole world was my asshole. I groaned as he kissed the inside of my thigh, his finger once more sliding over my ass lips.

"You like?" I could feel his smile as he breathed against my leg.

"Fuck, that feels good," I gasped, sucking hard on his monster dick, taking it as deep in my throat as I could.

He laughed, shivering as I swallowed against him. This time, when his finger went in, it dug deep. I groaned, long and loud, feeling the familiar jolt as he found what he was looking for.

"What have we here?" He rubbed again. I could hear the smirk in his voice. "Somebody wants his joy spot massaged?"

He pressed hard, and I cried out, an ooze of precome moving up my cock tube.

"Fuck, yeah, Jeff. Fuck, that feels good." I tried to arch against him. "Do it again, please!"

This time, his laugh gave me goose bumps. "I will, lover." I groaned as he rubbed, harder. "But I'm going to massage it with something designed specifically to make your slutty pussy purr."

He pulled his hand out. My nose twitched as the smell of coconut again filled the air. I jumped as I felt the nozzle against my ass lips. His fingers pulled my ass lips open, then the cool oil trickled into me, deep down into my hole, lubing it, getting it slippery wet.

"Jeez, man, that stuff is gonna wreck the rubber." The techie's voice sounded far away.

I was too far gone to even laugh. I sucked harder on Jeff's cock, getting it wetter, getting it stiffer for where it was going to go.

Jeff moved off me, his dick making a wet, plopping noise as it popped out of my mouth. He pressed the oil bottle into my hand. Then he was between my legs, lifting my thighs up and back, spreading them wide. I bent my knees and he pressed them back towards my shoulders, tipping my ass high in the air.

"You ready, babe?"

This time I did laugh. The head of Jeff's cock was pressed into my ass cheek—hot, demanding. I squeezed a huge puddle of oil into my hand, slathered the slippery grease over his cock, stroking, getting him even harder. I dropped the bottle next to myself and positioned him against me, rubbing his dripping dick head against my hungry, hungry hole.

"Jeez, man, what are they doing?"

"Somebody give them a condom!"

"Damn, Jeff's *huge!*"

Jeff grinned down at me. I smiled back. As we'd expected, our audience was shocked. My ass lips fluttered against him, kissing him. I stroked his shaft, slicking the oil over him one more time, looking right into his hot, velvety eyes—velvety as his dick skin.

"Fuck me," I growled.

"Jesus, he's going in bareback!"

I don't know who said it. I didn't care. I cried out as Jeff's monster cock started crawling up my hole. They'd said to do it for real, and that's the way Jeff and I fucked each other—only each other. Bareback.

"Marco, do you see what they're doing? Fer chrissakes, stop them!"

I gasped as Jeff pressed into me. It burned. Oh, god, it burned. It always did. Jeff's dick was so big and so thick and so fucking, fucking hard. I panted, keeping my mouth open, bearing down, willing myself to relax as my ass lips stretched. I felt like I was being split in two. It hurt and it burned and, fuck, I wanted it.

"Damn, that's hot." Whoever said it was completely out of breath. I knew we looked good. I lifted my head, watching Jeff impale me.

"I love watching my cock fill your hole." Jeff's words came out through gritted teeth. He was making himself go slowly, trying not to hurt me—trying not to come.

I gasped as he slid in another inch. My ass lips stretched—thinner, tighter.

"That's it, lover. Loosen up and take it all." He gasped, shuddering, as the sound of his voice seemed to open my hole. "God, you feel good! Unh!"

My sphincter relaxed in a rush, and Jeff slid in to the hilt. I lay back down, taking deep breaths, willing my body not to shake, not to panic at the sheer size of the cock buried deep in my rectum.

"Easy lover." Jeff's thumbs stroked the backs of my thighs. He was breathing hard, holding himself still over me. "It'll be OK in a minute. I'm gonna make you feel so good."

The pain passed, slowly, the way I knew it would. Gradually I became aware of another pressure, of the hard cock nuzzling against my joy spot. Pressing precome out of me. I looked up at Jeff. His face was flushed, his shoulders and arms and chest glistening with sweat. My cock twitched at the sight of him. I felt the jolt all the way around my asshole.

"Do it, you prick." I clenched my rectal muscles around him. "Fuck my horny ass until I come."

Jeff grinned. He leaned over and kissed me, shoving his tongue deep in my mouth. I sucked, hard. My ass lips kissed his cock, matching the rhythm of my mouth.

He closed his eyes and pulled back. His smile turned to a gasp, then to a grimace. "Damn, but you're tight."

The friction still burned, but at the same time it felt so good. So damn good. Then he was in again. And out. And in.

"You ready?" Jeff pressed hard, grinding his pelvis against me, his balls heavy against my ass cheeks as he once more looked down into my eyes.

I grappled on the bed for the bottle, slathered oil on my hand. Then I grabbed ahold of my long, hard pornstar cock and growled up at my panting lover. "Show me what you've got, fucker."

"Asshole," he snapped.

I yelled as Jeff shoved into me. Then he started fucking me, wild and fierce, his balls slapping against me. I cried out each time he punched my joy spot. I could tell I wasn't going to last long. Each time he hit my prostate, I surged closer, my juices boiling, ready to erupt. Ready to explode. I jacked myself faster, trying to match Jeff's rhythm. With each stroke I pulled waves of pleasure through my ever-expanding dick.

"Gonna come," I gasped. I shuddered as my hand stroked up. "Fuck me. Harder." My balls pulled up, tight. "Fuck me—damn it, *hard!*"

Jeff slammed his hips into me, punching into my joy spot—just the way I'd begged him to, just the way he knew I loved it. My hole clenched, hard and greedy. Then I howled as the orgasm washed over me. My dick and my prostate and my asshole became one continuous scream of pleasure. My come spurted out and I yelled until my throat hurt.

It was a helluva money shot. The wet splats landed on my chin and my neck and my tits. The last couple on my belly. Jeff ground his hips into me, twitching his dick inside me until I swear every drop of sperm in my balls shot out my cock tube. I shook like my bones were breaking.

I was totally wiped out. As my hand stilled, I looked up. Jeff was balanced over me, his arms shaking, his breath erratic, sweat dripping down onto me. His face was a mask of concentration as he arched his cock into me, prolonging my pleasure.

My arms trembled as I reached up and grabbed his tits. "I love you," I panted. I pinched, lightly. "You are one hot fuck."

Jeff gasped, his eyes glazing. We were the only ones in the world. My hole was raw and sore and stretched so loose it felt like it would never be tight again. I didn't care.

I smiled up at him, twisting the hard little nipples between my fingers. "Fuck me, lover."

Jeff's cry was incoherent as he started thrusting into me again, pounding toward his climax. His dick slurped in and out of me, wet and sloppy. I tried to tighten for him. I managed a light twitch before my muscles gave out. He felt it—he shivered.

His cock ravaged my asshole with fast, deep, full strokes. I tugged hard, rhythmically, on his tits. His breathing was so fast, I knew he was right on the edge. I lifted my hips, taking him as deep as I could, rocking back as he bottomed out, as his body stiffened.

"You fucker," I gasped, an evil laugh deep in my throat. He'd destroyed my hole. I was sore as hell and, damn, it felt good. I jerked hard on his nipples. "Do it!"

"Aargh!" Jeff's roar almost deafened me. He buried himself balls deep, his whole body shuddering, his thick, hard cock pulsing, stretching, throbbing against my poor battered ass lips.

"Get ready, this is gonna be one helluva shot..." This time I distinctly heard Marco's voice in the background mix. "When Jeff pulls out..."

"Um, it's too late, Marco."

"What?"

"Jeff just came up Zak's ass."

"What?! Nobody does that! Jesus H. Christ!"

"I'm not shittin' ya man, look! Jeff's whole ass is twitching."

"Jeff? Zak? Where's the come shot?"

"Man, I just came in my pants—and I'm straight!"

"Damn it! Where's my money shot? Zak? Jeff? Where's my fucking money shot?!"

Marco's curses degenerated into Italian. I tuned him out as Jeff collapsed on me. Jeff's breathing was ragged. He kissed me, clumsily missing my lips, then connecting. I lowered my legs and wrapped them around his waist, holding him to me in a ferocious bear hug.

Jeff pressed against me for a long time, his breathing slowly returning to normal. Finally he started to wiggle against me, his shoulders moving as he laughed into my neck.

"You liked?" He kept his voice low, just barely loud enough for me to hear.

I whispered back. "I'm gonna need diapers, you asshole. Damn, you're good."

He sucked on my neck. I could tell he was giving me a hickey.

"We gave them one helluva show."

When he could finally stop laughing, Jeff rolled off me, his dick pulling free with a loud plop. I reached down between my legs and felt my hole. It was puffy and sticky and about as well-used as a bottom boy's pussy can be. I knew it would be back to normal by morning—it always was. But for now, my butt positively purred.

Jeff grabbed the extra sheet and the blanket from the bottom of the bed and pulled them over us. Then he spooned himself up against my back and wrapped his arms around me. I clenched my butt muscles, enjoying the stretched feeling and the sticky, tacky pull of his drying come on my skin. The movement caused another trickle to leak out of my asshole and run down my leg. I shivered and pressed back against my lover, against his—for once—softly heavy cock.

"What are you two doing now?" Marco was beyond exasperation. He sounded genuinely perplexed. "What the fuck do you do for an encore?"

"We're rolling over and going to sleep," Jeff growled. "Just like in real life. Now shut up."

"Oh, fer chrissakes!"

Something heavy hit the floor. It sounded like Marco's clipboard. Then somebody started laughing—a lot of somebodies.

I closed my eyes and smiled as Jeff's breathing deepened. I knew we'd be getting our percentage. Marco was too greedy not to use a scene like we'd just given him. Jeff started to purr. I drifted right behind him. Marco's video was going to be great. And Jeff and I were even getting paid to sleep.

Heads and Tails
By M. Christian

"Suck it," he told me, and so I did. Willingly, eagerly. I opened my mouth, pushed out my lips and took his swollen cock head in. It would have been nice to say it was a sweet candy cane, but let's be realistic. It tasted like hard cock. A good hard cock, but a cock nonetheless: salt; the bitter bite of pre-come; the shit-tinge you always get down there; the musky reek of hormones, of excitement.

A good taste, a damned fine taste. A cock taste—and I tried to get every inch of it, and him, down my throat. I've sucked my share, some even bigger than this great beast filling my mouth, but for me—then, there—it was the only cock in the world.

I sucked him as he moaned, and not the first—or probably the last—I thought "playing the skin flute." A bad metaphor in its original antique context, but a favorite with my twist: yes, lips around. Yes, I was sucking and not blowing. But I really was playing him, applying my lips and making lovely music escape from him.

And what beautiful tunes I was making him perform: moans, groans, sighs, hisses—the entire scales of pleasure. I couldn't do my own singing, of course, with his instrument tickling the back of my throat, but I did hum and moan a bit in accompaniment.

Then it was time to stop—slowly, I opened my jaws even wider and let his hard cock slide free, the thick head popping up from my throat, glancing off my teeth, past the roughness, playfulness of my flickering tongue and then out. Shimmering, gleaming with a dribble of pre-come and lots of my spit, he came free, tapping against my nose with his strength, the iron of his shaft.

"Time to toss it, boy," he said, grinning wide and wonderfully mean.

Dancing in the light, twirling around and around, a sparkling bit of silver in the twilight room. Fast, so fast, he reached out and caught it—snatching the coin before he even fell past my eyes. A slap against his burly forearms. A peak under his hand, seeing the side—but showing me nothing but a wicked grin. "Tails."

I returned the smile, wiping my mouth free of my come-sucking drool. Keeping my eyes on his, relishing the hunger in his gray irises, I reached over and gently took up the bottle of baby oil.

Then I wasn't facing him—but rather a white wall, a small expanse of eggshell. I knew, soon enough, that I'd be memorizing, registering every crack, every deformation. I would never be able to look at that small spot of wall without thinking of what would come next.

Ass high, I offered myself to him—no, I gave him my asshole. He had the rest of me, or could have as much as me as he wanted, but I knew all he wanted right then was my asshole. I'd heard the compliments, so I showed my hole to him with pride. "A pink delicacy," "a fuckable rosebud," "such a pretty fuck-hole," and so much more.

His hand on my ass—hot, rough, strong. Just, at first, holding me, gripping one of my cheeks. Preparatory, a way he shakes hands with the ass he's going to fuck. Then a gentle pressure around that "wondrous asshole"—a slow, steady pressure around my "delicate hole"— and I know that he's in me. A finger, at first, but still he's within me. It feel good—a gentle invasion. Good, but not great—and so I growl, feral and hungry, demanding something greater, more powerful, more feral.

And he delivers. Up the gradient of sensation—passing the tickling entry of that finger and beyond...beyond even my own fingers, my own toys. He is not just big, he is not just huge. He is beyond all of that—and all of that is now beyond the lips of my asshole, deep within me.

And so, he fucks me. God, yes, he fucks me—in and out, a fucking, two-stroke engine of cock and legs, balls slapping against my ass. I can feel his hot invasion, his piston-stroke hammering deep inside me. I don't do it often, but I do it then—hot tears rolling down my cheeks, burning me. But they are not a sad leaking. No, they are tears of wonderful pain, wonderful suffering. It's a good kind of hurt, the sexy hurt of being fucked good and hard.

Then it's over, but not with the usual curtain call. No, this time it doesn't conclude with his hot come in the hot recesses of me. No, he pulls free long before that, long before the come boils free of his great, big, hairy balls.

Again, the shimmering ascent of the coin—a twirling dance in the dim light of my bedroom. For the first time I notice the denomination, and feel a delightful wave of shame that I'm only worth 5 cents.

He doesn't show me the side after he slaps it silly on his arm. Instead, he rolls back onto his wonderfully tight ass, showing me his rock-hard cock—and such a cock it is. I know where it's been, my asshole still throbbing from its absence, but that doesn't take away my hunger for it.

An echo, a touch of déjà-vu: "Suck it."

So I do, taking his thick cock into my hungry mouth. It didn't taste like shit—but then I wasn't in a position to really tell, or care. All that mattered was my mouth was around his cock, his head down my throat, his hairy balls tickling my chin. All was right in the world, I was sucking on my lord's cock.

I was somewhere else, lost in the sensation of his thick shaft sliding in and out of my mouth, fucking my tonsils, screwing my throat. I was lost, hovering beyond it all, in a place of pure lust and driving, hammering love. Distantly, I was aware my cock was throbbing, hard, and that my feverish hand was jamming up and down along it. It felt good, that was sure, but his cock down my throat felt even better.

Then, Jesus, he came—my Master, my Lover. He came. At first I thought it was just part of my sucking, the twitching that flowed up and down his throbbing cock, but then he started to fill my throat, up into my mouth—his hot, salty jizz, his steaming come. I swallowed and swallowed and swallowed some more, sucking his sticky come down my throat as I massaged him, squeezed his shaft with my mouth.

Sometime during this I came, too—jetting onto the sheets, my own orgasm quaking my knees, pulling myself free of his gleaming cock, to fall, panting, onto the sheets.

After a point, we slept, curled up in my tiny bed—a warm embrace of spent bodies—with just the tiny cool spot of a coin, pressed against my chest, to remind me of why were we sleeping.

Family Affair
By Bob Vickery

Nick and Maria ride up front in Maria's beat-up '74 Buick convertible, Maria driving like a lunatic, weaving in and out of the traffic, me wedged in the backseat with all the beach gear tumbling over me. The radio is turned on full blast, set to an oldies station belting out a Beach Boys tune. "I wish they all could be California girls," Nick sings along. He buries his face into Maria's neck and makes loud farting noises. Maria screams with laughter, and it's only by the grace of God that she avoids plowing us all into the highway's concrete median.

"Jesus Christ!" I cry out in terror.

Nick and Maria crack up—Nick wheezing, Maria's shoulders shaking spasmodically. "What the hell is wrong with you guys!" I shout. "You been sniffing airplane glue?"

"No," Nick says. "Drano." Maria breaks up again, laughing until she starts hiccuping.

"You two are fucking crazy," I say, shouting over the wind and the radio. "You're going to kill us all."

Nick turns his head and looks at me, grinning. "Lighten up, Robbie," he says. "We're supposed to be having a good time." I glare at him. He turns back to Maria. "I didn't know your little brother was such a tight-ass," he laughs.

"Oh, Robbie's OK," she says. She glances back at me in the rearview mirror and widens her eyes in comic exaggeration. I turn my head away sulkily and stare over on my left toward the ocean, which stretches out as flat and shiny as a metal plate.

We ride together for a few minutes in silence, then Nick reaches over and turns down the radio. He turns his head toward me. "So, Robbie," he says affably. "I hear you're gay."

"Jesus, Maria!" I exclaim.

Maria isn't laughing now. At least she has the decency to look embarrassed. "I didn't think you'd mind me telling him, Robbie," she says. But her guilty tone makes it clear she knew damn well I'd mind. She shoots a poisonous look at Nick. "You've got a big mouth," she hisses.

"He's not the only one," I say.

Nick's eyes shift back and forth between Maria and me. "Oops," he says. He laughs, unfazed. "It's no big deal. I'm cool. It's not like I'm a born-again Christian or anything." He looks at me. "So, are you just coming out or what?"

"I don't want to talk about it," I say frostily. Maria flashes me an apologetic glance in the mirror, but I just glower back at her. We ride the rest of the distance to the beach in silence.

It's still early: The sun has just started climbing high, and there are only a scattering of cars in the dirt parking lot. We start the trek to the beach—Nick and Maria leading the way, me lagging behind with the cooler. Nick leans over and says something to Maria, and she laughs again, her previous embarrassment all forgotten now, which makes my mood even pissier. At the top of the dunes the two of them wait for me to catch up. The sea stretches out before us, sparkling in the bright sun, the waves hissing as they break upon the sandy beach. "Bitchin'!" Nick says. He reaches over and squeezes the back of my neck. "You having a good time, Robbie?" he asks, smiling.

Though I hardly know the guy, I know that this is as close to an apology as I'll ever get. A breeze whips over the dunes, smelling of the sea; the sun beams down benevolently, and I see nothing but good humor in Nick's wide blue eyes. In spite of myself I smile.

"Atta boy," Nick laughs. "I knew you had it in you!" He lets go, and we start climbing down the dunes to find a stretch of beach isolated from everyone else.

After we've laid the blanket out Maria and Nick start taking off their clothes. I hurriedly pull my bathing suit out of my knapsack. "I'm going to change behind the dune," I say.

Nick has one leg raised, about to pull off a sneaker. "I'll go with you," he says abruptly.

I have mixed feelings about this but don't know how I can dissuade him. We circle the nearest dune, leaving Maria behind on the broad expanse of beach. Nick peels off his shirt, and I can't help noticing the sleek leanness of his torso, the blond dusting of hair across his chest. My throat tightens, and I turn my attention to my fingers fumbling with the buttons of my jeans. Nick kicks off his shoes and shucks his shorts and Calvins. The honey-brown of his skin ends abruptly at his tan line, and his hips are pale-cream. Nick turns his back to me and stretches lazily like a jungle cat, arms bent. His ass is smooth and milky, downed with a light fuzz that gleams gold in the sun's rays. Nick turns around and smiles at me. His dick, half hard, sways heavily against his thighs.

I turn away and quickly pull my jeans off. When I look back at Nick, he's still standing there naked, only this time his dick is jutting out fully hard, twitching slightly in the light breeze. He sees my surprise and shrugs helplessly. "Sorry," he grins, his eyes wide and guileless. "Open air always makes me hard."

"This isn't a nude beach," I say, trying to sound casual. "You have to wear a suit."

"In a minute," Nick says. "I like feeling the breeze on my skin." His smile turns sly, and his eyes lose some of their innocence. He wraps his hand around his dick and strokes it slowly. "You like it, Robbie?" he asks. "Maria calls it my 'love club.' "

"What the hell are you trying to prove?" I ask.

Nick affects surprise. "I'm not trying to prove anything," he says, his tone all injured innocence. "I'm just making conversation." I quickly pull on my suit and walk back to the blanket. Nick joins us a couple of minutes later.

Nick and Maria race out into the waves. She pushes him into the path of a crashing breaker, laughing as he comes up sputtering. They horseplay in the surf line for a while and then swim out to deeper water. Eventually, they're just specks in the shiny, gun-metal blue. I close my eyes and feel the sun beat down on me. Rivulets of sweat begin to trickle down my torso.

Suddenly I'm in shade. I open my eyes and see Nick standing over me, the sun behind him so that I can't make out his features—just an outline of broad shoulders tapering down. He shakes his head and water spills down on me. "Hey!" I protest.

He sits down beside me on the blanket. "The water feels great," he says. "You should go out in it."

"In a little while," I say. "Where's Maria?"

Nick gestures vaguely. "Out there somewhere. She didn't want to come in yet." He stretches out next to me, propped up on his elbows. "So why are you so upset about me knowing you're gay? You think I'll disapprove or something?"

"Jeez, what's with you! Will you just drop the subject?"

"I've gotten it on with guys," Nick goes on, as if he hadn't heard me. "It's no big deal." He grins. "You want to hear about the last time I did?"

"No," I lie.

"It was in Hawaii. Oahu, to be exact." Nick turns on his side and faces me, his head on his hand. "I was there on spring break last year. I started hanging out with this dude I'd met in a Waikiki bar, a surfer named Joe." He laughs. "Surfer Joe, just like in the song. Ah, sweet Jesus, was he ever beautiful! Part Polynesian, part Japanese, part German. Smooth brown skin; tight, ripped body; and these fuckin' dark, soulful eyes." He smiles. "Like yours, Robbie. Like Maria's too, for that matter," he adds, as if it was an afterthought.

"Anyway, I had a rented car, and we took a drive to the North Shore. Somehow we wound up lost on this little piss-ass road—nothing but sugarcane fields on both sides. It'd been raining, but the sun was just breaking out, and all of a sudden, wham! This huge technicolored rainbow comes blazing out right in front of us." Nick sits up, getting excited. "It was fuckin' awesome! The motherfucker just arced overhead like some kind of neon bridge and ended not far off in this little grassy patch beyond the cane. Well, Joe leaps out of the car—I tell you, he was one crazy bastard—and he races across the field toward the rainbow, and because I couldn't think of anything better to do, I do the same."

Nick's eyes are wide, and he's talking faster now. "Joe makes it to where the rainbow hits the ground, he pulls off his board shorts, and he just stands there naked, his arms stretched out, the colors pouring down on him. Blue! Green! Red! Orange! I strip off my shorts too and jump right in."

Nick laughs, but his eyes drill into me. "It was the strangest damn sensation—standing in that rainbow, my skin tingling like a low-voltage current was passing through me." He blinks. "Joe wrestles me to the ground, one thing leads to another, and we wind up fucking right there with all the colors washing over us—me plowing Joe's ass, Joe's head red, his chest orange, his belly yellow, his legs green and blue. When I finally came, I pulled out of Joe's ass, raining my jizz down on him, the drops like colored jewels." Nick gazes down at me, his eyes laughing. "Like I said: fucking awesome!"

"You are so full of shit," I say.

Nick adopts an expression of deep hurt. "It's true. I swear it."

"Fuck you. You can't stand in a rainbow, for chrissakes. It's against the laws of optics."

" 'The laws of optics,' " Nick snorts. "What are you, an optician?"

"You mean a physicist. An optician prescribes glasses. Jesus, you're an ignorant fuck."

But Nick refuses to be insulted. He laughs and picks up my tube of sunblock. "Here," he says, "let me oil you up again. You've sweated off your first layer." Nick smears the goop on my chest and starts stroking my torso. His hand wanders down my belly and lies there motionless. I can feel the heat of his hand sink into my skin. The tips of his fingers slide under the elastic band of my suit. He looks at me, eyebrows raised. When I don't say anything, Nick slips his hand under my suit and wraps it around my dick. "Do the same to me," he urges.

"Maria..." I say.

Nick scans the ocean. "She's way out there," he says. "She can't see anything." His hand, still greased with sunblock, starts sliding up and down my dick. I close my eyes. "Come on," he whispers. "Do it to me too. Please."

My hand seems to have a mind of its own. It slides inside Nick's suit and wraps around his fat, hard dick. His love club. "Yeah, Robbie, that's good," Nick sighs. "Now stroke it."

We beat each other off as the sun blasts down on us, the ocean shimmering off in the distance like a desert mirage. After a few moments we pull our suits down to our knees. Nick smears his hand with a fresh batch of lotion and then slides it down my dick. I groan. "Yeah, baby," he laughs. "You like that, don't you?" I groan again louder, arching my back as the orgasm sweeps over me. Nick takes my dick in his mouth and swallows my load as I pump it down his throat. Even after I'm done he keeps sucking on my dick, rolling his tongue around it, playing with my balls. He replaces my hand with his and with a few quick strokes brings himself to climax, shuddering as his load splatters against his chest and belly.

Maria staggers out of the surf a few minutes later and races to the blanket, squealing from the heat of the sand on her soles. Nick and I are chastely reading our summer novels under the umbrella. She flings herself down on the blanket, grabs a towel, and vigorously rubs her hair. "You guys enjoying yourselves?" she asks.

"Yeah, sure," Nick says, his mouth curling up into an easy grin. "Except your degenerate little brother can't keep his hands off me." He winks. Maria laughs, but she shoots me a worried look, checking to see if I'm offended. I shrug and smile back. I feel like shit.

Nick stops by my place a week later. It's the first time I've seen him since the beach. "Is Maria here?" he asks. "I swung by her apartment, but she wasn't home." He's dressed in a tank top and cutoffs, and he carries a summer glow with him that makes him shine like a small sun.

"No," I say, my heart beating furiously. "I haven't seen her all day."

Nick peers over my shoulder. "You alone?"

"Yeah," I say. My mouth has suddenly gone desert-dry. Nick regards me calmly, waiting. "You want to come in for a while?" I finally ask.

Nick smiles and gives a slight shrug. "Why not?"

As soon as I close the door behind us he's on me, pushing me against the wall, his hard dick dry-humping me through the denim of his shorts, his mouth pressed against mine. After the initial shock passes I kiss him back, thrusting my tongue deep into his mouth. Nick's hands are all over me, pulling at my shirt, undoing the buttons, tugging down my zipper. He slides his hands under my jeans and cups my ass, pulling my crotch against his.

I push him away, gasping. "This isn't going to happen," I say.

Nick looks at me with bright eyes, his face flushed, his expression half annoyed, half amused. "Now, Robbie," he says, smiling his old smile. "You're not going to be a cocktease, are you?"

I zip my pants up again and rebutton my shirt. I feel the anger rising up in me. "You're such an asshole," I say. I push past him and walk into the living room.

Nick remains in the hallway. I sit on the couch, glaring at him. He slowly walks into the room until he's standing in front of me. He looks out the window and then back at me again. "Why am I an asshole?" he asks. "Because I think you're fuckin' beautiful?"

"You may not give a shit," I say, "but Maria's crazy about you."

Nick sits down beside me on the couch. "Ah," he says quietly. A silence hangs between us for a couple of beats. "What if I told you I'm just as crazy about Maria?" he finally asks.

"You sure have a funny way of showing it."

Nick leans back against the arm of the couch and regards me with his steady blue gaze. He gives a low laugh. " 'Now, next on Jerry Springer!' " he says. " 'My sister's boyfriend is putting the moves on me!' " I look at him hostilely, not saying anything. He returns my stare calmly. "You know," he says, "lately every time I fuck your sister I think of you. It's getting to be a real problem."

"Will you knock it off!"

Nick acts like he hasn't heard me. "It's no reflection on Maria, believe me. She's a knockout. Great personality, beautiful..." He leaves the sentence hanging in the air, lost in thought. His eyes suddenly focus on me. "But there are things I want that she just can't give me."

I wait awhile before I finally respond. "What things?" I ask sullenly.

Nick's smile is uncharacteristically wistful. "You, Robbie. That's 'what things.' " I don't say anything. Nick lays his hand on my knee. "It's fuckin' amazing how much you look like Maria sometimes. The same dark eyes, the same mouth, the same way you tilt your head. It's like the excitement of meeting Maria all over again." He leans forward, his eyes bright. "Only...you have a man's body, Robby. That's what Maria can't give me." His hand slides up my thigh. "She can't give me a man's muscles, a man's way of walking and talking." His hand slides up and squeezes my crotch. "A man's dick. I swear to God, if I had the two of you in bed together, I wouldn't ask for another thing for the rest of my motherfuckin' life!" He looks at me and laughs. "You should see your face now, Robbie. You look like you just sucked a lemon."

I feel my throat tightening. "You're fucking crazy if you think that's ever going to happen."

"Maybe I am crazy," Nick sighs. His eyes dart up to mine. "But I'm not stupid." His fingers begin rubbing the crotch of my jeans, lazily sliding back and forth. He grins slyly. "If I can't have you and Maria together, I'll settle for you both one at a time." He leans his face close to mine, his hand squeezing my dick. "Come on, Robbie, don't tell me I don't turn you on. Not after our little session on the beach."

I don't say anything. Nick's other hand begins lightly stroking my chest, fumbling with the buttons of my shirt.

"You want monogamy, Robbie?" he croons softly. "I promise I'll stay true to you and Maria. I'll never look at another family."

"Everything's a joke with you," I say. But I feel my dick twitch as his hand slides under my shirt and squeezes my left nipple.

"No, Robbie," Nick says softly. "Not everything." He cups his hand around the back of my neck and pulls me toward him. I resist but not enough to break his grip, and we kiss, Nick's tongue pushing apart my lips and thrusting deep inside my mouth. He reaches down and squeezes my dick again. "Hard as the proverbial rock!" he laughs.

"Just shut up," I say. We kiss again, and this time I let Nick unbutton my shirt. His hands slide over my bare chest, tugging at the muscles in my torso. He unbuckles my belt and pulls my zipper down. His hand slides under my briefs and wraps around my dick.

"We're going to do it nice and slow this time," Nick says. He tugs my jeans down, and I lift my hips to help him. It doesn't take long before Nick has pulled off all my clothes. He sits back, his eyes slowly sliding down my body. "So beautiful..." he murmurs. He stands up and shucks off his shirt and shorts, kicking them away. He falls on top of me, his mouth burrowing against my neck, his body stretched out fully against mine.

I kiss him again—gently this time, our mouths barely touching. His lips work their way over my face, pressing lightly against my nose, my eyes. His tongue probes into my ear, and his breath sounds like the sea in a conch shell. I feel his lips move across my skin, down my torso. He gently bites each nipple, swirling his tongue around them, sucking on them. I can see only the top of his head, the shock of blond hair, and I reach down and entwine my fingers in it, twisting his head from side to side. Nick sits up, his legs straddling my hips, his thick cock pointing up toward the ceiling. He wraps his hand around both our dicks and squeezes them together tightly. "Feel that, Robbie," he says. "Dick flesh against dick flesh." He begins stroking them, sliding his hand up and down the twin shafts: his, pink and fat; mine, dark and veined. Some precome leaks from his dick, and Nick slicks our dicks up with it. I breathe deeply, and Nick grins.

Nick bends down and tongues my belly button, his hands sliding under my ass. He lifts my hips up and takes my cock in his mouth, sliding his lips down my shaft until his nose is pressed against my pubes. He sits motionless like that—my dick fully down his throat, his tongue working against the shaft. Slowly, inch by inch, his lips slide back up to my cock head. He wraps his hand around my dick and strokes it as he raises his head and his eyes meet mine, laughing. "You like that, Robbie?" he asks. "Does that feel good?"

"Turn around," I say urgently. "Fuck my face while you do that to me."

I don't have to tell Nick twice. He pivots his body around, and his dick thrusts above my face: red, thick, the cock head pushing out of the foreskin and leaking precome. His balls hang low and heavy above my mouth, furred with light-blond hairs. I raise my head and bathe them with my tongue and then suck them into my mouth. I roll my tongue around the meaty pouch. "Ah, yeah," Nick groans. I slide my tongue up the shaft of his dick. Nick shifts his position and plunges his dick deep down my throat. He starts pumping his hips, sliding his dick in and out of my mouth as he continues sucking me off. I feel his torso squirm against mine, skin against skin, the warmth of his flesh pouring into my body. Nick takes my dick out of his mouth, and I feel his tongue slide over my balls and burrow into the warmth beneath them. He pulls apart my ass cheeks, and soon I feel his mouth on my asshole, his tongue lapping against the puckered flesh.

"Damn!" I groan.

Nick alternately licks and blows against my asshole. I arch my back and push up with my hips, giving him greater access. No one has ever done this to me before, and it's fucking driving me wild. Nick comes up for air, and soon I feel his finger pushing against my asshole and then entering me, knuckle by knuckle. I groan again, louder. Nick looks at me over his shoulder as he finger-fucks me into a slow-building frenzy. "Yeah, Robbie," he croons. "Just lie there and let me play you. Let's see what songs I can make you sing." He adds another finger inside me and pushes up in a corkscrew twist. I cry out, and Nick laughs.

He climbs off me and reaches for his shorts. "OK, Robbie," he says. "Enough with the fuckin' foreplay. Let's get this show on the road." He pulls a condom packet and a small tube of lube out of his back pocket and tosses the shorts back onto the floor.

I feel a twinge of irritation. "You had this all planned out, didn't you?"

Nick straddles my torso again, his stiff cock jutting out inches from my face. I trace one blue vein snaking up the shaft. "Let's just say I was open to the possibility," he grins. He unrolls the condom down his prick, his blue eyes never leaving mine. He smears his hand with lube, reaches back, and liberally greases up my asshole. Nick hooks his arms under my knees and hoists my legs up and around his torso. His gaze still boring into me, he slowly impales me.

I push my head back against the cushion, eyes closed. Nick leans forward, fully in. "You OK, baby?" he asks. His eyes are wide and solicitous.

I open my eyes and nod. Slowly, almost imperceptibly, Nick begins pumping his hips, grinding his pelvis against mine. He deepens his thrusts, speeding up the tempo. I reach up and twist his nipples, and Nick grins widely. A wolfish gleam lights up his eyes. He pulls his hips back until his cock head is just barely in my asshole, then plunges back in. "Fuckin' A," I groan.

"Fuckin' A is right," Nick laughs. He props himself up with his arms and fucks me good and hard—his balls slapping heavily against me with each thrust, his eyes staring into mine, his hot breath against my face. I cup my hand around the back of his neck and pull his face down to mine, frenching him hard as he pounds my ass. Nick leaves his dick fully up there, grinding his hips against mine in a slow circle before returning to the old in-and-out. He wraps a hand around my stiff dick and starts beating me off, timing his strokes with each thrust of his hips.

We settle into our rhythm: Nick slamming my ass, his hand sliding up and down my dick as I thrust up to meet him stroke for stroke. There's nothing playful or cocky about Nick now: His breath comes out in ragged gasps through his open mouth, sweat trickles down his face, and his eyes burn with the hard, bright light of a man working up to shoot a serious load.

I wrap my arms tight around his body and push up, squeezing my asshole tight around his dick at the same time. I look up at Nick's face and laugh; it's the first time I've ever seen him startled.

"Jesus," he gasps. "Did you learn that in college?"

I don't say anything—I just repeat the motion, squeezing my ass muscles hard as I push up to meet his thrust. Nick's body spasms as he moans strongly. "You ought to talk to Maria," he pants. "She could learn some things from you." The third time I do this pushes Nick over the edge, making him groan loudly and his body tremble violently. He plants his mouth on mine, kissing me hard as he squirts his load into the condom, up my ass. I wrap my arms around him in a bear hug, and we thrash around on the couch, finally spilling onto the carpet below—me on top, Nick sprawled with his arms wide out.

After a while he opens his eyes. "Sit on me," he says. "And shoot your load on my face."

I straddle him, dropping my balls into Nick's open mouth. He sucks on them noisily, slurping audibly as I beat off. Nick reaches up and squeezes my nipple, and that's all it takes for me. I give a deep groan, arching my back as my load splatters in thick drops onto Nick's face, creaming his nose and cheeks, dripping into his open mouth. "Yeah," Nick says, "that's right, baby." When the last spasm passes through me I bend down and lick Nick's face clean.

I roll over and lie next to Nick on the thick carpet. He slides his arm under me and pulls me to him. I burrow against his body and close my eyes, feeling his chest rise and fall against the side of my head. Without meaning to, I drift off into sleep.

When I wake up, the clock on the mantle says it's almost 1 in the morning. Nick is gone, but he's covered me with a quilt from my bed. I'm too sleepy to get up, so I just drift back into sleep again.

Nick, Maria, and I are all sitting on Maria's couch watching Night of the Living Dead on her TV. Maria sits between us, nestling against Nick. We're at the scene where the little girl has turned into a ghoul and is nibbling on her mother's arm like it was a hoagie sandwich. "Gross!" Maria says.

Nick grins. "You're so damn judgmental, Maria," he says. "I don't put you down when you eat those Spam-and-mayonnaise sandwiches of yours."

Maria laughs and burrows deeper against Nick. As we continue watching the movie I feel Nick's fingers playing with my hair, and I brush them away with a brusque jerk that I make sure Maria doesn't notice. After a while, though, he's doing it again. When I don't do anything this time, Nick entwines his fingers in my hair and tugs gently. From where she's sitting, Maria can't see any of this. The ghouls are surrounding the farmhouse now, closing in on the victims inside. Eventually I lean back and sink into the feel of Nick's fingers in my hair.

Nocturne
By Barry Alexander

Darius walked down the empty street, between rows of houses shut tight against the autumn night. Piles of leaves smoldered at the end of driveways, and on porches, faceless pumpkins waited for the knife. Plastic skeletons hung from trees, their bones rattling in the wind. Cardboard tombstones sprouted incongruously from manicured lawns, and mummies beckoned from open caskets. Darius shuddered. He wondered at the eagerness with which people festooned their yards with the trappings of death.

A cold wind brushed his face, sweeping his soft brown hair back from his forehead. Darius tucked his hands deeper into his jeans pockets, wishing he'd worn his jacket as he kicked leaves that drifted along the curb. His legs ached, but he kept walking, restlessness compelling him down unfamiliar streets. The houses flanking the street became smaller and farther apart, the yards littered with toys abandoned for the night.

Streetlights faded away, and the blacktop gave out and turned to dirt. The road narrowed as trees closed in on either side. Soon Darius was following a path that meandered through the trees until his way was blocked by a tall, wrought iron gate, its black spikes stabbing the sky. Beyond the gate, the woods opened into a clearing that stretched into the distance, enticing him. Wind rippled the tall grass, shadows dancing over the undulating surface.

The place felt familiar, as if he had been there many times. Though how that could be he didn't know. A huge antique padlock secured the gate, so covered with rust he did not think it would open even if he had a key. Darius felt a wave of longing as he looked through the bars. Something lay beyond the gate, something that he was seeking, though he could not name it. He felt an overpowering need to pass through the gate. In frustration, Darius wrapped his hands around the bars. The cold bars pressed against his face as he peered through them. "Please," he asked, though he believed in no deity—there was no one to hear him. He only knew he had to enter.

Darius knocked, but no one came. He called; no one answered. He had the strangest sensation that he had done this many times before without response. He couldn't stop himself. He had to get inside. He beat on the gate until his fists were bloody. He felt a vibration beneath his hands. The lock snapped open and the gate swung wide beneath his touch. Darius shivered in anticipation. It was there, just on the other side. He stepped through.

Darius opened his eyes to darkness. He was shaking and he had no idea why. I just had the weirdest dream, he turned to tell Alex, then felt the kick in the guts he always felt when he remembered. God, you'd think the loss should be so ingrained in his soul he wouldn't have those half moments when he'd forget.

He stared at the ceiling—trying to get back to sleep—and listened as the wind rattled the window and moaned through the branches of a big maple tree. He tried to imagine that the tangle of blankets touching his side was Alex's body curled next to him. That he could lean over and touch him, feel his warmth, tangle his legs with his. It didn't work. It never did. Ten years of sleeping together, of bodies wrapped around each other every night, of listening to Alex snore— Darius just couldn't fall asleep easily anymore. He sighed and got up to take another sleeping pill.

He tried to remember his dream, but it faded before he could grasp the details. Weird. He felt like he'd had the same dream before, though how that could be, when he remembered nothing, he couldn't begin to guess. He felt a great sense of longing, and somehow he knew that if he could just dream the dream all the way through, all his questions would be answered.

Darius pulled the blanket to his chin, waiting for the pill to take effect. Wind rose and fell in tides that swept around his house, great currents of northern air washing in and sweeping away the last of summer. Then the sounds faded, became distant. Sleep claimed him.

The gate opened before him. Darius walked across a dark summer meadow. He heard the calls of night birds and the distant music of water. He followed the sound to a place of shadowy gardens where moon flowers bloomed between velvet-mossed stones at the base of a waterfall. A huge willow bent over a pool of black water, a thousand lightning bugs dancing among its swaying tendrils.

It was a place of magic. Darius was not at all surprised when the man stepped out from behind the tree, nor was he surprised to see that the man was totally naked. He had to be dreaming. Nothing human could be so serenely beautiful.

The man was tall and slim, his lithe body as pale as moonlight and as perfect. He walked like a king garbed in royal robes, no, like a god robed in night. Ripples of shiny black hair flowed over his shoulders. His deep-set eyes were as luminescent as black pearls, his check bones sharp as a scythe, his lips full and sensual. He looked young, but there were eons in the depths of his eyes.

Darius felt his cock swell and rise at the sheer beauty of the man. Then he realized that nothing had impeded his full arousal. Startled, he looked down. His cock stood proudly erect and fully exposed.

The man threw his head back and laughed. "You walk in dreams, Darius. All men are naked here, but only a few of your kind are permitted into my...garden."

"Who are you?"

"Do you not know, mortal? You have sought me for a long time."

"You seem...familiar."

"We met once, but you will not remember that here, unless I choose. Only one thing matters: Do you truly want me, Darius?"

"Who are you?"

"Death."

Br-r-r-i-i-i-ng!

Darius slammed his hand down, shutting off the alarm. God, he'd had that dream again. It felt closer this time, more real. He tried to remember, but the thoughts slipped away. He groaned as he dragged himself out of bed. He hated mornings. He glanced at the clock. Shit! Seven o'clock and it was still dark. Rain slashed against the window. He thought about calling in sick, but he'd already used up all his sick days.

He drove to work through the darkness, following the red glow of the taillights ahead of him. Hypnotized by the monotonous beat of the wipers, barely able to see anything but the red eyes in front of him, he almost missed his turn.

It was a shitty day. His supervisor was pissed over some stupid report. Everyone else seemed to be in a really bad mood. Darius wondered why the hell they cared. Did it really make a difference if Corporate got their expense report a day late?

Darius slogged through the day, counting the hours until he could go home. God, he was tired. And it seemed like once it started to get cold, he stayed chilled all day. He couldn't wait to go back and crawl into bed. A good night's sleep was what he needed.

He wasn't thrilled when Ben stopped him on the way out. Now what?

"Darius! We're going out and hit the bars. Friday, you know! We're gonna get dressed up and everything. You want to come along? I'm sure I can put a costume together for you."

"Thanks, but some other time, OK? I just don't feel up to bar hopping tonight."

"OK, but don't forget you promised to meet me at the Olive Garden for lunch tomorrow. And, we have to go out Saturday night. It beats staying home with a bowl of candy."

"Yeah, sure. See ya later."

Ben looked at him a little oddly, but Darius didn't really care. They'd been pretty good friends. The three of them—Alex, Ben, and Darius had gone everywhere together. But Ben was becoming a pest. He seemed to think he had to keep an eye out for Darius. Always trying to talk him into going out. Even setting up guys for him to meet. Fuck Ben. Darius wished everyone would just leave him the hell alone.

Darius grabbed a burger on the way home and ate it as he drove. Alex would have lectured him about junk food, but fixing supper for one seemed pretty pointless. He stopped and picked up a six pack, then swung by the pharmacy on his way home.

He still hadn't gotten used to the silence; the house echoed with it. Darius grabbed one of the beers and put the rest in the fridge. His nose wrinkled. Something was starting to go bad. He'd have to clean it out—one of these days. He flipped on the TV as he did every night now. Some inane sitcom was on—a bunch of ex-comedians being chased by a ghost—but Darius didn't bother changing the station. He sat down in front of the screen and read the paper, column by column, word by word—sports, finance, home and garden—all with equal disinterest. He finished his nightly ritual and glanced at the clock. Still too early for bed. He supposed he could do some laundry, but it didn't seem worth the effort. Darius got another beer and sat, watching the flickering images on the screen, waiting for the time to pass.

Darius settled into bed with a sigh of relief. No need to think about his job or Ben or anything. He didn't feel so empty here. He was warm and safe and he didn't think he ever wanted to get out of bed again. Sleep rose around him, dark and warm. He reached for it, welcoming it, and pulled it down into his arms.

Death's cock hung like a pale sword between his thighs. Even soft, it had an incredible length. Darius watched with awe as the slim weapon swelled and darkened until it was a battering ram of flesh.

Death smiled at the naked lust on Darius's face. "Come, taste what you have hungered for."

Darius dropped to his knees before him. Dark veins marbled the pale shaft. The foreskin still shrouded the dusky glans, forming a small sphincter of delicate skin. As he watched, a drop of moisture formed at the tip, hanging for a long moment as delicate as a drop of dew. Darius caught the single drop on his tongue before it could fall. Tasting its sweetness for the first time—warm and rich and earthy, like no other man Darius had ever tasted. His tongue dug inside the delicate skin, searching for more. He felt the shudder ripple through Death's powerful thighs as his tongue found the tiny slit and eagerly licked for more of Death's juices.

Darius gently eased the skin back, exposing the dusky glans to his attentions. His tongue flicked gently over the bulbous head. He opened wide and let the cock glide over his tongue. Warm flesh filled his mouth, widening his lips as he strove to take all. It bumped against the back of his throat, almost gagging him, but he swallowed and pressed closer and it slid down his throat. His nose pressed deep into the thick mat of pubic hair. The long hairs tickling the insides of his nostrils. He held there for a long moment, breathing deeply the scent of male musk. His hands stroked the broad thighs and moved to cup the hard round cheeks as he buried his face in the man's groin.

Slender fingers played in his hair but Death made no attempt to control his movements. Darius sucked slowly, letting the cock glide in and out of his mouth. It was so good, so big. He didn't even try to pleasure himself. All his attention was locked on the magnificent organ filling his mouth. He couldn't get enough of it. He drove himself onto the cock, again and again, taking it down his throat as far and as fast as he could. He worked his throat muscles and gave himself up to pleasuring Death, forgetting everything but the need to get as much of this cock as he could. Darius hungered to be filled, and he impaled his throat again and again, eager for the taste of Death.

With a groan, Death pushed him off. "Enough. Mortals may know the taste of Death, but no more while they wear living flesh. I have watched from the shadows of your dreams for a long time. You are more mine than you know. But it takes one final step. Now go. It is time for you to leave."

Darius looked at him in shock. "No, I don't want to. No, don't..."

But even as he protested, the garden blurred and shifted, and he was drifting in a dense fog. He couldn't move, his arms and legs seemed weighted as he slowly sank to the bottom. Cold tendrils of mist swirled about him, fingering his naked body. For a long time he could hear nothing. Then he heard the distant moan of wind, rising until it filled his ears with its roar. His body seemed very far away, and he floated helplessly, unable to move as he listened to the wind. The fog broke apart, leaving only darkness and the wind rattling his window.

Darius woke to a great sense of loss. This time he remembered. Everything. The images were so intense they were more real than the room around him. He belonged there. There was nothing else for him. He had to go back. Had he ever felt such desire for anyone? Even the pain of Alex had receded to a dull ache, like something he'd dreamed long ago. All he could think of was his overwhelming desire for Death.

He tried to pull sleep around him like a blanket, seeking the beginning of the dream, the path through the trees to the meadow and the gate. He drifted in and out of half-dreams, clinging to sleep, but unable to go deeper. And then he remembered the pills.

Darius sighed as he sank back into bed and pulled the covers up around him. His body settled into the familiar hollows with contentment. He pushed his feet into the coolness at the bottom of the sheets and shivered as he snuggled the thick blanket around him. He could drift off to sleep warm and safe and forget about everything.

He was close to sleep but an annoying sound kept intruding. It took him a moment to identify the sound. The phone rang and rang and rang. He tried to ignore it, but it wouldn't shut up. Groggily, Darius picked it up.

"Uh'lo?"

"Darius? I've been ringing for ages. Why didn't you meet me?"

"Forgot."

"My God, it's one in the afternoon. Are you all right?"

"Fine," Darius said with a yawn. "Sleepy, call you later." He dropped the receiver on the bed, but he could still hear Ben talking. Why wouldn't he just shut up.

"Maybe you should see someone. Darius, I'm worried about you. It's been a year. Darius?"

Darius fumbled with the phone, aiming it at his mouth, forcing himself awake. "Fuck off, Ben. I'm fine I tell you. Just leave me alone."

Darius pushed the phone off the bed. No more interruptions.

Darius drifted down into the warm, silent darkness. Sleep, like a great weight, dragged him down. Let go, the voice told him. Just let it happen. He was so tired. There was nothing he wanted more than sleep. To walk in dreams. So warm, it was so warm here. He drifted down into darkness.

Darius fell back on the grass, knees raised, offering himself for Death's pleasure. Death stood silhouetted against the darkness. His pale body bright against black. He looked like some ancient god towering over Darius, and for a moment, Darius felt incredibly vulnerable. But he wanted that giant cock inside him, spreading him open and filling him like no one had ever done before. He parted his legs in eagerness, exposing his tight hole.

Death knelt between his legs and leaned forward, supporting himself with his arms on either side of Darius's head. Slowly, he lowered himself, so close that Darius felt his body heat, but Death didn't actually touch him.

"Do you want me? I must hear you say the words." His face was so close, his breath softly touched Darius's face. Darius couldn't take his eyes away.

The grass was thick and cool against his bare back and a thousand, thousand stars danced overhead, but Darius saw only the ones that glittered in Death's eyes.

"I want you. I think I've always wanted you." His head lowered, his long dark hair shrouding Darius's face in darkness, just before his lips enveloped Darius's. His chest pressed against Darius, the skin smooth and warm.

Death plundered his mouth. His lips locked around Darius's, the soft, moist underside sucking at Darius's lips and teasing them apart. His tongue delved into the back of his throat. He caught Darius's wrists in his hands and held them over his head as he ravaged Darius's mouth.

Darius raised his hips, offering himself. Death's cock brushed against the portal. He moved his hips to center his member. Darius's hole fluttered against the cock head pressed against it, inviting it to enter.

Death's eyes speared Darius as he paused before entering.

"Take me."

Death rocked forward, plunging his cock deep inside. Darius opened to him, unable and unwilling to resist the determined assault. The cock moved forward, pushing wide the inner walls of Darius's bowels and claiming the space for itself.

Darius clung to Death, feasted on him as he was filled like he never had been before. He could do this forever he thought, as Death's cock plunged in and out of him. His own cock beat against his stomach aching for release.

Death reached between them and wrapped his fist around Darius's cock. His hand pumped in time with his thrusts. Darius groaned as the huge cock pummeled his guts. It felt so damned good. And then he couldn't hold back anymore. He stiffened and shuddered, splattering his come all over Death's chest and stomach.

His muscles clamped around the cock plunging so deeply inside him. And then he felt a great surge as Death shuddered against him. A torrent of hot fluid filled him and he sighed in total satisfaction.

He clung to Death, his head pillowed on his chest and Death's arms wrapped tightly around him. Sleep rose to claim him once more. The wind sang to him. Voices mingled with the wind, but the sounds were distant. He thought he could hear Ben's voice, but his words broke into sounds without meaning.

"Dare us! how man y p ills ? Dare us!"

And then it didn't matter—falling into the abyss—more sounds in the air.

"O Ga... Call n ambu nce... dun wor... ang n... Dare... Dare..."

But, there were the warm arms of Death, the falling, a gentle whisper, "Sleep, my love, sleep. You have nothing to fear. Even life can't last forever."

Snowbound

By Lee Alan Ramsay

I hadn't seen a highway sign in maybe 40 minutes, not that I was traveling that fast. Since there was close to half a foot of snow on the ground, I wasn't sure I was on a highway at all; it could have been a mere trail. If this was indeed the shortcut I saw on the map, then I would be breaking out onto 89 within the next five miles.

However, the deeper I got into the thick, heavy forest and the narrower, bumpier, and more twisted the roadway—whatever it was—became, the more I started thinking I had taken a very wrong turn. When flurries added to the already blowing snow, I decided to find a wide place to turn around. With the gas gauge indicating that I had about a quarter of a tank, I didn't have the luxury of a lot of time to experiment, and roads that the state kept plowed were preferable to the meandering thing I was on. It would be dark in another hour.

I saw a slight break in the trees to the left. I headed the hood ornament slowly in the direction of the gap, came to a stop, and put the car in reverse. I was just about to stop and begin another swing when the right rear of my Saturn gave way with a loud metallic bang.

There must have been a ditch—a very deep ditch by the feel—on the right-hand side of the roadway, and I was now partly in it. When I put the transmission into drive once again, the heavy clanking and whirring sounds issuing from the rear of the vehicle told me I was also in serious trouble.

I got out and surveyed the right rear tire, which was at a crazy angle to the rest of the car. I had broken an axle.

Getting back into the driver's seat, I did some quick thinking. I had a heavy parka that would keep me warm through the night. On the seat beside me were a half-filled bag of Doritos and a quarter of a cup of cold coffee. Even with nothing to eat, I could last the night.

It was too close to dark to strike out on foot in any direction, and at least with the closed car, I'd have some protection from the wind. And if I idled the engine for just a few minutes at a time, I could provide myself with a little heat. In the morning I could head back to the road and flag someone down.

I tried not to think too much about how stupid I'd been to turn off the marked roads. It wasn't like I was desperate to get back home to L.A. or anything.

It was then that I noticed a small sign up ahead, partially obliterated by the swirling snow. I squinted just in case desperation was making my eyes play tricks on me. No, it was a small white sign with black letters, which I couldn't read at that distance. I zipped up the parka and got out again.

On closer inspection I saw that the sign read ranger station 3 mi., with an arrow pointing up, indicating straight ahead.

I looked back at my stricken Saturn and decided to try for the station. If it was locked up solid, I still had enough daylight left to get back to the car. But plan B held out the hope of warmth, a little food, and a means to communicate with the outside world. I trudged off in the deepening snow; I hadn't a moment to lose.

After 20 or so minutes, I saw light in the distance. It was still snowing lightly, but I could see square yellow windowpanes. A few more steps, and I could discern the outline of a rude cabin.

The cabin was small and square with a sharply pitched dormerless roof, and smoke poured from the huge stone chimney. On the wide front porch, raised and relatively sheltered from the snowfall, was a stack of cut wood.

I hammered on the rough-hewn panels of the windowless door and shouted, "Is anyone home? "

I heard stirring from inside, and eventually the knotted panels of the door creaked open. A huge bearded man in black briefs and a red tank top stood there to greet me. He was frowning heavily and seemed outrageously disturbed by my presence.

"Yeah?"

"Uh, sir...I broke an axle down your road a ways, and I wonder if you have a phone."

I could feel the warmth of the cabin flowing out the open door. The stranger seemed not to mind the cold air replacing it around his scantily clad body. He stood there mute and scowling.

"Maybe I could also warm myself by your fire while we're waiting for the tow truck?" I added tentatively.

The man was large; he must have been six-five at least, and he was heavily muscled. But there was a bigness about him that went beyond stature, a presence that must have commanded attention when he walked into any room. His ruddy, florid face was surrounded by unruly wisps of black hair and a full beard of the same raven shade. Dark eyes shone out from his face, twinkling even in the gathering dusk.

It seemed that the stranger needed a long time to frame his comments, as if he were being charged money for words and had to be efficient with them. "No tow trucks comin' out on a night like this. No business on this road anyway."

I was cold and beginning not to feel my feet anymore. And it suddenly occurred to me that this man was being cruelly hostile. I'm only five-six and certainly represented no threat to this Paul Bunyan.

"Gee, I'm sorry to have bothered you," I snapped. "I'll just knock on your neighbor's door instead. Maybe he'll be a little more civil than you."

The stranger snorted. "Snotty little article. You'd never know I hold out salvation for you."

"Not if you don't let me in," I countered, unflustered by his blustery manner.

At this he stood aside from the doorway and bid me enter with a gesture.

The interior of the cabin was clean but claustrophobic. The single room was no bigger than the average square living room. One side of the chamber was dominated by an overstuffed easy chair and a double bed with heaps of plain cotton quilting. There was a braided rug in earth tones on the floor. The other side of the room held a huge black wood-burning stove of ancient vintage and a small wooden kitchen table of perhaps the same decade of manufacture as the stove; it had plain sturdy square legs and a distressed mahogany-colored surface. There was a single kitchen chair of a different design from the table.

Behind the table and stove was a wall of shelves, floor to ceiling, obviously the pantry. The deep shelves were lined with cans, bags, and boxes. To one side of the shelving was a niche with a two-way radio. My spirits brightened when I spotted that detail, not having seen a telephone in my opening scan of the room.

"My name is Oscar," I said, pulling the parka hood off my head. "I was heading back to L.A. from Greenboro—that's a little town in the upper northeast corner of California. Thought I'd see a little of the Sierras on my way back. I saw a chance to cut 20 miles off the trip with a little shortcut. Guess that map's mismarked or something..."

From the stranger's stark silence, I suddenly realized I was carrying on like a demented magpie. I offered my hand.

"Darien," he said. He had a firm handshake, tough but not bone-crushing. He went to the stove and poured me a mug of coffee from the speckled blue pot. He moved with a pantherlike grace, silently on bare bony feet that had to be size 15s at least. He handed me the steaming mug and pointed to the easy chair, bathed in a pool of bright light from a floor lamp with a yellowing fringed shade. There was a book facedown on one of the arms; I had interrupted his evening reading. I glanced at the title as I sat: Lady Chatterley's Lover.

Darien pulled the kitchen chair into the center of the room and sat within conversation distance of me. He had beautifully sculpted thighs, which he spread wide, and a bulge in the black briefs that could possibly have taken my breath away had I been at liberty to stare at it for a few consecutive minutes. From the rather rude greeting this man had given me so far, I decided not to press my luck.

I looked over at the radio. "So can we contact the outside world from here?"

"Sure."

There was nothing more. No more words, nothing in the way of movement toward the sacred microphone that might have spared me any more anxiety over my situation. I pondered what I was doing wrong. Was I not communicating my desire to leave? Was there some kind of a language barrier? Perhaps I was to use the radio myself. Perhaps Darien needed to be told exactly what I wanted: Darien, baby. I want you to go to the radio, activate it, call the nearest similar radio, and relay the message that Oscar has a broken-down car, a reasonable amount left on his MasterCard, and a stern desire to return to the

City of the Angels, otherwise known as La-La Land.

It seemed that my host had an inertia problem. Bodies at rest tend to remain at rest...

"Darien, sir...I realize I've interrupted a quiet evening at home for you, but if we could just make some kind of call out to civilization..."

My host interrupted me. "What makes you think this place is uncivilized?"

The question gave me cause to ponder a moment. "Well," I began slowly, "I don't see a gas station nearby. There aren't exactly a lot of hotels and bars around with lighted signs. We're not in the real thick of a lot of people."

"And lights, buildings, people make up civilization?" Darien asked matter-of-factly. "One person alone can't be civilized?"

It was warm in the room in more ways than one. I used the time to pull off my parka to think. "I'm sorry if I've offended you, sir. I didn't mean to demean your situation here. As rustic as it is, it is obviously not uncivilized."

For the first time Darien smiled. The beautiful Santa Claus lips spread wide, and the thick hair around his mouth moved. "I could call now, but no one'd come out till morning, maybe day after tomorrow morning if it snows all night. Why don't you just plan on staying the night, and we'll bring someone out for your car when we can?"

"Sounds like a plan to me," I said. I sensed my host was growing a trifle more at ease with my presence. Perhaps he was one of those people who is shy with strangers; that could account for his apparent status as a hermit in a rather inhospitable section of wilderness. Surely he was not bothered by very many visitors, even if he was a forest ranger.

I was in the mood for a hearty meal and a good stiff drink or two, but if he had already eaten and was a teetotaler, I could survive. At least I was warm.

My spirits brightened significantly over the next moment.

"I was about ready to start supper," said Darien. "Can't offer much more than tinned stuff, but you're welcome to join me."

"I'm pretty handy in the kitchen, sir. And though I've never cooked on a wood stove before, it's always been a fantasy of mine to try. Maybe you could let me put something together, and you could go back to just relaxing with your book. A little effort on my part to thank you for your hospitality."

Darien nodded, his pensive lips extended. Oh, those thin rust-colored lips in that vast nest of black hair! At length he made a slow sweeping gesture to the pantry shelves and indicated the row of clean pots and pans on the warming shelf over the stove. He pointed to the stack of wood in a huge hod next to the firebox.

He sank into the easy chair I'd just vacated, absorbing himself immediately in the pages of Lady Chatterley's sexual Olympics. Pity, I thought. Hairy, masculine, built, hung...and getting his jollies off on a het sex book. Sigh.

I found some chipped beef, one jar among dozens on the shelf. Though nonfat dry milk was no substitute for the real thing, I mixed it thick enough for a creamy nuance; there was enough thyme and oregano to bump up flavors and make cream chipped beef over soda biscuits, something you'd order again at a truck-stop beanery. I tested the heat of the oven for the biscuits by sticking my hand into its dark depths, like I knew what 350 degrees felt like on my bare skin! And when I finished preparing a side of French-cut string beans heavy with garlic powder, I was ready to call my host to the table.

During that half hour I watched him "unconsciously" scratch his crotch 14 times by actual count, and I got the feeling it was not because his bulging genitals were itchy. He sat in the huge wing chair—done in a faded gold brocade that looked like a relic that had tarnished—with his legs as wide apart as when he was sitting in the kitchen chair, which point raised the serious question of where I was going to sit at the dinner table. There was only one table chair in the tiny room.

That's not all there wasn't.

There was no sink and consequently nothing to draw water into. But this was no tragedy since there was nothing to draw water from either, not even a pump with a curved metal handle. I ladled water for the meal from a huge pot on the stove; I guessed it was melted snow.

There was also no door in the room leading to anything resembling a bathroom, which I was going to need within an hour or so.

And since I had been on the road a day and a half without bathing, I was especially curious about this strange home's other sanitary facilities.

"It's soup," I said to my host.

He looked over the top of his book and smiled. Setting the volume down on the brocaded chair arm, he rose and went to the door. A gust of cold snowy air burst in; he didn't bother closing the panels for the time he was on the porch. After 30 seconds of chilly blasts, he returned with a captain's chair in scuffed and warped maple, which he slid toward the table. That answered the question of where the second of us was to sit for dinner. My other questions—and some I had not even thought of—would be answered within the hour.

My host was apparently not used to eating in close quarters with other people, at least not people with genteel tastes. Darien hunched over his plate, clamped all four fingers over the handle of a spoon, and shoveled food into his mouth like an Aborigine. I tried not to notice, though his table manners and the fact that he chewed with his mouth open were nauseating.

I disarmed the situation with chitchat.

"So I was visiting my Aunt Charity, she's the one I told you about earlier, the one who's been real generous with me over the years, especially at Christmastime. Anyway, I wanted to make sure she was settled in the new retirement community, Lazy Acres; you remember, I mentioned that earlier too. Well, I just wanted to make sure the place was decent and that they were taking care of her OK. Anyway, I talked to the resident manager and made sure she'd get the best of care, then I just headed home. Aunt Charity isn't too coherent anymore." I paused in my monologue to make a twirling-finger gesture at my temple.

"Anyway, it's not that I really need to get home or anything. I can't tell you why I decided to even look for a shortcut back to L.A. I have this dippy roommate, Greg; I told you about him. Well, I'm not exactly desperate to get back to his craziness." Though in Chatty Cathy mode, I decided not to go any further with the part of my story concerning Greg, my ex-lover. "And I mean, like, a mail-room job at Moist Erotic Entertainment Enterprises isn't anything you'd want to put on a résumé these days. I think they could actually struggle through an extra day or two without me. Besides, stuffing Harvey Takes a Dive and Bambi's Audition into boxes for shipping isn't anyone's idea of a career these days, take it from one who knows."

I'm not sure when I noticed it, but I was the only one talking during dinner. I'm not even sure Darien acknowledged my efforts at conversation with the proper grunted monosyllables. I just prattled on as if what I was saying was the most important talk in the world.

When I finally sat back and relaxed in the captain's chair, sated and silent at least for a moment, Darien stood and in a single motion lowered all the dirty dishes into the water pot on the stove. It was my guess that they'd simmer for the night, a very convenient and most effective dishwasher, and the water would be discarded in favor of new snow in the morning.

My host checked the firebox, threw in another two chunks of split wood, closed the wrought iron door, and damped it down to nearly zero air for the gentle blaze within. "That'll go the night."

Starve the blaze of air, and it lasts a long time.

I decided the time was right to get bold about sanitation facilities. "Uh, Darien, sir, I need to use the euphemism, if you could point me in the right direction. And if it wouldn't be a huge imposition on your hospitality, I'd like to shower...or bathe, as the case may be in your establishment."

My host stood in the middle of the room and deliberately pulled the red tank top over his head, revealing a thickly muscled chest, tanned and covered with a matting of black hair. The man then casually bent over and lowered the black briefs from his crotch. I had to stifle a gulp.

He was gorgeous. No more than a 30-inch waist, yet he bulged everywhere else: pecs, ass cheeks, biceps. His thick flaccid penis dangled a quarter of the way to his knees, and his heavily muscled thighs pushed the softball-size nut bag out from his body. And all of it was covered with black hair—not thick, kinky, fluffy hair but smooth black fur that hugged his ruddy skin. I was having a lot of difficulty remaining civil.

Standing buck naked in the middle of his single room, my host bowed slightly at the waist and gestured to the front door, the only door. Maybe he misunderstood what I had just asked for. Then again, I was the one most likely to misunderstand anything in this realm.

Darien motioned with one upturned palm that I was to stand. I complied. Then he pinched at garments he no longer had on and gestured "nakedness." I shook my head in disbelief but complied with his oblique orders. I sat to take off my shoes and socks, pulled my T-shirt over my head, lowered my jeans, and stripped off my Jockey briefs.

"Hul-lo," I said. "Bathroom? Shower? Toilet?"

The huge man grabbed me by the wrist and pulled me to the cabin door, opening it with his free hand. I was led out onto the porch and down the front steps into a pool of moonlight on the snow-covered front lawn.

I couldn't believe what was happening. He took me to the side of his home, where he squatted and promptly relieved himself. Unable to come up with a reason why not, I imitated him, right beside him, though my bare feet were being assaulted by icy knives of cold.

He moved a few feet from his steaming pile of urine and excrement and began scooping up handfuls of snow, first to wipe his crotch area and then, with new clumps of white powder, to scrub the rest of his body: armpits, face, chest, legs.

I was getting shivery with the cold, so as long as this was going to be my evening toilette, I decided to make it quick. I moved away from my own relievings and doused myself wildly with snow. Actually, I have to admit, not only was the notion of bathing in snow just kinky enough to make it exciting, but romping about on a mountaintop naked with this incredible hunk of male sinew was beginning to turn me on. I rubbed snow thoroughly in my crack area and shampooed my reddish brown hair with snow as well.

Then I felt the cold invading me to a point that I knew was dangerous. Beginning to shiver more violently, I scrambled up the steps of the cabin and raced inside, followed by my bounding, laughing host. Our bare feet pounded on the rough boards and braided rug.

"As long as the core doesn't get cold..." he bubbled.

I raced for the stove and spread my arms, putting as much of my body in contact with the radiating heat as I could. I felt both clean and invigorated. And my natural functions had been satisfied as well.

As rude as his ways might be, I was somehow getting in tune with this rough mountain man.

Darien turned toward the bed and bent over, showing his beautiful hairy cheeks and his livid wrinkled ball sac sagging between the backs of his thighs. He began turning the quilts down. "OK," he pronounced, "I'm turning in. Ya got yer choice. The floor, the easy chair, or in here with me."

"Uh..." I fumbled, still not sure of my status in this household. "I guess I'd better tell you straight out so there's no misunderstanding: I'm gay—you know, homosexual—and it might be best if I take the floor or the chair, just so nothing untoward happens during the night."

Even as I delivered the last of that ridiculous line—like I would force myself on this man, who was roughly twice my size and weight—I realized how utterly stupid I could get sometimes. Then I realized I was even stupider still.

Darien stood up from arranging the bed and turned toward me to reveal a semi-hard-on that was beginning to angle away from his magnificent loins. The thick penis was still curved slightly downward, but it was veined and rugged, like the mountaintop we were both standing on, tough and demanding. He had an almost exasperated expression on his face, as if to say, "Gay? Why, whatever do you mean?"

"Oh, God," I heard myself saying into the yellow light of the cabin. Then something like "Darien, please, could we just sit and talk about this for a minute..."

My host simply snapped his fingers in the direction of his open bed. I must say, I've been seduced by the direct and very effective "Let's fuck" line in bars before, but Darien had these amateurs beat by light-years!

I left the warmth of the stove and slid under the quilts; Darien slipped in beside me and immediately enfolded me in his arms. He extended his tongue and licked around my neck slowly, like a snail leaving trails. Then he journeyed up my neck to an earlobe and began nibbling on it. I could feel the steady puffs of air on the side of my face.

I became a puddle of goose pimples. I let out a guttural moan of pleasure that has meaning only in an animal realm. I let my hands roam about his massive back; he was hairy even there. As he pressed our bodies closer and closer together, I felt his mighty organ growing stiff between us. This was the kind of penis that moved solid objects out of the way as it engorged itself.

He began caressing me slowly, very delicately. His palms were rough, like sandpaper, but he put so very little pressure on my skin that the sensation of iron fist–velvet glove sent me into waves of shivering ecstasy: my arms, my chest—with lingering stops at the nipples—my abdomen, my thighs. I had been hard for some minutes now but became totally aware of just how aroused I was only when he closed his fist around my throbbing dick.

Aroused? This man was arousing me in ways that went way beyond the mere physical. It was as if I were not a slave to just my nerve endings anymore—or perhaps he was stimulating nerve endings in my mind and imagination. His clean, musky scent invaded my nostrils, unclouded by manufactured perfumes.

I got bolder. I wanted to caress him too. No, that was a lie—or at least not the complete truth. I did want to let my palms explore his hairy skin but only after I thoroughly explored and fondled his penis and testicles. I wanted to hold the organs in my hand, actually feel their bulk and weight. Perhaps I wanted to feel how demanding they were becoming. I reached down and drew my fingers around the warm, pulsating cock. I inched a few centimeters closer to utter erotic insanity.

He did not thwart my efforts to grope him. Rather, I sensed he might have shifted his body ever so slightly to give me room to probe his crotch.

As I let my fingertips explore the hard shaft of male flesh, I think I made some trashy reference to the Almighty. I let my fingers inch their way down to the rod's base, where I gathered up the balls and pressed them against his hairy crotch. The bulging sac felt like a living cactus plant, bristling with black stubble. I fondled each testicle in turn and returned to holding the cock in my curved fingers.

Then I delivered the line of all ridiculous lines: "Are you going to rape me with this piece of meat?"

"It's going up your ass. If you don't want it there, then I guess it'll be rape."

I deserved that.

I could have simply said, "Fuck me." I could have just rolled over and presented my upturned cheeks to let him know that I wanted to be fucked. In the end, though, I just succumbed to his pace, his way of making things unfold. I didn't become a limp, unresponsive blow-up buddy doll, by any means, but I would do what he wanted us to do. And I definitely opted for not saying anything further.

He rolled on top of me and pressed his lips against mine. I allowed his tongue to begin a long, slow exploratory journey into my mouth. With the actual invasion of my body, I soon realized just how strong and passionate Darien was. Perhaps it was pent-up desire, a long time in the wilderness without another body nearby to seek release. Yet somehow, in some tiny remaining chink of reason—reason was quickly being swept away by my own passions and animal lusts—in a small recess of reason, I wondered if this man ever really wanted for anything. He could not be in love with me: We'd known each other only a few hours. But there was something, a galvanic force that was almost literally drawing me toward him.

I felt his mighty legs shifting position under the quilts. They were between mine now, and he was forcing my legs apart. I offered no resistance whatsoever. In a quick succession of movements that did nothing to shatter the sublime mood, he threw off the quilts, reached to the floor next to the wall for a towel and grease, slathered his dick along with my upturned hole, and positioned my ankles for the optimum angle of thrust. The cabin's air was still warm; there was no chill on my naked skin.

I braced myself. I'd taken some huge dicks in my time, but this one was going to take concentration. I didn't want to ruin everything by wimping out or, worse yet, screaming in pain. I would have to relax. I let my head fall back into the pillow and released both nerve endings and muscles to the inevitable. He sensed when the moment was right.

Oh, God, did he go slow! At times I thought he wasn't moving into me at all, then I could feel the next increment spreading me apart. Slowly, ever so slowly, he came down and into me.

I opened my eyes for a brief second, just to see his face. He was staring intently at the place that connected us, staring fixedly, face contorted in riveted concentration. Then, when he sensed that enough of his organ was inside me, he relaxed, pushed forward in one long, brazen thrust, and sent me over the edge.

I felt no pain, just massive bulk and pressure, as if I were inflated. He locked my legs in the crooks of his elbows and slumped down on me. I felt my body doubling up, my knees pressing against the sides of my chest. I was completely helpless, and yet I was soaring the updrafts of raw, unadulterated lust for another man. My mind started to reel out of control as if the room itself were spinning on an unseen axis. I was intoxicated.

Then he started to stroke, slowly at first, then with a mounting savagery that pushed me even further into the oblivion of passion. The lower regions of my body started to catch fire with the friction of his huge pole. I started to squirm within the limits of my entrapment beneath him but not in an effort to get away by any means. Rather, I wanted him deeper in me if that were possible. I wanted to open myself further to him, to press myself up toward him even harder than he was pounding me. I let out a long moan that must have shaken dust from the rafters of the cabin.

Then, almost without warning, I heard his voice begin to fill the cabin's air: low and raspy at first, then mounting inexorably to a steady roar over my head. He slammed his pelvis home, welded it there, and then in another few seconds the whole room quaked with an orgasm I was certain was affecting seismographic equipment in at least three states.

I could feel his mighty organ pumping into me, shooting load after load of liquid. Though I could not see inside my bowel to make certain, I would have bet he set records with the amount of sticky fluid he was releasing. He seemed to go on twitching for hours; the concept of time had long since shattered for me. Then, breathless, he slumped onto me as if he'd just died. I was breathless too, though he had done all the work. I just lay there, looking up into the rafters of the cabin, glassy-eyed, content—and I had not even shot yet!

When he finally rose from atop me, he smiled. With only a slight adjustment of position—he let me lower my legs a bit—he took my right hand and wrapped the fingers around my still-hard, throbbing cock. Without words he told me it was my turn.

Though enough time had gone by for him to start growing soft inside my fuck hole, I discerned no noticeable change in the bulk of his organ. I started to stroke my own meat and again sank into the nether realms of passion. His mighty piece was pressing agonizingly against my prostate. I could feel the pressure, and two or three times I almost exploded without touching myself.

So it did not take too many strokes for me to send myself into the fiery cauldron of orgasm. The hot little droplets spilled over my chest, searing little globs, probably paltry in comparison to the amount this huge man had released into me, but I enjoyed my come as much as he did. As the monumental tickle overtook me, I threw my head about on the pillow and screamed, bucking my hips to exercise the organ that was still inside me, to press it ever closer against my twitching and draining prostate. Now it was my turn to collapse, incoherent, at peace, into the mattress beneath my back.

When I was still at last, he slowly withdrew and made very quick work of the mop-up: my chest, his dong, my crack. Then the towel went to the floor, and he came to my side and enfolded me in his huge arms once again, smiling into my face from mere inches away. I nuzzled my face into his hairy upper chest; he pulled the quilts up around us, and the whole cosmos suddenly became warm and womblike.

I usually thrash around a lot when I sleep, needing at least three quarters of the width of a bed for my restless nights. But now I sank almost immediately into a dreamless sleep and woke up in exactly the same position I last remembered the night before, in his arms with my face nestled into his hairy chest.

Darien yawned and rolled away, the back of his head in his folded palms, and looked up at the ceiling. The hair in his armpits was musty and pungent.

"When was the last time you had sex?" I inquired, still half convinced that the "pent-up desires" theory explained his ardor of the night before.

He looked at me and smiled through the shiny black beard surrounding his mouth. "Why is that important?"

"I was just wondering. You were pretty wild last night. I thought you might be a little on the hungry side."

Darien's only answer was a quiet snort. Then he went back to staring at the ceiling. Gray light was beginning to replace the blackness beyond the few curtainless windowpanes in the cabin. It was now chilly in the room.

There was something about this man that intrigued me. He was not being enigmatic just to impress someone. Sometimes people do that: purposely put on a cloak of mystery so others will try to pry and find out what is beneath the shroud. To these pseudosophisticates, mysteriousness is a contrived way of getting attention, and the surprise inside is hardly ever worth the effort to discover it.

Darien was definitely not trying to attract anyone's attention, not in the middle of nowhere. He was a real enigma, not seeming to care who figured him out or who didn't. I suddenly realized he might be with the most real person I'd ever encountered.

"Ever have anyone else live up here with you?" I inquired offhandedly.

"A boy. Once."

There was some sort of a spin on the word "boy" that led me to believe we were not talking about a child.

I frowned in a bit of confusion. "One small dresser," I stated, referencing the smallish, almost dollhouse-size bureau. "No closets. Only one easy chair..." I couldn't see two people living in the place, and I made my confusion known.

Darien snorted once again. "He didn't wear clothes, and he wasn't allowed to use the furniture."

My blood suddenly froze in my veins. "Come again?"

"You heard me. He was a boy. A dog boy really."

"You mean you lived here with a sort of slave-type person you humiliated on a daily basis?"

"No."

I raised myself up on one elbow to look at him directly. "Excuse me. Being kept naked and not being allowed to use the furniture is humiliation from where I sit."

"Fine," responded Darien. "It wasn't for him." He obviously didn't care what I thought on the matter.

I decided it was time for me to make some motion to leave this place. I slipped out of bed, and, rather than act rude, I went to the wood hod and opened the firebox in the stove. There was a layer of gray ash on the grate; I blew on it to reveal a thinner layer of live embers underneath. I carefully lowered a few small and medium chunks of split wood onto the glowing bed. It caught almost immediately, but it was a while before the room became comfortable again.

"Completely naked?" I inquired. "All the time?"

"Buck ass."

I didn't know exactly why at the time, but my dick started getting hard. The thought of a man submitting to this woodsman was doing something to me. I remembered certain scenes from movies that involved a power shift, sometimes bondage and seminudity...

I decided not to fret about the matter. I didn't feel in any danger; if Darien had wanted to do me harm, he could have done so long before this.

I grabbed the bucket with the dishes in it and went out the front door into the chilly dawn. I quickly emptied the dirty water, scrubbed its interior and all the dishes with snow, and filled the bucket with new snow, packing it down hard. Then I took a leak and scurried back into the relative warmth of the cabin.

Darien was still in bed. I warmed up the biscuits left over from the night before, whipped up a large batch of oatmeal, and, when the snow was melted in the bucket and the water was hot, made a pot of tea.

I could feel Darien watching me as I worked—I actually stayed busy so I could escape noticing how intimately he was studying me. Yet—and don't ask me why—I didn't bother to put any clothes on. The thick walls of the cabin held the heat very well, and soon it was warm inside once again.

Darien got up for breakfast; he didn't bother to put any clothes on either. And as I suspected, he consumed enough for any three of us. How he kept trim was anyone's guess. But then I suppose tramping around the wilderness in below-freezing conditions eats up a lot of calories.

He stood up from the breakfast table and took a long, careful look at me, his arms folded across his massive hairy chest. Then with new purpose he went to the top dresser drawer and drew out something black made of leather with a chain attached to it. It was a heavily studded collar, which he instantly snapped round my neck.

"Uh...Darien..." I stammered. "Uh..."

He gently pushed down on one of my shoulders, indicating I was to go to the floor. I was not afraid, just totally confused. I had not indicated I was submitting to this—well, maybe I had with a hard dick as we were talking about it earlier. But that wasn't exactly consent.

He wrapped the chain around one of the stove legs and slipped the snap hook at the end into one of the links. Without a word he dressed quickly in his briefs, socks, jeans, blue flannel shirt, and hiking boots. Still without a word he grabbed a thick parka from a peg next to the door and left.

I could barely believe what had just happened. I was crouched on the floor, completely naked, with a dog collar around my neck, my knees on the braided rug of a cabin, God only knew how many miles from the nearest neighbor, with my ass high in the air.

I don't know how long I stayed in that position. Perhaps I thought he might come back and do me harm if I was not in the same position he had left me in.

Harm?

What harm? What harm had he done me so far? None, pure and simple. When I did sit up, I realized there was enough slack in the chain to actually get comfortable, away from the searing front surface of the stove.

I suddenly burst into peals of uncontrollable laughter. Laughter at my own folly, laughter at my own foolishness.

There was no lock on the collar, nor on either end of the chain. The door was not bolted from the outside. My clothes were within easy reach. I could take the collar off, put my things on, walk to my car and the road beyond, hail a fellow motorist, and contract to have my car towed away and eventually repaired. I could report Darien to the authorities...

I started laughing louder than before. Report what?

The man had fed me the night before, let me sleep warm and safe in his bed, given me the best sex of my life, and shared his breakfast with me. "Oh, this is true dementia!" I screamed into the empty room. "The monster!"

Tears were springing into the corners of my eyes as the laughter went on undiminished. I pounded my fists into the braided carpeting in a vain attempt to bring the mirth under control. I would have a lot of trouble turning Darien in for anything illegal.

Then, as the laughter calmed and I could think a little more clearly, I began to chill myself with some thoughts and notions. The collar actually felt good around my neck, not cutting and chafing as one might think but substantial and comforting, like an old pair of shoes. When was the last time anyone thought enough of me to perform such a bold gesture?

After the last argument Greg and I had had as lovers, he smashed all my begonia pots and shredded the plants into practically powder. That was indeed a bold gesture, but it was meant to drive me away, to hurt me, to take something away from me, to vent blind rage on an innocent object. It was pettiness pure and simple, albeit bold.

The collar around my neck said exactly the opposite. It meant "Stay!" It meant "Learn!" It meant "See a new world with rules I did not make up." It meant "Dare to be adventurous, cut yourself loose from what you know, and see a new horizon—even if it is from the floor of a rude cabin in the wilderness." In short, the collar around my neck was, in some manner I could not fully understand yet, a way of giving me something.

Several times that morning I undid the chain and had my Jockey briefs poised to slip into, only to journey back to the stove leg and sit there thinking some more. Several times I looked up at the silver box housing the two-way radio, thinking I might figure out how to use it myself. Mostly I just sat and thought, occasionally shoving more wood into the fire to keep the place warm.

Since Darien hadn't taken any lunch with him and I didn't think there was a convenient diner nearby, I assumed he would come home around noon, hungry. I made some more biscuits, heated up a small tinned ham, and prepared some mixed veggies on the side.

I don't know exactly what time it was—there was no clock in the cabin, and my watch had stopped—when I heard Darien stomping up the steps and across the front porch. I reattached the chain around the stove leg and assumed the same position he had left me in: on my knees, upper chest on the floor, ass in the air, and legs spread wide. I think I was more interested in offering him a good noontime fuck than trying to impress him with how obedient I could be.

Without a word he sat down to his meal. After two bites he tossed a few things onto a plate and lowered it to the floor next to his boot, snapping his fingers to indicate that this was my share.

I ate silently with my fingers. I was really hoping he didn't want me to gobble it up with my mouth on the plate. Mercifully he let me sit and pick things up.

When he finished he left the dirty dishes on the table and retired to his easy chair. There had still not been a single word passed between us.

I was growing uneasy because there were some things I wanted to clarify, some detailing I needed to understand, and two or three items on a list I needed done for me.

"Can we talk?" I ventured at length.

I had obviously interrupted some sort of postlunch quiet time, a private reverie he did not appreciate having broken, but he did not explode with anger. He stood up calmly from the chair and reached for a flat riding crop that had been hanging by the door. Slowly and quietly he unhooked the chain from the stove leg and bent me over the captain's chair.

I received a smart slap on each cheek; neither hurt all that much, but I took this to mean that if I broke rules in the future, he might not be so lenient. I would like to have seen or at least heard a list of the rules, but because of his silence, I figured that would not be forthcoming. I had my choice: Accept the situation as it was presented or leave.

I have to be very honest: At this point I was so curious about Darien and the life he was offering me, I would not have left even if his punishment with the crop had left me black-and-blue. He replaced the crop on its hook next to the door, pulled on his parka, and left.

I sat in a quiet quandary for several minutes: naked, chained in a warm cabin, with a benefactor I was at a loss to figure out. But then as I pondered, I realized there was very little to figure out. He had not punished me for releasing my chain in order to cook for him. I figured housekeeping and tending to my natural functions would come under the same blanket dispensation. He just didn't want to talk. The "why" would take me a while to figure out, but for the time being I decided to go along with this weird scenario. I did not feel in danger in any way.

I found a broom and dustpan and gave the cabin a fluffing. I made the bed and tended the dirty dishes. Something was nagging at me, though, something I had to communicate with him even if it meant punishment.

While I was dusting around the base of the bureau, I noticed that the bottom drawer was open a few inches. I wondered at the time if that had been done on purpose. The corner of something complicated and metallic caught my eye.

I pulled the drawer open and found an ancient black Underwood typewriter. Next to it, nestled in the bottom of the drawer, was a thick stack of blank paper and two spare ribbons still sealed in their cellophane.

I'd never done any commercial writing. I'd spent some time as a secretary, writing business letters—which my peers told me were quite effective—and correcting a middle-level management executive's corrupt English to make him look good to his superiors, for which I was never thanked.

Writing...writing.

Surely the duties of taking care of this household would not take up much of a day's time. I had already pondered what life would be like here as Darien presented it to me, and the notion of sitting chained to a stove or bureau all day was nothing short of abhorrent because of the boredom.

Writing...writing.

When Darien came home late in the afternoon, I was ready for him. Not only was there a meal on the table, but I also had the typewriter set up beside his place with a sheet of paper in its carriage. I also had my clothing stacked neatly next to the stove.

When I heard him stomping across the porch, I attached my chain to the bureau leg—I wanted to see just how much flexibility I had with the way I presented myself to him as he came through the door. And I assumed my ass-in-the-air position, still hoping for a good fuck. I waited.

He was obviously reading my note before he reacted to anything else.

I had written:

Sir,

I'm not sure why yet, but I would like to stay with you for a time. I will learn your rules in whatever way you wish to teach them to me, and I will obey those rules to the best of my humbled ability.

There are some people in L.A. who will miss me if I do not return in a few days, and so I will beg you to communicate to Greg Rafferty at (310) 555-1918 that I will not be coming home and for all I care he can go fuck himself. He may have all my possessions in the apartment, and it is my sincere hope that he meet and fall in love with someone who will bash his face in if he does the cruel and dastardly things he did to me. Ask him please to call my place of employment and tell them they can take their job and shove it.

I will never again intrude on your privacy by addressing communications to you, sir. We will communicate with each other your way. And if this note offends you, I am prepared to suffer your punishment.

Your obedient servant,
Oscar

I had my face to the floor so I couldn't see the expression on his features. He took an agonizingly long time to move. At length he walked across the room to me. I wasn't sure he had the riding crop in his hand; I braced myself for stinging slaps on my upturned and waiting ass. Instead he reached down and unhooked the chain. He spoke not a word.

Once released, I went directly to my pile of clothing, which included my shoes. I opened the firebox door on the stove, and, one item at a time, I tossed them into the blaze within. Then I assumed my position next to his dining table chair. Still without a word he sat down to his meal, and we ate as we had eaten lunch.

After dinner he turned the chair around and activated the two-way radio. He did an accurate job of relaying my message, except he cleaned up the expletives.

It was almost eerie to hear his voice, knowing I would never hear actual words directed to me. Communicating with him on baser and simpler levels would be not only challenging but also intriguing. I would try to work things in the future so that I was out of the cabin when he checked in for the evening. I did not want the crutch of hearing his voice.

That night he set the tone for our evening time together. He sat in his easy chair and patted his thigh for me to join him. It was like curling up with Grampa for story time. He opened Lady Chatterley's Lover and began to read. I simply read along with him. I read a little faster than he did, so I was always ready when he turned the page.

He absently stroked my hair as if I were a favorite spaniel. And I think for the first time in my life, I was totally comfortable being near another human being. I did not feel threatened by human contact, perhaps because it was dawning on me exactly where I stood with Darien. No pretenses, no chance for lies.

Was it that my new friend was shy around strangers? I think not. A man of his stature need not fear what others think or do. Was it that he hated humankind in general? I doubted he could really hate anything or anyone. Perhaps he just wanted to be alone. It would be a while before I figured him out; but that was not high on my list of priorities. Being his proper pet and silent companion, learning and fine-tuning exactly what he expected of me—that was on my list.

Someday I would seek a broader cosmos. I was certain I would not stay with Darien forever; there would be a calling that would tell me that my new lessons had all been learned and that it was time to seek a greater place in the world. Perhaps I found comfort in Darien's tiny cabin now because I wasn't finished yet and needed a little more gestation time in a womb.

Lying next to this man at night, my sphincter throbbing from his penetrations, I would have multitudes of hours to give the matter careful, sublime thought.

He did communicate one thing to me that first night—silently yet in terms totally understandable: He did not put the typewriter away.

Writing...writing.

Gravity
By Greg Wharton

It started with a kiss: one tender, soft kiss. We were parked out by the Henderson's old place; you know, by that house out on AA that has the billboard in the front yard, big enough for the cars traveling south on the interstate to see: ASK JESUS TO MAKE HELEN WELL. Only nobody knows who Helen is—or was.

Coal and I had just got out of work. We closed down the Dixie Queen together. It was summer, hot, boring. Just out of school, nothing going on, nothing much to look forward to but a cold beer. We drove past my house and I grabbed a couple six-packs from the fridge and motored down to AA where we could watch the lights of the interstate as cars drove past on their way somewhere else.

There was a bit of breeze, just shooting the shit together in his beat up Camaro. Coal and I always did get along well in school, but never talked much other than locker room lies. Then this old sappy song came on the radio ...God, I miss the girl... and he was babbling like a baby. Crying and saying how he didn't understand how Deb could hurt him like she did. Deb was his girlfriend.

"Shit, Coal. I'm sorry man. Don't cry, shit."

And I took him in my arms. It was OK; he was hurting. I took him in my arms, and squeezed. He let me. I squeezed his strong body to mine hoping I could make him stop hurting. Before I knew I was doing it, my hands took his sweet face and pulled it to mine. I kissed a tear that was slowly weeping down his cheek, then his eye. I gently ran my tongue over his lips, then between to his bright white teeth, surprised at my sudden aroused state. It was like my chest was supporting a great weight, like the witches in old New England that were tortured by being laid down and having stone after stone placed on them. Only it felt good. Real good and I was hard. I was touching Coal and I was hard.

He looked into my eyes. We kissed: one tender, soft kiss. My life was suddenly very different.

"Gravity, mother fucker! Gravity!" he yelled as he bounced up from the bed on his strong legs and tapped his palm on the ceiling. "Gravity."

We were so looped. A double feature at the Zucker Drive-In, two tabs of blotter acid each, and a bottle of spiced rum looped. Coal said he wanted to fuck me in a hotel, and I wanted him to, so we drove to Tipp City and while he hid in the car giggling like an idiot, I got a room.

"Come on, Vic. Come on! Gravity!"

I was watching him from the other bed as he did his trampoline jumps, his fat cock bouncing up and slapping his brown tanned belly with every descent, large heavy balls making thumping noises against his thighs. My vision was blurred; his leaps whether slowed down or speeded up I couldn't tell, but he was just a white blur of light and motion with a hard-on.

A hard-on I wanted to eat. I wanted to eat him. I pictured it on a bed of lettuce with a slice of Wonder bread and a couple fluorescent pickles.

It was a week since the kiss. He had kissed me back, but then said he had to get home and drove like a bastard out of hell to get me back by my place, dropping me off and speeding away without a word about what had happened. I ran in the house, into the bathroom and jerked off, coming on the mirror above the sink in an explosion with just five quick jerks of my fist.

Nothing was said until earlier today at work when he showed me the acid and asked if I wanted to see the monster pictures at the Zucker.

"Gravity!" And he was suddenly flying across the room at me knocking me off the bed with a loud thump with his full weight. His hand grips my cock through my boxers and starts pumping, keeping time with his other hand wrapped around his own.

I'm laughing, uncontrolled and hard, the effect of the drug or the rum or him. My head bends to the plate of cock, but first I flick away the pickles. I lick the bead of come off his piss slit, then wedge the head into my mouth. Not knowing what to do with the slice of Wonder bread and lettuce, I fling them across the room sending trails of color with them. His cock's head seems to be larger than my mouth, but somehow I manage to make it fit.

The stinky brown shag carpet burns as we twist and bend over and around each other, but I don't care. I am too enthralled with the taste of his body, the pinpricks of sensation my skin is experiencing, his deep musky scent, like the locker room at our old school, but better. I have already come once, in his mouth. But he hasn't stopped stroking me with his lips. I have my middle finger up his ass and he is fucking hard into my throat, his knees on either side of my head, balls flapping heavily against my eyes with each thrust. His ass swallows my finger, then two. I think of my arm up inside him and then he's pulsating, his cock expanding, contracting, pumping, emptying. My mind flashes greens, then blues, then bright white-silver. I think gravity, Coal, gravity. His fat cock finally shoots, and I know I love him. He pushes farther into me, down my throat. His come tastes like the pepperoni sausage we put on the mini-pizzas at the Queen, and I pull his thick red cock out with my hand and squeeze and it sprays my mouth and lips and tongue as I mouth I Love You I Love You, and his ass squeezes my fingers tight and he screams "Vic, oh, Vic, oh!"

For two weeks we meet every day, as best friends. As lovers. We explore each other's bodies, we talk, get high. I can't believe it, but I feel as if somebody really, finally, knows me. Nobody at work suspects the truth that two of Piqua's recently graduated have joined the ranks of faggot brotherhood. That the king jock from Piqua High, Coal, goes down on cock: mine.

We meet before work, after work, and on nights when we close the Queen alone we suck and fondle and paw between customers. I let him fuck me. When he shot deep inside me the first time I heard him say it. He said, "I love you, Vic." Soft and sweet as anyone could possibly say it. He didn't know it, but I cried as his cock plowed hard into my ass again exploding within minutes of the first.

He said that he wanted to go away; get out of Ohio. Maybe Chicago. That we were good together. Who cares about what people would think? He didn't. I didn't anymore.

And then it ends. No kiss. No tender soft kiss, just cold, flat words through the phone wires. He calls me on the phone and severs my life force just as if he took his favorite hunting knife and slit deep into my throat.

"Why not, man. What happened? What the fuck happened?"

"It's just over, Vic. Forget it!"

"Forget it? Coal, shit. I love you! I thought—"

"Shut up, you do not! Stop sounding like a fag, Vic! It's over!"

It was over, just like that. I pull my cock out and roughly, angrily, grind as I think about what he said. I wrap the phone cord tightly around my balls until they look like they will burst; I start to cry. He said Deb was pregnant and wouldn't have an abortion. Somehow his dad found out and now Coal was getting married. Married! I felt like my life just ended. I want to feel his soft lips on mine again.

I imagine his blade forcing its way into my throat and the pain it causes. I see Deb's face smiling as he kills me, my blood flowing freely, draining.

I come all over my sneakers just as the alarm sounds, not even realizing what the alarm means. I rub the spunk from my hands on my jeans and wander out the front door staring at the sky's dark green color. My dick is hanging out and I don't care and I walk out to the cornfield in a daze.

I am peeing on the old weathered scarecrow my dad and I put up when I was nine when I first hear it. Thunder? The wind whips the stream of pee on me and I fall down yanking my jeans off, not concerned with anyone seeing just wanting to be free of them. I pull off my T-shirt and rub my hands over my chest and belly, yanking on my nipples as if I could pull them off. Nobody's around. There's never anyone around. I hate it here! I hate...

It sounds like a train is headed right at me and a smile forms on my tear-stained face. It's a fucking tornado! Huge and black, covering the entire horizon. Electricity sparkles around me and my body hair stands at attention. I watch it pick up Aunt Felice's house and devour it, then the barn across the field. I am awestruck and my cock juts out strong and stiff. Running isn't even an option I consider. I raise my arms to the sky and think of what happened the past couple weeks with Coal. I picture his bright teeth when he smiled at me.

My Coal, my love. Over. I have nothing; feel nothing. I ask Jesus to make me well. Fuck Helen. I am lifted from the ground violently; arms spread skyward like a rocket launching, my eardrums bursting from the overwhelming roar, and I am flying into my new destiny.

Gravity, mother fucker, gravity.

The Act
By Dale Chase

I didn't get the part. Never mind how long I'd known the director or how many times he'd fucked me in the past, he gave the role to someone else, and I had to wonder if Derek Fall was really a better actor or just a better fuck. Watching him prowl the stage only complicated things. Every time I looked at him, a battle started inside me: jealous fury squared off against overwhelming desire.

The part was the best thing to come along in years, and every young actor in San Francisco auditioned. Six of us were called back to the ancient Lindsay Theatre for a second reading, and it was then that I knew I was in trouble. Not only did Fall's reading match my own, I got hard watching him. Winning a lesser part was little consolation, and I found rehearsals of the four-man, two-act play more difficult than anticipated—because in addition to mastering my supporting role, I had to balance envy and lust, which caused me more than once to forget my lines and endure an embarrassing silence that Fall seemed to relish. At those moments I could feel his smirk, even though his gorgeous James Dean face never betrayed a thing.

After a week's rehearsal I was clearly undone, and writer-director Abel Groff, gay theater patriarch, called me on it. "If you're in some kind of snit at not playing the lead, please get over it, because you are not doing justice to the part you've been given, not at all. Don't you see, Brian is trapped by his feelings, he's tangled without hope, he's suffering! All I'm getting from you is distraction."

I couldn't respond.

"All right," Abel sighed, "just work on it, will you? You're a fine actor, Carl, and you'll do a wonderful job if you'll let yourself get into the role." He studied me then as only a man whose dick had been up my ass could do. "You probably just need a good fuck," he added, glancing at his watch. "I'd do you myself if I didn't have an appointment." And then he was gone.

I remained in the cramped communal dressing room long after the theater was dark. Fall's image clung to me. He'd made a production of changing from jeans to tight black slacks, enjoying, I was certain, my unease around his exposed cock. He'd revealed it slowly, sizable shaft lingering in the mirror, and I'd feasted on the sight: long, thick, and half hard. My asshole had clenched involuntarily, my own dick stirring.

Anyone else I would have already approached, but Fall had a way of daring me to make a move while threatening me if I did, all of it accomplished in a charged and brutal silence. I hated the way he hoarded his words, saving everything for the stage, and the way he toyed with me like some defenseless prey.

His looks, of course, drove me wild. Never mind how cold the blue eyes, they bore into me like a rigid cock. His blond hair and exquisitely cut features—he was James Dean incarnate—seemed almost crafted, and yet his presence was truly animal, so base and raw that I was continually unsettled. Abel was right, I did need a good fuck. And I knew from whom.

Things were no less difficult onstage. Every time I was put up against Fall, it was my erection prodding, never mind Brian, my poor tormented character. I passed that first week in bittersweet misery, and Fall knew it and played me accordingly. We existed in a state of near perpetual arousal, and at night I devoured anonymous cocks to exhaustion. By next day's rehearsal, however, I was desperate all over again. And then, after Abel's admonishment, when I decided to forgo everything for a quiet night, an unattended asshole and lone jerk-off, the door opened, and I looked up into the mirror and saw Derek Fall in all his glory.

He approached me as if it was scripted, and while I hated his arrogance, I stood for him, pulled down my jeans, and presented the ass he had owned from day one.

"Pussy boy," he growled, as he shoved his cock into me. He said it again as he began a vicious stroke, and I responded as I knew he wanted. "Your pussy boy," I said, riding his dick and crazy with heat because I knew how the scene would play, because it was a scene, Abel Groff's scene, although onstage the sex was simulated, clothed in shadow. Now it was alive, and as Derek Fall rammed his sizable dick up my ass, I knew we were playing our respective parts, but, of course, didn't care. I had what I wanted, I was getting my fuck, and as I writhed on that magnificent tool, all that mattered was that cock up this ass, never mind if the ass was Brian's or mine.

Fall didn't utter a word during the entire act and, outside of the rhythmic slap of flesh, the room remained silent. I longed to cry out but didn't, taking his hose to the root and still wanting more. I couldn't get enough of him now that he was inside me; it felt like a cobra sliding up into my bowels, and my asshole pulsed in exquisite delight as it swallowed what seemed a mile of cock. Other than hands on my hips and dick up my ass, Fall gave me nothing, and once he'd pumped his cream into me in a massive gusher, he simply withdrew. His exit was as abrupt as his entrance, and I remained bent over the dressing table as I heard the door close.

He didn't seem to care that I too had delivered a massive load, milky puddle validation that we had indeed shared the act. My hand was still on my cock, as if it needed consolation, and my asshole throbbed in recollection. I stood up slowly and stared at the door, knowing it was Fall who had fucked me but having the eerie feeling the encounter had been with his character, that Jake Cavett's prick had been the one up my ass.

"No, no!" Abel Groff screamed the next morning during rehearsal. "I told you how to play it. Can't you follow simple directions?" He was onstage in seconds, shoving me aside to show me Brian's move toward Jake. When he turned to me after the demonstration, I offered nothing, and this enraged him further. "Well?" he shouted.

"Yes," I managed, glancing at Fall, who leaned against the sofa back, erection prominent inside his jeans. Approaching him was agony, my own need overwhelming poor Brian's. I didn't care about scenes or characters or any of it anymore. I just wanted to pull out Fall's dick and climb on.

I managed to get through rehearsal but suffered a near-collapse at day's end and again remained behind in the dressing room. I half expected Fall to come in for a repeat—he knew it a given—but heard instead fading chatter and the clicks and groans of a theater shutting down for the night. For a while I considered quitting the play—an eager understudy could step in—but knew I'd go on, unable to resist Fall's promise. Exhausted, I finally forced myself out the door.

A single light illuminated the stage, and I paused in its meager stripe to remind myself I was an actor in a play and would perform before hundreds of people. It was, after all, an act; I should simply get on with it. I had gathered a bit of calm when I heard footsteps in the wings. Derek Fall stepped from the shadows and strode toward me, and I thought of Brian, who lusted after Jake so pathetically— and yet I dropped my pants and waited.

Fall freed his cock, and as I stared at the magnificent pole I wondered if it ever went soft. The head was blue-purple and swollen with need, precome oozing in stringy gobs. He backed me to the sofa, and I eased down and raised my legs, offering him the only thing he wanted. I watched his face darken as he slid his piston up my alley, and when he began pumping it was with a jackhammer fury that sent shock waves of pleasure through me.

As he fucked me I wanted more than anything to pull away his clothes and confront the animal who took me with such authority. I wanted everything of his—lips, tongue, nipples, balls—but for now took what was offered, the pile-driving cock that tore into my ass.

My dick stood tall, and I wrapped a hand around it and jerked madly as Fall's prick drove deep into my rectum. He never let up, hammering my ass with his fat bone, searing my chute until my gut began to churn. I searched his face for some kind of reaction, some bit of pleasure, but he remained expressionless even as he slammed into me, balls banging my ass. I could tell his load was rising only by his urgency, frantic now, cock wild and untamed, insatiable and pumping furiously. My own prick was on fire and ready to let go, but still I kept watching his face. I wanted to see him at that most vulnerable moment; I wanted something of his besides another pint of cream, a grimace or groan or squeal, a man instead of an animal.

When Fall finally came it was another gusher, as if he hadn't gotten off in weeks, but still he didn't react up top. I'd never seen a dick so disconnected, all that fury trapped inside his meat as if it had a life of its own. My own cream spurted in reply, arcing up onto my shirt in answer to his own long climax. Never before had so much juice sprayed out of my cock, but even after I was empty my balls felt heavy, ready for another go. Only then did I begin to realize the enormity of my need for Derek Fall.

As before, once he'd gotten his fuck he abandoned me. I kept my legs up long after I heard the outer door slam, its echo like a cell door closing. My flaming hole faced empty seats, but I saw instead an imaginary audience who, I decided, were entitled to a better finale. I squeezed and stroked my softening prick, come gathered at the slit; I cupped my balls and pulled at my bag; I slid a finger into my dripping pucker and played in the fresh come; I let the audience linger where Jake Cavett had been.

"Oh, Christ," Abel Groff said when I ran into him that night at a club we both frequented. "He's fucking you, isn't he."

I nodded.

Abel sighed, shook his head, then reconsidered. "Maybe it's not a bad idea. Maybe...tell me, has he used any of Jake's lines?"

"No," I lied.

"But you're his Brian."

Was I? Brian was ineffectual, weak, so incredibly needy. Anyone could fuck Brian. "I don't think so," I told Abel. "It feels very...me."

Abel eyed me. "You're a good little pussy," he mused, "and maybe for the good of the play, if Jake is fucking Brian, then we've got a bit of reality, don't we? What more could a director ask?"

Abel refused to fuck me that night, even when I presented myself to him in the men's room at 2 a.m. He was at the urinal, dick in hand, and I went limp when he turned me down. "For the good of the play," he said, adding quickly, "I know, I know, it's unheard of, Abel Groff begging off, but I want it pure, don't you see? Jake and Brian and nothing else. You've got his come up your ass and that's purity." He zipped up and patted my shoulder. "Go home," he said softly. "Let Brian sleep."

It was an awful night, passed in dreams as frustrating for their lack of clarity as for their paltry payoff. At one point I lay in the dark clutching my dick, trying to figure out if it had been Brian or me, deciding finally it didn't make any difference.

Fall and I had a culmination scene late in the second act that was to be the focus of the following morning's rehearsal. So far we'd skated through it; Abel concentrating on earlier bits, leading us up to it much as Jake led Brian. It wasn't the play's climax, however—sex in that context would have been cliché even for Abel Groff. No, the climax was Jake's suicide just before the curtain fell.

Now Fall and I were alone onstage. The rest of the cast had been called for afternoon, and we had just a few crew members. The old Lindsay had never seemed more cavernous. Even though it was just a rehearsal, I'd dabbed makeup over dark circles that shadowed my eyes. My entrance was calculated and determined; I wasn't Brian, and I wanted them to know it. I was Carl, and it was all an act.

Partway through Abel's instruction, I tuned him out because he didn't matter anymore. Derek Fall—Jake Cavett?—was in charge, and he and I knew it, possibly even Abel knew it, although no director is ever going to admit a loss of control. My dick began to fill in anticipation of Fall's body against mine, and I glanced down to see the all-too-familiar bulge at his crotch.

The scene was Jake's ultimate acquiescence to Brian's advances, which had for most of the play been limited to mutual hand jobs and cock sucking—all shadowed, all simulated. Now Brian was to be granted his wish. Jake would, with all his rage pooled inside his balls, fuck him full-on. This required the usual bit of nudity, and Abel reminded us yet again what we didn't need to hear but what he obviously enjoyed saying: "Remember, you can get it out, you just can't put it in."

Part of Abel's success had been controversy over the "getting it out" that was such an integral part of his plays. Audiences could always count on at least one or two cocks making an appearance, and this had brought attempts to shut down every one of his productions, but San Francisco's liberal majority had prevailed, and exposed cocks had been allowed to stay. The new play, however, went a step further, and word was already out that an erection would be visible in the second act. Talk was heavy; Derek Fall's prick was going to be famous.

Abel insisted we take it all the way during rehearsal, which meant Fall had to produce a stiff prick. All I had to do was bare my ass, but the foreplay, that long arduous scene in which Brian pleads for his sexual life, was so emotionally demanding that by the time Cavett presented his cock I was as battered as Brian.

The entire second act took place in Jake Cavett's bedroom, much of it his raging soliloquy on love and loss. Bottle and glass stood empty on the dresser, bedclothes were tangled, and Jake had retreated to an overstuffed chair and opened his jeans. He had a hand down inside, working his cock, eyes closed as if this was the only solace. At this point I made my entrance.

It didn't matter that Fall had fucked me. I was Brian now, and Jake Cavett was going to do it because we were onstage and had an audience, however limited. There was something extra in slipping inside someone else for a sexual act, in playing a part, but this time I knew it was different, and as much as I tried to be Brian, to assume his need instead of my own, I played the scene for myself. When it was time for Jake to push Brian over the arm of a chair and enter him, to present the much anticipated and highly visible erection for all to see and for me to receive, I felt myself open to him, asshole begging even as he slid his rigid prick between my legs in a masterful simulation.

The fuck was real, never mind theater. As we writhed for Abel and the few others present, I squeezed my thighs together and took him, massive dick working me with a steady thrust. His meat skated my balls as it plowed blindly forward, and I wanted more than anything to grab my dick and jerk off but, of course, that wasn't in the script. I had to take him without any visible response other than gratitude, and take him I did, thighs slippery with his precome, asshole pulsing with the mere proximity of that swollen sausage.

Jake cries out "Pussy boy" as he gives it to Brian. He has succumbed at last to love and its attendant pain; he rails against it all, professes love and hate as one, swears, then comes. The audience could not see his cream spurting between my legs, or my own seconds later. I had not touched myself. Derek Fall's heat and the raw pleasure of his skin against mine had been enough to send me over.

Cavett's disintegration begins at this point. His dick is still up Brian's ass when he starts to come apart and lashes out in his own brand of cruel self-preservation, closing with, "You're just a fuck, Brian. A good one, but that's all you'll ever be."

"Wonderful!" Abel Groff shouted. "Let's stop there."

Fall's dick was softening, and I let it slide from between my legs. My heart was pounding, and I heard an awful rush in my ears. I managed to pull up my jeans and gather enough strength to face our director, but when Abel saw me, he knew I was in trouble. "Let's take a break, shall we?" he said. "Ten minutes."

We both watched Fall hurry away, then Abel put his hand on my shoulder. "It's fabulous, you know. The energy between you is absolutely electric; it plays all the way to the balcony. Opening night, there won't be a limp dick in the house. The theater will reek of come."

"Abel..."

"I know, but it's what we want, Carl. Anguish, pain, passion, two men unable to connect except with cock and ass."

"It's exhausting," I said.

"I would imagine. We'll work on the dialogue next." He looked into my eyes. "And remember who you are. He's rejecting Brian, not Carl."

We picked up exactly where we'd left off: Brian enduring Jake's wrath because he'd stirred him above the belt as well as below. It was devastating for Brian, and the scene ended in shouts, broken glass, and slammed doors. We ran through it so many times, I began to lose myself, and Abel called it a day when I finally broke into tears.

Derek Fall didn't fuck me again until opening night. As the play was finely tuned I gradually came unglued, managing to keep Brian alive while Carl went under. I continually sought out fresh cock but found myself accepting only James Dean types, surly blonds who invariably disappointed, never mind how big a sausage they crammed up my ass or how beautiful the owner. I finally had to admit I was hopeless about Fall and, worse, that it was probably a one-way street.

The dressing room was frantic opening night—too many well-wishers and hangers-on. Fall had kept his distance but managed to stand half naked long enough to catch me looking at his prick. Once he'd accomplished that, he gave it a long artful stroke, put on his costume—torn jeans and T-shirt—and left.

It was a packed house, and where I usually enjoyed exhilaration I now felt anxiety. My hands shook, I snapped at assistants, and I pushed one fellow actor so far, he stormed out after a single departing comment: "Get fucked, Brian."

I was alone in the dressing room when Abel came in. Seeing my distress, he said, "You'll do fine. Let Brian have his night, OK?" He kissed my cheek and left, not waiting for comment.

"Five minutes," someone called outside the door.

When I walked onstage I had no idea who I was. Brian and Carl had finally become one, and I felt hundreds of eyes watching this hybrid creature who played the part for real, who said the lines and hit the marks and lived the agony Abel Groff had scripted. By the end of act one I had nothing left. I ran outside and stood in the alley, taking deep breaths, trying to regain some bit of balance for what lay ahead. I halfway wanted Abel to come out and console me, but he didn't. I think he knew we were beyond that.

When act 2 began, I watched Jake Cavett's raging soliloquy from the wings, fighting what I knew was fast becoming a truth. Tears were in my eyes when I made my entrance.

Brian's move toward Jake was calculated, almost coy, but as his failure became apparent, as Jake sat unblinking, hand inside his jeans, Brian grew desperate and began to plead, offering unconditional love in addition to his body. When Fall stood and pushed me toward the chair, I dropped my pants, baring the ass I so wanted him to have. He came up behind me, erection brushing my crack, and then instead of sliding between my legs he pushed into my asshole in one long, glorious stroke.

I didn't care there was an audience. I wriggled back onto his cock and clenched my muscle because I wanted him to know I was there, Carl not Brian, and he responded with a full-on fuck, one I'm sure Abel thought the ultimate mastery of sexual simulation. And never mind Fall had gone in before. This was a whole new game, and as I felt that long prick shoving in and out of my channel, I hoped desperately that what had happened to me was happening to Fall as well, that Jake had been pushed aside and now, onstage, before hundreds of eager faces—and who knows how many stiff pricks—he might at last be himself.

Thanks to creative lighting and carefully planned angles, the audience could not see what has happening to me. Confident they were watching a simulation, they enjoyed an innocent thrill while I received the prick of a lifetime. Their presence made the entire act so incredibly public that my swollen cock began to throb and I unloaded into the chair while Jake raged behind me, driving his dick into me with renewed fury. I took it all, letting his angry words flow past as that snake of his plowed my channel, and when he came I squeezed for all I was worth, sucking dick with my ass to quench an unbearable thirst.

The rest of the scene—Jake's retreat, denial, shouts, the hurled bottle—was just that, a scene. I let Brian endure it and at the appointed moment made my exit. Standing in the wings, I had only a minute's respite before the finale began, Jake's suicide. I forced myself to watch him down the pills and liquor; I felt an awful dread even as his come dripped from my ass.

The lights dimmed as Jake fell to the bed, then everything went dark, and when they slowly came back up to an eerie shadow, they found me onstage. I felt for a pulse and let out a cry; I had no trouble with the requisite tears.

Jake Cavett was on his side, curled slightly, eyes closed. I climbed in beside him and took him into my arms, kissed his cheek, and placed my hand over his crotch to knead the lifeless prick. Not a single sound, barely my own breathing, then a slow fade to darkness. When the curtain fell, it took the audience a moment to react. Stunned silence, then applause.

I was grateful Fall didn't leap from my arms. He lay still and let me prod his dick until others rushed onstage to pull us up, hug us, congratulate us. I didn't want to let go but rose to take my bows with the rest of the cast, then just the two of us side-by-side, and finally Fall alone to thunderous applause. From the wings I joined in.

Abel had arranged a party at a friend's penthouse, and after an hour of backstage crowds and champagne I was finally alone. Before leaving, Abel made me promise I'd be along soon. "You're sure you're all right?"

"Fine," I told him. When he raised a brow I added, "OK, not so fine, but I survived."

"You were wonderful, Carl." He patted my shoulder and left.

I needed to change but managed only to take off my makeup. Time was what I wanted now, room to absorb what had happened, to sort out performance from...performance. I wandered out onstage in a confused sort of elation, reminding myself the man had fucked me in front of 500 people. I flopped onto the bed and burrowed into the covers. Fall's scent was there, and I closed my eyes and inhaled deeply.

"Carl."

He'd crept in like a cat and stood leaning against the headboard, beautiful in the half-light. I rolled onto my back and opened my arms. When he slid on top of me, I felt no bulge at his crotch and none of that awful tension he usually carried. He seemed to have uncoiled, as if the play had solved him, and yet I still wasn't sure just who I had here.

There was no urgency now. Fall simply hung on for a few minutes, burying his face in my neck while I ran my hands up under his shirt and kneaded his back. He was lean and smooth, taut as an animal, and I explored every inch, gradually working down into his jeans. I squeezed his ass and he groaned softly, then pulled back and began to strip. I lay paralyzed at the sight of him, skin tawny-gold, cock quiet, flaccid yet still so formidable, something that belonged on a lion, not a man. His chest was hairless, well-defined, nipples ripe; his stomach had a stripe of hair that splayed out into a golden bush engulfing the cock I coveted. Just looking at the whole of him sent me into a frenzy, and I reached out and took his sizable prick into my mouth.

He eased back onto the bed and lay beside me as I swallowed all I could of him, tongue inching down his shaft, squeezing and sucking until he began to fill. As he stiffened I licked him to the root, then pulled back and fixed on his knob until I could feel him oozing juice, and I raised up off him to finger his dripping slit and stroke this magnificent meat. And I realized only then what he was giving me, that this was the first time he hadn't arrived fully primed.

When he began to pull at my crotch, I stopped working his cock long enough to shed my clothes, then slid back down to him but in reverse, my dick in his face, his in mine. We took each other then and lay sucking pricks onstage, bare as newborns and playing to that imaginary audience.

I wanted it to last forever, my hand cradling his heavy balls as I sucked his fat knob and licked that long, sweet shaft. Everything was in slow motion now, the feast of a lifetime, and as much as I wanted to shoot my wad I wanted more to keep eating, to suck my way to infinity or die trying.

Fall's prick finally began to grow hot inside my mouth, jamming into my throat with a thrust that told me an eruption was imminent. My own load was churning as well, and I began to push into him, to fuck that beautiful mouth I had never so much as kissed. Fall was moaning and slurping, lapping at me as I jammed into him while I took his massive meat deep inside my throat, sucking it until it began to squirt. Seconds later my own explosion hit, and we lay feeding off each other, hands squeezing ass as we swallowed gobs of cream in the ultimate exchange.

Even after we were spent, we didn't let go. I buried my face in his balls, inhaling his musky scent while he ran his fingers through my dark bush. He was so incredibly gentle, I had to remind myself it really was Derek Fall's dick in my face. And then he slid a finger into my crack and further, into my pucker, probing lightly, as if he hadn't been there before, then pulling out to gather spit and sliding back in. I knew then, as he finger-fucked me, that we would go on to Abel's party and later, behind a locked bathroom door or on a remote terrace corner, he would fuck me. Derek Fall would fuck me.

Gorgeous Tits
By Roddy Martin

Harvard was lounging on his patio—robe more off than on, pectorals brushed by creamy brown shadows. He stretched and you could see all the way down his hip. I knew what kind of day this would be.

I went to buy my wife sweet nothings.

I first glimpsed the florist through his shop window. Well, I glimpsed his thigh. He had his boot on a crate. The thigh was burnt umber and shapely. Ding! I hurried inside.

The man himself had clear, savvy eyes. He wore cut-off overalls that went down to here and up to there. I stood gaping. The collarbone! The hollow at the base of his throat! And moving lower...

"You're late," he purred.

"Late?"

"You're not my 11 o'clock? Oh. Never mind. What can I get you?"

"I'd like a dozen yellow roses."

He went in the cooler, bent over the blooms. You could see the side of his pec, a flash of underarm. It wasn't enough.

"How's this?" he asked, coming out.

"Beautiful."

"Likewise. You want" —his voice dropped an octave— "long stems."

"The longer the better."

"Baby's breath?"

"Oh, yes."

Holding my gaze, he unhooked his suspender straps. The bib fell foreword. What gorgeous tits! I had to fondle them, mash them, taste every inch.

"Whoa." Him dragging me by the belt to a back room. He undid his hip snaps, which left the overalls barely hanging. Now I could worship the pert nipples, the way muscle glided to muscle.

"You just gonna stand there?" he asked.

"Uh-huh." I dived for his chest. He grabbed my head. He arched his back and went, "Uh!"

This was what I lived for.

Panting, he stretched out on a table covered with green floral wrap. Off came the overalls, leaving him naked except for boots, socks, and garden gloves. His cock was big and black, straight up. I pulled up a stool and swallowed until it jabbed the back of my throat.

Only then did I realize that the shop was a front for some type of high-class, illegal fuck pad, and that the roses might cost $200.

"Don't you…" he gasped. "Don't you want to get comfortable?"

"Oh no. I'm married. I've got to be good."

"You call this good?"

"Don't you?" I shoved two fingers up his butt. Zing, found his prostate, and he moaned. I've always loved pleasuring a guy while I played with his tits, and the florist's were—"Oooh!" From some angles, you might have wished his nipples were a quarter of an inch rounder, but on the whole, the package was A-minus, at the very least.

Presently his balls got high and his breathing labored. "Oh, I'm close."

The bell in the shop rang. "Hello?" called a baritone voice. Possibly the real 11 o'clock. Or the cops.

"Don't stop," the florist panted. I was frigging him now. A handful.

"Hello? Anyone here?"

"You stop, you die…Oh! Oh! Oh!" The florist shot all over his chest. It pooled there, looking gorgeous. I sprinkled it with yellow petals.

As you may have guessed, windows were my friends.

Ever seen one frame a topless guy with his arms folded, biceps tight against pecs? Or a bottomless guy? He seems twice as naked, peeling a tee-shirt over his abs. Such was my great fantasy, to see Harvard on a water bed that way, while the wave machine makes wave after wave after….

OK.

Once the swelling subsided, I caught the uptown train at Christopher. Across from me stood a Spanish boy with lithe arms and cute little biceps. His tee was baggy, but a portfolio strap crossed his heart. You could see what he had, for sure. He was so sweet and innocent. I wanted to spank him.

By Penn Station the car was SRO. I found this hip in my face. It looked shipshape in taupe pleats. I bet the guy's chest was that way too. His shirt clung like a milk mustache.

He smiled and lifted a brow. My eye traveled back down, watched something stiffen and stir. Slipping off a loafer, I rolled my toe around his ankle-bone. He flopped his tie aside, undid his collar, and the next button and the next. He glanced left. He glanced right. He flashed a pec.

How I wished I was wearing a butt-plug.

This incident reminded me of a man my mother dated when I was 18. I went to his apartment after they broke up—ostensibly as a go-between, but in truth to practice techniques from How to Land in the Feathers (with Practically Anyone)!

Steven appeared to be dressing for a date. He was a brisk, tailored optometrist. His slacks worked butt magic. His shoulders strained his expensive undershirt. I cooed, "You don't mind my Coming?"

"Quite the opposite."

"So, no Hard Feelings?"

"None."

"Why do Hard Feelings make us Come Again and Again...to a bad End?"

"Don't try to con me," he said evenly, rolling deodorant in a virile underarm. "I know that seduction routine." Still, he let me sit on his lap and suck his tits.

I arrived at the foundation where my wife works 12-hour days, something I need not do. I'm kept, baby. Kept, kept!

You probably wonder about the roses. You think, "Her birthday, and he's acting like a wretch." Not so! We want to make a baby. When we conceive, Daddy-O's going to give us a fuck load of cash. True, my behavior with the florist was inappropriate, but most people wouldn't call it adulterous.

Raised my sperm count, didn't it?

In the foundation building, glass elevators scale a vast atrium. Elevator boys wear ties and navy jackets. Mine that day was angel-faced, round-eyed, and sensuously dark. "New here?' I asked.

"Yes, sir. Nice roses."

"Nice uniform."

We passed seven, eight, nine floors. I scanned them all. Once in this very shaft I happened to witness an assignation involving the most beautiful pair of—

The elevator ground to a halt.

"What's wrong?"

"I don't know." The elevator boy hovered by the control panel with a vague air of premeditation. "Might be here a while. I hope you don't mind"—adorable stammer—"tight places."

"Rather enjoy them."

"Isn't it getting kind of warm, sir?"

(Yes well. The truth is, I can land in the feathers with practically anyone.)

I tossed his jacket on the floor, groped him through his immaculate cotton shirt—one of my favorite things, by the way, along with scoop tanks, open collars, bathrobes, strategically cupped hands, and all types of underwear.

"You're built like a football player," I said, opening his fly. "Go to college?"

"Rutgers."

His cock was thick and ready. I started unbuttoning his shirt from the bottom up. "What major?

"Social work."

"Sexy. Tell me, has a man ever done social work on your tits?"

"Ah!"

Thought he'd come all over me. Stepping back, I crunched my wife's roses and felt a pang. After all, I made certain promises when I married her. But she must have known they'd be tough to keep, and I'd be house-bound soon enough, with a little boy or a little girl and Daddy-O's $4,000,000, which we could then double and triple. Our brokers had explained this.

Only we had to conceive, like fast. Because...trust me, it's complex.

I set to work on the elevator boy from behind. Pants-humped his butterfly buns. Felt up his obliques, his violin-shaped abdominal crest, the ridge that bisected it. Yes! Great abs meant great tits.

I knew his would be. I was foaming at the mouth.

I thrust my pelvis, pinned his to the glass. Forced him to fuck it, 10 and a half stories high. His shirt slipped down. White cloth, brown skin. Drove me wild. I bit his shoulder.

My fingers brushed the bottom curves of his pecs. Felt so good, I grabbed. I kneaded. O-o-oh! Wide, smooth, nipples low on the muscle. I was like, Wanna come, wanna come. Ah, ah! I want to come!

"Oh sir!" cried the elevator boy.

Close call. I slumped, panting.

The elevator boy's virility rolled down the pane. It dawned on me that if we could see out, others could see in.

Sticky. Ick. Dripping down.

Time to regroup.

The way things were going, I skipped over to 8th Avenue for lubricant and a cheap butt plug. The bookstore clerk was atypically handsome. He caressed my palm with $1.75 change. "Would you like a bag? Or should I insert that for you?"

"Please." I dropped my pants....

By now it was 4 o'clock. Times Square evangelists were out, exhorting the brothers. "Do you suck up to the white man and the white woman?"

Not unless they have gorgeous tits.

I took the #9 down to the flower hook shop, where I found the florist clad in cap and leather harness. I said, "I need another dozen yellow... Did I interrupt something?"

From behind the counter arose a john with a studded belt in his teeth.

"I can't think of a snappy bon mot," said the florist. He looked at the john, who nodded. They advanced hungrily. "11 o'clock, meet 5:30."

I shouldn't. I couldn't. I had to get home, make dinner, wash the guys off my skin... 5:30 grabbed his shirttail and pulled it up. I thought maybe I'd stay a few minutes.

He was a Playgirl "Real Man of the Month" type. You know, 30ish

WASP in upscale shoes. Nice abs, though. Nice pecs. Too much hair. Overall effect was B-plus, but I could raise that. I produced the clippers I carried for such occasions.

5:30's eyes grew wide. "Oh, no. No way." I switched on the instrument. Its buzz cut the air.

Somewhat later—

"Not the bush! Not the bush!"

"Just going to shape it." Buzz. The clippers bit into the wiry hairs, forming puffs that floated onto the florist's head. He didn't care. He knelt with foam and razor, shaving 5:30's nuts.

I left 5:30 a quarter of an inch.

"My cock's bigger," he exclaimed, staring in amazement. "My cock's 20% bigger." He swung it thigh to thigh.

I also left him a dusting on his chest, for accent. Vast improvement, brought out the lines. Now I could watch his beef-red tits rub against the florist's brown ones.

(You might think me a solipsist with a fetish, but I know this is passing phase.)

"Want me to go down?" the florist asked, addressing his client but looking at me.

"Yeah."

Watching those pillow lips slide instilled a desire to have them for myself. I knelt beside the florist. "Let him have it," gasped 5:30. "Let him suck it."

We took turns. Sucked fast, slow, lazy, macho. Did lollipops, corkscrews. 5:30 didn't know the florist and I were showing off, teasing each other, closer and closer. Our mouths met on the tip of the cock and I kissed him, put my heart into it.

"How do you feel?" he asked.

"Great, man. Real good."

He reclined. I swallowed. I felt 5:30's hands on my basket, on my hard-on. I felt his mouth on my balls. I let the daisy wheel spin....

When I spun out of the wheel like a roulette ball, there was a righteous cock in my mouth. Biggest I ever. I didn't care who it belonged to. I was about to come, and from the taste of it, about to swallow a forbidden, unsafe load. I got a mental picture of $4 million in a sack with wings, flying out the window.

I opened my eyes. The cock was mine.

The florist stood fucking 5:30's tits, the most potent sex act in the world. "Fuck him, baby," I growled, zipping up as best I could.

Cocks are potent. Pecs are potent.

"Fuck him, he's a whore. The john's the one who's a whore... Baby, I'm getting fucked too." Not the actual case, but if you say it, it's so. And I knew how to work a butt plug. I have great suction. I squeezed it. I squeezed and squeezed.

Oops.

Took me 15 minutes to dig it out.

Afterward I took baby steps to the street. Anything more definite would have meant a case of wham pants. Not that you could tell the difference, with all the precome.

We'd conceive tonight, no problem.

I tumbled into a cab on Seventh Avenue. "Hey!" Someone grabbed the car. "Mind if I share?" My eye took in the cut-offs, the massive thighs, the chest.

"You are most welcome."

Ten minutes later I was prostrate in the body-builder's lair, drooling as his ass gyrated. Down came the cut-offs, up went the tank-top. His waist was narrow, his back broad and bronze. Whipping a sleeveless flannel shirt over it, he spun front.

Sweet voyeuristic torture! The round inner pecs. The flat stomach, the flat navel. The cock solid enough to provide ballast for tits whose masculine fullness I could but imagine.

"Oh baby," I groaned. "Masturbate for me."

He rolled his hips and worked it, two-fisted. Inflation—who'd have thought? Despite its heft, his was a blood cock. "Lick my boot," he said, sticking it in my face. I licked. I didn't care, barely noticed when he tied a jimmy on his shaft with both of my shoelaces.

And yanked off my pants.

Of course, when the first inch popped my bubble, then I noticed. "Ouch, ouch, ouch!"

"Fuckin' take it."

"Ah."

He hit a spot—that spot—again and again. My blood turned to buttered rum. "Harder," I gasped.

"Shut up." He knew how to build.

There was a mirror. I saw his butt pump. I saw his Adam's apple, the veins in his biceps. I had to see the rest! I reached for his shirt. He grabbed my wrists and held them over my head. Struggle as I might, there was nothing I could do but watch his shirt as it slid, thrust by thrust by thrust thrust thrust. Until—

"I love your tits! Oh, I love your tits!"

My wife left a message, "Be home late." Good. I thought I'd unspool with a soak and my hidden stash of non-explicit but outlandishly erotic soft-core gay videos. Those Czechoslovakian boys look great without shirts.

Harvard was out again, lounging in a very full red thong. He squeezed it, slipped his hand... I ran for binoculars.

What a show. I could feel a fresh $4,000,000 spawn in my testicles. Presently Harvard reached for his cordless. My phone jangled.

"You're watching." His voice was low and hot. "I can feel it. You watch often."

"Well, you have gorgeous tits."

"Hold that thought."

He went inside. I could see him bending in silhouette, presumably skimming the thong off. I was so excited I couldn't breathe. Then the cops came and dragged me away for invasion of privacy.

Opportunities
By James Anselm

I have a better day job than most people, but it's the night work that brings in the best money—and, besides, I have more fun doing it. "Escort" is the nice name for it, but I whore because I like whoring! I get such a rush from turning some guy on, from making him more and more excited, from coaxing a big load out of him, and shooting my own right after his.

Looking in the mirror, I check everything out, and what I see is first-rate. I'm just back from a week in Florida, sporting a really nice tan, so my skin is a golden brown that looks really hot with my soft blond hair. I'm not built extra big, but my definition is razor-sharp—you won't see better abs. A quick glance assures me that my bubble-butt is where I left it.

A few easy strokes get my cock nice and hard. My fingers feel around for stubble, but there is no need to shave again. My erection is just over seven inches, thick enough so it looks even bigger, with a nice fat head. I tense my stomach and my cock points straight up. The clients like that.

I have three appointments in my book for this evening, which isn't bad. I don't do that much work every night, but these are all regulars, and I know what they want and like.

Rob, my first client, is married, with three kids. (How do I know? I've seen the pictures when I checked his wallet while he was in the shower. I would never rip anybody off—I don't need to—but I like to make sure they're not the law.)

As always, he has called me the day before, and arrives on the button for his session. Directly from the office, never the same day of the week twice in a row. I'm sure he "misses" his train and gets home just a little late for his suburban dinner.

He has me suck him off, and that's all he seems to want, so it's easy money. He could get the blow job cheaper a few other places, but I guess he somehow figures if he does it with a guy, he isn't cheating on his wife.

I'm only wearing gym shorts and a T-shirt, and Rob strips efficiently, folding his clothes as he puts them aside, so they won't get messed up. Mrs. Rob feeds him too well, but there's still plenty of muscle below the soft layer. He must have been a football player in college; maybe he still goes to the gym. We don't make conversation, so I don't know.

He sits on the edge of the bed, spreading his legs, and closes his eyes. Kneeling in front of him, I go to work. Sometimes he'll let me stroke his chest and stomach, but today he gently pushes my hand away.

My tongue circles the head of his cock a few times, then slides up and down his length. I feel his dick twitch as the blood starts to pump into it. Teasing his ball sac with my fingers, I vacuum him into my throat as he ever so slowly fills out. It takes him a long time to get completely hard, and it's no wonder: Rob's erection is truly awesome, close to ten inches long and thick in proportion.

Circling the base with my fingers, I give him the occasional squeeze, and the head of his cock swells between my lips as the whole thing pulses bigger and bigger. Up and down my mouth goes on his rod, teasing its tip with my tongue.

The bigger his tool gets, the more I have to work at not choking on him, but I'm up to the challenge. Keeping the saliva flowing, I can swallow quite a bit of it—more than his wife ever tries to, I'll bet.

Rob's handsome face is impassive, and gives little clue as to whether he is enjoying what I do. Once he reaches his full extension, though, he never goes soft. Getting warmer, I whip the T-shirt off over my head. I pull my rod out of my shorts and stroke it as I suck on his; why should he have all the fun?

Bit by bit, I become aware of his breathing getting faster. I ease back on the suction, enjoying how large he is, and my own part in bringing him there, close but never too close. We hang there for a few minutes, both of us getting high on his big, hard cock.

When his fingers suddenly dig into my shoulders, I know he's ready to shoot, and I bring my hand up to finish him off. His chest expands, he tenses, and he delivers his load onto my torso—one enormous rush of it, then a few little squirts before he relaxes and exhales. Some of it dribbles down along my stomach, and hits my cock, which is throbbing hard now.

Rob turns his back while I wipe myself with a towel; why, I don't know. Does it freak him out to know he excites me so? Bringing the fabric close to my face, I revel in the aroma and potency of his jism, the manstuff that's already brought three gorgeous boys into the world. I'm so turned on by him, it's all I can do not to jack myself off into the same towel...but it's far too early in the evening for that.

He always showers before he pays me; then he says "Thank you; I'll call about next time." I'm quite taken aback when he throws his arms around me and hugs me. I resist the temptation to give him a kiss, and let him out.

Billy is still in school, and hasn't shed his baby fat yet. I don't know where he gets the money to pay me, even at my lowest rate—he has no degree yet, no job, no place of his own, and very little self-confidence.

I always contrive to be out of the room when Billy undresses, since I realized the first time he visited me it makes him uncomfortable if I watch. He doesn't have a bad body, even if it is a bit soft, and his face is very cute.

He likes to cuddle first, which is a nice way to start, and I let myself get a bit hard for him, but not fully erect. I can feel his heart thumping against his ribs, but he betrays no other excitement.

We ease ourselves down onto the mattress, and he spreads his legs for me. I wriggle one finger into his hole, and Billy's cock perks up right away. It's amazing how fast he goes from nothing to a real boner.

He watches me carefully as I tear open a condom packet, slicking my cock with lubricant. "Oh, man," he breathes, as I bring it to full stretch and make myself thoroughly stiff, "Oh yeah."

I check the rubber, and slip it over the head, unrolling it bit by bit, squeezing my dick from the base as I go. Once it's rolled down to the bottom, I squirt some more lube on it, and slick the outside as well. Then Billy gets on all fours, and presents his backside to me.

My finger goes back into his crack with a little more lube, then I spread his cheeks for my entry. The head is the hardest part, because of its size, but there's no way except to push it in.

Billy winces only once—most people wouldn't even notice, but I do—then takes a deep breath, and relaxes. Once the head pops through his ring, the rest is easy: an inch in, then back half an inch, then the second inch in, the third, then back just a bit, then inch after inch until I'm all in.

Some guys wilt as soon as they're filled up, but not Billy! I can see him jutting out like a broom handle, the head so red it's almost glowing. Reaching around his waist, I gently stroke him in time with my own motion inside his guts.

This is one of the most difficult things I do...I always have to be so careful not to get carried away, to remember that it's the customer who needs to have a good time, not just me. It has to go on long enough that he gets his money's worth, and I have to stay hard to accomplish that. Fortunately, I can stay hard forever, and I love to fuck!

At first, I just sort of rock back and forth, one hand braced in the small of his back, the other gripping his dick, my leg muscles doing all the work. Before long, Billy is pushing his ass against me, looking for more.

So I give it to him, thrusting harder. He knocks the pillow off the side of the bed as his hand reaches back to hold onto me. Then I pick up the pace till we're both grunting.

"Oh God, yes!" he cries, his feet writhing and his hands thrashing about. "Deeper, deeper—make me come!"

I pull back, to the verge almost of slipping out, then give him every inch I have with one steady thrust. I lean my body against his for maximum penetration, tensing every muscle to make myself as big as I can possibly get. I feel my cock expanding as his tight hole spasms around me.

Billy is clutching the bedsheet with both hands now. "Aaaawww, shiiiiiit!" he wails as the first wave of his orgasm hits him, and the come blows out of his balls. His insides clutch at me, but I keep perfectly still, holding myself just below climax, saving my load for later.

Billy shoots six times, each one a ribbon of white streaming from his tool to land on the bedding with a soft plop. After a while, I pull out of him, but Billy keeps playing with my still-hard cock as he dresses and pays me. He gives it one last squeeze before I open the door, and then he's gone.

My last job of the evening is one of my favorite customers. Steve is in his mid-forties, and into body worship. As I wait for him to ring the bell downstairs, I do some quick sit-ups and pushups, so my muscles will be pumped and tight.

I greet him at the door in only my jeans—no shirt or shoes. His eyes light up, and I can see his cock start to grow even as he enters the apartment. He rests one hand on my arm, and I flex the biceps for him to feel. "You're looking good," he tells me. "I am good," I reply in a voice a little deeper than the one I normally use.

I sit on the edge of my bed, and Steve climbs around behind me, to massage my shoulders and neck. His hands are strong, and he works his fingers deep into the muscle. For just a moment, I feel like the client as he relaxes me. When I do give this up, I'd like to settle down with somebody like Steve, I think.

When he comes back to stand in front of me, his fingers soon move down over my chest, kneading my pectoral muscles and brushing against my nipples. The whole pulse of my body begins to shift from relaxation to arousal. My hand rises to his basket; the woody he's been sporting since he walked in the door is now as hard as a rock.

I start to pull down his zipper, but he says, "Not yet," so I just fondle him through the fabric. He unbuttons his shirt, though, and tosses it aside. He's got a nice body for his age, firm pecs and a flat belly, and it's easy to get turned on for him. I let my cock start to grow now, blood pulsing into it.

Once he's got my nipples teased out as big as they'll go, he helps me to my feet and puts his arms around me. Spreading my lats to make my back as wide as I can for him, I pull his crotch close to mine, so he can feel my hard-on against his own.

This time, when I reach down to open his pants, he offers no objection. Every move I make he mirrors, so we are soon naked, our hands gently teasing each other's hard dicks.

Expanding my chest to its maximum size, I strike a pose for him. He sits on the edge of the bed to enjoy the private show. I flex my biceps and tense my abs, feeling the hard muscles swell against the skin. Then I drop to one knee, clenching my balls to make my cock stand straight up.

Steve's hands are literally trembling with excitement, and grips the side of the bed to keep them off his cock. "Oh, that's beautiful," he whispers.

"Do you want it?" I ask—as if I don't know, as if that isn't why he's here. I turn my back on him, showing him the globes of my ass, tensing and relaxing the muscles to make my cheeks dance for him. "Or is this what you really want?" I can hear his breathing grow ragged, but he doesn't answer me.

"Make me come, and maybe you can have it," I tell him. He's off the bed in a flash, and roughly turns me to face him. We kiss furiously, tongues in a tangle, as he tries to suck the air out of my lungs.

His kisses move rapidly from my mouth to my chest, then his tongue darts across the lines of my stomach. A moment later, my dick is in his mouth.

Gently tickling my piss-slit, he sweeps around the helmet, then moves along, tracing a throbbing vein down the side as he heads for my balls. First one nut, then the other, gets thoroughly swabbed before he returns his attention to my rod itself. At the same time that Steve sucks my cock, I can feel myself getting excited over Rob again, and working myself into Billy's canal—it's like I'm having sex with all three guys at once, and even I can't control myself any more.

"That's it, Steve," I warn him: "I'm gonna come!" His mouth is replaced by his hand, just in time, as nothing can hold me back now. I'm so turned on that it's just that last stroke, then I explode into orgasm, come flying across the room.

Steve keeps milking me as settle ourselves on the bed, and I straddle his torso. I let his hard-on slip between my ass cheeks—just nesting there—and he slides it up and down, moaning and shaking as he does so. Then his hands are on my thighs, gripping the muscles as I tense them to lift my body higher.

Only a handful of clients have ever fucked me; I make damn sure they know what they're doing first. Steve knows what he's about, waxing his shaft and slipping the rubber on it with no wasted moves. A quick coat of lube for the outside, then he slips the same finger into me to slick the path. I can relax with him, I admit the finger readily.

Though I brace myself instinctively, I know he won't hurt me. I'm always surprised that something as big as Steve's dick—and while he's no Rob, I've seen enough men to know he is big—penetrates me so easily. He doesn't force his way in; he doesn't need to.

Once the head makes its entry, I let myself down onto him. My ass seems to know him as he fills me, and welcomes each new inch of him.

Steve likes to do it in all different positions, a couple of minutes each way. With each new position, he does more and more of the work, but far from tiring, he seems to get stronger the longer we go on.

Next I'm on my hands and knees, and his tongue is slobbering around in my crack. I'm getting a fresh hard-on, and he reaches over to play with my nuts. Meanwhile, his dick is finding its way home again, and he's soon pumping in and out from behind me.

He turns me over then so I lay on my back, and lifts my feet over his shoulders, pressing in deeper as he pulls my body closer to his. I spread my legs to make room for him, and almost before I know it, his balls bump my backside.

"Oh, Steve," I grunt as I squeeze my ring around him, "you're so big."

"And I'm getting bigger," he tells me. "Can you feel it?" Sure enough, there's more blood pumping into his erection, and I feel his size increasing in me.

"God, yes, I can." It's almost a surprise to me when I hear my own voice begging him, "Fuck me, man; fuck me with that bullcock of yours."

Now he starts thrusting without mercy. Both of us are soon grunting and gasping, in time to the squeaking of my bedsprings. Steve shoves his cock as deep in as he can, bumping my prostate on the down strokes.

Big as he is, my ass can't get enough of him. He rips into me, and I love it. My cock seems impossibly hard, too, bouncing against his midsection each time our groins meet, which seems to turn him on even more.

Then the climax seizes him, and Steve's head flies back. He lets out a roar with each burst of jism into the condom and, to my amazement, I find myself blowing another load along with him. There's not as much as before, but it squirts up to coat his torso. Finally, he drops onto me, and it glues us together as his cock has its last spasms.

He stays in me when he's done shooting, and it's fully five minutes before either of us begins to go soft. Still, we don't move.

There's an odd sadness in seeing him leave; we linger as I kiss him good-bye. I even wait until I hear the elevator door close before I count the money he gave me.

Boystown
By R.J. March

Maybe we weren't getting a lot of studying done; maybe we were always this close to academic probation. "But maybe ass really is more important than the social structure of England in the 16th century," McFeeley said in all earnestness, burning his fingers on what was left of a big fat joint.

McFeeley and I got together at orientation. We were standing in line to register for freshman comp. He stood behind me. I'd seen him all weekend—he looked like a man to me and not at all like some prefrosh 18-year-old. He'd worn the same clothes all weekend: a scruffy yellow Polo button-down oxford-cloth shirt and a pair of chinos with a tear in the ass that hung open like a toothless grin, exposing a variety of boxers throughout the three days. On this particular day I noticed tattersall, which tugged at me somewhere inside, becoming meaningful for no apparent reason. I had, I guessed, a tattersall fetish.

I straightened my shoulders and pushed out my chest when he came up behind me. I glanced back casually—you know, checking out the lines and shit, and mumbled a "How ya doin'?" He smiled, his green eyes on me, and nodded. He chewed gum, his dimples working in his cheeks.

It was a slow-moving line, inching up a little at a time. McFeeley was moving a little faster, though, and I felt the wind of his spearminty breath against the top of my head. I was afraid to move—I didn't want to turn and bump into him, and I didn't want to get any closer to the girl in front of me, and I didn't want to stop feeling the heat his body generated radiating toward me.

I got up to the table to register, my hands shaking, my cock just about hard. After a few moments of floundering, I found a class that sort of fit my schedule. I put the pencil down and turned, McFeeley having pressed up against me the whole time I was bent over the table.

"Wait for me," he said uncoyly. I nodded, a sudden slave to his whim and my boner.

I went with him to his room. His roommate for the weekend, an Asian he called Duck Soup, was at the getting-to-know-you party in the quad. McFeeley unbuttoned his shirt, his chest thick with hair and muscle.

"You gonna wrestle?" he asked, stretching out on the bed, his chino pants going taut over his crotch and accentuating the McFeeley log.

"Now?" I asked. "Oh, for school." I shrugged, feeling more than stupid. "Thinking of it, I guess."

"Me too," he said, his hand going behind the curtain of his shirt.

I still don't remember exactly how he got me on his lap. I recall his scratching an itch on his back and then having taken off his shirt. "Is this a fleabite?" he asked me, wanting me to come closer so I could inspect the thing. The next thing I knew, his big black-haired chest was tickling my ear, and his hand rumbled over my hard-on.

"You suck dick?" he asked. "You've got pretty lips. Pretty eyes too. Don't look like a cock sucker, that's why I didn't bust a move the first night at that asshole dance." We'd pissed together at the dance, wordlessly, shyly. I didn't look at him or anything. A feat in itself, I thought at the time.

His voice lulled me but not my cock. He played with it to distraction.

He had me stand for him, undoing my pants. My dick poked up stiffly in my briefs. He slid them down. My pointer vibrated as he regarded the pouting snout of my foreskin. "Cool," he said, leaning forward and taking the frilly end into his mouth, teething on it, pulling it, tonguing into the turtleneck of it. His hands circled my waist, fingers resting in the crack of my behind. He pressed his cheek against my prong, inviting me to hump his face, and I did for a while, but I had to pull back. "I'll shoot," I said, and he looked up at me, his face all serious.

"Oh, no," he said. "Don't do that yet."

He had me sit down to watch him strip off his pants. He was solid, already a man, and I felt so fucking pubescent looking up at him, with my boner all sticky between my thighs. He stood before me in his tattersall boxers, the front dotted with leakage. He was prickly with hair, his legs carved columns, slightly bowed. His toes lay on the linoleum like fingers, his feet wide and white.

He stepped up to me, pushing me backward, crawling over me, straddling my middle. He bent over and pushed his mouth against mine, the stubble of his face burning mine. He licked around my lips and into each nostril and then across my eyelids. I could feel the big press of him against my chest, still wrapped in tattersall. I wanted to haul it out and feel its hot skin and slimy leak; I wanted to taste it.

"Never sucked dick?" He pulled my arms up over my head, tipping his hips forward, butting the soft underside of my chin with his cock. I shook my head slowly to feel the head of it down there.

"You picked a roommate yet?" I had: Kevin Stein, bright and innocuous and unattractive—but only because he asked me.

"You wanna room with me?"

I nodded slowly, his huge dick restricting the full movement of my head. "OK," I said quietly, my spit thick and making it hard to speak. I wanted him fiercely, pointedly. All the things I'd ever wanted to do rushed through my head like a porn flick on fast-forward as his cock rested against my throat.

He rolled off and lay beside me.

"Go to it," he said.

McFeeley's log was thick and long and straight. It did not taper to a point like mine; instead it stayed the same circumference from base to head, a frigging telephone pole of a dick. I held it in my fist, impressed with its being there. I'd always wanted to suck dick, forever and ever—I just hadn't had the opportunity. There had been a couple of close calls, I guess—jacking off with a buddy, trying to pretend it was a matter of course, meaningless. Cases like that, you just jack, come, and act like nothing ever happened.

But this time there was no pretending, no need to pretend. It pulsed in my hand, wanting my mouth. I pressed my lips against its flat red-rimmed head. I took it into my mouth and tried to swirl my tongue around it. His fingers played over my shoulders, and I laid a hand on his thigh, stroking the fur on it. His nuts, two racquetballs in a bushy bag, bobbed as I ran my bottom teeth along the tender front of his cock. There was no way I could take half of it in my mouth, but I was satisfied, and I think he was too. I used my hand to take care of the rest, a firm sliding grip that banged against his pubes.

"Oh, my God," McFeeley said, an arm slung over his face. "That's a sweet fucking mouth."

He rolled me over, his dick planted in my mouth, and began to fuck me that way. He screwed my face gently, taking care not to choke me. I gripped his fleecy ass, fingering into his crack, loving the feel of him in my hands. His bung hole pushed out like lips waiting to be kissed. I poked around it, the hairs there coarse, thick. "Touch it," I heard him say, and I fingered the plushness, the wrinkled, winking gash turning hard and tight. I pushed in and found him wet as a whore. He fed me a little more dick. He throbbed on my flattened, useless tongue; he throbbed into the aching cave of my throat. He stopped breathing, and his whole body tightened. He brought his fanny down hard on my finger.

"Oh, fuck," he whispered as his cock chugged in and out of my mouth, its split opening and hosing my tonsils with the warm pudding from his balls. His thighs tensed against my cheeks, and he pulled out to finish the job by hand, gushing sweetly over my lips and chin.

He turned around and grabbed my pecker. "Never played with one like this before," he said, fisting it, exposing the head. I shot up into the air between us, splashing us both.

"Jesus," McFeeley said, wiping his eyes. "You could have warned me."

McFeeley liked games. His favorite was "I'll Get Him First." I guess he made it up. I mean, it doesn't exactly sound like the kind of game you'd play in the backseat of a car, your miserable parents up front trying to get you to Disney World.

When we moved off campus from the room we shared in Boynton Hall—Boystown Hall, we used to call it—we realized the freedoms we just didn't have on campus. McFeeley liked loud sex, a lot of loud sex—something that living in the dorms didn't foster. And I liked screwing the swim team, but discretion made up a small part of their valor, and smuggling the breaststroker Dickerson into my twin bed (with McFeeley feigning some pretty awesome snoring and drunken mumblings, all the while jacking off and watching us have at it) was no small feat. "No more mower sheds for us!" we rejoiced, toasting ourselves with shots of beer our first night, trying to get a quick buzz before Dickerson came by to our private housewarming party.

There was this new guy—Val Palmer was his name—a transfer from the Midwest. Mack and I spotted him at the student union."Mine," I said, as though calling him first would give me dibs on this blondie with the falling-down socks and big switching ass, his homemade tank top riding his little pink nipples into some kind of hardness.

"To the victor go the spoils," McFeeley said with some smugness, and a week later I came home from biology and walked in on the two of them, McFeeley naked on his knees, his big dick disappearing into the fat-lipped mouth of Mr. Palmer, who lay spread-legged on the floor, his little flopper hanging out of his undone jeans.

I stayed where I was. Mack liked an audience anyway, although he didn't see me at first. He was too busy staring lovingly at Palmer's widened mouth. Val hummed and kissed the red end of McFeeley's joint and licked the thick shaft and slack-skinned balls that swung mid-thigh. He took them into his mouth, and McFeeley lowered himself onto Val's face. He unbuttoned the boy's shirt, uncovering those now-famous—with me, at least—nipples, firmly puckered, like his lips.

His chest was free of hair except for a pretty feathering of the stuff narrowing up from the big blond bush that surrounded his impossibly white, nicely thick, and strangely soft cock. He moaned under the touch of Mack's fingers.

Mack was a big-ass monster. His beefed-up arms were leglike in their girth, and he was more interested in the gym than the gridiron for a couple of fairly obvious reasons I don't feel it necessary to go into. But he didn't mind making the occasional tackle, throwing himself headlong at one of those big, sweating guards from Penn State.

Unlike Palmer, McFeeley was all haired-up with black curlies, but under it all his skin was as white as a salt lick. He was as pretty as a picture—to me, at least—his face nicely sculpted, his cheek and chin always carrying a shadow of beard no matter when or how often he'd shave, his mouth full and always smiling, reminding me of kissing. His green eyes were closed as he squatted himself on Val's face.

The boy under him squirmed and scrambled, his hands impotent weapons against McFeeley's sequoia thighs and boulderlike glutes. I noticed Val's prick twitching to life.

It was then that I also noticed that I'd been noticed, McFeeley blinking up at me with a shit-eating grin. He reached down and swung Palmer's little bat at me. "You snooze, you lose," he said.

"Hmm?" Val mumbled with a mouthful.

I gave Mack the finger.

"Feels awesome, baby," he said, his voice dripping with sex. "C'mon, buddy, clean me up."

I left them alone, myself in some sore need of attention. I drove fast to the bookstore on Route 222, where'd I'd stop every now and then after class. I walked sheepishly past the attendant, trying to look like I wasn't here for a blow job. My dick felt as obvious as a shoe in my pants, though. I got some quarters and roamed the place—it was a big room lined with stalls, featured movies posted outside each door. My peers today were familiar faces: two old men sucking Luckys and giving me the glad eye. "Cold enough for you?" they both asked as I walked past.

Out of a booth fell a thin boy wearing sad bicycle pants, wiping his lips with the edge of his T-shirt. He looked up at me like I was his next meal. From the same booth exited Monty Viceroy, patting the wet spots on his crotch and checking his zipper, his car keys already in hand. He saw me and glanced away quickly, but he knew he was busted, so he gave me a little nod. I'd seen him here before and in the library john at school, so I was not surprised to see the president of the student council looking so postcoital. He ducked his red head and did some fancy stepping around his trick and the two smoking fogies.

Present company did not present any likely or likable suck candidates save for Viceroy, him only for the sheer pleasure of doing someone in politics. I viewed some video sex and yanked on my pud. McFeeley and Val were probably covered with goo and in each other's arms right now, I was thinking. McFeeley had probably already turned on Mighty Morphin Power Rangers, which he never missed, his dick soft and heavy and sticky and reeking of Palmer's ass.

I sighed, feeling lonely. I heard someone getting change and checked my watch. The screen went blank. My Sambas smacked on the sticky floor, sounding as though I'd walked in wet paint. I wondered why there weren't any good fuck films about hockey players. I tucked my rock away, the stubby, flat-ended thing with its frill of skin. I sniffed my fingers.

Standing to the left of my door, wearing a tank top and warm-ups and startling me when I emerged, was someone who looked vaguely familiar. I was pretty sure I hadn't boothed it with him before, though. His hair was flattopped, and he had the long, stretched-out muscles of a basketball player. He looked at me, then away, his hands restless in his pockets—I could hear them rustling in the nylon. What I could see of his chest was free of hair; there was a russet peek of titty when he worked his shoulders into a purposeless shrug.

I left him standing there. As eager as I was to see him with his filmy pants about his ankles, he didn't seem the type to suck or be sucked. There were a lot of players who just liked to garner some attention, showing off their tent poles before secreting themselves and their cocks away in a video closet and adding to the sticky mess on the floor, going home chaste to the wife or girlfriend. I walked away from this one, trusting my judgment.

Sometimes I'm wrong, though, and so when this one turned and followed me, staying a few doors behind me, I figured I was going to have to reconsider my initial impression.

He mumbled a greeting, and I said hey, and he leaned toward me and said he felt here the same way he felt in church when he was a boy. "You know—a lot of whispering and thinking bad thoughts when you're supposed to be praying," he said, his voice barely above a whisper. He had long white teeth and was clean-shaven. He looked to be about 30.

"You go to Kutztown," he said, and I looked at him a little more closely, wondering if I should know him. Had we already boothed it?

"I was coaching tennis there," he said. "Name's Nicholson. I re-member seeing you around. You're what's-his-name's roommate."

And Nicholson was the one what's-his-name told me about, the coach let go when rumors of sexual impropriety started circulating. "He was probably screwing Velakos," McFeeley speculated. "But fucking Velakos is fucking with fate, man, 'cause the fucker's nuts. Probably went to the dean with a butt full of the coach's come." McFeeley had a good eye for such things—Palmer, for instance, who was probably walking back to his dormitory room with a butt full of McFeeley's man juice. Good fucking eye, Mack.

I didn't feel right about this one, though, not trusting my own eye. He was nice to look at—very nice—with his short brown hair and his heavy brow and his pants rustling like a flag in the wind. I caught sight then of someone familiar, a black man whose dick never seemed fully engaged, who took a long time to come. We nodded—it was nice to be remembered. The huge vegetablelike curve of his dick was apparent through his zebra-stripe workout pants. I looked over at Nicholson. He scratched his bared tit.

The two old guys shuffled off, giving us whippersnappers dirty looks, and Bicycle Shorts left, miffed at being so completely ignored. It was just the three of us then, circling the outer walls, every now and then popping individually into a booth to refreshen our tumes-cences.

There was an alcove out of sight of the security cameras, which hovered and flashed little red lights over our heads. It was a favorite resting area for me when I felt like loitering outside a booth, and it was also a handy place to gather a small group of daring pud-pullers. I'd seen as many as seven guys in the tight little space doing all sorts of shit. I stood and waited. It was a proving ground—I figured if Coach came around and stopped too, it was a done deal.

He came around, parking himself in a doorway, gripping the front of his pants. He stepped into the booth and looked at me, but I stayed where I was. I fingered the outline of my dick, making it hard. He kneaded himself through the blue nylon, producing a sizable erection. He pulled it out and shook it at me, the second time I'd been wagged at like that today. Second time's the charm, I told my-self and undid my jeans. My cock hit the air running, thrusting up with a snap. I did not have the coach's length or girth, but I made up for it with a wealth of foreskin. I could see his lips wet with drool, and I figured I knew what his favorite food was.

I pinched the end of my pecker and twirled it around for him like a bag of Shake 'n Bake. I skinned the head back and fingered the hard bluish head. I pushed my jeans down my hard-muscled quads and lifted my shirt. My chest and stomach were covered with a fine stubble of see-through hairs. I pinched my right tit and rolled it under my thumb, circling it, feeling the rasp of mowed-down hairs all around it.

Nicholson's prick was monolithic. His grip failed to cover half of it, and his fingers could not close around it. It was by far the longest johnson I'd ever seen. He worked it in his fist and squeezed out a ladle's worth of juice, leaking as much as I ejaculate. He wiped his sticky hand on his stomach as though the stuff were offensive, while I was thirsty for some of that.

There was the sound of someone getting change, $5 in quarters falling and reminding me of Atlantic City. Nicholson's cock was gone in a flash. I peered around the corner. Another old shuffler, probably a retired trucker, got himself into a booth and stayed there.

I gave Coach the all-clear. I still had mine out; it was buzzing in my hand. I watched the slow unveiling of Nicholson's member and decided then and there to bend at the waist and have a taste. I was not normally inclined to the act, though certainly no stranger to it. The fat gusher appealed to me—its fat knob, the trim and taut shaft that looked suntanned, a brown ring running around the middle of it, marking the beginning of the deep end.

"We could watch a movie," he said.

"I'm claustrophobic," I told him. "It's all right here; nobody can see." I liked it outside the narrow, coffinlike cubbies. I liked the chance of an audience, the dangerous thrill of being caught by the club-armed attendant.

The black guy pulled up like a shadow, soundlessly. Nicholson quickly turned shy, but I kept playing with mine. The man stepped into the alcove with us, between the coach and me, his back against the wall, and let out his hose. It was similar to Nicholson's in size and shape, and it was the color, almost, of an eggplant. He kept his eyes on my prong, which seemed hardy and useful and insistently hard. His head was shaved, and he wore a Tommy Hilfiger T-shirt through which he rubbed his rubbery tits. Coach eyed us both, shrugging his shoulders and dropping his pants, and we were all unimpeded. I reached out and plucked at one of Coach's rusty nipples—it shrank up and pointed at me. I twisted until I heard him sigh.

I wanted them side by side, their similar, contrasting bangers swinging toward my mouth. Tommy's curved downward as though tugged by gravity and its heavy purple knob. He smacked it against his thigh until it left wet marks. Coach's cock was bone-hard and ruler-straight. I decided then and there to blow them both. I wasn't much of a cock sucker—not much!—but when would this ebony-and-ivory opportunity present itself again? I went to my knees in the alcove between them, and they both stepped up.

I licked Tommy's salty tip and held on to Coach's staff, jacking the rocky thing as I nosed under the plummy hang of Tommy's balls. I looked up to see the two of them fiddling with one another's pecs, their hands pawing, their faces coming closer and closer. I switched to the concrete head of Nicholson's dick, forcing it to the back of my throat. I heard his sigh and the smack of lips, and I squinted up to see Tommy's snaking tongue bathing the stubble of Nicholson's chin. I felt my own leaky piece twitch. Tommy thrust his dick in my face, and someone's fingers tangled in my hair.

I sucked one and then the other, switching back and forth. I was pretty pleased with my performance, and my cock was feeling as though the head would come off in a gooey blast. I pulled on it until I felt my nuts suck up into my insides, and my pecker vibrated over and over again.

Coach was close too, I could tell, but there was no telling when Tommy would get off. I decided to concentrate on Nicholson's sticky knob, using my hand to get to where my mouth couldn't. His hands cradled my head, holding it still, and he fucked into me, and I swallowed an amazing amount of dick. He made a noise, something between a moan and a growl, and he pulled out, swearing and panting, looking down at his pipe. He aimed for my mouth, his own gaping, and shot five or six blasts into me, thick and stringy.

Tommy grunted with approval and lust and turned my head with a finger and added his own deposit of come, adding to my already sizable postnasal drip.

"Ah, shit," I said, feeling like a cat stretching in the sun. I tossed a big load onto the gray linoleum, getting a little on Tommy's Filas.

I got home after dark, and McFeeley was on the couch watching The Ren & Stimpy Show. He was wearing a pair of boxers and some dark-heeled socks. He lifted his hand in greeting.

His boxers were the tattersall ones, my favorites, and I found myself wishing I hadn't just wasted my time and come at the 222 Adulte Shoppe. I could see the warm, soft, fuzzy sac that leaked out of the leg of Mack's shorts. I felt a little wistful.

I went into the bathroom, ready for a shower. Mack followed me. I turned on the water and started undressing. Mack sat on the lidded toilet watching me. "What?" I said, getting down to my shorts and finding my dick glued to the inside of my briefs. I gave a little yank and felt as though I had ripped off a chunk of skin. I checked for bleeding. McFeeley snorted.

"Where were you?" he asked, smirking. "Who was sucking your dick?"

"Sex, sex, sex, McFeeley—is that all you think of?" I said, my cock pulsing upward.

Contributor Biographies

Derek Adams is the author of a popular series of erotic novels featuring intrepid detective Miles Diamond. He has also penned over 100 short stories, which, he insists, are ongoing chapters in his autobiography. He lives near Seattle and keeps in shape by working out whenever he can find a man willing to do a few pushups with him.

Barry Alexander's erotic fiction has appeared in magazines such as *In Touch, Indulge, Men, Freshmen, Honcho*, and *Playguy* as well as the short story collection *All the Right Places*. Alexander has stories in several anthologies including *Friction 1, 2,* and *3, Heat Wave, Boys on the Prowl, Feeling Frisky, Skin Flicks 1* and *2, Casting Couch Confessions, Rent Boys, Freshmen Club*, and *Divine Meat*. He lives in Iowa with one dog and a cat with a porcelain fetish.

James Anselm, since his debut as a writer of erotic fiction in 1981, has made regular appearances in all your favorite magazines, including *Men* and *In Touch*. Genius, he says, is 1% inspiration and 99% ejaculation. Outside of sex, his interests include books, classical music, and theater. (Inside of sex, he prefers smooth, blond muscle boys.) The author is single and lives in New York City. Two of his stories can also be found in the Alyson anthology *Up All Hours*.

A native Californian, **Bearmuffin** lives in San Diego with two leatherbears in a stimulating ménage à trois. He has written gay erotica for *Honcho, Torso, Manscape*, and *Hot Shots*.

Mark Caldwell is the name the author uses because it is the name of the boy who was both the object of greatest desire and the source of greatest torment during the author's youth. He has written for *Stroke* magazine since 1980.

Michael Cavanaugh has worked as a waiter, a doorman at a luxury hotel, and a model. He is currently ready to set sail as a steward on board a private yacht bound for the South Seas. He is confident that Mr. Right is definitely out there somewhere.

Dale Chase has had over 50 stories published in *Men, Freshmen, In Touch,* and *Indulge.* His work has appeared in several anthologies including *Friction 2, 3,* and *4, Twink,* and *Bearotica.* One story has been acquired by independent filmmaker Edgar Bravo and will soon reach the big screen. Chase lives near San Francisco.

R.W. Clinger lives in Pittsburgh, where he works as an administrative manager and part-time private investigator. He spends his evenings and free time with his life partner and his writing. His short stories have appeared in *Blackmale, Indulge, In Touch, Locker Room Tales,* and *Friction 2* and *3.* His first novel, *The Last Pile of Leaves,* will be released later this year.

M. Christian is the author of the critically acclaimed and best-selling book of erotic stories *Dirty Words.* He is editor of *The Burning Pen: Sex Writers on Sex Writing, Guilty Pleasures: True Stories of Erotic Indulgences, Midsummer Night's Dreams: One Story, Many Tales,* and *Eros Ex Machina: Eroticising the Mechanical.* He is coeditor, with Simon Sheppard, of *Rough Stuff: Tales of Gay Men, Sex, and Power.* His short fiction has appeared in more than 100 anthologies and periodicals. He lives in San Francisco.

Grant Foster is the author of *Long, Slow Burn* and has contributed short stories to a number of magazines and anthologies. In addition to fiction he also writes articles about travel and gay history. When not writing, traveling, or doing historical research, Foster gardens at his home in rural Washington state.

Derek Kemp would like you to know that Max the DJ is real. Though some of the elements of "The Hot Nine at 9:00" are fictionalized, most of it is very real. If Max is reading this, he knows Derek's phone number and should call. Derek would very much like to get on with Round Three.

Phillip Mackenzie Jr. is a freelance writer and entertainment consultant who lives in Los Angeles.

R.J. March is the author of *Looking for Trouble: The Erotic Fiction of R.J. March*. His work has appeared in numerous magazines and anthologies and is also featured on the Web site Nightcharm.com. He is currently at work on another collection of erotica, due to be published in late 2002. He lives in Pennsylvania.

Roddy Martin's work has appeared in Volumes 1, 3, and 4 of *Friction, Best Gay Erotica 1998, Unzipped, Freshmen, In Touch, Indulge, Blackmale* and in magazines for children and teens.

Alan Mills has been published in three previous editions of *Friction*, as well as *Casting Couch Confessions, Quickies 2, Divine Meat, Skinflicks*, and *What The Fuck*. Alan was once the editor of *In Touch, Indulge*, and *Blackmale*, and his work has been featured in those magazines as well. He currently lives in West Hollywood, Calif., works in the film industry, and is actively looking for more material to write erotica about.

Christopher Morgan is a 30-something born-and-bred New Yorker who has been writing and editing gay erotica for ages. His first novel, *Musclebound*, has been an excellent seller in both English and Japanese and was cited in Will Roscoe's scholarly work, *Queer Spirits: A Gay Men's Myth Book*, in his chapter "The Way of Initiation." Other short stories of Morgan's have appeared in *Boy Next Door* and *Country Boy* magazines and in *Southern Comfort*, edited by David Laurents, and *Western Trails*, edited by Gary Bowen.

Scott Pomfret is an attorney and writer in Boston. His work has previously appeared in *Friction 4* and *5* and *Indulge*, as well as numerous literary journals and gay publications.

Lee Alan Ramsay is the pen name of Daddy Bob Allen. Daddy Bob has a 16th-century torture grotto carved out of his garage, which at times has been booked as much as six weeks in advance. He has built an international reputation as a leatherman; it has been said that he has forgotten more about S/M than most people will ever know. He has been writing for *The Leather Journal* since its inception in 1987 and is now its news editor. He is also the fiction and photo editor of *Eagle*. He is the author of two books, *The Only Reason I Mention This* and *The Wings of Icarus*.

A New York-based writer, critic, poet-playwright, **Lance Rush** has been published in *Empire Magazine*, *In the Family*, and *New York Daily News*. His erotica has graced the steamy pages of *Coming Out*, *FQ*, *Honcho*, *Inches*, *Mandate*, *Torso*, and several of the better anthologies. *The Long Blue Moan*, his long-awaited novel, will be published in spring 2002 (under the name L.M. Ross).

Dominic Santi, a former technical writer turned rogue, is coeditor, with Debra Hyde, of the sex and politics anthology *Strange Bedfellows*. Santi's dirty stories appear in *Friction 2, 3,* and *4, Best Gay Erotica 2000, Best Bisexual Erotica 1* and *2, Best Transgendered Erotica, Tough Guys*, and dozens of other smutty anthologies and magazines.

Simon Sheppard is the author of *Hotter Than Hell, and Other Stories*, and coeditor, with M. Christian, of *Rough Stuff: Tales of Gay Men, Sex, and Power*. His short fiction has appeared in several editions of *Friction* and *Best American Erotica*, along with numerous other anthologies and magazines. His nonfiction column, Sex Talk, appears in gay papers nationwide. He lives in San Francisco.

Mel Smith is a single mom working as a locker room attendant at a high school. I was in the fire service for four years and in law enforcement for 13. In my spare time I live my dream by writing. Only one of my stories has actually been published, but three more are due for publication—two in *In Touch* magazine and one in the anthology, *Best Gay Erotica*.

Jay Starre lives in Vancouver, British Columbia, where he sits at his desk pounding out gay erotic tales. His stories have been published in magazines such as *Honcho*, *Blueboy*, *International Leatherman*,

Torso, and *In Touch* magazines, and in the anthologies *Hard Drive*, *Rent Boys*, *Friction 4*, and *Skin Flicks 2*.

Bob Vickery (www.bobvickery.com) is a regular contributor to various Web sites and magazines, particularly *Men* and *Freshmen*. He has three anthologies of stories: *Cocksure*, *Cock Tales*, and *Skin Deep*. He has stories in numerous anthologies, including *Friction 1, 2, 3,* and *4*, *Best Gay Erotica 1999* and *2001*, *Best American Erotica 1997* and *2000*, *Quickies 1* and *2*, *Best Bisexual Erotica 1* and *2*, and *Queer Dharma*. In his spare time he bakes muffins for a zen Buddhist monastery in northern California.

David Wayne resides in upstate New York, where he is completing his Ph.D. dissertation in, of all things, physics. Countless hours of his formative years were expended poring over the good bits of his mother's accumulation of Harlequin Romances. He started writing erotica for himself at the tender age of 13. "For the Asking" is his first story intended for public consumption.

Greg Wharton is the founder and publisher of Suspect Thoughts Press, and editor of the webzine suspect thoughts: a journal of subversive writing, and www.suspectthoughts.com. He is the erotica editor for VelvetMafia, at www.velvetmafia.com, and editor of the Suspect Thoughts Press anthology *Of the Flesh: Dangerous New Fiction*. His short fiction, reviews, and creative nonfiction has been widely published online and in print. He is hard at work on a collection of short fiction and a novel.

Dante Williams is a pen-name used by Alan Mills, profiled above.

Thom Wolf is the author of *Words Made Flesh*. He lives and works in the United Kingdom. He has been writing erotica since he was 18. His work has appeared in *In Touch*, *Indulge*, *Men*, and *Overload*, and in the anthologies *Friction 3*, *Twink*, and *Bearotica*. He likes yoga, music, and, of course, sex, and is a rabid Kylie Minogue fan. He is now working on a new novel.

Sean Wolfe lives in Denver with his partner of 11 years. In the past two years he has been published in *Men, Freshmen, Playguy,* and *Inches* magazines. His work has also appeared in *Friction 3* and *4.* He is not, however, a sex maniac. He just completed his first non-erotic gay novel, and is hard at work on his second. He facilitates a weekly gay men's writer's group, and works at Category Six Books, Denver's only bookstore dedicated to gay men.

Publication Information

Blackmale ("Side Effect," "Gorgeous Tits") can be contacted at (800) 637-0101.

The Boy Next Door ("In-Tents Encounter") can be reached at Sportomatic Ltd., P.O. Box 470, Port Chester, NY 10573.

Classifieds ("Fantasies," "Looking for Mr. Right") was launched in 1992. With its September 30, 1997, issue, however, the magazine began publishing under the name *Unzipped*. For subscription information, call (800) 757-7069.

Eagle ("Snowbound") can be contacted by fax at (213) 656-3120.

Firsthand ("For Real") can be contacted at Firsthand Limited, 310 Cedar Lane, Teaneck, NJ 07666.

Freshmen ("Boystown," "Family Affair," "Plaza del Sol," "Three-Penny Dare") can be contacted at (800) 757-7069.

Hard Drive ("Almost Better Than Sex," "Pig") was edited by Miguel Angel and published by Alyson Books, www.alyson.com.

Honcho ("Assume the Position") can be contacted at (888) 664-7827.

Indulge ("Chain Male," "Constantine's Cats," "Nocturne," "Revelations," "Shelter," "Thug Life, Thug Fiction," "Working Up a Sweat") can be contacted at (800) 637-0101.

In Touch ("Joe Pornstar," "Nasty," "Now and Then," "Opportunities") can be contacted at (800) 637-0101.

Mach ("Getting Even") can be contacted at Brush Creek Media, 367 Ninth St., San Francisco, CA 94103.

Men ("The Act," "For the Asking," "The Hot Nine at 9:00," "Karma" "The Porn Writer") can be contacted at (800) 757-7069.

Nightcharm.com ("Heads and Tails") is online.

Stroke ("Bringing Up Robbie") can be reached at Magcorp, P.O. Box 801434, Santa Clarita, CA 91380-1454.

Torso ("Ripped Rasslers," "The Training Session") can be contacted at (888) 664-7827.

ExquisiteCorpse.com ("Gravity") is online.

Vulcan America ("He") can be reached at (888) 919-0822.